THE SECRET PLACE

OTHER BOOKS BY AL LACY

Angel of Mercy series:
A Promise for Breanna (Book One)
Faithful Heart (Book Two)
Captive Set Free (Book Three)
A Dream Fulfilled (Book Four)
Suffer the Little Children (Book Five)
Whither Thou Goest (Book Six)
Final Justice (Book Seven)
Things Not Seen (Book Eight)
Not by Might (Book Nine)
Far Above Rubies (Book Ten)

Journeys of the Stranger series:
Legacy (Book One)
Silent Abduction (Book Two)
Blizzard (Book Three)
Tears of the Sun (Book Four)
Circle of Fire (Book Five)
Quiet Thunder (Book Six)
Snow Ghost (Book Seven)

Battles of Destiny (Civil War series):
Beloved Enemy (Battle of First Bull Run)
A Heart Divided (Battle of Mobile Bay)
A Promise Unbroken (Battle of Rich Mountain)
Shadowed Memories (Battle of Shiloh)
Joy from Ashes (Battle of Fredericksburg)
Season of Valor (Battle of Gettysburg)
Wings of the Wind (Battle of Antietam)
Turn of Glory (Battle of Chancellorsville)

Hannah of Fort Bridger series (coauthored with JoAnna Lacy):
Under the Distant Sky (Book One)
Consider the Lilies (Book Two)
No Place for Fear (Book Three)
Pillow of Stone (Book Four)
The Perfect Gift (Book Five)
Touch of Compassion (Book Six)
Beyond the Valley (Book Seven)
Damascus Journey (Book Eight)

Mail Order Bride series (coauthored with JoAnna Lacy):
Secrets of the Heart (Book One)
A Time to Love (Book Two)
Tender Flame (Book Three)
Blessed Are the Merciful (Book Four)
Ransom of Love (Book Five)
Until the Daybreak (Book Six)
Sincerely Yours (Book Seven)

The Secret Place

SHADOW OF LIBERTY BOOK TWO

AL & JOANNA LACY

Multnomah® Publishers *Sisters, Oregon*

This is a work of fiction. The characters, incidents, and dialogues are products of the authors' imaginations and are not to be construed as real. Any resemblance to actual events or persons, living or dead, is entirely coincidental.

THE SECRET PLACE
published by Multnomah Publishers, Inc.

International Standard Book Number: 1-57673-800-0

Cover image by Aleta Rafton
Background cover image by Tony Stone Images
Design by Chris Gilbert/Uttley DouPonce DesignWorks

Printed in the United States of America

For information:
MULTNOMAH PUBLISHERS, INC.
POST OFFICE BOX 1720
SISTERS, OREGON 97759

Library of Congress Cataloging-in-Publication Data

Lacy, Al.
The secret place / by Al and JoAnna Lacy.
p. cm – (Shadow of liberty;bk. 2)
ISBN 1-57673-800-0
1. Physicians–Fiction. 2. Switzerland–Fiction. I. Lacy, JoAnna. II. Title.
PS 3562.A256 S45 2001
813'.54–dc21 2001002101

01 02 03 04 05 06 07 08 — 10 9 8 7 6 5 4 3 2 1 0

To Cammy Jacobson,
a faithful fan and a very special young lady.
God bless you, Cammy.
We love you!

PHILIPPIANS 1:3

Prologue

In the 1870s a group of French citizens celebrate the centennial of the American Revolution by commissioning the construction of a statue of "Liberty Enlightening the World." The statue was to be presented to the people of the United States to demonstrate the harmonious relationship between the two countries.

The statue, monumental in size, would be the creation of the talented French sculptor, Frédéric-Auguste Bartholdi, whose dream was to build a monument honoring the American spirit of freedom that had inspired the world.

In the United States, government leaders were pleased with the kind gesture and set about to raise the $300,000 needed to build a pedestal for the huge French statue, which would be erected on Bedloe's Island in New York Harbor. Promotional tours and contests were organized to raise the money. During these fund-raising campaigns, American poet Emma Lazarus—the daughter of a prominent Jewish family in New York City—wrote the poem "The New Colossus" which was inscribed on the pedestal just prior to the statue's dedication by President Grover Cleveland on October 28, 1886.

Emma Lazarus's words transformed the French statue of Liberty Enlightening the World into the American Statue of Liberty, welcoming the oppressed of the world within its borders to have opportunity to make their dreams come true. The "New Colossus" on Miss Liberty's pedestal reads:

Give me your tired, your poor;
Your huddled masses yearning to breathe free,
The wretched refuse of your teeming shore.
Send these, the homeless, the tempest-tossed to me,
I lift up my lamp beside the golden door!

Castle Island in New York Harbor served as the chief entry station for immigrants between 1855 and 1891, though it was diminutive in size. In order to enlarge the facilities for processing immigrants, New York authorities began considering another site in the harbor. Eyes shifted to Governor's Island, but that was already occupied by the United States Coast Guard. Attention turned then to a larger island just a few hundred yards north of Bedloe's Island, where Lady Liberty held high her torch. (Bedloe's Island was later named Liberty Island).

The choice island was originally called Kioshk, or Gull, Island by Native Americans in the 1600s; Gibbet Island in the early 1700s when criminals were hanged there from a gibbet, or gallows, tree; and later Oyster Island because of its abundant population of shellfish. In the early 1780s, the island was purchased by wealthy merchant Samuel Ellis from whom it derived its present name. New York state bought Ellis Island in 1808, and used it as an ammunition dump until June 15, 1882, when the immigration facility—built at a cost of $500,000—officially opened its doors. From that time, Ellis Island was the entry station for immigrants and remained so until 1943.

The hopeful message on the Statue of Liberty's pedestal has greeted millions of immigrants from countries across the seas who left their homelands behind in search of a better life in the United States of America.

According to the Statue of Liberty–Ellis Island Foundation, more than a hundred million Americans can trace their roots to ancestors who came to this country through Ellis Island. This means that approximately half of today's Americans are the offspring of pioneering ancestors who registered into the country through the immigration station which stands virtually in the shadow of the Statue of Liberty.

Martin W. Sandler, author of the book *Immigrants,* says, "Our cultural diversity is our greatest strength, for we are more than a nation. Thanks to those who dared to be immigrants, we are a nation of nations. It is a heritage of which we should all be proud."

Well-known American historian Oscar Handlin said, "Once I thought to write the story of the immigrants in America. Then I realized that the immigrants were America's story."

They came from many countries across the Atlantic Ocean. For many the journey was treacherous, and the good life they came for was just a dream. For others the sailing was smooth across the oceans, and they prospered in the new land. Both kinds of people created the rich and diverse country in which we live today.

They heard talk. About a place where all men were free. A place of compassion. But what about the cost? Not just money for the passage, but the emotional toll. For most immigrants, grandparents, aunts, uncles, cousins, and friends would be left behind. The same was often true of wives and children. The men would have to go alone and send for their families later. Many of the children, who came with their mothers later on, would see their fathers for the first time in months—sometimes years—in the shadow of the Statue of Liberty.

The immigrants were driven by pain and fear and hopelessness; by poverty and hunger; by religious persecution; or by the simple need to survive. These things they all had in common, as well as the hope of a better life.

They all shared a common destination: New York Harbor.

They came with nothing but the clothes on their backs; a pocketful of dreams; a flimsy suitcase, trunk, or lidded woven basket; and some crumpled bills carefully stashed in pockets or purses. There are countless stories of new friendships and relationships that were begun while aboard ship, or while waiting at the process station to be approved by physicians and government officials to enter the country.

None who entered this new land and found their place within its borders did so without having their lives changed forever.

A Note from the Authors

It is with great pleasure that we present this series of novels about America's immigrants. We have walked the grounds of both Liberty and Ellis Islands and caught the spirit of those men, women, and children who left their homes in faraway countries, traversed the oceans, and came to the Land of the Free.

Passing through the same buildings on Ellis Island where they took their medical examinations and their verbal tests in hope of entering this country, we felt we could almost hear the shuffle of their weary feet, the murmur of voices, the laughter of children, and the crying of babies.

The walls of the buildings are covered with photographs of the immigrants, their faces displaying the intimidation they felt, yet showing a light in their eyes that revealed the hope that lay within them for a better life in America.

We have purchased many historical books that have been written about the immigrants. Some tell us of statements that were made by them during and after their arrival in New York Harbor. Stella Petrakis, a Greek immigrant, said, "I felt grateful the Statue of Liberty was a woman. I felt she would understand a woman's heart."

Those readers who know our other fictional series are fully aware that our stories are filled with romance, adventure, and intriguing plots designed to make the books hard to lay down. They are interlaced with Scripture that will strengthen and encourage Christians, and as always, the Lord Jesus Christ is honored and His gospel made clear.

Since the books in this series are about the people of Europe, which is comprised of many countries and tongues, and because a great number of them spoke several languages, we will not weary the reader by continuously pointing out what language they are speaking. We will simply give it to you in English.

It is our desire that the reader will feel as we did when we walked those hallowed halls, deeply impressed with the courage of those people who helped settle this land we call home.

He that dwelleth in the secret place of the most High
shall abide under the shadow of the Almighty.

PSALM 91:1

Introduction

Early in the second half of the nineteenth century, many European countries saw the rise of working-class influences. Home industry was being displaced by factories, where wages were much lower than the money independent industrialists could earn working in their own private shops.

This trend brought about outbreaks of machine smashing and factory burning by those who feared the loss of livelihood and independence. Often this resulted in violence, bloodshed, and death.

To counter the low wages and poor working conditions in the factories, cooperative labor unions were formed. Though factory owners objected to the unions, they were forced to give in to pressure placed upon them, but there was continual conflict between the two. In time, the unions—which were established with the proper purpose—were infiltrated by greedy men who brought graft into the system, and misdeeds became common within their ranks.

This industrial revolution was the cause of a great number of Europeans to pull up stakes and sail to America, where they were free to make a living in home industry. One of the last European countries to be transformed into an industrial state was Switzerland, which came late in the nineteenth century. And that is where our story starts.

One

On Monday morning, May 23, 1892, in the eastern Switzerland town of Chur, the sun was shining out of a crystal clear azure sky. It was a perfect spring day. Warm weather was slow coming this year, but it had finally arrived in glorious fashion.

Birds were happily chirping in the trees as stores and shops opened for the day's business. While children merrily hopped and skipped on their way to school, horse-drawn vehicles and men on saddle horses moved along the town's main thoroughfare, and the board sidewalks were showing increased activity. Women who wore colorful kerchiefs covering their hair were busily polishing storefront windows and sweeping the planks of the boardwalks in front of their places of business.

On the main thoroughfare just south of the central business section, things were not so peaceful. An angry crowd of men were gathered in front of the Wilhaus Furniture Factory and harassing employees as they arrived for the day's work.

In the factory office, which was on the second floor, factory manager Durbin Thorpe stood at the window. Flanking him were his twenty-four-year-old son and assistant manager, Helmut, and his lovely bookkeeper, Metryka Baume, who was a year younger than Helmut.

Metryka's raven hair was tightly braided and wound around her head to form a coronet across the top. She was wearing a sky-blue cotton dress, sprinkled with white polka dots. A white sash encircled her slender waist. Her eyes were almost the same shade of blue as her dress, but at that moment they were taking on a darker shade, reflecting the fear in her thudding heart. A frown wrinkled her ordinarily flawless brow as she watched the scene below and heard the independent woodworkers expressing their anger and frustration toward the factory employees.

Durbin's lips were colorless as he turned to Helmut and said levelly, "Son, slip out the back way and run to the police station. Tell Metryka's father he'd better send some officers over here in a hurry. We've got real trouble brewing this time, for sure."

Metryka's eyes were wide with fear as she watched Helmut dash out the back door of the office. When she turned to Durbin, the skin of her face was like parchment. "Oh, Mr. Thorpe," she said with trembling voice, "I'm afraid."

"Me too," admitted Durbin, licking his lips. "I should have sent Helmut sooner. I hope your father gets his men here quickly."

Across the street from the factory, grocer Jabin Faulk was arduously sweeping the boardwalk in front of his store while keeping a sharp eye on the potentially violent scene in front of the factory. His white shirt and dark trousers were covered with a crisp apron and the bright morning sun reflected off his shiny bald head.

He paused in his sweeping when two of the factory workers shouted at the taunting woodworkers and seemed about to resort to fisticuffs. Other factory workers were trying to calm their two coworkers down.

At that moment, Faulk's attention was drawn to the large delivery wagon that was coming down the street. The driver was looking at the scene across the street while angling his vehicle toward the boardwalk in front of Faulk's Grocery. As the wagon rolled to a halt, Jabin let his eyes roam over its side, where bright lettering identified it as being from the Feinman Grocery Distributors in Zurich.

Alighting from the wagon seat, the driver glanced across the street, then smiled at the bald man as he stepped up on the boardwalk. "Mr. Faulk, I presume."

Returning the smile, Jabin nodded. "Yes, sir."

"I'm Roydan Maar. The new driver on this route."

Extending his right hand while holding the broom with the left, Jabin said, "I'm glad to meet you, Roydan. You can call me Jabin."

When they had shaken hands, Jabin said, "Hector told me on his last delivery that he was retiring and I'd have a new driver this time. I'm glad you're here. My shelves are getting low on several items."

"I'll get right on it," said the driver, turning toward the wagon.

"Would you like some coffee, first?" asked Jabin.

Roydan paused, smiling, and looked over his shoulder. "I'll never turn down a cup of coffee."

"Good! Come on in."

As he was following the grocer through the door, Roydan glanced back across the street where the angry clamor filled the air. Jabin closed the door, muffling the agitated voices in front of the factory.

Going to the potbellied stove, Jabin lifted the ever-present coffeepot and poured two mugs. The new delivery man was staring out the window at the display of emotion going on across the street as Jabin drew up. As Roydan turned to meet him, Jabin handed him a steaming cup. With a toss of his head, Roydan said, "So what's that all about?"

Jabin took a sip from his own cup. "You're aware that Europe's industrial revolution is now making its mark in Switzerland."

"Yes," said Roydan, taking a sip.

"Well, it finally came to Chur. As you can see, the sign over there says it is the Wilhaus Furniture Factory."

A blank look was on Roydan's face.

Raising his bushy eyebrows, Jabin said, "You do know who Eiger Wilhaus is?"

"No, sir. I'm fairly new in Switzerland. My wife and I came to Zurich from Austria only a few weeks ago. So who is Eiger Wilhaus?"

"Only one of the richest men in this country. He owns the Wilhaus Industries, which are headquartered in Bern. This factory, and many others like it in Switzerland are part of the Wilhaus Industries, along with several other types of manufacturing companies."

"I see. And the angry men out there are independent furniture makers whose business is being stolen by the factory."

"Precisely. You see, the factory opened just a week ago. And the independent woodworkers are already feeling the financial pinch. They are fast losing their livelihood. They gathered here Wednesday, Thursday, and Friday last week, protesting against the factory. They have even threatened violence."

Glancing back through the window as the muffled sound of loud voices still filled the air, Roydan said, "I think they mean it."

"No doubt about it. A lot of those men are ordinarily quite peaceful, but the leader among them is a big rough, tough fellow, who I'm sure is capable of violence. He has bloodied up many a man in drunken brawls at the town's taverns over the years. His name is Alexander Metternik. There's enough warrior in him that some of his friends have dubbed him 'Alexander the Great.' His furniture-making business has been the most flourishing of all, so he has the most to lose."

"I really can't blame Metternik and his friends for being angry. If it were me, I'd—"

Maar's words were cut off by the sight of several men in dark blue uniforms charging into the crowd of vociferous woodworkers, waving their nightsticks threateningly, and loudly demanding silence.

"Looks like the police have decided to take control of the situation." Jabin peered out the window. "See that big, thick-bodied man who's leading them?"

"Yes."

"That's the town's chief magistrate, Burgomaster Koblin Baume. He's a tough one, himself. That man beside him is the factory's assistant manager. His name is Helmut Thorpe. His father is the manager, and I'm sure we'll see him shortly."

In the office above, Durbin Thorpe was experiencing an ever-tightening knot in the pit of his stomach as he looked down on the noisy scene with his bookkeeper at his side.

It was Metryka Baume who first caught sight of the law officers coming down the street with her father in the lead. "There's Papa and a bunch of his men, Mr. Thorpe!" she said with elation.

Durbin's tongue was thick and dry and clung to the roof of his mouth. Working it loose, he headed for the door, saying, "You stay up here, Metryka."

She watched her boss hurry down the stairs and move quickly to her father and Helmut, who had positioned themselves with their backs to the gate, facing the angry woodworkers. Her father said something to Durbin, then shouted loudly for the angry men to get quiet.

Helmut looked up at Metryka and gave her an assuring smile. She tried to smile back, but her fear kept a smile from developing.

Even though the police officers were waving their nightsticks in a threatening manner, the woodworkers were shouting heatedly at Durbin Thorpe, demanding that he close down the factory.

Koblin Baume's beefy features were beet red as he boomed above the babel of their voices, telling them to get quiet or they would be arrested. Because of his size and form, Baume's voice was powerful, and the thunder of it finally brought a hush over the crowd.

Drawing a deep breath, the burgomaster said loud and clear, "Listen to me! I want you to know that Mr. Eiger Wilhaus was informed by wire from my office on Friday of your three-day protest here at the factory. The wire was sent with the knowledge of Mr. Durbin Thorpe. Mr. Wilhaus wired back just moments ago, saying that he is traveling by rail from Bern on this coming Thursday, so he can talk to all of you on Friday morning. He is bringing two of his vice-presidents with him. I haven't even had opportunity to advise Mr. Thorpe of the wire. I was going to suggest to him that we spread the word all over town in the next four days, so you would know about it. Mr. Wilhaus will be here to address you at the gate at eight o'clock on Friday morning."

"Why does he want to talk to us?" shouted a man from the crowd.

"Mr. Wilhaus fears the threats of violence on your part against his employees and factory property. He is eager to make peace with you."

One angry woodworker, an ominous, dark look on his face, shouted, "If Mr. Moneybags wants peace, all he has to do is close down this factory!"

Moving a bit closer to the burgomaster's side, Durbin Thorpe said, "Sir, Wilhaus Industries has gone to a lot of trouble and expense to build this factory in your town. We still need lots of workers. All of you could have jobs in the factory if you would accept them."

Another man threaded his way through the press to get closer to the manager. Fixing Durbin with blazing eyes, he said, "The wages are too low, Thorpe!" His tone expressed a venom of disgust.

"Right!" bawled another, who stood close. "We can't live on wages like Wilhaus pays!"

"Wilhaus doesn't care about us! All he cares about is getting richer!"

Choosing to ignore the double accusation leveled at Eiger Wilhaus, Baume said stubbornly, "You would have to tighten your belts for a while if you went to work in the factory, men, yes. But look at it this way: The factory has already helped put Chur on the map. People across Switzerland are now hearing about Chur. Not only that, but the factory's presence has already helped the town's economy. The fifty-five new workers and their families who have moved into town from Bern have boosted sales in the stores. Most of them are living in the hotel while their homes are being built. This is helping the hotel, but even better, the construction business is flourishing. And I might add that the taxes paid by the factory will strengthen Chur's treasury."

Helmut Thorpe looked at Baume. "May I say something, sir?"

"Certainly," said the man.

Running his gaze over the strained faces of the woodworkers, Helmut said, "Gentlemen, I have already done some figuring on what our burgomaster was just pointing out. With the taxes the factory will be paying, Chur will be able to build a town square I've been told you have been talking about for years. This will make Chur more like a big city and bring prestige to our community."

A woodworker in the middle of the crowd spat angrily, "Town square? Prestige? This means nothing to us as long as our families are going hungry!"

There was an uproar of agreement.

Koblin Baume raised his hands for silence. Lifting his voice, he said, "Your families would not go hungry if you took jobs in the factory! Like I said, you would have to tighten your belts for a while, but you would make it even though your income wasn't as high as you had been making in your own shops. And please note—I said for a while. When the factory's income goes up, the pay scale for the employees will go up, too."

"We have no guarantee of that, Koblin!" shouted one of the men. "Ol' Moneybags Wilhaus will keep the profits for himself!"

"Yeah! That's right!" cried out another, and the woodworkers began to shout for the factory to be shut down.

Baume called for silence once more, warning the people that they would be arrested if they kept it up.

When the din was lessening, another man shouted, "You don't have to worry about keeping food on your table and paying your bills, Koblin! Of course you're happy—your daughter works as the factory's bookkeeper. Her job has added income to the Baume household. The rest of us don't have that luxury!"

The man's words were like a sudden wind striking a campfire. The flame of fury began to spread through the crowd, and the woodworkers were shouting threats against the factory if it wasn't shut down.

Koblin Baume cried out for his officers to arrest them, and as the uniformed men were replacing their nightsticks with revolvers, a tall figure threaded his way through the angry men, raised his hands, and cried loudly for their attention. It took a few seconds, but when the woodworkers saw their leader at the front, they were soon quiet.

Every eye was on Alexander Metternik as he said, "Men, listen to me! This whole thing is getting out of hand. Now, just calm yourselves. It won't help our cause at all if we end up in jail or if somebody gets hurt!" He took a quick breath. "Let's all assemble here on Friday morning at eight o'clock and meet peacefully with Mr. Wilhaus and his two vice presidents. Certainly something can be worked out so everybody will be happy and satisfied."

A woodworker named Croft Susack stepped closer to the front, a cold, white fury in his eyes. "Alexander, I'm surprised at you! The only way we will be happy and satisfied is if this rich man's factory is closed down!"

"That's right!" bellowed another woodworker, whose name was Eldon Mott. Everyone knew Mott's two-year-old son, Borgen, had been recently stricken with a rare disease and was in a hospital in Zurich. The medical bills were already staggering.

Metternik raised a palm and said, "Eldon, I'm aware things are tough with your boy sick, but—"

"But nothing!" snapped Mott. "My wife and I can't make it, paying the medical bills for Borgen and keeping food on the table, too! Our income is next to nothing since this factory opened its doors. I say let's burn it to the ground!"

This brought loud cries of agreement.

Mott waved his hat in the air and shouted, "Let's burn it!"

Koblin Baume saw one of his officers looking at him questioningly.

Baume nodded, and the officer moved to Mott and lined his revolver on him. "All right, Eldon, you're under arrest. You're going to jail."

A friend of Mott's stepped up and growled at the officer, "You can't do this! Eldon's got enough problems without being locked up."

Another officer moved in and said crustily, "Back off, Ernst, or you'll be his cell mate!"

"Wait a minute!" shouted Metternik. "There's no reason that anybody should go to jail. Eldon, I'm sorry about your boy, but burning down the factory isn't going to solve his problem. Just calm down now. You too, Ernst." He turned to the burgomaster. "Koblin, please don't put Eldon in jail."

Baume looked at Mott. "You ready to take back before these men what you said about burning the factory?"

Mott scrubbed a shaky hand over his eyes, then looked at Metternik.

Nodding, he said, "I'm sorry, Koblin. I...I just lost my temper. I...I didn't mean it."

"All right," said Baume. "Let's everybody settle down."

"Yes," said Metternik, running his gaze over the faces of his friends. "Let's at least meet with Mr. Wilhaus and his executives Friday morning and see what they have to say."

There was silence.

Since no one spoke back, Metternik looked at the factory's manager. "Mr. Thorpe, we will be here Friday morning."

Obviously relieved, Durbin said, "Good. Mr. Wilhaus will be glad that he will have an opportunity to work things out."

Metternik looked around at his friends. "All right, men, let's all leave peacefully."

As the crowd began to break up, some of the woodworkers grumbled as they walked away, moving down the street in small groups.

A quietness finally settled over the small community. Stores and shops were open, and people who had been standing afar off went about their business on the beautiful spring day as a tentative peace settled over the town.

Two

Metryka Baume stood at the window in the factory office, watching the woodworkers fading from the scene below as the Wilhaus employees headed into the building to go to work. The threat of violence that had hung like a cloud in the air left its marks etched in her face. Wisps of hair hung limp and lifeless on her forehead.

Metryka stepped out of the office and descended the stairs, looking down at her father who was dismissing his officers, telling them to go back to headquarters. Koblin was about to say something to Durbin and Helmut Thorpe when he saw his daughter move off the bottom step and rush toward him. He opened his arms to her and felt her body trembling as she said, "Oh, Papa, I was so afraid there was going to be bloodshed."

Kissing the top of her head as he held her close, Koblin noticed Durbin and Helmut looking on as he said, "Well, honey, it didn't turn out that way, thanks to Alexander Metternik. If he hadn't stepped in..."

"That really surprised me, Papa. Alexander is usually the one to swing his fists first."

Koblin chuckled. "Yeah. He surprised me too. Pleasantly, I might add." He sent a glance toward the last of the woodworkers, who were now out of earshot, and said, "But I despise him, anyhow. Just like I despise the rest of those troublemakers."

Durbin stepped up with his son on his heels. "I feel the same way about them, Koblin. If I had my way, every one of them would be behind bars."

"Yeah," put in Helmut, "and the key would be thrown away."

Metryka looked at Helmut as if she were going to say something but decided against it.

"Well, son," said Durbin, "we'd better get back up to the office. We've got plenty of work to do. Metryka, you stay and talk to your father as long as you need to. I know this thing has been a harrowing experience for you."

Metryka nodded silently.

Helmut gave her a thin smile, then followed his father up the stairs.

When they had gone into the office, Metryka eased out of Koblin's grasp, touched up her hair, and said in a cautious manner, "Papa, I...I don't understand how you can despise those poor men."

Koblin's eyebrows arched and his eyes widened. "What? 'Poor men'? Why do you call them poor men?"

"For the most part, Papa, they are good, hardworking men who love their wives and children and want to provide an honest living for them by operating their wood shops. I've seen the fear and concern reflected in their eyes. There is no other way in this small town that they can make a decent living."

Koblin's back arched. "They've been offered jobs in the factory."

"Yes," she said hesitantly. "At less than half the income they were bringing in by working in their own shops. Papa...the factory's presence in Chur is going to force them to move elsewhere in order to provide enough income to care for their families. No wonder they're upset. They feel beaten down, with nowhere to turn. I realize I am employed at the factory, and I am glad for the income it gives me, but this industrial boom is not a good thing when it causes so much heartache for so many people. And what's going to happen to Chur's economy if they all pack up and move away?"

Koblin Baume's face was twisted into a scowl as he looked down at his daughter. A faint sigh passed over her lips as she shook her head and stared off into the distance.

Koblin set his mouth in a thin, bitter line. The agitation of his beefy face preceded a convulsive wrestling of his wide shoulders. "Metryka," he said stiffly, "you shouldn't defend Metternik and his bunch of troublemakers! They're standing in the way of progress. The industrial boom is here, and they need to get in line with the times."

"What about their wives and children, Papa? Have you thought of how they must feel? They've got to be frightened. Especially the wives. They need compassion and understanding."

Koblin set his jaw and hissed through his teeth, "I don't like what I am hearing from you, Metryka. Ever since that fanatic Erik Linden talked you into becoming one of those born-again Christians, you've lost your good sense. You need to get your eyes off of individuals and be concerned about what is best over all for the town. The factory is a boon for Chur. It's the best thing that has ever happened to it."

"Oh, Papa, come on, now," she said defensively. "I had compassion for people before I ever met Erik. But what about you? Chur's burgomaster should think about those poor wives and children and what they are going through. Like Eldon and Veronica Mott. And little Borgen. How are Eldon and Veronica going to pay the medical bills for that poor little boy? Their income is gone."

Koblin was finding it difficult to answer her and was glad when Durbin Thorpe appeared at the top of the stairs. "Koblin, I need to talk to you. I know you'll be heading back for your office pretty soon. Could I walk along and talk to you, then?"

"Sure," he said, flicking a glance at Metryka, then looking back up at Durbin. "I'm going right now. I need to let Metryka get back to work, anyhow. Come on."

Giving her father a pleasant smile, Metryka said, "I'll see you this evening, Papa." With that, she headed for the stairs, and the two men moved down the street.

When she entered the office, Helmut looked up at her from his desk, smiled, and said, "Are you all right?"

Metryka took a shallow breath, nodded, and said as she moved to her desk, "I'm fine, now that the threat of violence is past. At least for the present."

Helmut left his chair as she sat down, stood over her, and said, "I was listening at the window and heard your father's comment about the 'born-again Christian' thing."

Metryka chuckled drily. "Yes. Papa brings it up quite often."

Bending down so as to put his face on her level, Helmut said, "Well, sweetheart, pretty soon your father won't be bringing that up to you anymore." Then he reached out, cupped her chin in his hand, and leaned close to kiss her.

Jerking her head back, she looked toward the window. "Not now, Helmut. Somebody might see us."

Cupping her chin in his hand again, he said, "If anybody's going to approach the window or the door, we'll hear their footsteps first. Then he kissed her. "June 26 is barely more than a month away, Metryka. When are you going to tell Erik?"

A wry smiled curved her lips. "As soon as I get a chance. And the sooner the better. He'll be back from Bern on Thursday's train. I'll tell him the wedding's off as soon as I can get him alone after he gets back."

At the west edge of town, Alexander Metternik and three of his men had stopped in a grove of evergreen trees and were discussing the incident at the factory's gate.

Croft Susack laughed and said, "Oh, I understand now, Alexander. You were only acting peaceful in front of Baume and his bunch to make it look good."

"That's it," said Metternik. "I want them totally off guard for what I've got in mind."

"Well, I hope it's good, Alexander," said Arthur Wengen. "This meeting with Eiger Wilhaus on Friday isn't going to accomplish a thing."

"Right," put in Thomas Allman. "It's a waste of our time and his."

"For sure," agreed Metternik. "Ol' Moneybags is nothing but a greedy scoundrel who has no concern for other people. No matter how long we meet with him, he isn't going to raise the pay scale for the factory's employees. But I'll tell you what he will do. He'll try to convince all of us independent woodworkers that lower income is better than no income, and that we should come to work for him."

"Sure," said Susack. "So we can help produce even more money for him."

"So what have you got in mind, Alexander?" asked Wengen.

"You men agree that something has to be done about Wilhaus, right?"

All three nodded and spoke their agreement.

"Well, I've been devising a plan."

"We're all ears," said Allman.

"You men are aware that there is only one train per day from Bern to Chur."

Again, they nodded, listening intently.

"The train leaves Bern at ten-thirty every morning, and since it has two stops along the way, it takes two and a half hours to cover the one-hundred-mile distance between Bern and here."

"Correct," said Susack.

A wicked sneer captured Metternik's features. "On Thursday, Ol' Moneybags and two of his vice presidents will be aboard the train. It's time the big money people in this country and the Swiss government leaders learn a much-needed lesson. In its journey from Bern to Chur, the train passes through Nidwalden Tunnel in the Alps, right?"

All three nodded once more.

"And how long is the tunnel?"

"Six miles," said Wengen.

"Exactly," said Metternik. "I need my three friends, here, to help me. A little dynamite positioned in just the right place in the tunnel, with fuses long enough for us to get out before it goes off, will be sufficient to teach the big money people and the government leaders that they can't push us common folks around."

"Dynamite?" said Thomas Allman, his brow puckered. "You mean blow up the train?"

"Exactly!" Metternik laughed. "And that will take care of Ol' Moneybags and his two cohorts."

"Hey, that's good!" said Croft Susack. "That'll be enough to make the Wilhaus Industries take another look at their Chur factory, and it'll teach the rest of the big shots in the country the lesson they need. And Ol' Eiger won't be around to persuade them differently."

"Great idea, Alexander!" said Arthur Wengen. "We'll put some fear in them for sure."

Thomas Allman's face was a gray mask. "But...but innocent people will die, too, Alexander. We shouldn't—"

"That's the breaks of war, Thomas," cut in Metternik. "Innocent people always get killed in wars. And this is war! It's either let our families starve...or do battle. As for me, I'm going to do battle!"

"Me too!" said Susack. "We've put up with the big money people in this country long enough."

"Right!" agreed Wengen. "Let's do it!"

Metternik set steady eyes on Allman. "Well, Thomas, are you in the battle with us, or are you going to be a conscientious objector?"

Sweat glistened on Allman's pallid face. He blinked and wet his lips with his tongue.

"Well?" demanded Metternik with the other two glaring at Allman.

Thomas swallowed with difficulty, took a short breath, and nodded. "I...I guess it is war, isn't it? And I've got to protect my family. All right. I'm in the battle with you."

"Good!" laughed Metternik, clapping a hand on Thomas's back. "Now let me explain my plan..."

On Tuesday evening, May 24, a crowd was gathering in the spacious auditorium at the University of Bern for the graduation ceremonies of the university's highly esteemed medical college.

People were greeting one another with warm smiles as they were taking their seats, and there were little bursts of laughter punctuating the air as the university orchestra was playing from the orchestra pit.

Soon the medical school's top administrators entered from a side door just off the side of the elevated stage in their caps and gowns. With them was the graduation speaker, who was flanked by Dr. Richard Clough, president of the university, and Dr. Jacob Plenz, chief administrator of the medical college.

When the people on the platform were standing in place, the orchestra conductor signaled for the musicians to fade their rousing number and go into the processional.

On cue at the back of the auditorium, the graduating class of medical students began filing down both aisles and moving into the reserved section of seats directly in front of center stage.

When the graduates were seated, Dr. Plenz approached the podium, welcomed the guests warmly, and the graduation ceremonies began.

Some fifty minutes later, after the valedictorian had spoken and all other necessary things had been said and done, Dr. Richard Clough stepped to the podium. "Ladies and gentlemen," he said, smiling and running his gaze over the sea of faces, "it is my distinct pleasure to introduce the speaker for our 1892 graduation. Dr. Erik Linden—"

There was an instant burst of applause.

Lifting his hands, Clough signaled for silence. "I know most of you have heard of our speaker, and many of you know him personally." He chuckled. "But please allow me to inform those who do not know him of his accomplishments."

Laughter swept over the crowd.

Clough cleared his throat. "Now, as I was about to say, Dr. Erik Linden is an 1888 graduate of Bern University Medical College. He is on record as being among the top five students in his scholastic achievements to graduate from this institution. In addition to his high grades, Dr. Linden was on the honor roll consistently from the first semester of his freshman year until he graduated in May of 1888.

"Our graduation speaker was also senior class president and valedictorian of his graduating class. As I said a moment ago, most of you have heard of Dr. Linden, and are aware that at twenty-six years of age, he has had remarkable success in these past four years. Upon graduating, he was hired by the esteemed Dr. Joseph Danzig at the Chur Medical Clinic, and just one year later, Dr. Danzig made him a partner. Since then, we have read in our newspapers of the great number of difficult surgical operations Dr. Linden has performed, every one of them being successful. He has broken ground for new thought in certain surgical procedures, and his ideas have been adopted by surgeons all over Switzerland, and Germany. Those same procedures have also been adopted by our surgical professors here at Bern University Medical College."

Clough then turned, gestured toward the speaker, and said, "Ladies and gentlemen, may I present our distinguished speaker, Dr. Erik Linden."

Applause spread over the auditorium as Dr. Linden stepped to the podium and shook Dr. Clough's hand. Clough sat down, and Linden smiled at the crowd. The applause diminished quickly, leaving silence over the crowd.

Dr. Erik Linden captured the audience's attention immediately with his warm and charming personality and his superb speaking ability.

When Linden finished his encouraging and uplifting speech, directed mainly to the graduates, he closed off by clearly and unashamedly giving credit to his Lord and Saviour Jesus Christ for the success he had enjoyed thus far in the medical profession. These remarks were met with loud and long applause.

Soon the graduates passed across the stage to receive their diplomas, and when this was done, the time for congratulations arrived. Dr. Linden found himself swamped with admirers who commented favorably on his speech and some complimented him on his boldly giving glory to the Lord Jesus Christ. Most of the compliments on the latter were from people with whom he was well acquainted because they were from the church he had attended during his years at the university. Among them were his special friends Hyram and Elsa Quolvey, whose son Derek—also twenty-six—had been Linden's closest friend during his four years in Bern. The Quolveys waited till everyone else had passed by, then approached the young doctor.

Elsa hugged him. "Erik, that was some speech. You really did a marvelous job."

Erik kissed her cheek and said, "Thank you, Elsa."

Hyram shook hands with Erik. "That Dr. Clough sure made you sound bright and intelligent. I could tell him how I helped you with your studies all the way through medical school, but I wouldn't want to steal your thunder!"

Elsa laughed. "Oh, sure, dear husband of mine. Since when did bricklayers know anything about medicine?"

Erik chortled, laid a hand on Hyram's shoulder, and said, "Why, since I started to medical school, Elsa. Didn't you know?"

The three of them had a good laugh together, then Hyram said, "You're still going to spend the day with us tomorrow, aren't you, Erik? Like you said in your letter, when we wrote and asked you?"

"Sure am. Since I'm going home on Thursday, tomorrow is my day to spend with my favorite people in Switzerland's capital city."

"We're looking forward to it," said Elsa. "And...we have a big surprise for you."

"Surprise? Does it have anything to do with Derek?"

Elsa giggled as Hyram's smile spread all over his face. "It sure does!" she said. "Derek and Marla are coming from Luzern to see you! And they'll have their new baby boy with them! They'll be here late tonight."

"Wonderful!" exclaimed Erik, his hazel eyes twinkling. "It will be nice to finally meet Marla. I haven't heard what they named their baby."

Hyram said, "We're not going to tell you what they named him. We'll let Derek and Marla tell you."

Erik chuckled, shook his head, and said, "Well, I know they didn't name him 'Elsa' after his grandmother!" His dark brown, wavy hair caught the light.

Elsa giggled again.

Putting on a mock frown, Erik looked at her husband. "Oh, no! Don't tell me they named him 'Hyram'!"

"Well, you're just going to have to wait till tomorrow to find out," said Elsa. "We'll have a picnic in the backyard in the afternoon.

But we want you there by nine o'clock in the morning. All right?"

"Sure!" said Erik. "It will be so good to see Derek again."

Three

On Wednesday morning, Dr. Erik Linden was rinsing his face at the small table in his hotel room after shaving, and as he applied the towel to his face, he smiled at his reflection in the mirror. "Well, Erik, old boy, tomorrow afternoon you'll hold that sweet girl in your arms again."

When his face was dry, he closed his eyes and said, "Oh, Metryka, it's only a month and two days until you become my blushing bride." Then opening his eyes, he looked at his reflection again. "Erik, old boy, you have been blessed beyond measure. In addition to being partner to the greatest physician and surgeon in Switzerland, the Lord has given you the most beautiful and wonderful woman in the whole world. Metryka, my sweet, we are going to be so happy!"

With light heart, Erik combed his hair and dressed, checking the ticking clock on the dresser. "Seven-thirty," he said to himself as he picked up his necktie. "Plenty of time."

When the tie was knotted perfectly, the man put on his suit coat, picked up the room key off the dresser, and stepped out into the hall. Inserting the key in the lock, he turned it, pocketed the key, and headed down the hall toward the staircase.

He was just about to the bottom of the stairs, when he glanced across the lobby and saw the two distinguished-looking men come in from the street. Smiling, he hurried toward them, extending his right hand. "Dr. Clough, Dr. Plenz, what an honor that you would join me for breakfast!"

"We are the ones who are honored," said Dr. Richard Clough.

"Yes, we are," said Dr. Jacob Plenz. "We are so proud of you, and do we ever brag about you whenever the newspapers carry another story of your new surgical methods! It's such a pleasure to tell people that you are one of our graduates."

Erik blushed. "I appreciate that, gentlemen, but whatever contributions I've made to the medical profession would not have happened if the Lord hadn't given me the knack for them in my mind. He made me as I am, so the credit goes to Him."

"Not to take anything from the Lord, son," said Clough, who was the oldest in the trio, "but there has been some deep thought and hard work on your part, too."

"Well, gentlemen," said Erik, looking toward the restaurant at the end of the lobby, "how about some breakfast?"

Soon the three men were eating, and between bites, the two university executives talked to Erik about some of his innovations in improving surgical methods. He had improved on eighteenth-century French surgeon J. L. Petit's effective tourniquet for leg and arm amputations which controlled blood flow while the surgeon carried out his normal ligatures.

They discussed Erik's procedures on amputations for a few minutes, then Dr. Clough brought up the article he had read a year ago in the *Bern Chronicle* on Erik's new method of performing a lithotomy. He asked how Erik came up with removing a bladder stone so quickly without developing complications, and when the young physician explained it, both men agreed that Erik's method was marvelous.

Dr. Plenz then referred to another article in the same newspaper some six months ago, which told of Dr. Erik Linden's accomplishment in coming up with a new approach to ovariotomies that had given them a higher percentage of success, and even more, his improvised handling of cesarian sections, which had been copied already by a great number of European surgeons.

By the time the older men had heard Erik's explanation of these last two innovations, breakfast was over. Complimenting the young doctor on his work, both men said once more that they were proud to name him as a graduate of the University of Bern Medical College, and took their leave.

Erik checked the time and saw that he must hurry to make it to the Quolvey home by nine o'clock.

While Dr. Erik Linden was speedily making his way to the home of Hyram and Elsa Quolvey in Bern, a hundred miles away in Chur, Adolf Combray was busy stocking shelves at Chur Hardware, of which he was proprietor.

He looked up to see one of the independent woodworkers enter the store, and greeted him with a smile. Paul Gressman returned the smile and said, "I need some wood screws and some varnish, Adolf."

"Well, I'll be glad to sell them to you, my friend," said the proprietor, laying aside the materials he had in his hands.

As the proprietor and his customer walked to the shelves where the needed materials lay, Adolf said, "Apparently you've still got some work."

"At this point, yes," said Paul. "It's a cabinet job I started for farmer Wald Malford three weeks ago. You know—before the no-good factory opened up." He took a deep breath and sighed. "This is the last job I have. The factory will have all the business that would have been mine. I can't compete with Wilhaus's prices. It's the same for the rest of the independent woodworkers. There's no more work."

Adolf nodded. "How well I know. It sure has cut my business way down. Since you woodworkers don't have jobs anymore, you don't buy anything from me."

Paul's jaw muscles rippled, and his skin had taken on a red tint. "This situation with the factory is not going to be settled just because Eiger Wilhaus is coming to talk to us. It will never—"

Both men were looking toward the front door and saw the large frame of the burgomaster enter. Spotting them, Koblin Baume moved that direction. Paul said, "I have to go, Adolf. I'll come back and get the screws and varnish later." With that, he headed toward the door, avoiding eye contact with Baume.

The burgomaster stopped, turned, and said, "Hello, Paul."

Gressman did not so much as look back. He was instantly out the door, and gone.

Shrugging his wide shoulders, Baume looked at Combray. "What's his problem, Adolf?"

Before Adolf could respond, the door opened again, and he saw his wife and daughter enter. Their faces clouded when they saw the burgomaster.

Adolf tried to lighten things. "Well, there are the two most beautiful women in the world!"

Farina Combray and her twenty-one-year-old daughter quickly changed expressions and moved toward the two men.

"Good morning, Chief," said Farina. She said to her husband, "And don't you forget that, dear."

"That's right, Papa," said blond Dova. "Hello, Chief Baume."

Obviously nervous, Adolf chuckled hollowly and said, "How could I forget that the Lord gave me the two most beautiful women in the world?"

Baume touched his hatbrim, nodded, and said, "Good morning, Farina, Dova. It is nice to see you." Then to Adolf: "Back to my question. What is Paul's problem? Have I offended him in some way?"

"I'm surprised you have to ask," said Adolf. "He is an independent woodworker, and you have sided with Eiger Wilhaus and Durbin Thorpe. Paul was telling me he is on his last job, which he started before the factory opened. He has no more work lined up when this cabinet job is finished."

Baume jutted his jaw. "He could take a job in the factory."

"Oh yes," said Farina, "and struggle to keep food on the table, let alone keep the house warm in the winter and clothes on everybody's back in the family."

"It'll be more than a struggle if he doesn't take the factory job," the burgomaster said flatly.

"And what about us, Koblin?" said Adolf in a level tone.

"What do you mean?" queried Baume stiffly.

"Have you any idea how our business has gone down since the factory opened? More than half of what we have sold here in the store since we opened twenty-two years ago has gone to the woodworkers. We're hurting too, Koblin. Will the factory hire me? All I know how to do is run a hardware store."

The burgomaster frowned, but did not reply. Clearing his throat, he said, "Adolf, I came in to buy a new hammer. I'm doing a little work on my back porch in my spare time, and I broke the handle to the old hammer I've had ever since we came to Chur."

While Adolf was selling Koblin the hammer, Farina and Dova went into the office. When Koblin was gone, Adolf entered the office and sighed. "I wish Eiger Wilhaus had kept his Wilhaus Industries in Bern. He's brought nothing but trouble to this town."

Dova nodded. "You're right, Papa. Could you tell Pastor Helms was on the verge of saying something like that in his sermon Sunday night when he was preaching about trials and troubles coming into Christians' lives?"

Adolf grinned. "I see I'm not the only one who sensed his feelings about that."

"Well, that makes three of us," said Farina. "And I imagine there were many more who were sitting in the pews thinking the same thing."

"Papa, what are we going to do?" asked Dova. "How are we going to make a living?"

"We'll just have to trust the Lord, honey," replied Adolf. "We trusted Him with our souls when we opened our hearts to Jesus, didn't we?"

"Yes."

"Well, if we can trust Him to take our souls to heaven when we leave this world, I believe we can trust Him to take care of us while we're still here, can't we?"

While Dova was thinking on her father's words, Farina sensed the fear in her daughter's heart and laid a hand on her arm.

Dova nodded, set her blue eyes on her father, and said, "Yes, Papa. We can trust Him to take care of us."

They heard the front door of the store open, and Adolf headed for the office door, saying, "Sounds like more business, praise the Lord."

When Dr. Erik Linden knocked on the door at the Quolvey home in Bern, it was three minutes before nine o'clock. He had seen the curtain on the parlor window stir as he mounted the porch steps, and even while he was knocking, the door came open. A smiling Derek Quolvey lunged for him, and the two friends embraced.

The reunion was a sweet one, and when they let go of each other, Erik saw Hyram and Elsa standing with a lovely young woman, who was smiling at the scene before her. Elsa was holding a chubby baby boy.

Derek introduced Marla to Erik, then told Erik it was all right for him to hug her. When that was done, Marla giggled and said, "Derek, darling, I don't understand."

"Don't understand what?" asked Derek.

She giggled again. "You told me Erik was ugly. He's not ugly. I think he's quite handsome!"

Derek's face reddened. "Erik, when you get to know this woman I married, you'll realize she's got an ornery streak."

Marla laughed. "I think Erik has already figured that out, darling!"

Then everybody laughed, including Erik.

Elsa stepped forward and said, "Erik, there's someone else for you to meet."

Erik's eyes lit up as he looked down at the gurgling baby. "May I hold him?" he asked.

"Of course," said Elsa, placing the baby in his hands.

Marla chuckled. "Little Erik should be safe in the hands of a prominent physician and surgeon, wouldn't you say?"

The doctor's jaw sagged, and his eyes widened. "Did you say—"

"Yes," Marla said, giggling again. "Derek insisted on naming him after this ugly friend of his."

Everybody laughed again, and Erik tickled the fat cheeks of his namesake. "Well, little Erik, for sure you're not ugly. You're one handsome little man!"

"He gets that from his grandfather," Hyram said emphatically.

"Yes," said Marla, "my papa is one good-looking fellow!"

There was more laughter, then in a serious tone, Erik expressed his deep appreciation for Derek and Marla naming their baby after him.

The rest of the morning was taken up with Erik and Derek exchanging facts about what had happened in their lives since they last saw each other four years ago.

What Elsa called a picnic was more like a feast. She had gone all out in preparing for the celebration of the reuniting of her son with his best friend. The day was warm and cloudless, and a delightful breeze wended its way through the many trees in the yard. The air was perfumed both with the pungent scent of evergreens and the mouth-watering aroma rising from the table laden with tasty delights.

After Hyram had offered a prayer of thanks for the food and for the Lord making the day's occasion possible, everybody dug in. While they were loading their plates, Hyram said, "Marla, did Derek ever tell you that when Erik was here going to medical school, people at the church used to say how he and Erik were so alike that they could have been twins? Not in their physical features, but in personality."

"No, he didn't, Papa Hyram," said Marla.

"Well, there were lots of people in the church who delighted in calling them twins. Their names even rhymed: Erik and Derek."

A mock wicked grin curved Derek's lips. "I'm sure glad it wasn't our physical features, as ugly as he is!"

Erik chuckled, reached across the table, and playfully punched Derek's chin. "Take that, you meanie!"

Elsa laughed, and said, "It's like nothing's changed in four years!

You two still carry on like you always did!"

"I'll probably have to spank them both before the day's over," said Hyram, chuckling.

Questions then were asked of Erik by Derek and his parents about the clinic in Chur. Though Chur was only a midsized town, all of them knew of Dr. Joseph Danzig and his exceptional medical practice. Erik told them some of the most interesting surgeries he had done, and explained that he was doing more and more of the surgeries in the clinic because Dr. Danzig was unable to perform surgery like he used to.

Erik went on to explain that Dr. Danzig's wife had died eight months ago, and he hadn't been the same since. He would soon be seventy-six, and his age was preventing him from being able to carry the normal workload. Erik was putting in long hours to keep up with the workload, which he didn't mind, but he was growing more and more concerned about Dr. Danzig.

"I'm sure Dr. Danzig is very glad to have you as his partner," said Marla.

Erik grinned. "He seems to be."

Derek took a sip of lemonade, set the glass down, and said, "Now, old pal, I want to know if there is a young lady in your life."

"I was going to ask about that," said Hyram.

Elsa chuckled. "And so was I."

Erik's face beamed as he said, "I'm very happy to tell you that I am engaged to a beautiful young lady of twenty-three whose name is Metryka Baume. She has coal black hair and dark blue eyes. Her father, Koblin Baume, is Chur's burgomaster."

Hyram raised his eyebrows. "Well, I'm impressed! Your future father-in-law is a burgomaster!"

"That's really something," said Derek. "With all of the esteem the burgomasters carry in Europe, it won't hurt your career to be related to one of them!"

Erik shrugged coyly. "What can I say?"

The others laughed, then Derek asked, "How did you meet Metryka?"

"Well, it really was quite simple. The Baumes have gone to Dr.

Danzig for many years. In fact, Dr. Danzig delivered Metryka when she was born. I had become acquainted with her while caring for her when she had influenza about two and half years ago. She was sick for quite a while, and during that time, I witnessed to her of her need to know the Lord Jesus Christ. She listened politely but made no move to be saved. Then about a year ago, when she was in the clinic for a minor infection, I talked to her about Jesus again. The seed of the Word had done its job in her heart, and I had the joy of leading her to the Lord. We fell in love shortly thereafter."

"Have you set a wedding date?" asked Marla.

"Yes," he said, light dancing in his eyes. "It's barely more than a month away: Sunday afternoon, June 26. It will be at our church and a large crowd is expected, since Metryka's father is the burgomaster."

"I'm sure that's true," said Hyram. "I assume Metryka wasn't raised in a Christian home."

"No, sir. Koblin Baume is very much opposed to anything related to God, His Son, the Bible, and churches that preach the gospel. He is a big, blustering man and has a hot temper. Mrs. Baume is afraid to even consider becoming a Christian. Metryka's father gives her a hard time about having become a Christian. One good thing, though, he hasn't tried to interfere with his daughter marrying me, even though he blames me for persuading Metryka to become a Christian. I figure it's because he sees some prestige in his daughter being married to a medical doctor."

Hyram nodded. "I can understand that."

"Since your wedding is so close," said Derek, "do you have a place to live?"

"Yes. Metryka and I are having a house built in Chur. It's almost finished."

"Well, it sounds like things are going very good for you, my friend," said Derek. "I'm really glad for you."

"We all are," said Elsa. "As hard as you worked in medical school, and as faithful as you are to the Lord, you deserve success and happiness."

"So how's your family, Erik?" asked Hyram.

"Everybody's doing fine, sir. Papa's still doing well as Chur's blacksmith, and Mama's busy taking care of the house. Of course, she gets a lot of help from Justina." He shook his head. "It's hard to believe that my little sister is twenty-one now."

"They grow up in a hurry," said Elsa, running her gaze to Derek. "Before you know it, they have flown from the nest and made their own nest."

Derek grinned and shot a glance at Marla.

"Let's see," said Hyram. "It's been so long since we met your family at your graduation. How old are your brothers, now?"

"Ludwig is nineteen, sir. And Brandt is seventeen. They are quite the young men. Ludwig is showing interest in following Papa's line of work, and of course, Brandt is still in school."

"I sure hope we get to see them all sometime," said Hyram.

"Maybe we can go for the wedding, dear," said Elsa.

Smiling broadly, Erik said, "You would sure be welcome, I'll tell you that."

"We'll have to put some thought to it," said Hyram.

"Maybe we can, too," said Derek.

"Be sure I get your address," said Erik, "and you'll get your formal invitation. So will you, Hyram and Elsa."

On Wednesday evening in Chur, the Linden family sat down to supper. Their guest for the meal was Justina's best friend, Dova Combray. The Linden and Combray families were close friends and regularly sat on the same pew together at church.

When they had joined hands around the table, Frederic led in prayer, thanking the Lord for the food and asking Him to bring Erik safely home to them tomorrow.

As they began to eat, the conversation turned to Erik. His mother, Mura, said, "I'm so honored that Dr. Clough asked Erik to be the graduation speaker."

"Me too, sweetheart," said Frederic.

"I'm so proud of him," she said, then ran her gaze to Justina, Ludwig, and Brandt. "I'm proud of these other children too, because each one of them loves the Lord and is seeking His will for their lives."

"We couldn't ask for better children, Mama," said Frederic.

Ludwig smiled. "And we couldn't ask for a better sister-in-law, either. I'll be glad to have Metryka in the family when she and Erik get married."

"The rest of us feel the same," said Mura. "My heart is so heavy for her parents. I so much want them to be saved."

"Me too," said Brandt. "From what Erik has said, I guess they've never let him talk about the Lord."

"Well, one thing for sure," said Ludwig, "Pastor Helms always puts a clear gospel message in his wedding ceremonies. The Baumes will hear it then."

Frederic nodded. "Indeed they will. You know, at first it looked like Koblin was going to refuse to walk Metryka down the aisle because he hates the thought of being inside a church building."

"I'm sure glad he gave in to it," said Mura. "It would have broken Metryka's heart if he hadn't. It would have broken Kathlyn's heart, too, because if Koblin had refused to enter the church building, he wouldn't let his wife go to the wedding, either."

"Well, I'm glad Koblin's going to do what he ought to do," said Frederic.

"Me too," said Ludwig. "And I'm proud to be one of the ushers."

"It's going to be a beautiful wedding," said Brandt.

"Yes," said Justina. "And one reason is that Dr. Danzig is going to be Erik's best man. I'm sure it meant a lot to him when Erik asked him to be his best man. And Metryka's best friend, Sonya Waltman, told me with tears in her eyes how happy she is to be Metryka's maid of honor. I'm quite happy to be one of the bridesmaids."

As she spoke, Justina's gaze wandered to Dova Combray, whose eyes had a distant look. Bending her head a little, she said, "Dova, don't you think it's going to be a beautiful wedding?"

Still preoccupied, Dova continued to stare distantly.

"Dova," said Justina a little louder, while the others looked on.

Dova's head turned. She blinked and said, "I'm sorry. What did you say?"

"I asked if you thought Erik and Metryka are going to have a beautiful wedding."

"Oh...ah...yes, of course."

Justina frowned. "Honey, are you all right?"

"Why, yes. Please forgive me. I've got something pretty heavy on my mind."

"Oh, of course," said Justina. "This furniture factory thing."

Dova blinked again. "Yes. The furniture factory thing. I'm so concerned about what's going to happen. I'm afraid there's going to be bloodshed."

"I seriously doubt this meeting Eiger Wilhaus and his two vice presidents are going to have with the woodworkers on Friday will accomplish anything good," said Frederic. I'm afraid it's going to end up in a big fight like has happened at some of the other factories in Europe."

"It will unless the burgomaster and his officers can somehow put the fear in the woodworkers," put in Mura.

"And even if they are able to do that," said Ludwig, "it won't surprise me if the woodworkers break into the factory some night and destroy all the machinery."

"And maybe burn the place down," said Brandt. "Like what other men have done to factories all over Europe."

Dova brushed a lock of blond hair from her forehead. "Papa is predicting bloodshed. Since he has sold the woodworkers their building materials for all of these years, he knows them pretty well. He has told Mama and me that he doesn't trust Alexander Metternik. By Metternik's past bloody fights in the taverns, he has proven he has a quick temper. I know he put on a good show in front of the crowd on Monday, but Papa says there's something underlying his act. He really expects Metternik to lead the woodworkers to riot if Eiger Wilhaus doesn't meet his demands in this meeting."

"I suppose the woodworkers being out of work has hurt your father's business," said Frederic.

"Very much so," said Dova. "It's cut the store's income drastically."

"You all know woodworkers David Cowan and Colter Glumac," said Mura.

All eyes turned to her. "I got to talking to their wives at Faulk's Grocery this morning. They told me that they are going to take their families and go to America where work is plentiful and people can control their own destinies in the 'land of the free.'"

"Well, I can't blame them," said Frederic. "I've heard much the past year or so about the lure that America presents to people from all over the world. Certainly many Europeans are going there to start life anew. I hope it works out well for the Cowans and the Glumacs."

It grew quiet at the table for a few minutes, then Brandt said, "I just thought about it. Since Eiger Wilhaus and his vice presidents are to arrive here tomorrow, they will be on the same train as Erik."

"Yes," said Ludwig, "I guess they will."

"Well, if they happen to be in the same coach," said Brandt, "they could get to talking. Erik is smart. Before he left for Bern on Monday, he was saying that the only way they will be able to avoid bloodshed is if Mr. Wilhaus will hire Chur's independent woodworkers and pay them a fair wage. Otherwise, Erik said, there is going to be a head-on collision between them."

"Erik is right," said Frederic, "but Eiger Wilhaus is so greedy, he will not pay the kind of wages it will take for the woodworkers to accept the jobs."

"If Mr. Wilhaus would listen to Erik," said Brandt, "he might be able to convince him that there is going to be real trouble unless he offers the woodworkers reasonable wages and hires them all."

Mura sighed. "I'm afraid Mr. Wilhaus will not give in, no matter what he is told. Besides, chances are slim that Erik will be in the same car with him. And even if he should be, the wealthy Eiger Wilhaus probably won't have anything to do with a small-town doctor."

Four

It was another glorious spring day with a flood of morning sunlight streaming down brilliantly over the city of Bern as Hyram Quolvey swung his carriage into the parking lot at the railroad terminal. A fragrant breeze wafted its way through the surrounding trees, fluttering the leaves, while birds twittered happily in the branches.

Derek Quolvey stretched his neck to get a view of the train that stood under the long canopy in the depot. "We're all right, Erik. That's your train."

Even as Derek was speaking, the sound of the conductor's voice calling for all passengers to board echoed from the depot across to the parking lot.

As Hyram pulled rein, he said, "Erik, I'm sorry about being late to pick you up at the hotel."

"It's all right, Hyram," said Erik, grasping the leather handle of his overnight bag. "I'll make it."

As Erik hopped out, Derek started to get out. "Don't bother, Derek. I've got to make a run for it and get right on the train."

Derek smiled and said, "Sure was good to see you. We'll be

expecting the wedding invitation."

"Us too," said Elsa from the rear seat.

Erik smiled. "I'm sure Metryka will have them in the mail soon. Good-bye, Marla, and take care of my little namesake."

"I will," Marla said, matching his smile, and looking at the baby in her arms.

"Good-bye, Elsa. Thanks for the delicious meal yesterday."

"My pleasure," she said.

"Good-bye, Hyram. I'm sure glad you didn't have to spank us boys."

Hyram grinned.

Erik cuffed his friend on the chin and said, "Take care, Derek."

With that, he turned and ran toward the train.

The train that ran between Bern and Chur had three coaches behind the coal car, and a dining car behind the last passenger coach. As Erik drew up to the train, the bell on the engine was ringing, and steam was hissing from the boiler. The conductor saw him coming and pointed to the third passenger coach. Erik nodded and veered that direction. Two men were mounting the metal steps, and when Erik moved inside behind them, they were picking seats on the aisle in a coach that was nearly full.

Erik's eyes ran ahead, and he saw a seat midway in the coach occupied singly by a well-dressed man, who was sitting next to the window. He was in animated conversation with two other well-dressed men in the seat ahead of him. Hurrying to the seat, Erik stopped, smiled down at the man and said, "Has anyone claimed this seat, sir?"

"No," replied the man. "It's all yours." He smiled as he spoke.

"Thank you," said Erik. He placed his bag in the overhead rack.

The three men went back to their conversation as Erik wearily lowered himself on the seat. The whistle on the engine blew and there was a series of dull, thumping sounds as the engine lurched forward, setting up momentum between the cars.

It had been a tiring and emotional trip, and Erik was looking forward to easing back on the seat and gathering his thoughts. As the train rolled out of the terminal, he eased back and closed his eyes.

His mind went immediately to his beautiful Metryka and the upcoming wedding. He felt a throb in his breast as he envisioned her lovely face and the smile she so often gave him.

After a while, he began to mentally tick off the items that he needed to tend to before that glorious day arrived.

Erik opened his eyes when he heard the front door of the coach open and close and the conductor call out, "Tickets, please! Have your tickets ready, please!"

The man next to Erik eased back on the seat and took his ticket from an inside pocket of his suit coat. When the conductor had punched both their tickets and moved on down the aisle, the man extended his hand and said, "My name is Agno Lutrey. I'm with the Wilhaus Industries. You probably know about our company."

Erik felt his stomach turn over. Gripping Lutrey's hand, he forced a smile and said, "Yes, of course. I'm Dr. Erik Linden."

Lutrey's eyes widened, and his smile broadened. "Oh! Dr. Erik Linden of the Danzig Medical Clinic in Chur?"

"Yes, sir."

"I've read about your work, Doctor. And I must say, I am quite surprised to see that you are so young."

Erik chuckled softly but could think of nothing to say.

"Let me introduce you to Mr. Eiger Wilhaus, Doctor." Leaning close to the two men in the seat ahead, Lutrey said, "Mr. Wilhaus, you'll never guess who is sitting next to me."

Both men turned around in their seats and smiled at Erik.

"Dr. Erik Linden," said Lutrey, "I want you to meet Mr. Eiger Wilhaus."

The silver-haired Wilhaus smiled warmly, reached over the back of the seat, and shook Erik's hand. "We've all read of your outstanding accomplishments, Dr. Linden. I'm very happy to meet you. This gentleman next to me is also one of my vice presidents: Zugg Hinwill."

Hinwill shook Erik's hand, also complimenting him on his medical achievements.

Meeting Erik's gaze, Wilhaus said, "You are aware of our new furniture factory in Chur, Doctor?"

"Yes, sir." Erik's stomach turned over again.

"And I suppose you know about the trouble that has developed with the independent woodworkers since we opened the factory."

"Yes. I'm aware that the woodworkers were on the street in front of the factory last Wednesday, Thursday, and Friday, voicing their protests against it. It looks to me like the situation is on the verge of violence."

"Yes. My vice presidents and I are on our way there to see what we can do about the problem. We're meeting with the woodworkers in front of the factory tomorrow morning."

"I see. Well, I sure hope it will serve to avoid violence."

"We'll do everything in our power to reason with them," said Zugg Hinwill.

"We sure will," said Wilhaus.

The coach was swaying as the train charged full-speed eastward with the steady rhythmic sound of the clicking wheels beneath them. Dark clouds of smoke floated past the windows then disappeared.

Erik adjusted himself on the seat, looked Wilhaus in the eye, and said, "What basis of reasoning will you use, sir?"

"I'm going to offer every one of them a job in the factory."

Erik nodded. "Apparently you told Durbin Thorpe you were going to do this. He has already mentioned it to the woodworkers."

"Yes, I did tell him. But I feel it will set better with the woodworkers if they hear it from me and my two vice presidents."

Moving his head back and forth, Erik said, "I doubt it, sir. From what I heard, the wages you pay your factory employees are much lower than the money the woodworkers were making in their own businesses before the factory opened and started taking their customers."

"This is true, Doctor, but our reasoning will be that if the woodworkers take the jobs we are offering in the factory, at least they will have income. We hope to help them see that earning some money is better than earning none."

"And something else, Dr. Linden," said Zugg Hinwill, rubbing his temples with the tips of his fingers, "from what Durbin Thorpe has told us, the factory has already been a boon to Chur's economy."

"I'm glad for that," said Erik, "but my heart goes out to the independent woodworkers and their families for what they are going through. They're frightened, and it bothers me to see them hurting financially. I just hope some kind of peace can be made so there won't be any violence. They're desperate and getting more so with each passing day."

"All we can do is try to reason with them," said Wilhaus. "We certainly don't want any blood being shed."

Erik rubbed his chin. "Well, sir, everybody in Switzerland knows that your company is a financial giant. If you really don't want anyone getting hurt, I strongly suggest that you come up with sufficient wages for your factory employees in Chur. It will make the independent woodworkers happy. They'll take the jobs you are offering and bring peace in the whole matter."

Lutrey and Hinwill exchanged uncomfortable glances, then looked at their boss. Eiger Wilhaus looked out the window and pointing to a spot along the edge of a nearby forest, said, "Look, there! A whole herd of deer!"

It was obvious to Erik that the conversation was over.

As the train rolled across the rugged land toward the towering Swiss Alps, Agno Lutrey asked questions about Dr. Joseph Danzig's health and the future of the clinic. Erik explained that he and Dr. Danzig had discussed the future, and at the moment, plans were for him to purchase Dr. Danzig's portion of the partnership when the elderly physician felt it was time for him to retire.

There was a pause in the conversation, then Lutrey asked, "Is there a Mrs. Dr. Erik Linden?"

"Not yet, sir, but there soon will be. I am marrying a wonderful young lady on June 26. Her name is Metryka Baume. Her father is Chur's burgomaster."

"Oh, really!" he said, eyes lighting up. He leaned forward and tapped Eiger Wilhaus's shoulder. "Mr. Wilhaus, Dr. Linden just told me that he is engaged to Koblin Baume's daughter! They're getting married next month"

Wilhaus looked over his shoulder, smiled, and said, "I've known Koblin for many years. Haven't talked to him for a while, or I'm sure he would have told me that Metryka was getting married, especially to Chur's prominent young physician and surgeon. Congratulations, Doctor."

"Thank you, sir."

Zugg Hinwill rubbed his temples. "Yes, congratulations, Doctor. It never hurts to marry into a well-known family like the Baumes."

Erik frowned. Ever the physician, he looked into the man's eyes, and saw the pain dulling them. Laying a gentle hand on his arm, he asked, "Do you have a headache, Mr. Hinwill?"

"Mm-hmm." He nodded and continued massaging his temples. "I have them quite often. And more often of late, since this Chur problem has come up."

Erik stood up, took his overnight bag down, and opened it. He took out his medical bag and returned the larger one to the rack. Opening the medical bag, he extracted a packet marked: Salicylic Acid Powder.

"I'll go to the dining car and get some water, Mr. Hinwill," said Erik. "A good salicylic acid mixture will help alleviate your pain."

Even as he was speaking, Erik saw one of the porters enter the car. They had passed through several times since the train had pulled out of Bern. When he saw Erik looking at him, he asked, "May I be of help to you, sir?"

"I'm Dr. Erik Linden. My friend, here, has a severe headache, and I was about to go to the dining car and get some water to mix these powders for him."

"I'll get you some water, Doctor," said the porter.

"About half a glass is what I need," said Erik. "And a spoon, please."

"Be right back, sir," said the man, and hurried toward the rear of the coach.

Eiger Wilhaus looked up at Erik and said, "Thank you, Dr. Linden. I appreciate your kindness to Zugg."

"Not as much as I do," said Hinwill, his fingers pressed tight against both temples.

"That's what doctors are for," said Erik. "I'm glad to help."

The train made a slight turn, and Agno Lutrey looked out his window eastward. "I can see the mountains," he said. "They look fairly close, but how far away are they?"

"About sixty miles," said Erik. "They do fool you."

"That's for sure," said Wilhaus, peering through his window. "You'd think they were no less than thirty miles from here."

The porter returned with the glass of water and the spoon. Erik thanked him, and quickly poured the white powder into the glass. While using the spoon to mix it good, he asked, "Mr. Hinwill, have you ever taken salicylic acid mix?"

"No. My doctor has given me an alkaloid drug for my headaches, but he warned me not to take it often."

"Right. Alkaloids can be addictive. Salicylic acid is not addictive, but it will relieve your pain. The bad taste will be worth it, I guarantee you. I want you to drink all of it."

Hinwill accepted the glass gratefully, put it to his lips, and drank the bitter brew without stopping to take a breath. There was a sour look on his face when he finished. He shook his head, blinked, and scrubbed a palm across his mouth. "Whew. You're right about the taste. But I'll be very glad if it relieves this throbbing pain."

"It will," said Erik. "Now, put your head back on the seat and close your eyes for a while."

"Gladly, Doctor," said Hinwill, and slid down a bit in the seat so his head could rest against the hard back.

Erik put the remaining portion of the powder back in his medical bag and set it at his feet. Agno Lutrey brought up Europe's industrial revolution once more, and they discussed it at length. The young doctor had to admit that one day the new machines being used in the factories would be good for the people of the continent, but stated that the transition period was going to be a rough one.

As the train drew closer to the mountains, many passengers were pressing their faces against the windows to get a good look at them. Soon two of the porters came into the coach and lit the wicks of the six kerosene lanterns that hung above the aisle. One of the male passengers, who was obviously Russian, asked in his language why they were lighting lanterns in the middle of the day, and was told through a passenger who acted as an interpreter that they would soon be passing through six-mile-long Nidwalden Tunnel. Without the lanterns, the coach would be black as midnight.

A new subject was introduced between the doctor and Agno Lutrey. They talked about the tunnel, and what a task it must have been for the engineers and workers to blast their way through the mountains with dynamite to provide the tunnel for the railroad.

Time passed quickly, and soon someone shouted, "There it is! We're coming to Nidwalden Tunnel!"

A few minutes later, the train plunged into the black mouth of the tunnel. Some passengers spoke of how much they now appreciated the lanterns.

Erik noted that Zugg Hinwill hadn't moved since first placing his head on the back of the seat. Eiger Wilhaus was listening to a conversation between two women who sat in front of him as they excitedly watched the glowing sparks from the engine's smokestack flying past the windows.

Erik and Lutrey sat in silence for several minutes while the train charged full-speed inside the tunnel. Erik said, taking the subject back to the low wages paid by the factory in Chur, "Mr. Lutrey, has the Grutliverein Labor Union given indication that they will get involved in your Chur factory as they have in other Wilhaus factories to force you to pay higher wages?"

"We haven't heard anything from the union as yet, but I have no doubt they will do so."

"I'm interested to know if the union has been able to force the wages in your other Swiss factories to come up to a pay scale that would make the independent woodworkers in Chur change their minds about going to work for you."

Lutrey shook his head. "No. Not that much."

"Tell me. Am I right that the Wilhaus Industries could afford to raise the wages at Chur so they would entice the woodworkers to—"

Suddenly, there was a loud roar in the tunnel ahead, and the brakes of the train were screeching on the tracks. Women were screaming and men were shouting words of concern when just as suddenly the train came to a sudden stop, throwing passengers from their seats and making luggage sail through the air from the overhead racks.

Dr. Erik Linden, being on the aisle, abruptly felt himself hurled helplessly from his seat. He flew through the air for a short distance, felt a sharp pain in his left leg when it connected with something solid, then slammed into the back of a seat across the aisle, and fell to the floor.

There were screams and cries that seemed to fade in and out as his head reeled, and he nearly passed out. His brain seemed to be spinning inside his skull as he fought to remain conscious. After a few minutes, his head began to clear, and he was struggling to get to his feet amid the moans and wails of children and adults in pain. Many were crying out for help.

Only a single lantern was still burning in the coach. It hung toward the rear, swinging and casting moving shadows. The impact had doused the flames in the others, but Erik could see smoke filling the tunnel and floating past the windows. His left leg was shooting pain as he finally was able to stand up and look around at the other passengers.

He saw Eiger Wilhaus lying on the floor in the aisle, clutching his left rib cage in agony. Limping to him, he bent down and said, "Mr. Wilhaus, I'll be back to check on you shortly."

Then limping further, he saw Zugg Hinwill sprawled under a seat across the aisle from where he had been sitting. He was breathing, but unconscious. Taking another couple of painful steps, he saw immediately that Agno Lutrey was in a heap between the seats, and bent over to check on him. His forehead was split open, and he was dead. It was obvious that the impact had slammed his head into the seat in front of him.

The interior of the coach was a bedlam of weeping and wailing as Erik looked about for his medical bag. He saw a man about his age on his feet, a bit dazed, and trying to find someone. When he saw Erik, he said, "We've got to help these people. I'm trying to find my wife."

"I'm a medical doctor," Erik said, a bit thick-tongued. "I'm looking for my medical bag. Could you use that burning lantern to light a couple more so we can see better?"

"Sure," said the man, and went to do so.

Erik paused at the crumpled form of Eiger Wilhaus as he limped forward in the coach and told him he would be back to help him as soon as he could. Gritting his teeth while still clutching his ribs, Wilhaus nodded.

Trying to ignore his own pain, Erik worked his way further forward in the cluttered coach, telling people he was a medical doctor, and was looking for his medical bag. He would get to them as soon as he possibly could.

The coach brightened as the man fired up one of the other lanterns. Erik commended him, saying it was better already.

Suddenly a woman's voice rose above the din, calling out, "John! John!"

The man who was lighting lanterns turned to look and said, "Oh, Ruth! I couldn't find you! We needed more light, so I'm trying to provide it."

"I was under the seat," she said. "I heard you and the doctor talking. Don't worry about me. I was just dazed. I'm bruised up a little, but I'm all right."

"That's good, honey," said John. "Just sit down and rest."

"I'm going to see if I can help some of these people," she said in return. "I'm all right."

Erik spotted his black bag lying on the floor against the leg of a seat. Hurrying to it, biting his lips as pain shot through his injured leg, he bent down to pick it up. His eyes fell on a little girl about five years old, crumpled under a seat, her nose bleeding profusely. She was conscious, but dazed.

Passengers were begging the doctor to help them. Some were parents, calling out that their children were hurt. "I'll get to all of you as soon as I can!" he called out. "Right now, I have a little girl who will bleed to death if I don't take care of her!"

An older man who was bent over on a seat, his mouth bleeding, said in a hoarse voice, "Doctor, the little girl's mother is over here by me. She's unconscious."

Erik gave him a nod. "Thank you for telling me, sir. I'll get to her and to you as soon as I can."

A quick glance showed Erik that John was still trying to light the remaining lanterns. Amid wails, moans, and weeping, there were still cries from the passengers, begging the doctor for help.

In order to be heard above the discordant sounds, Eric raised his voice and cried, "Is there someone here not badly hurt who can help me assess the injuries?"

Erik saw a young man whom he estimated to be in his early thirties stand up near the rear of the coach. "I can do it, Doctor! I was traveling with my mother and she…she just died." His voice broke. "Tell me what you want me to do." As he spoke, he hastened to the doctor.

The young man had a cut on his cheek, and it was leaking blood as he pressed a handkerchief against it, but otherwise he was uninjured.

"You sure you're all right, friend?" said Erik. "I'm so sorry about your mother."

"Yes, sir. I'll be fine. Now, tell me what to do."

"Now that we can see better, I just need you to go through the coach and look at each injured person. See if you can tell how bad they are hurt, and when you're done, you'll have to tell me who to look at next. Right now, I have a little girl who's losing blood fast."

"I'll hurry, Doctor," said the young man. "By the way, my name's Charles."

"Thank you, Charles," said Erik, then put his full attention on the five-year-old.

Concentrating on stemming the flow of blood from the child's nose, Erik's mind was still able to pick up the moans and cries of the passengers, and the surprisingly soothing, competent voice of Charles as he moved among them.

What a fine young man, Erik thought. *His own mother was just killed, but he has the wherewithal to encourage and comfort others while his own heart is breaking. When this is over, I've got to find a way to thank him.*

Charles returned just as Erik had managed to stop the girl's bleeding. He reported only two dead: his mother, and a man whose head was split open. Erik told him he knew about the man. Charles led the doctor to an older woman who was also bleeding at the nose, saying he thought she should be tended to next.

Staying by Erik's side, Charles looked on as he worked on the woman and said, "What is your name, Doctor?"

"Erik Linden, Charles. I'm partner in a medical clinic in Chur."

Charles nodded, then said, "Dr. Linden, I think it had to be an explosion of some kind. It sure sounded like dynamite going off to me. I'm in the road-building business, so I'm acquainted with it. I've been around dynamite quite a bit."

"Well," said Erik, "I'm no expert on dynamite, but it sure sounded like an explosion. It was more than just a wall of the tunnel caving in."

At that moment, the rear door of the coach squeaked open, and the conductor came in. His head was wrapped in a bandanna, which was soaked with blood. Seeing the two men bending over the older woman, he hurried to them, and said, "I wanted to check on the passengers in here. I've already been in the other two coaches. I was in the one just ahead when we crashed." Suddenly he noticed the open medical bag, and looking at Erik, said, "Are you a doctor?"

"Yes," said Erik without looking up. "I'm partner with Dr. Joseph Danzig in Chur."

"Oh, wonderful!" exclaimed the conductor. "There are people in the other two coaches who need your help, Doctor."

"I'll get to them as soon as possible," said Erik, this time looking up at him. "As you can see, I have my hands full here."

"Of course," said the conductor. "The engineer and the fireman are no doubt dead. There is no way I can get out there to see about them. We have three dead people in the first car, and two dead in the second car."

"We have two dead in here," said Erik.

"Some of them in both of the other cars are seriously hurt, Doctor," said the conductor. "I've got those who aren't hurt so bad trying to help them. I hope you can get to them before they die."

Grimacing from his own pain, Erik said, "I do too, sir. Charles, how about you going with the conductor and assessing the injured in the other cars for me?"

"Of course," said Charles.

As Charles and the conductor hurried out of the coach, Erik's features stiffened and went white. He felt for a pulse in the neck of the older woman he was attending. There was none. She had just died.

Five

With heavy heart, Dr. Erik Linden looked around for something to use as a cover for the dead woman. A shawl lay in the aisle next to the leg of the seat in front of him. He picked it up and spread it over her face.

A woman in the seat just behind him wailed, "Oh, Bruce! That lady died! The doctor just covered up her face!"

She broke into sobs, and others in the coach who were already making fearful sounds became even louder. Her husband, in pain from a dislocated shoulder, put his good arm around her, speaking soft words of consolation.

Erik wiped the back of his hand across his mouth and picked up the black bag, trying to ignore his own pain and looking around to figure out who needed him most. Charles had not indicated which one he thought should have the doctor's attention next.

A man toward the front of the coach, where much luggage had piled up in the crash, raised a hand and said, "Doctor, my wife is unconscious. I can't rouse her. She hit her head on something. There's a big lump on her temple."

Erik hurried to the spot and was assessing the woman's condition when the conductor returned, saying, "Dr. Linden, there is a nine-year-old boy in coach number two who may have a broken neck. His parents are frantic. Charles told me to get you in there immediately. He's in coach number one now."

"Give me just a moment here," said Erik, then made a quick examination of the woman's bruise. He assured her husband that there was no permanent damage, and that she would soon regain consciousness.

He picked up his bag, called out to the passengers that he would be back as soon as possible, then paused to look down at Eiger Wilhaus, who still lay in the aisle. Wilhaus was still clutching his ribs, teeth clenched, eyes closed. Ejecting a tiny moan, he nodded. Erik then hurried into the next car.

Charles was just coming in from car number one as Erik rushed into number two behind the conductor, who led him to the nine-year-old boy.

Charles told him of at least four people in car number one he felt were critical. Erik knelt down beside the boy, who was in his father's arms, and said, "I'll get to them as soon as I can, Charles. Please tell them for me."

"I will, sir," said Charles, and dashed out the door.

Moments later, he returned, telling the doctor that he had delivered the message. Every person who was able was doing what he or she could to help the critical ones until he could get to them.

After examining the boy, Erik was relieved to tell his parents that his neck was not broken. They both wept with relief. Then Erik gently chastised them by saying that they should never move a person who might have a spinal column injury. The parents nodded.

While working on the next patient, Erik asked Charles to enlist the help of the less seriously injured passengers in every coach to do everything they could to help those who needed it. It would help if he could get some water to them. Charles immediately went to work on it, and the conductor sent a man to the dining car to see if the cook could supply him some cups and water.

The conductor then excused himself to Erik, saying he needed to do what he could to check on the engineer and the fireman.

Erik worked on, trying to save as many lives as possible and to relieve as much suffering as he could.

Some two hours after the crash had taken place, Erik was able to kneel down beside Eiger Wilhaus, who still lay in the aisle. Zugg Hinwill was now conscious and standing over his boss. By the look on his face, it was obvious that he had an excruciating headache. "I tried to move him, Doctor," he said, "but because of the pain in his rib cage, he would not allow it."

"I understand," said Erik, who had a stethoscope dangling at his neck. "I'll give you some more salicylic acid mixture as soon as I can. I can tell you're hurting. It is your head, isn't it?"

"Yes, sir, and it's like someone is beating the inside of my head with a hammer. But don't worry about me. I'm concerned about Mr. Wilhaus."

Bending over Wilhaus, Erik said, "Mr. Wilhaus, I know you're in pain, but I need to see just how badly you are hurt. I may have to inflict a little more pain to do so. Understand?"

The silver-haired man, whose features were lined more than usual because of his agony, nodded.

Weeping and moaning sounds continued to fill the coach.

After a few minutes Erik said, "Mr. Wilhaus, you have two broken ribs. There's nothing I can do for you, here. Whenever we can get you to the nearest clinic or hospital, we can work on the ribs."

He frowned and looked down at the pulse throbbing in the side of Wilhaus's neck. Putting the earpieces of the stethoscope in place, he listened to Wilhaus's heart. His frown deepened.

"What is it, Doctor?" Wilhaus asked in a strained, gravelly voice.

"Your heart is beating erratically. Do you have a heart problem?"

"Never have."

"It could be because of the extreme pain you've been in for two hours. I'm going to give you some medicine to relieve the pain and a sedative to help ease the tension you're experiencing."

Wilhaus swallowed with difficulty. "Th-thank you."

Erik began mixing powders in a glass of water.

At that instant the front door of the coach squeaked open, and the conductor came in. "Doctor," he said, "I took two of the male passengers with me into the tunnel with lanterns. There is no question that someone set off dynamite in the tunnel. The blast caused a huge section of the tunnel to collapse. The engine was partially engulfed in the collapsing rock and dirt. We found the engineer and the fireman in the engine's cab, dead."

"I'm sorry to hear that," said Erik, pausing with the glass in hand.

"I estimate, Doctor," said the conductor, "that we are about four miles into the tunnel. So, any help we get will have to come from behind us. Those same two men who went with me to the engine volunteered to go for help. They left just now. It will take hours for them to bring help, but at least we're working on it."

"Good," said Erik. "In the meantime, I'll keep working as fast as possible." He then lifted Eiger Wilhaus's head and administered the mixture.

"I'll keep moving through the coaches, Dr. Linden," said the conductor. "If there is anything you need me for, I won't be hard to find."

"All right. Thank you."

As the conductor moved away, Erik quickly mixed powders for Zugg Hinwill and handed him the glass. "Mr. Hinwill, watch Mr. Wilhaus closely, please. If there is any change before I get back to check on him, come and let me know."

"I sure will, Doctor," said Hinwill.

The next three patients on Erik's agenda were in coach number one.

When he entered that coach, he found Charles busy trying to help the injured as best he could, and being an example to others to do the same. He called Charles to him and told him of the dead engineer and fireman, but added the encouraging news that two men had gone for help. Charles was glad to know that help was on the way. He thanked Erik for telling him, and went back to his task.

With supreme effort and prayer, Erik was able to ignore his own pain and continue his work on those in worse pain. All the while, he was aware of the moans and cries of the suffering passengers around him, but was pleased to hear the calm voice of Charles as he encouraged the passengers by telling them help was on the way. Many of them, in turn, tried to comfort the most fearful and to calm those who were near hysteria.

Erik had been in coach number one for little over half an hour when Zugg Hinwill dashed through the door, calling out, "Dr. Linden, I think Mr. Wilhaus is having a heart seizure!"

The doctor's face blanched. He looked down at the middle-aged man he was treating and said, "Mr. Wolfram, I'll be back as soon as I can." Then he said to Wolfram's wife, "Press this cloth tightly against the cut and hold it there till I get back. All right?"

"Yes, Doctor," said the small woman, fear evident in her eyes.

As Erik hurried through coach number two behind Zugg Hinwill, passengers called out to him. He paused long enough to tell them he would get to them as soon as he could, and hurried into car number three.

A young woman was kneeling beside Eiger Wilhaus, holding his hand as Hinwill drew up with the doctor on his heels. Wilhaus was a pallid gray color and was gasping for breath. His eyes had a vacant stare.

Erik dropped to his knees beside her. She let go of Wilhaus's hand and moved aside. "Thank you for watching over him, ma'am," he said.

Using the stethoscope, Erik checked Wilhaus's heartbeat. Glancing at Hinwill, he said, "He is definitely having a heart seizure."

Bending low over him, Erik said, "Mr. Wilhaus, can you hear me?"

The man's eyes came back into focus as he looked up at the doctor, grunted, and nodded.

"I've got to sit you up so you can breathe easier. Understand?"

Wilhaus nodded again, his breath coming in short gasps.

Erik eased him to a sitting position and immediately his breathing became less laborious and more even.

"Mr. Hinwill," said Erik, "I need you to sit down here on the floor and press your back against his. I've got to massage his heart, but I need him steadied as much as possible."

While Hinwill was getting into position, the young woman said, "Is there anything I can do, Doctor?"

"Yes. Move over here close and hold his hand. It will help calm him."

While Zugg Hinwill and the young woman did as they were told, Dr. Erik Linden worked at massaging Eiger Wilhaus's chest, pressing hard in order to affect the heart. His own leg was shooting pain, but he ignored it, working furiously to save the man's life.

After nearly half an hour the heart was beating regularly again, and Eiger Wilhaus was breathing normally. Erik looked at his helpers and said, "He'll be all right now."

Still quite pale, Wilhaus licked his dry lips and said with shaky voice, "You saved my life, Dr. Linden. You saved my life. Thank you."

At the Danzig Medical Clinic in Chur, nurse Louise Levron glanced at the clock on the wall as she stood at the foot of the examining table. It was almost 12:45. She hoped the train from Bern would be on time.

On the table was an eight-year-old boy who had fallen from a tree in his yard and broken his arm.

With shaky hands, Dr. Joseph Danzig had set the boy's arm, but was having trouble shaping the cast he was putting on it. Sweat was beaded on the doctor's brow and began to run into his eyes. Beside him was his other nurse, Amelia Folchert.

Amelia and Louise exchanged glances, studied the trembling hands of the aging physician, then looked at each other again.

Amelia, who was the oldest and most experienced of the two, touched Dr. Danzig's arm and said, "Doctor, you seem to be quite shaky. I've done many casts just like this one. Why not let me finish for you?"

The old man nodded, brushed sweat from his eyes, took a deep breath and sighed. "All right."

He stepped back and glanced at the clock. "The train is due to arrive in fifteen minutes. Dr. Linden will be here shortly. If you have any problems, he can help you. I...I think I'll go home and lie down."

"You go on, Doctor," said Louise, moving up to the opposite side of the table. "Amelia and I will take care of Johnny."

Dipping a plaster of paris strip into the water bucket that sat on the cart next to her, Amelia took up where the doctor left off.

Dr. Danzig made a shuffling move to the door, paused, and looked back. "I'll tell Johnny's mother you ladies will have him ready to go in a little while, okay?"

"Yes," said Louise, smiling at him. "You go home and get some rest."

When the door went closed, Amelia paused in her work, looked at Louise, and shaking her head, said sadly, "I fear the dear man's work here at the clinic is rapidly drawing to a close."

Tears misted Louise's eyes. "Yes. Rapidly."

At the Wilhaus Furniture Factory, Durbin Thorpe rose from his desk, and running his gaze between his son and Metryka Baume, he said, "I'm going now. The train will be here in a few minutes. I'll take Mr. Wilhaus, Mr. Hinwill, and Mr. Lutrey to the hotel. If they haven't eaten on the train, I'll take them to lunch. Either way, I'll be gone a while. I need to talk to them about tomorrow's meeting with the independent woodworkers. Once everything is set, I'll be back. It could be late this afternoon, though."

"Tell them hello for me, Father," said Helmut, "and that I'll look forward to seeing them either this evening or in the morning."

Putting on his hat, Durbin said, "I'll do that."

When his father was gone, Helmut left his chair, moved to stand over Metryka, and said, "We're alone."

As he was bending down to kiss her, Metryka stiffened, glanced at the large window, and said, "We can't be sure."

Holding her gaze with his nose only inches from hers, he said, "I don't hear any footsteps."

Before Metryka could say anything else, he kissed her then stood to full height. "I want you to tell Erik today. Enough of this being afraid to show our love to each other while we're here in the office."

"I will tell him today, darling," she said softly. "But I have to have things just right. I still think a lot of Erik even though I'm not in love with him anymore. I want to make this as easy as possible on him."

"All right, if you think it has to be such a delicate thing. But I want it done today."

"Whenever Erik has traveled somewhere and comes back to town on a weekday, he always comes here first before going home or to the clinic. When he shows up here in a little while, I'll say I want to go for a walk. Then I'll tell him."

"Good. And what about Justina and Dova? Aren't they still working on your wedding dress?"

"Yes."

"So when are you going to tell them the wedding's off, and they can throw the dress away?"

"As soon as possible after I tell Erik. It's only right, Helmut, that Erik knows it first."

"All right, all right. Just so it's all done today."

Metryka sighed. "Justina and Dova are going to be furious, just as Erik will be. But I agree—it simply must be done today so you and I can get on with our lives and plan our marriage."

Both of them went back to the work at their desks.

The factory foreman came in wanting to see Durbin, but when he was told by Helmut that his father had gone to the depot to meet Mr. Wilhaus and his two vice presidents, the foreman snapped his fingers and said he forgot that the train was due in at one o'clock.

Metryka and Helmut had lunch together in the office then went back to their paperwork. Every few minutes one of them glanced at the door, expecting Erik to appear at any moment.

It was nearly two o'clock when Helmut left his chair, went to the door, opened it, and glanced outside. Shaking his head, he closed the door. "What's keeping him?"

"Maybe the train is running late," Metryka suggested.

Heading back to his desk, a frustrated Helmut said, "Wouldn't you know it would pick this day to be late?"

Time dragged on as the pair stayed at their paperwork.

When Metryka looked at the clock again, it was five minutes after three. Unable to concentrate any longer, she laid her pen down and pushed the scattered papers into a pile. Sighing, she looked at Helmut and said, "It's after three o'clock. The train can't be this late. It sure never has been before. I can't understand why it's taking him so long to get here."

She rose from the desk. "I've got to go see if I can find him. My heart is in my throat. I've got to get this over with as soon as possible. It isn't fair to Erik to let him go on thinking everything is all right, and it isn't fair to you and me to have to hide our feelings for each other any longer."

Helmut grinned. "I agree. We've labored long enough under this delusion."

Picking up her purse from the corner of the desk, Metryka said, "I'm going to go find Erik right now. My nerves can't take any more of this."

She moved to the door, opened it, and looked out, hoping to catch a glimpse of Erik coming her way, but there was no sign of him. She glanced back at Helmut. Her voice shook with pent-up emotion as she said just above a whisper, "This is so hard, Helmut. But it's got to be done. I'm going to the clinic first to see if he is there. If he's not, then I'll go to his apartment. Maybe he went there for some reason."

Metryka stepped outside, closed the door, and Helmut could hear her footsteps on the wood floor of the walkway as she headed for the stairs. Rising from his desk, he went to the window. His eyes followed her as she descended the stairs, went to the street, and soon disappeared from sight.

A frown furrowed his handsome brow, and he lowered his head into his hands.

Louise Levron was at the desk in the clinic office, looking for something in a drawer, when Metryka Baume came through the door. At the moment, there was no one in the waiting area.

Louise smiled warmly at Metryka. "Hello, future Mrs. Linden. How are you?"

"I'm fine physically, Louise," Metryka replied, forcing a smile, "but not emotionally. I've been expecting Erik to come by the office and see me, but he hasn't. It isn't like him. May I see him, please?"

"He's not here," Louise said, closing the drawer and placing the envelope she had retracted from the drawer on top of the desk. "Amelia and I have been quite busy up till now, and there hasn't been time for one of us to go to the depot and see if the train has been delayed. Dr. Danzig had to go home just after noon. He isn't feeling well."

"I'm sorry to hear that," said Metryka. "If Erik comes in and hasn't seen me yet, please tell him I need to talk to him."

"Will do," said Louise, as the young woman hurried out the door.

On the boardwalk, Metryka mumbled to herself, "There's no way the train is late. Maybe in winter, but not in nice weather like this. He must have gone to his apartment."

She could not get an answer to her knock at Erik's apartment and learned from the man in the adjoining apartment that Erik had not been home. She headed for his parents' house.

When Metryka walked into the Linden yard, she saw Justina and Dova on the front porch. They were sitting at a small table with the lovely white wedding dress spread out between them.

Dova was just rising from her chair when she saw Metryka. "Oh, hello, Metryka," she said warmly. "We were just enjoying this beautiful spring weather while working on your wedding dress."

A wide smile was on Justina's lips as she said, "Come see our progress, honey."

Making her act look real, Metryka examined the dress and said, "My, my! You have really gotten a lot done since I saw it last. You are doing a beautiful job!" She looked around the yard then at the front door. "Is Erik here?"

"No, he isn't," said Justina. "He didn't come to see you when he got in?"

"Sure didn't."

"Well, then, he must have gone to the clinic."

Shaking her head, Metryka said, "He isn't there, either. And he's not in his apartment. I thought for sure he'd be here."

Even as she was speaking, Ludwig and Brandt came out the door.

Brandt said, "Did I hear you right, Metryka? Erik didn't come to see you when he got in, and he's not at the clinic or his apartment?"

"You heard me right," she replied.

"Then I know where he is," said Ludwig. "For the past month or so, he's gone to your new house every day to see how the construction is coming along. That's where he is. You know, after being gone a few days, he probably wanted to check on it."

"But the train's been in since one o'clock," Metryka said. "He wouldn't stay at the house this long."

"He might, if the builders are at a particular spot he's interested in," said Brandt. "Ludwig and I will go over there and see. Come on, Ludwig, I'll race you!"

The boys took off running, and soon rounded the corner and vanished from view.

Justina looked down the street the opposite direction and said, "Here comes Papa home from work."

At the same time, Mura came out of the house. She spoke to Metryka, then said, "Justina, where are the boys?"

Justina was explaining where Ludwig and Brandt had gone, when Frederic drew up to the porch. "I doubt Erik would stay at the new house this long, Metryka," he said. "The train must be delayed for some reason. I know whenever he's been gone, Erik always looks you up first when he comes home."

Dova said, "Come to think of it, when I was walking over here to work on the dress with Justina, I did notice a small crowd standing in front of the depot. That was about one-thirty. I hadn't given it any more thought until just now. They must have been waiting for the train."

"I'll go over to the depot and check on it right now," said Frederic. "Be back in a little while."

Just as Frederic was turning from the porch, he and the women heard Ludwig's voice calling, "Papa! Mama!"

Every eye was instantly on the boys as they came on the run.

Frederic waited for the boys to come in the yard. Panting as they drew up, they gasped for breath, and Ludwig said, "While we were running to Erik and Metryka's new house, we met up with Mr. and Mrs. Bolton. They have been at the depot, expecting their daughter and son-in-law to arrive on the Bern train. They told us the train is not in yet, but a telegram came in just a few minutes ago to the station manager from the burgomaster in Vaudron, saying the train has been wrecked inside the Nidwalden Tunnel!"

Faces lost color, including Mura's as she gasped, "Wrecked! Oh no! Did the Boltons say how bad it is?"

Brandt took hold of his mother's hand. "They told us the wire said that a few passengers were killed, and many were injured. A dynamite charge had been set off in the tunnel when the train was moving through it. It wrecked the train about four miles from the west entrance of the tunnel."

Mura burst into tears, saying, "No! No! Erik was on that train! What if—what if—"

Frederic folded her into his arms as she broke into uncontrollable sobs, wailing incoherently, while the others looked on.

Metryka's heart skittered in her chest. She opened her mouth to say something, but she couldn't get the words past the lump in her throat. Even though she had known for better than a month that she was no longer in love with Erik, she still was fond of him, and greatly admired him.

Gathering her fragmented thoughts into a semblance of order, she spoke to Justina, Dova, Ludwig, and Brandt above Mura's wailing: "We have to do something. We have to know about Erik."

Ludwig put a strong arm around Metryka's shoulder. Above his mother's wails and his father's words of comfort to calm her down, he said, "As soon as Mama quiets down, we'll tell you what's being done about the situation."

Brandt stepped close to Metryka and laid a palm lovingly on her cheek. His voice cracked as he said, "I know how much you love my big brother. Your heart must be bleeding right now, not knowing whether Erik is dead or alive. We'll know soon, as Ludwig and I will explain. But don't give up hope, Metryka. I feel in my heart that Erik is alive and all right. You'll have your wedding and your future together, just as planned."

Guilt ripped through Metryka Baume. She wanted Erik to be alive and well...but if he was, what were these people going to think of her when she announced to Erik that she was in love with Helmut and going to marry him instead?

While Metryka Baume was in the grip of her guilt and the young Linden brothers were trying to comfort her, the others in the group were weeping under the shock brought on by the news of the train wreck.

In spite of the fear that raked at his own heart, Frederic held a sobbing Mura in his arms with tears coursing down his cheeks and said to all, "We must trust the Lord in this. Erik could be among the survivors."

"Yes, Papa," said Brandt. "I just feel in my heart that Erik is still alive."

Mura took a shuddering breath. "Yes! Oh, dear Lord, please! Let our boy be alive!"

Frederic pulled Mura's head against his chest and ran his gaze to his sons. "You boys were going to tell us what's being done about the situation."

"Yes, Papa," said Ludwig. "Mr. and Mrs. Bolton told us that Mr. Borszich, the railroad station manager, is calling for volunteers—both men and women—to ride a special train from Chur to the tunnel to help get the survivors and...and...the bodies out of the tunnel. He is sending men all over town to spread the word. The train will be leaving at eight o'clock tonight."

Mura sniffed, wiped tears, and said, "Well, I'm going."

"I don't think you should, sweetheart," Frederic said levelly. "It would be too much for you. The boys and I will go. You ladies should stay here."

Mura shook her head vigorously. "Frederic, I'm Erik's mother! I've got to go."

"I want to go too, Papa," said Justina.

Metryka knew they would expect her to insist on going, also. "Me, too," she said, running the back of her hand over her cheeks to remove tearstains.

"I am going too," said Dova.

Mura stepped away from Frederic, put an arm around Dova, and said, "Honey, you don't have to go."

"Oh, but I do," she said. "I'm Justina's best friend, and Erik is her brother. I must go."

Justina took hold of Dova's hand. "I appreciate it, honey. I want you to go. Thank you for being such a true and caring friend."

Caressing Justina's cheek, Dova smiled. "Nobody ever had such a wonderful friend as you. Your whole family is special to me…including Erik. I want to be with all of you when you arrive at the tunnel and find him alive and well."

Mura kissed Dova's cheek. "Yes. We want you there when we find our boy alive and well."

Brandt put an arm around Metryka's shoulder and said, "And when Metryka finds her husband-to-be alive and well. Right, sister-in-law-to-be?"

Metryka's insides were churning. She could only look at Brandt, compress her lips together, and nod.

"I need to hurry home and tell my parents I'm going on the special train to the tunnel," she said. "I'll come back here so I can walk with you to the depot. First, I need to go to the factory and get permission from Mr. Thorpe."

"I'm sure he will let you," said Frederic. "You need to go home, too. Since you live closer to the depot than we do, why don't you just meet us at the depot at seven-fifteen? In the meantime, I'll go tell Peter Borszich he has seven volunteers."

Metryka agreed and hurried away.

Dova said she would be back to the Linden house before seven o'clock and headed for home, which was the opposite direction.

With their hastily made plan in action, the Lindens were feeling a measure of relief. The boys stayed with their mother and sister while their father headed for the railroad station to advise Peter Borszich of the volunteers he had from their family, their future daughter-in-law, and Dova Combray.

Metryka's heart was in her throat as she climbed the stairs to the factory office in the light of the lowering sun. At first she was surprised to find the office closed, then she realized that Helmut and his father had received word of the train wreck, and no doubt quite shaken at the news, had gone home.

Less than fifteen minutes later, she knocked on the door of the Thorpe residence. When there was no answer within a reasonable amount of time, she knocked again. Footsteps were heard, and when the door opened, she found herself looking at the pale, drawn face of the man she loved.

"Oh, hello, Metryka," said Helmut. "Sorry to take so long to answer your knock. We're in pretty bad shape around here. Come in."

As she stepped in, Helmut said, "I assume you've heard about what happened to the train."

"Yes. I need to talk to your father for just a moment."

"Sure. He and Mother are in the library."

Helmut put an arm around her waist as they moved down the hall, then let go just before they passed through the library door.

Lynelle Thorpe was seated in an overstuffed chair, eyes fixed on her husband, who was wringing his hands and pacing the floor in front of the fireplace.

When Helmut led Metryka into the room, both looked at her, and Lynelle said, "Hello, Metryka."

Without breaking his stride as he paced, Durbin, whose face was pale and drawn to a greater degree than his son's, said, "Metryka, you know about the train wreck?"

"Yes, sir. That's why I'm here. I need to talk to you."

Still on the move, Durbin said, "About what?"

"Do…do you know about the special train that's going to the tunnel from Chur at eight o'clock?"

"The volunteers Peter Borszich is asking for. Yes." He paused in his pacing, and said, "I don't know what I'll do if those three men were killed…especially Eiger Wilhaus."

"I hope they're all right," she said weakly.

Pacing again, Durbin said, "I would like to go on that special train, but I have to prepare to meet with the independent woodworkers tomorrow morning without Mr. Wilhaus and his vice presidents. I need Helmut in the office, so he can't go, either."

"Well, sir, that's what I wanted to talk to you about. I would like your permission to go."

Durbin stopped again, his face twisting. "What? You go?"

"Yes, sir."

"I don't know about that."

Metryka looked to Helmut for some support. "Sir, I really need to go."

Helmut remained silent, a slight scowl on his face.

"Durbin," said Lynelle, "the girl is engaged to Erik Linden, and as I recall, he was supposed to arrive home today on that train."

"Oh," said Durbin. "I hadn't realized—"

"I really do need to go, Mr. Thorpe," Metryka said with a tone of urgency in her voice.

Helmut's scowl deepened.

"Everybody in the Linden family is going, sir," said Metryka. "And…and Dova Combray, too. I really need the time off so I can go with them. Besides, it would look good for the factory if someone from the office was among the volunteers."

Durbin began to nod, staring at the floor. Then he looked up again. "Yes. You're right, Metryka. All right. You can go. And I hope you will find all three men alive and well."

"Thank you, sir," she said with relief evident in her voice. "I hope I do, too. Well, I'll be going."

Metryka's eyes flicked to Helmut once more, and the look on his face told her he was upset. He stepped closer to her and said, "I'd like to talk to you outside before you leave."

She nodded to him, then said, "I'll report in as soon as I return, Mr. Thorpe."

"Please do."

"See you later, Mrs. Thorpe," Metryka said.

When Metryka and Helmut were moving down the hall, he whispered heatedly, "What on earth are you doing? You're not engaged to Erik anymore, even though he doesn't know it. Why do you need to go? And don't give me that business of wanting to make it look good for the factory in front of the town."

By this time, they were in the foyer, and Metryka preceded him through the door onto the porch. Stopping, she turned and said, "Just use your head, Helmut. If I don't go to the tunnel—"

"You still have feelings for him, is that it?" Helmut's features were beet red.

"No. That's not it. Not romantic feelings. I've already told you that I still think a lot of Erik, even though I'm no longer in love with him. But like I said...just use your head. You and I are the only two people on earth who know that I am about to jilt Erik. Because of that, I do have to make it look good, don't I? If I don't go to the tunnel, everyone will wonder why."

A light seemed to come on in Helmut's eyes. "Oh. Sure. I hadn't thought of it like that. You're right."

"I knew you'd see it my way if you just gave it some thought."

"All right. You go. But be careful and come back to me quickly, won't you?"

"I will."

He looked deep into her eyes. "I'd sure like to kiss you good-bye, but someone might see us."

Moving off the porch, she said, "See you when I get back."

Helmut let her take a few steps, then said, "Metryka..."

She stopped, and turned around. "Yes?"

"You will tell Erik the first chance you get, right? If he's still alive."

"Yes. If he's still...alive."

Metryka wheeled and hurried away.

It was almost seven-forty-five when railroad station manager Peter Borszich stood before the small crowd of volunteers and thanked them for coming. He explained that he received a wire from Vaudron's burgomaster, which said there would be several wagons sent to take them off the special train at the east end of the tunnel and carry them the six miles over the mountain road to the open end on the west side.

Borszich pointed to nurse Louise Levron of the Danzig Clinic, and told the crowd that she had brought along bandages, medical supplies, and blankets, and would need help carrying them aboard. Hands went up, indicating they would help her.

Burgomaster Koblin Baume and his wife, Kathlyn, had come along with Metryka. Koblin had also brought two of his officers with him. Borszich pointed them out to the crowd. With the attention on him, Koblin spoke to the crowd and told them he had brought along Officer Conrad Meyer and Officer Othmar Ramus to investigate the explosion in the tunnel.

A man in the crowd called out, "Burgomaster Baume, do you think it was the independent woodworkers who blew up the tunnel?"

A grim look settled over Koblin's features. "Yes I do," he said. "They knew Eiger Wilhaus and his two vice presidents would be on the train. I think it was their way to punish Wilhaus for building the factory here in Chur."

"I agree!" shouted another man, whom everyone recognized as an employee of the furniture factory. "I figured those troublemakers would get violent...and they did!"

There was a low murmuring in the crowd. "Let's get aboard, folks," said Koblin Baume. "We need to get to the tunnel!"

Moments later, the train chugged out of the depot, heading west across the rolling land. Kathlyn and Metryka sat close to the Linden family and Dova Combray. Knowing a mother's heart, Kathlyn understood the deep anxiety Mura was experiencing over Erik and tried to comfort her.

Sitting next to Justina, Dova laid her head back and closed her eyes. "Dear Lord," she said in a low whisper, barely moving her lips, "please keep Your hand on Erik. He just has to be alive. He just has to..."

Metryka sat in silence on the seat with her mother, next to the window. While Kathlyn was turned in the seat, talking to Mura, who was behind her, Metryka kept her gaze on the darkening landscape. She was barely aware of the conversations going on around her as she tried to prepare herself mentally for whatever was to come. If Erik was dead, she would feel bad, but at least she would be spared the task of telling him the wedding was off. If he was alive...the task would still be hers.

In the tunnel, Dr. Erik Linden was working as fast as he could to save lives and relieve suffering. His own injured leg was giving him a great deal of pain, but he endured it, limping as he moved back and forth from coach to coach, caring for the passengers in order of the seriousness of their injuries. Many took notice of him wincing from his own pain as he knelt down beside his patients.

As the hours passed, the lanterns in the coaches began to run low on kerosene, which was in short supply because the train ordinarily ran only in daylight hours.

Soon the conductor was forced to leave two coaches at a time in total darkness in order to conserve kerosene so Dr. Linden would have light to work by.

Erik had finally found a moment to ask Charles his last name and learned that it was Krodin. Charles stayed with the doctor wherever he went, carrying two lighted lanterns to give him plenty of light to work by.

As Erik was working in coach number three on a fourteen-year-old girl who was bleeding from a deep gash on her arm, her mother sat next to her, holding her hand and speaking to her in low tones. Her father stood over them, looking on with concern.

While Erik was stitching up the gash, Charles's attention was drawn to the front door of the coach when he saw a short, stout man come in.

"Dr. Linden," said Charles in a subdued voice, "it's Blair Tolman. He looks angry."

"I told him I would get to his wife as soon as I can," said Erik, without looking up. "He'll just have to understand."

"Should I intercept him?" asked Charles.

"If you can."

Both lanterns were positioned to give off the best light. Charles turned and headed for the man. As they met up, he blocked Tolman's way. "Sir, Dr. Linden will get to your wife as soon as he—"

"Out of my way!" boomed the heavyset man, and knocked Charles aside with his shoulder.

Charles stumbled and fell against a man who was seated. "I'm sorry, sir." He righted himself and hurried after Blair Tolman.

Dr. Linden had looked up when the scuffle took place and saw Tolman drawing near, his moon-shaped face a deep red. He was concentrating on his work when Tolman stomped to a halt. Without looking up, he said, "Mr. Tolman, I told you I would tend to your wife as soon as possible. Please do not bother me."

Tolman's voice was sharp-edged. "She can't wait any longer, Doc! I want you to tend to her right now!"

This time, Erik paused, and looked up at him. "Is she worse than when I examined her?"

"Yes. Her pain is worse."

"But is she bleeding much through the makeshift bandage I put on her?"

Tolman cleared his throat. "Well, no." Then in a hard tone, he said, "But she's really hurting!"

"Mr. Tolman, I wish I could treat every injured person on this train at once. But it is impossible. This girl has a deep gash on her arm and is bleeding worse than Mrs. Tolman. I'm stitching it right now."

"Well, leave it like that and come tend to my wife!"

"I can't. If I don't finish it, she will bleed profusely again. She could bleed to death. I'm telling you, your wife will be all right. Now let me get this done."

"I said for you to come right now!"

The girl's father inched closer to the angry man. Keeping his voice steady, he said, "Sir, from what I heard Dr. Linden say, your wife is not as seriously injured as my daughter. Please. You are hindering him from finishing his work on her."

Breathing hard, Blair Tolman looked down and saw one of Dr. Linden's scalpels lying on a cloth next to his medical bag. Shoving the concerned father aside, he moved quickly, bent down, and grasped the scalpel. Instantly locking Erik's head in the crook of his muscular arm, he pressed the tip of the scalpel's razor-sharp blade against his throat. "You come now and tend to my wife, or I'll cut your throat!"

Charles tensed, as did the girl's father. The mother let out a tiny squeak, her face twisting into a mask of fear. The girl—already pale—went sheet white. The other passengers looked on with fear and astonishment on their faces, but nobody moved.

The conductor had come in, and stood like a statue, noting the blade that was so dangerously pressed against the doctor's throat. He had never felt so helpless.

Sweat was beaded on Tolman's round face, and his breathing was becoming more ragged. "Now, Doc!"

Blood was now trickling from the part of the gash on the girl's arm that was not yet stitched.

Remaining absolutely still, Erik said in a low, level tone, "Mr. Tolman, I understand why you are concerned over your wife's condition, but when I examined her earlier, I felt her condition was not as urgent as some of the other passengers. Listen to me. If you cut my throat, there will be no one to take care of your wife at all. Then what?"

Tolman's rapid breathing slowed, but he did not reply.

Taking advantage of the moment, Erik said, "Indeed, your wife needs medical attention, Mr. Tolman. And she might die before any help comes from the outside if I don't get to her soon. But I can't let this girl bleed to death. I must finish with her before I go to your wife. Every second you hold that scalpel to my throat is one less second your wife has to live if I can't get to her in time."

Suddenly, Blair Tolman's beefy features wrenched beneath his skin. He sucked in a ragged breath and starting weeping. Slowly, he removed the scalpel from Erik's throat and laid it down where he had found it. There were countless sighs of relief.

"I'm sorry, Dr. Linden," Tolman said, the harsh edge gone from his voice. He sniffed and wiped tears from his eyes. "Please forgive me. It's just that—"

"I understand, sir. You go to your wife, and I'll be there as soon as I finish with this young lady."

The girl's mother was softly stroking her daughter's cheek. Her father's bulging eyes were fixed on the short, stocky man.

Tolman turned slowly and brushed past the conductor on his way to the door.

Erik released a pent-up breath and went back to work on the girl.

When Blair Tolman opened the door, he saw a small group of people approaching the coach, carrying lanterns. Some had blankets rolled up under their arms and others were holding canteens.

Two men stepped up and explained to Tolman that they were the men from the train who had gone after help. They had brought these people from Vaudron. Tolman explained that they were running low on kerosene. He told them Dr. Linden was working in number three, and that the conductor was with him. Quickly, Tolman reentered the coach and called for the conductor. When the conductor came, he smiled at the sight before him, and thanked the two men who had gone after help. Tolman went back to his wife.

The two men introduced a middle-aged man to the conductor as Aaron Reust, explaining that he was the group's leader. They had brought water and blankets in case the injured people needed them.

A smile broke across the conductor's face. He welcomed them all, then explained about the passengers who had been killed instantly when the train wrecked and of others who had died since.

"These two men told us you have Dr. Erik Linden aboard, sir," said Reust.

"Yes, thank the Lord," said the conductor. "He is one busy man."

"I'm sure that's true. I have a message for him."

"Well, all right. I'll take you to him."

Turning to his Vaudron group, Reust told them to go into the darkened coaches with their lanterns and give out water and blankets as needed then to check in coach number three.

Aaron Reust was ushered into coach number three by the conductor. They found Dr. Erik Linden just finishing his work on the girl. As he gently tied the knot on the bandage, he said, "There you are, Heather."

The girl smiled and thanked him as did her parents.

The conductor introduced Aaron Reust to the doctor, explaining that Reust had brought a group from Vaudron with blankets, water, and lanterns, and that Reust had a message for him.

Picking up his medical bag, Erik smiled and said, "Yes, sir?"

"Dr. Linden," said Reust, "you are acquainted with Vaudron's physician, Dr. Glynn Domire?"

"Yes. Fine man."

"Well, we alerted Dr. Domire about the wreck of the train here in the tunnel just as he was climbing into his buggy to follow an anxious husband to his farm, so he could deliver his wife's baby. We told him that you were aboard the train and tending to the injured passengers. He said to tell you that as soon as the baby was born, he would come to the tunnel and help you."

A tired smile curved Erik's lips. "Well, those babies don't ask if it's convenient for us doctors to deliver them when they are ready to enter the world. They just do it. I certainly understand. But I'll be glad to have him here. There's plenty of work yet to do."

At that moment, some of the Vaudron group came into the coach bearing water and blankets and carrying lanterns.

Dr. Erik Linden thanked Aaron Reust for coming, then excused himself, saying he had to get to his next patient. Charles carried both of his lanterns just in case the doctor would need them and followed him out the front door of the coach, knowing the next stop would be Mrs. Tolman.

When Erik had finished with Mrs. Tolman in coach number one, he limped to number two and began working on a man named John Berwick, whose chest had been punctured with a splintered piece of metal. He wasn't bleeding badly but was in a great deal of pain. The metal was buried some three inches deep.

Berwick's frantic wife was beside him as Erik knelt down, grimacing with his own pain, and opened his medical bag.

"Mr. Berwick," he said softly, "as I told you when I examined you earlier, I am going to have to do some surgery in order to remove this piece of metal properly."

"Yes," said Berwick, nodding weakly.

"I hate to tell you this, sir, but I'm out of what little chloroform I had in my medical bag. I'll have to do the surgery with no way to ease your pain."

Through clenched teeth, Berwick said, "I understand, Doctor. You go right ahead."

Lela Berwick bit her lower lip, shook her head, and said, "Dr. Linden, John is already in so much pain, I'm afraid when you start cutting, the increased pain will kill him. Could someone be sent to the doctor in Vaudron to get some chloroform or ether?"

"Well, ma'am, it so happens that Dr. Glynn Domire is delivering a baby on a farm somewhere outside of town and isn't available. I could send someone to try to find his nurse so she could get into the office tonight, but there really isn't time. Your husband has already had to wait a long time for me to get to him. The longer that broken piece of metal from one of the coach seats stays in his body, the more susceptible he is going to be to infection. I really need to get it out of there right now."

Lela's eyes filled with tears. John took hold of her hand. "It's all right, dear," he said in a whisper. "I won't die from the pain. Dr. Linden is right. He has to do the surgery now."

Lela made a thin, wordless sound of anguish as tears blurred her vision. Her breath came in quick shallow gasps as she put her hands to her mouth and nodded.

At that instant, a woman from across the aisle stepped up and put an arm around Lela's shoulders. "I couldn't help but hear what was being said, ma'am. Here. Hold onto me."

Lela blinked against her tears, gripped the woman's hand, and said, "Thank you." She looked at Erik through the veil of tears. "All right, Doctor. Go ahead."

Seven

With the terrified Lela Berwick looking on while in the grasp of the woman from across the aisle, Dr. Erik Linden asked Charles Krodin to place his hands on the patient's shoulders and hold him down. When Charles was in position, the doctor began his surgery.

As the scalpel bit into already tender flesh, John winced and jerked.

Charles bore down, saying, "I'll help you all I can, Mr. Berwick."

John opened his eyes, breathed a weak "thank you," and closed them again.

Seconds later, as the scalpel dug deeper into flesh, John ejected a cry. Lela stiffened, and the woman gripped her harder. Charles squeezed tighter on John's shoulders, pressing him firmly on the seat where he lay.

In a sweat, John tried not to cry out as the scalpel probed around the piece of metal, but once again, let out a cry.

Lela's eyes bulged. "Doctor, stop!" she wailed. "You're killing him!"

Erik concentrated on his task. "Ma'am, I know this is hard for you to watch, but he won't die from the pain. If it gets much worse, he will pass out."

"Please, honey," said the woman. "Try to relax."

"I can't relax!" screamed Lela. "He's killing my husband!"

"Shh...shh..." the woman said. "You're distracting the doctor."

John moaned, cried out, and shook his head. "I'm sorry, Doctor," he said with a quivering voice. "I just can't help it!"

"Stop it, Dr. Linden!" wailed Lela. "Stop it!"

Looking up at her, Erik said, "Please, Mrs. Berwick. I can't stop now. In a few minutes, I'll have it out."

Again, John jerked and let out a moan.

"Stop it! Stop it, I say! You're killing him!"

Looking up at the woman who was holding onto Lela, Erik said, "Ma'am, would you take her to another coach so I can get on with the surgery? Please?"

The woman gripped Lela's shoulders and turned her toward the door. "Come on, honey. Let's go."

Lela twisted free, screamed at the woman to leave her alone, and shoved her away.

Suddenly, a man appeared, wrapped Lela in a powerful set of arms, and hurried her toward the door. The woman went with them. Lela was wailing at the top of her voice all the way, but soon they passed through the door, heading for the next coach.

An eerie silence descended over the coach as Lela's cries dulled, then were gone.

John Berwick, face wet with perspiration, looked at the doctor with languid eyes. "I...I'm sorry about Lela."

"Don't be," said Erik. "I understand what she's going through. Ordinarily when I do surgery the family members are in the waiting room. Not in the operating room."

John closed his eyes, nodded, and passed out.

As Erik was about to continue with the removal of the broken piece of metal from John's chest, the man who had taken Lela out entered the coach and approached the spot where Erik was.

Erik looked up and asked, "How's she doing?"

"We got her seated in the next coach. Mrs. Reinhold—that's the lady who's with her—is trying to calm her down. Is there anything I can do to help, Doctor?"

Erik smiled. "You've already helped a great deal, and I thank you for it. Right now, since I have Charles here to hold John down if he regains consciousness, everything is under control. But stay close. I may need your help later."

"My wife and I are seated right over here," he said, gesturing toward a seat across the aisle, some ten or twelve feet away. "By the way, my name is Martyn Thake, Doctor."

Erik smiled again. "Mr. Thake, I'm glad to make your acquaintance."

Thake made his way around the small bits of debris on the coach floor to his wife, and Erik resumed his work with the scalpel.

Bright lanterns hung on the sides of the four wagons as the special train from Chur chugged to a halt near the east entrance of Nidwalden Tunnel.

Burgomaster Koblin Baume was the first to step off the train, and while he was offering his hand to Kathlyn to help her down, a man stepped up and said, "Hello, Chief. You don't know me, but I know you. I'm Ruger Jagman, from Vaudron. I'm sort of the leader here. I'm glad you could come along. And I assume this lovely lady is your wife."

"Yes," said Baume.

"Glad to have you here, ma'am," Jagman said, doing a slight bow.

"Thank you," said Kathlyn.

"Chief," said Jagman, "I'm on horseback, and when we get close to the west mouth of the tunnel, I'll hurry on ahead and let the train crew know the wagons bearing help from Chur are not far behind."

"Mr. Jagman," said Baume, "can you tell me how it is with the people on the train? You know—deaths and injuries."

"No, sir. We headed this way under the directions of our burgomaster. We haven't had any contact with the people on the train. But the quicker we get your group off the train and into the wagons, the quicker we'll have some answers to your questions."

"I'll hurry everybody along," Baume said, climbing back into the coach.

Ten minutes later, the Chur people were aboard the wagons and moving up the winding mountain road in the ring of light provided by the lanterns. Ruger Jagman was riding alongside the first wagon.

While the wagon wheels squeaked and thumped on the rough road, many of the group were in silent prayer, not only concerning Dr. Erik Linden, but for others on the wrecked train who were injured or grieving over the loss of a loved one.

Justina and Dova were sitting together in the bed of the same wagon occupied by Justina's parents and brothers. There was a half moon in the starlit sky.

After a while, Justina heard her best friend sniffle and saw her press a handkerchief to her nose.

"Honey, you all right?" asked Justina.

Dova dabbed at her nose, sniffed again, and nodded. "Yes."

"You sure?"

"Yes," said Dova, turning to look at her. "I've just been talking to the Lord in my heart, and asking Him to let everything be all right with Erik."

Justina took hold of her hand, squeezed it, and said, "I really appreciate you caring so much about my brother."

There was a brief silence, then Dova said, "Erik is such a fine man. I really admire him. And, of course, he is my best friend's brother."

The wagons continued to climb the steep road toward its crest and talk was minimal.

Dova Combray spoke to the Lord in her heart. *Dear Lord, forgive me for covering the truth a moment ago. You are fully aware that I more than admire Erik. I—well, You know…*

Dr. Erik Linden finished his work on John Berwick, who was still unconscious, and while Charles Krodin was buttoning John's shirt over the bandage on his chest, Erik was cleaning his instruments with alcohol.

While doing so, Erik caught Martyn Thake's eye and motioned for him.

Hurrying to him, Martyn said, "Yes, Doctor?"

"I'm all finished here. Would you go tell Mrs. Berwick she can come back in now?"

"Certainly," said Thake, and hurried out the door.

Charles looked at the pale features of the patient. "How long do you think he will be in this unconscious state, Doctor?"

"Hard to tell exactly, but I'd say he'll come out of it in another fifteen or twenty minutes."

"Who's next?"

"The elderly lady in coach number one."

"Oh. Mrs. Yelman. The one with the cut on her scalp."

"Yes. We'll go as soon as—"

Lela Berwick plunged through the door, ran down the aisle ahead of Mrs. Reinhold and Martyn Thake, and skidded to a halt where her husband lay across the seat. Her eyes widened as she looked down at him. "Oh, no! He's dead! He's dead!"

The outburst drew the attention of the other passengers, who looked on, some straining their necks to observe the scene.

"No, no," said Erik. "He's just unconscious. He's breathing. See?"

When Lela focused on the rise and fall of John's chest, she let out a quivering sigh, and her knees buckled. Martyn grabbed her and held her up. "Your husband will be fine, ma'am."

Lela drew a shuddering breath, looked back at her breathing husband, then at Erik. "I...I'm sorry, Doctor. I thought—"

"He indeed will be fine, Mrs. Berwick," said Erik. "I was able to remove the piece of metal without doing additional damage to the area. When the wound heals, he'll be good as new."

Tears began to spill down Lela's cheeks. "Dr. Linden, I want to thank you for taking care of John. And...and—"

"Yes, ma'am?"

"I...want to ask you to forgive me for the way I acted before... when you had to have me removed from the coach. I am so sorry. I was very rude to you. Please forgive me."

Rising to his feet, Erik patted her arm. "There is no apology needed, ma'am. I understand the trauma you were experiencing. John should come around in a few more minutes. I'll be back to check on him later."

Erik picked up his medical bag, motioned with a turn of his head to Charles, and limped toward the front door of the coach under the admiring eyes of the passengers, with his young assistant on his heels.

When Mrs. Yelman's scalp cut had been tended to, Erik said wearily, "Charles, that takes care of our list of the most seriously injured. We'll begin on that lady with the broken nose in coach number three in a little while, but I've just got to get off this leg and rest this body for a few minutes."

Gesturing toward an empty seat a few steps away, Charles said, "Here's a place for you to sit down, Doctor."

Limping that way, Erik said, "Tell you what. While I'm taking a small break, will you take a walk through all three cars and see if anything has changed with those I've already worked on? Or if someone who hasn't been treated yet has gotten worse? I'm especially interested in Eiger Wilhaus, since his problem is mainly his heart. Be sure to check on him for me, won't you?"

"Sure will, Doctor," said Charles. "I'll start back in number three and work my way back in here."

As Charles headed toward the rear of the coach, Erik lowered himself stiffly onto the empty seat and stretched his cramped legs out in front of him. Pain shot through his left leg, causing him to eject a cry, which he stifled in time to keep the other passengers from hearing it.

Wondering what time it might be, he took out his pocket watch and had to look twice to make sure his eyes were not playing tricks on him. "One twenty-five in the morning!" he breathed to himself, slipping the watch back in his pocket. "I wouldn't have guessed it was this late." Erik laid his head back on the seat, feeling the effects of the emotional strain he had been under since the train had wrecked. His injured leg was throbbing mercilessly. He thought of Dr. Glynn Domire, and said in a low whisper, "Lord, please get him here soon. It's not going to be long before I'll need medical attention, myself."

Erik saw an elderly woman, her silver hair shining in the light of the lanterns, making her way unsteadily along the aisle toward him. Her shuffling feet were scattering some of the debris that lay in her path. His gaze went to her shaking hands, and he saw that she was carrying a cup, and water was sloshing over the rim.

As she came nearer, she set her eyes on him and smiled. "Dr. Linden, I'm Rose Vandlik. You look awfully tired. May I offer you this cup of water?"

Erik looked up into her deeply lined features. A grateful smile found its way across his face as he lifted his hand to accept the woman's humble offering. "Well, bless your heart, you sure may. Thank you so much."

Rose placed the cup into his hand. "Thank the Lord, as frail as I am, I'm only bruised a little. When the train crashed, I took a little flight, but I slammed into a heavyset man. He cushioned me quite well."

"Praise the Lord, indeed," said Erik in a fatigued voice, lifting the cup to his lips.

Rose watched him as he drank down every drop without stopping to take a breath. Raising her eyebrows, she said, "I'll go get you some more, Doctor."

"That won't be necessary, thank you," he said softly, as he placed the cup back into her shaky hand. "It was very kind of you to do this."

Erik scrubbed a palm over his eyes, used the seat in front of him to help him rise to his feet, and took a few seconds to gain proper balance on his bad leg. He patted Rose's cheek and said, "Thank you, again, ma'am, for the cup of cool water."

Rose gently nodded her head, smiled, and made her unsteady way up the aisle.

Erik was about to choose the next person to tend to when Charles entered the coach. "Good news, Dr. Linden!"

A man was on Charles's heels whom Erik did not recognize.

The eyes of the passengers were quickly on Charles and the stranger as they headed toward the doctor.

Charles introduced Erik to Ruger Jagman, and let Jagman tell him that a group of volunteers from Chur had come as far as the east end of the tunnel by train. He explained that he was from Vaudron, and had led four wagons over the mountain road to the east mouth of the tunnel, and that the wagons would be arriving at the west mouth any minute. The Chur people were coming with blankets and medical supplies, and had a nurse with them.

They would have to walk the four miles to the train, since the tunnel was not large enough to accommodate the wagons on either side of the tracks.

Elated to hear this good news, Erik thanked Jagman, then told Charles that they needed to get back to work. Jagman excused himself and left the coach. The passengers were talking happily about the group coming from Chur with a nurse and medical supplies.

Charles told the doctor that Eiger Wilhaus was sleeping peacefully with Zugg Hinwill watching over him, and that in his estimation, the next person in need of his attention was a woman in car number three who possibly had a broken arm.

When the Chur people arrived at the west mouth of the tunnel, Ruger Jagman was just riding out of the tunnel on his horse. From the saddle, he explained to them that they would have to hike to the train, then quickly trotted back to see if he could help in any way at the scene of the wreck.

The men carried the medical supplies and lanterns for Louise Levron, and some of the women carried blankets.

As they walked into the tunnel and headed toward the spot where the dynamite had stopped the train, Frederic Linden said to his family, "I wonder if Jagman knows anything about who survived the wreck. I should have thought to ask him before he rode away so quickly."

"I guess we should have told him who we are before he came ahead of us to the train in the first place," said Mura. "If we had, he could have told us just now if Erik is all right."

"I still feel that he is, Mama," said Brandt. "You'll see. We'll be there in a little while."

In less than an hour, the hikers drew near the wreckage. By the light of the lanterns they carried and lanterns that burned outside the train, they saw that the engine was partially buried under dirt and rocks and was askew on the twisted tracks. The coal car had left the tracks, and lay on its side. The three coaches had buckled on impact, and each one was partially off the tracks.

Metryka's heart was pounding in her chest. Was Brandt right? Would she still have the unpleasant task of telling Erik the wedding was off? A wave of nausea washed over her.

Eager for the arrival of the group from Chur, the conductor was waiting on the rear platform of coach number three with Martyn Thake, where a pair of lanterns hung to give off sufficient light. When he saw the Chur group drawing near, he stepped off the platform and smiled at them. "Hello, folks," he said with a smile. "I'm Hyman Fields, the conductor. This is Martyn Thake, one of the passengers. Are we ever glad to see you!"

"That's for sure!" said Thake. "We have so many people who need care. The doctor on board has had to spread himself plenty thin, doing surgery and setting bones, and those passengers who weren't hurt so bad—like myself—have been trying to help him, but—"

"You're talking about Dr. Erik Linden, sir?" cut in Frederic as he stepped forward.

"Yes," said Thake. "You must know him."

"Know him? I'm his father!"

Mura was instantly beside her husband, her eyes filling with joyful tears. "Oh, praise the Lord! My Erik is alive!"

The rest of the Linden family, along with Dova and Metryka, crowded up, joining in with words of praise.

As though the entire group from Chur had been holding their breath, a collective sigh was released. Many voices were raised in praise and thanksgiving to the merciful God of heaven.

"Where will we find Erik?" asked Mura. "We're his family. We want to see him."

"He was in coach number one the last time I saw him, ma'am," said Fields. "But he may be in another by now. He's been moving back and forth in all three, trying to treat the injured in accordance with the seriousness of their injuries."

"I'll go find him," said Martyn. "I'll tell him his family is here, and I'm sure he'll come just as soon as he can."

"Tell him his fiancée is here, too," spoke up Justina.

"Yes," said Metryka. "That's me."

Dova glanced at Metryka and brushed a tear from her cheek as she thanked God in her heart that Erik was alive and able to care for the injured passengers.

As Martyn dashed away, Brandt said, "See, Mama! Didn't I tell you Erik was all right?"

Both boys hugged their mother, and Frederic put an arm around Justina.

Hyman Fields smiled at Mura. "Ma'am, your son has become a real hero to all of the passengers and myself. He is quite a man."

Koblin Baume stepped forward and introduced himself to the conductor as Chur's burgomaster. "I am wondering, Mr. Fields, about three men who are on this train. Mr. Eiger Wilhaus and two other executives of the Wilhaus Industries. Are they—"

"Mr. Wilhaus is injured, sir. He had a heart seizure, but Dr. Linden was able to help him. He was sleeping the last time I passed through his car."

"I'm so glad he's alive," said Baume. "And what about—"

"Mr. Hinwill has a minor injury, sir. He is with Mr. Wilhaus. Mr. Lutrey was killed, I'm sorry to say."

"Oh. That's too bad."

Kathlyn gripped her husband's arm. "But at least Mr. Wilhaus and Mr. Hinwill have been spared, Koblin."

"Yes," he said, patting the hand that gripped his arm. He said to the conductor, "We have a nurse here, Mr. Fields."

As Louise Levron stepped forward, Fields smiled at her. "Yes. So I was told. Dr. Linden will be happy to see you, ma'am."

"So where do we start, Mr. Fields?" queried Louise.

"It would be best if we talk to Dr. Linden first," said Fields. "He can direct you. I'm sure he will be here shortly, when he learns from Mr. Thake that you're here."

Koblin Baume introduced Officers Conrad Meyer and Othmar Ramus to the conductor, explaining that he had brought them along to do a thorough investigation into the explosion. Fields welcomed them, and said they could go to work whenever they wanted to. Meyer and Ramus hurried forward in the tunnel each carrying a lantern.

Dr. Erik Linden was examining the bruised arm of a forty-year-old woman in coach number one with Charles Krodin at his side when he saw Martyn Thake come in, his eyes dancing.

"Dr. Linden!" he said, smiling broadly. "The people from Chur have arrived! They're waiting beside coach number three. They want to see you."

"Oh. Good. I'm glad they're here."

"Your family and your fiancée are among them."

Erik's eyebrows arched. "Oh! Well, double good! Tell them I'll be there in a few minutes. I have to finish with this lady first."

"All right," said Martyn, and quickly disappeared out the door.

The Linden family and those with them were still standing at the rear of coach number three with the conductor when they saw Martyn Thake running alongside the train. As he drew up, he said, "Dr. Linden was happy to learn that his family and his fiancée are in the group. He said to tell you he will be here in a few minutes. He's in coach number one."

Everyone in the group was tense as they waited for Erik to appear on the platform of one of the coaches.

Standing beside Mura, Metryka said, "Mrs. Linden, when he comes, you go to him first, since you are his mother."

Mura smiled. "Thank you, dear. I appreciate my future daughter-in-law being willing to let his mother go first."

A pang of guilt jolted Metryka's heart.

Suddenly Erik came into view on the rear platform of coach number one. When he stepped down from the platform, everyone saw that he was limping alongside the jumbled coaches as he headed toward them.

"Oh, Frederic, he's been hurt!" gasped Mura.

"It can't be too bad, honey," said Frederic.

Erik was running his gaze over the brightened faces as he drew up, and Mura lunged into his open arms. Weeping for joy, Mura stroked his face tenderly. "Oh, my precious son, I was so relieved when we were told that you were alive! What about this limp?"

"The thigh was bruised in the crash, Mama, but I haven't had time to look at it."

"I'm just so glad you're alive!" Mura said, embracing him again.

Erik looked over his mother's head and smiled at his father, brother, and sisters. Noticing Dova, he gave her a smile, then did the same with Koblin and Kathlyn Baume.

His eyes lit up when he set them on Metryka.

She found a smile for him as she moved up close. Her heart was beating so loudly she was sure everyone around her could hear it. *I can't let on now that I'm no longer in love with him,* she thought. *I've got to give a good performance. But just as soon as possible, I must unburden myself to him. For his sake as well as my own.*

Erik kissed his mother's forehead, then she let go of him, knowing he wanted to see Metryka.

As Mura stepped aside, wiping tears from her cheeks, Metryka took another step toward him, then stopped. Her mind flashed to the soon coming moment when she would have to break his heart, and her blood turned cold.

Erik was alerted to the flow of emotions passing over Metryka's face and the troubled look that was fixed in her eyes. Mentally shaking himself, he reached for her and folded her in his arms. *Whatever it is will have to wait,* he told himself as he held her tight.

Looking up into his eyes, Metryka said, "Oh, Erik, I'm sorry about your leg, but I'm so glad you're alive."

Meeting her gaze adoringly, Erik said, "The Lord was good to me, sweetheart. I love you so very, very much."

Metryka forced a false smile. "Me too," she said weakly.

Justina was next to embrace him, followed by Ludwig and

Brandt. Frederic followed and put a bear hug on him, saying how glad he was to learn that he was alive.

Last to move up was Dova, who smiled at him, saying how happy she was that he was all right.

Erik gave her a brotherly embrace.

In the emotion of the moment, Dova wanted to tell Erik that she was in love with him, but swallowed the words even as they started to form on her tongue. Guilt also stabbed her heart for feeling the way she did, but she was helpless in her battle to rid herself of the love she felt for him. She had continually asked the Lord to forgive her for loving Erik because he was promised to her dear friend Metryka.

As Erik released his hold on Dova, she blinked at her tears and said, "Erik, I prayed so hard on the train and in the wagon that the Lord would let you live if you were injured. You have so much to give to those who need your compassion and tender care in your medical work."

Erik smiled down at her and folded her in his arms again. "Dova, you have such a wonderful way about you."

As he held her, Dova thought, *This is all I will ever have of him,* and tried to imprint the feel of his strong arms deeply in her mind. *How can he help but be aware of the flow of love from my heart?*

Erik released her and she stepped back, smiling at him with quivering lips.

Brandt rushed up and said, "Erik, I told everybody from the moment we heard about the explosion and the train wreck that I knew you were alive."

Dova felt hot tears at the backs of her eyes and put a trembling hand to her mouth to smother the sob that was threatening to escape. The tears were surfacing, and she quickly turned away so no one could see them.

Erik had a hand on Brandt's shoulder about to say something to him, but his eyes went to Dova. In his peripheral vision he had seen what she did, and he was puzzled by it.

Erik said his few words to Brandt, then saw Kathlyn Baume standing close with her husband behind her. When he embraced

Kathlyn, she told him how glad she was when she learned he was alive.

Koblin then stepped up, smiling, and shook Erik's hand. "The conductor told me that in spite of that injured leg, you have worked hard to save lives and relieve suffering. I'm so proud that you are going to be my son-in-law."

Erik was both surprised and pleased to hear Metryka's father say this. Up until that moment it seemed that Koblin Baume was merely tolerating him because he was engaged to his daughter. He knew that Koblin despised what he stood for and was carrying a grudge because he had led Metryka to the Lord.

Metryka was standing between Dova and Justina and clearly heard what her father had said to Erik. Her heart suddenly felt heavy. This was going to make it even harder to break it off with him.

The rest of the Chur people stepped forward to tell Erik they were glad he was alive, and to commend him for the work he was doing with the injured passengers.

While this was going on, Frederic Linden asked the conductor if there was anything he and his teenage sons could do to help him. Fields told him they and some of the other Chur men could carry the dead passengers out of the coaches so they could be loaded in the wagons and taken to the undertaker in Vaudron. He pointed to Aaron Reust, who was standing by, saying they could work with him. Fields said he would use the other Chur men to help clean up debris and remove broken seats from the coaches.

Erik was talking to Louise Levron when he saw his father, brothers, and three other Chur men heading toward the rear door of coach number three, being led by Aaron Reust.

Louise was asking Erik where she could best be used. He told her he would take her to a couple of patients who needed extra care. At the same time, Mura asked her son how she and the other women in the group could help. Erik said he would take Louise to coach number one first, then come back and assign the women places in the coaches where they could tend to the injured passengers.

As doctor and nurse walked toward coach number one, he said,

"Louise, how has Dr. Danzig been doing while I've been gone?"

"Not so good, Doctor," she said. "Amelia and I have had to send him home a couple of times. He was so tired and shaky."

Erik shook his head. "I'm sorry to hear that."

"We just have to face it, Doctor," said Louise. "He has worked hard all of his life, and his age is slowing him down increasingly."

"Yes," sighed Erik. "Retirement may be upon the man much sooner than he has planned."

"I'm afraid so," Louise said sadly.

Eight

It was just after four o'clock in the morning when a drowsy Aaron Reust lifted his head at the sound of a horse whinnying softly. It was one of the horses that was hitched to the Vaudron wagons that were collected at the west entrance of Nidwalden Tunnel. Aaron was seated on the ground with his back against the tunnel wall.

Another horse whinnied, then Aaron heard the sound of hoofbeats and spinning wheels, and realized the horses had heard the horse and buggy coming before he did.

Rising to his feet, he yawned and looked toward the west. In the pale light of the moon, he saw the buggy coming his way. It took only seconds for him to recognize the driver, and a smile broke across his face.

As the buggy drew up, the driver pulled rein and said, "Hello, Aaron."

"Hello, Dr. Domire," Aaron said warmly. "I'm sure glad to see you, and Dr. Linden will be too. He sent me to wait here for your arrival, so I can take you back to the train."

"I'm later than I expected to be. Mrs. Zeldrick had some complications giving birth. I understand the train is past halfway in the tunnel."

"Yes, sir. It's about four miles in."

Looking around at the collection of wagons and horses, Dr. Glynn Domire said, "Can't take the wagons in?"

"No way to turn them around in there, unless you want to take a chance on breaking an axle trying to get the wheels over the tracks."

"Be the same for my buggy, I guess."

"Yes, sir. There isn't much room on either side of the tracks. Just a little more than enough to run the trains through."

"Well, I guess we'll walk then," said the doctor, picking up his medical bag and hopping out of the buggy. When his feet touched ground, he glanced at the nearest wagon and saw three lifeless forms in the bed, covered completely with blankets.

"Those are three of the passengers who were killed in the crash," said Aaron. "There are four more bodies over there in that next wagon. Two of them are the engineer and the fireman. They were both killed on impact when the dynamite exploded and the train crashed into the rocks and dirt as that part of the tunnel collapsed. Some of the passengers were killed on impact, and others died a little later. Dr. Linden has had his hands full. And...he's injured, too."

"Oh?"

"His left leg. He's limping pretty bad, but hasn't had time to examine it."

"Well, I'll examine it," Domire said. "Let's go. You can give me more details as we walk."

Dr. Erik Linden moved from coach to coach, observing the men and women of Chur who were doing what they could to relieve the suffering of the injured passengers and checking on the passengers. There were a half dozen that he still considered critical, and kept a close eye on them, wishing he could stay with each one. He was praying fervently that the Lord would bring Dr. Glynn Domire speedily, so he could help watch over the critical ones.

Nurse Louise Levron had worked on the two passengers to whom she was assigned first, then under Dr. Linden's directions, worked on others as her services were needed. Erik had given her Charles Krodin to assist her. From time to time, she sent Charles for the doctor when she needed his professional help or advice.

As Erik continually limped his way from coach to coach, he paused each time he passed through coach number three to check on Eiger Wilhaus. Most of the time he found Wilhaus sleeping soundly and resting well. Zugg Hinwill was sleeping some, but awakened often to make sure his employer was all right.

Each time Erik came upon his mother, sisters, Dova, and Metryka, who were spread throughout the train, it was a joy to him to see them sincerely doing everything they could to make the injured passengers comfortable. He noted that Dova chose to work with the children as much as she could, and it pleased him.

Once, while moving slowly through coach number two, Erik came upon Metryka as she was giving water to John Berwick while a sleepy-eyed Lela looked on. Metryka looked up and smiled at Erik.

He bent over and said, "I've got you in good hands here, Mr. Berwick."

John swallowed the last of the water in the cup, and as Metryka took the cup from his mouth he said, "She is a fine young lady, Doctor."

"That she is," said the doctor. "Well, I must move on. Both of you try to get some sleep."

"We will," said Lela.

The front door of the coach opened, and two men stepped in.

"Dr. Linden," said Aaron Reust, "I have Dr. Domire here."

Domire stepped ahead of Aaron and beelined for Erik.

Erik shook his hand, saying how glad he was to see him, and introduced him to Metryka, telling him that they were going to be married soon. Domire offered his congratulations, and butterflies flitted in Metryka's stomach as she watched the two doctors leave the coach with Erik limping. Aaron Reust followed them.

When the three men stepped to the ground, Aaron said, "Dr. Linden, if you don't need me for anything else right now, I'll go help the Chur men with the chores you gave them."

"You go right ahead," said Erik. "And thanks for bringing Dr. Domire to me."

"My pleasure," said Aaron, and walked away.

Domire looked down at Erik's left leg by the light of the lanterns that burned outside the coaches and said, "How bad is that leg hurt?"

"I'm not sure. I've been too busy to look at it."

"Mm-hmm. That's what Aaron told me. Where can we go so I can take a look at it?"

"There's no time for that right now, Doctor. There are too many passengers who need your help and mine. I've got some who are critical, and I've been spread plenty thin trying to watch over them. I need you to take over some of them."

Domire sighed. "As you wish, but as soon as possible, I want to see that leg."

"All right. Now—"

"How did you injure it?"

"Well, when the train came to a sudden stop, I didn't. While I was flying through the air, I hit it on something. I think it was the back of a seat."

Domire nodded. "I'm sorry. I sure hope it isn't broken."

"Me too. Now, as I was going to say, let me take you to the passengers who need you most."

At dawn, the two doctors left their patients long enough to discuss the situation. Standing on the rear platform of coach number two, Dr. Domire said, "I suggest we take all the injured passengers and their families to Vaudron, since it is closer than Chur. We can use what space I have at the office for the critical ones, and make a hospital out of the town's meeting hall for the others, plus sleeping quarters for their families. What do you think?"

"I like the idea," said Erik. "We could sure give them better care that way than using the cramped quarters we have in those three banged-up coaches."

"Right. Since Ruger Jagman has his horse, I'll send him to town right away and have him talk to Mayor Eli Kenisaw. I know the mayor and his wife will jump right in to help us. They'll have the meeting hall ready by the time we get there."

"Sounds good to me," said Erik.

As the sun rose, spreading its golden light over the land, the injured passengers were being loaded in the wagons, accompanied by their loved ones.

While Dr. Erik Linden was supervising the loading process, he saw his mother step out of coach number three and head toward him.

"Good morning, Mama," he said, giving her a slanted smile. "You look pretty tired."

"No more than anyone else, son," she said. "I want you to have Dr. Domire look at your leg."

"He and I have already discussed it. When we get to his office, he's going to examine it."

"Good. I feel better now."

At that instant, Koblin Baume approached, flanked by his two officers. Mura excused herself, and moved back toward the coach.

Frowning, Erik gave the three men a smile. "Conrad, Othmar, what are you doing here?"

"I didn't get a chance to tell you, Erik," said Koblin. "I brought these two officers with me so they could do an investigation on the explosion."

"Oh. I see. Then you two have been in the tunnel ever since you got here?"

"Sure have," said Othmar. "At both ends. We used one of the wagons to go to the east end so we could get a good look there."

"What did you come up with?" queried Erik.

"We felt sure it was dynamite when we saw this end of it," said Conrad, "and our assessment of it was confirmed when we went to the other end. The culprits who planted the dynamite used a long fuse. We followed a long thin line of burned powder from the east entrance all the way to the spot of the explosion."

"They timed it just right with the train's arrival in the tunnel," said Othmar, "so they could make a run for it and get out before it went off."

"It's too early to more than speculate who the culprits were," said Koblin, "but my speculation is that it was independent woodworkers."

"Well, if it was," Erik said in a low tone, "it had to be a small minority of them. The majority—as upset and angry as they are—would never approve of murder, especially the murder of innocent men, women, and children on the train. Whoever they are who did it are vicious and heartless. They were willing to kill a train full of people in order to take the life of one man—Eiger Wilhaus. Or should I say three men? Hinwill and Lutrey too."

"When these two men and I get back to Chur, the woodworkers will be questioned," said Koblin. "Hopefully we can trip somebody up and nail the guilty ones."

"Yes, sir," said Erik. "The guilty parties must be punished."

At that moment, Erik saw his father step out of the last coach and head toward him. Excusing himself to the burgomaster and his officers, he made his way in that direction.

As father and son met, Frederic asked, "What are your plans? Are you going to stay in Vaudron for a few days, or come home with us?"

"I'll have to stay, Papa. I'll wire you and let you know when I'm coming home. I talked to Louise about it, and she said she was sure Dr. Danzig could handle things at the clinic barring some cataclysmic event. I should be able to bring Mr. Wilhaus and Mr. Hinwill to Chur in about a week."

"All right. Keep in touch, won't you?"

"Yes. From what I understand, someone in the Vaudron group will wire the depot in Chur so a train can be sent to pick all of you up shortly after you get to that side of the tunnel."

Frederic chuckled. "If they get back here with the wagons in a hurry so we can get over the mountains."

"I'm sure they will."

Erik's family was gathering around, along with Metryka and Dova.

He told them he would be home in about a week, he thought...depending on how well Mr. Wilhaus did at the clinic in Vaudron. He hugged each one, and was told once more by his mother to get the leg checked by Dr. Domire.

Erik gave Dova another brotherly embrace, then took Metryka by the hand and moved a few steps away. She explained that the first thing she had to do when she got to Chur was to give a report to Durbin Thorpe. He would be anxious about Eiger Wilhaus. They embraced, and Erik kissed her cheek, knowing they were in public.

"Dr. Linden!" came the voice of Ruger Jagman. "We're ready to roll!"

"All right," Erik called back.

He kissed Metryka's cheek again. "We'll be husband and wife pretty soon, sweetheart."

Feeling a pang of guilt once again, Metryka nodded.

The group watched as Erik headed for one of the wagons, medical bag in hand, and climbed in. As the wagons started westward, Erik turned and waved. Everyone in the group waved back.

As Dova Combray watched Erik's wagon move away with the others, her hungry eyes lingered on the man she loved until he was carried from view. *Dear Lord, what am I to do?* she said in her heart. *Please take away this love I have for Erik. It is too much for me to bear.*

Julia Kenisaw, wife of Vaudron's mayor, had been busy all morning organizing the town's women in setting up the makeshift hospital. Cots had been placed a few feet apart for the injured passengers at one end of the town hall and others at the opposite end as sleeping quarters for their families. All cots were made up with clean, crisp sheets and soft pillows.

The place was a beehive of activity as Julia looked on.

In her midsixties, Julia was a small woman, full of energy and a zest for life. She was adored by her husband and loved by the community.

As she stood in the center of the hall, giving orders and suggestions, a stiffly starched apron covered her green spring dress. Her snow-white hair was in its usual style, swept up into a bun on top of her head and firmly secured with numerous hairpins.

Periodically, Julia's eyes turned toward the hall's kitchen where pots of chicken soup and kettles of beef broth with carrots and potatoes were simmering at the back of the large stove in preparation for the arrival of the people from the train at any moment. Tea was steeping in warm cozies and coffeepots were bubbling merrily, giving off a pleasant aroma. Baskets on the cupboard held slices of freshly made bread slathered in butter.

Satisfied that all was in readiness, Julia moved to the center of the hall and turned a bright smile on the group of women who had cheerfully given of their time and effort. "Ladies, I want to thank you one and all. Whatever would I have done without you?"

Modest smiles lit up radiant faces as the women looked admiringly at the mayor's wife.

One lady who stood near a window said, "Mrs. Kenisaw, I hear wagons coming!"

By noon, most of the injured passengers had been made comfortable in the makeshift hospital at the town hall. Those in serious condition were on cots at Dr. Glynn Domire's small clinic.

While Dr. Domire's nurse and other Vaudron women looked after the patients, Erik lay on a table in the examining and surgical room while Domire examined his leg.

When he was finished, Domire said, "Your thigh is severely bruised, Doctor, but the bone is not broken."

"Praise the Lord for that," said Erik, sitting up. "Now I can get back to my patients."

Durbin and Helmut Thorpe were busy at their desks in late afternoon when they heard feminine footsteps on the walkway outside the door. Both looked up to see Metryka move past the window. They were out of their chairs and moving toward the door when she entered.

"You're back!" said Helmut, releasing a toothy smile.

"Come sit down," Durbin said, gesturing toward her desk.

Releasing a wearied sigh, Metryka moved that direction. "I'm very tired, but I wanted to report the news as soon as possible to both of you. Let me tell you quickly that Mr. Wilhaus was injured, but he is alive, thanks to the efforts of Erik. The injury brought on a heart seizure shortly after the crash, but Erik worked at massaging his chest and saved his life. He is doing better now. Mr. Hinwill was injured slightly, but is doing fine. Mr. Lutrey wasn't so fortunate. He was killed by a blow to the head when the train crashed."

Father and son exchanged glances, then Durbin said, "I'm sorry about Agno, but I sure am glad Mr. Wilhaus is alive."

Durbin and Helmut drew up wooden chairs and sat down as Metryka sat onto her padded desk chair.

"So will Mr. Wilhaus still be able to come and meet with the independent woodworkers?" asked Helmut.

"Erik says he will. He may have to be in a wheelchair, but Erik said he hoped to have him and Mr. Hinwill here in about a week. This will depend on how Mr. Wilhaus fares, and how quickly the railroad people can clear the tunnel so they can get trains through. Erik said he would wire his parents and my father to keep them advised as to exactly when they will be here. Papa will stay in touch with you on it, Mr. Thorpe."

"All right," said Durbin, rising from the chair. "I'll go right now and advise Alexander Metternik of this."

"So how did the meeting go without Mr. Wilhaus present?" asked Metryka.

"No real problems. All the woodworkers knew about the explosion in the tunnel by then, so after I promised them I would keep in touch with Metternik when I had any news, they left peacefully." As Durbin moved toward the door, he said over his shoulder, "Guess I'd better go keep my promise. We'll set up the woodworkers' meeting with Mr. Wilhaus as soon as possible after he arrives."

When Durbin was gone, Helmut left the chair, leaned over Metryka, and kissed her tenderly.

Then looking into her eyes, he asked, "Did you tell Erik the wedding is off?"

"No," she said quickly. "We didn't have a minute alone in the tunnel. I'll tell him as soon as possible after he returns home."

Helmut's face clouded as he stood up straight, and a frown laced itself across his brow. "Well, dearie," he said crisply, "you should've talked to him in private, anyhow. Couldn't you have just told him you needed to see him alone?" There was anger in his eyes.

Metryka was taken aback at Helmut's insensitivity and retorted sharply, eyes flashing, "Injured passengers were needing his help, *dearie.* Some were at the point of death. It was hardly the time or place to corner him and bring up such a personal matter. How can you even suggest such a thing?"

The anger quickly left Helmut's eyes. He dipped his head, then looked at her and said in a subdued voice, "I'm sorry. You're right. Forgive me for seeming to be so uncaring. It's…it's just that I want all of this to be over so I can declare my love for you openly."

"I know," she said quietly, placing her hand on his arm. "So do I."

Covering the hand with his own, Helmut said, "You'd better tell Erik as soon as he arrives. June 26 isn't that far away."

"I'll take care of it," she assured him.

Exactly a week later, Dr. Erik Linden, Eiger Wilhaus, and Zugg Hinwill were seated together on the train as it chugged into the station at Chur. Railroad crews had worked around the clock and had been able to clear the tunnel sufficiently for trains to pass through. Complete repairs would take months.

Erik had wired his family, Koblin Baume, and Dr. Joseph Danzig of their arrival time. The Lindens were there to meet the train along with Durbin Thorpe. Louise Levron was there with a wheelchair from the clinic, which Erik had requested for Eiger Wilhaus's use.

Thorpe had a buggy ready and took Wilhaus and Hinwill toward the hotel, saying he would explain on the way about the upcoming meeting with Alexander Metternik and the independent woodworkers.

After Mura Linden had embraced her oldest son, she thanked him for telling them in the wire about his leg. And as they walked away from the station, she remarked on how much better he was walking already.

"Are you going to the factory first, son?" asked Frederic.

"Yes, Papa. I'll see you later at the house. I want to see Metryka, then I'll go to the clinic and check in with Dr. Danzig."

Climbing the stairs to the walkway at the factory was a bit of a task for Erik, but there was only slight pain as he turned the knob and opened the office door.

Metryka was at her desk, and on the other side of the room, Helmut was just settling onto his padded desk chair.

"Hello, Erik!" Metryka said, leaving her chair and embracing him as Helmut glared at her covertly. "I'm glad to see you. How's the leg?"

"Quite a bit better," said Erik, warming her with a smile.

"I was glad to hear that it wasn't broken."

Putting on a fake smile, Helmut moved toward Erik and said, "Yes, I was glad to hear that it wasn't broken, too, Dr. Linden. I guess since it's doing better, you'll be able to do your normal work at the clinic then."

"Yes," said Erik. "In fact I've got to get over to the clinic right now and see Dr. Danzig." Then to Metryka he said, "I'll come by the house and see you tonight."

"All right," said Metryka. "Tonight."

They embraced each other for a brief moment, then as Erik turned to leave, his eyes fell on a revolver that lay on Helmut's desk, causing him to stop.

Helmut said, "My father and I have been keeping revolvers in our desks since the woodworkers began stirring up trouble. I had just cleaned and reloaded mine a few minutes before you came in. I hadn't put it away, yet." A sneer formed on his face. "If Metternik and his bunch decide to storm the office, they'll be sorry."

Erik sighed. "I hope it doesn't come to that."

"Me, either," said Helmut, "but if it does, I'm ready."

Erik told Metryka one more time that he would see her that evening and left.

Helmut turned to Metryka, his jaw squared. "You didn't have to be so warm to him. And you certainly didn't have to hug him so tightly—twice."

"Helmut, what's the matter with you?" she said crisply. "If I wasn't warm to him and didn't hug him like that, he'd wonder why. I have to keep up the facade until I tell him I'm not in love with him anymore and the wedding is off."

"You'd better tell him tonight," he clipped.

"I will if I can get him alone," she said levelly. "Papa is wanting to talk to him and may dominate him the entire evening."

Helmut frowned. "Metryka, I can't stand much more of this. He's got to know real soon."

"I'll get it done," she said. "Trust me."

"All right," he said, going to his desk and opening a drawer. He dropped the revolver in it and shoved it closed. "I've got a couple of errands to do for my father. I'll be back in a little while."

With that, he was out the door.

Nine

Metryka Baume's heart was thumping heavily in her chest as she walked to the window, and the faint metallic taste of dread filled her dry mouth.

She watched Helmut descend the stairs. Just as he reached the ground, the factory foreman called to him, coming from one of the wood shops on the first floor. Helmut talked with him for a moment, then as the foreman headed back into the building, he hastened down the street.

Metryka broke into tears and moved slowly to her desk. Dropping onto the chair, she put her elbows on the desktop and laid her face in her hands. Tears ran through her fingers and down her arms, staining the sleeves of her dress as she struggled with her problem.

She knew she was in love with Helmut in spite of the fact that he didn't always treat her right. She knew also that she had deep respect for Erik and didn't want to hurt him.

"But you don't have any choice," she said to herself in a broken voice. "You've got to tell him about Helmut and get it over with."

The strain of it all was too much for her, and she broke into sobs.

She wept for several minutes, then taking a handkerchief from a desk drawer, she dabbed at her eyes as she contemplated the moment when she would tell Erik the truth. Not only was he going to be hurt to learn that she was in love with Helmut, but he was going to be shocked when she told him she hadn't been honest when she supposedly became a Christian. She had only gone through the motions and made a profession so he would want her.

At that moment, Metryka heard light footsteps on the stairs. She quickly wiped the tears from her eyes, blew her nose, and tossed the handkerchief into its drawer. As the footsteps drew near the door, she acted as if she was poring over some papers that lay before her on the desk.

As the door came open, she looked up to see the smiling face of lovely Dova Combray.

"Hello, Dova," said Metryka, pressing a smile on her lips.

Dova closed the door behind her and moved to the desk. "I was just passing by on my way to do some shopping and decided I would come up and see you for a moment."

Metryka gestured toward the wooden chair that stood in front of her desk. "Sit down, honey. It's nice of you to stop by."

As Dova was settling on the chair, she looked closely at Metryka. "Your eyes are swollen and bloodshot. Have you been crying?"

Knowing it would be foolish to deny it, Metryka replied, "Yes. I have been crying." Then she lied. "Dova, I was crying because I'm terrified over this woodworkers' problem. I'm afraid that when Eiger Wilhaus, Zugg Hinwill, and my boss meet with Alexander Metternik and his bunch, there's going to be violence and bloodshed."

Dova reached across the desk, took hold of Metryka's hand, and said in a comforting tone, "If Mr. Wilhaus is reasonable with the woodworkers, there won't be any trouble."

Metryka let her gaze drop to the desk, paused briefly, then looked at Dova once more. "I don't think Mr. Wilhaus will give in and raise the wages enough to entice the woodworkers to go to work for the factory."

Letting go of Metryka's hand and patting it, she leaned back in the chair. "Then, honey, we just have to leave it in God's hands. Let's pray about it right now."

Metryka's body stiffened, then quickly forcing herself to relax, she said, "Yes. We...ah...should pray about it."

"All right, honey," said Dova, "you pray first, then I'll follow."

Metryka's mouth went dry, and her nerves tightened. "Ah... Dova, you've been a Christian for a long time. You know how to pray about something like this better than I do. You go ahead and lead us."

After she had prayed about the problem facing the factory and its leaders, Dova's face was beaming. "Oh, Metryka, isn't it wonderful that we can carry our burdens to the Lord and know He hears us and will answer our prayers?"

"Yes. Of course."

"Being a born-again child of God is so marvelous. We have our heavenly Father to watch over us all the way through this life, then we have all eternity with Him when we leave this world. Isn't it a blessing to know that because our sins have been washed away in Jesus' blood, we never have to fear going to hell? We know that heaven is our eternal home."

Metryka nodded.

"Honey," said Dova, "I was so happy the day I learned that you had opened your heart to Jesus."

Metryka forced another smile only to keep Dova fooled. In her heart, she was in agreement with her father. All this business about being born again and washed in the blood was poppycock. Besides, there wasn't any hell to worry about. Her father had taught her since she was a small child that when a person died, that was the end of them. There was no afterlife.

Meeting Metryka's gaze, Dova said, "Are things shaping up for the wedding?"

Metryka rolled her tongue in her dry mouth. "Yes, of course. Everything is on schedule."

"I can imagine how excited you must be."

Forcing a third smile since Dova had entered the office, Metryka said, "There's no way to describe it."

Dova let a few seconds pass, then said, "Honey, you are so fortunate to be marrying Dr. Erik Linden. He is such a fine man."

"You're right. Erik is indeed a fine man."

"I hope the two of you will be very, very happy."

"Thank you." Metryka's conscience was stabbing her like a dagger in her heart.

Rising to her feet, Dova said, "Well, I'd best be going. It's been nice talking to you."

"You too," said Metryka, pushing her chair back and standing up.

Dova moved to her, gave her a hug, and said, "Please don't cry over this woodworker problem, honey. The Lord will work it out in His own way."

Metryka did not comment. She followed Dova to the door and opened it for her. "Thanks for coming by."

"My pleasure," said Dova, and stepped outside.

Metryka closed the door, then stepped to the window and watched Dova descend the stairs and head down the street. "You're right, Dova. Erik is a fine man, but I'm in love with Helmut. And besides...I wouldn't be able to stand all that fanatical church nonsense."

As Dova headed down the street, something about Metryka was troubling her, but she couldn't quite put her finger on it. She pondered it while she walked past stores and shops, and when she came to the first intersection and waited for two wagons to pass, she said aloud, "Lord, I know what it is. Something about Metryka just doesn't ring true."

Dova crossed the street, and when she reached the boardwalk on the other side, she stopped, shook her head, and said, "Forgive me, Lord. I shouldn't have said that about her."

Continuing down the street, Dova tried to put her mind on something else, but her few moments with Metryka wouldn't leave her thoughts and kept troubling her. She paused in front of a clothing store and let her eyes rove over the women's clothing that hung on hangers, all the while thinking about Metryka.

Suddenly, as though she had walked from a dark room into bright sunlight, she knew what was bothering her. Every time she was around Metryka, she got the strange feeling that something was missing. Now she knew what it was. "There is no witness of the Holy Spirit between us as there should be, Lord," she said softly. "That's what it is. Metryka says she is saved, but why isn't the witness there? I can't see her heart, and I don't mean to be her judge, Lord. But as I see it, the witness of the Spirit isn't there."

She crossed the next intersection, and drew up in front of the shop on the corner. "I'm afraid Metryka doesn't really know You, Lord," she said, a small frown of concentration puckering her brow. "Help me to know how to reach her."

As she spoke, she opened the door and entered the shop.

That evening after eating supper with his family, Dr. Erik Linden walked the few blocks to the Baume home and knocked on the door.

Metryka opened the door. "Hello, Erik. Please come in. Papa's been waiting for you."

Stepping in, Erik said in a low voice, "'Hello, Erik'? What happened to 'darling'?"

"Oh, I'm sorry," she said shaking her head. "Hello, darling."

Erik was about to take her in his arms and kiss her when he heard Kathlyn's voice and footsteps at the same time. "Hello, Erik," she said, coming into view. "It's nice to see you."

"You too, ma'am," he said, giving her a warm smile.

"Everything all right at the clinic?"

"Yes, ma'am. Busy, as usual."

"Is Dr. Danzig feeling all right?"

"He got a little worn out while I was gone, but he'll get some rest now that I'm home."

"Erik!" came the booming voice of the burgomaster as he came from the rear of the house. "Glad to see you!"

The young doctor found himself a bit off balance. Koblin Baume had never been so warm toward him.

Koblin drew up, vigorously shook Erik's hand and said, "Let's you and I go into the parlor." He gave Metryka a sly grin. "You can visit with my daughter later."

Kathlyn giggled, patted Metryka's arm, and said, "Don't keep him too long, dear. They have a wedding to plan, you know."

A cold ball formed in Metryka's stomach as she watched the two men enter the parlor.

Koblin pointed to an overstuffed chair. "Have a seat, Erik."

Sitting in a chair facing the young physician, Koblin said, "First, let me tell you about our pursuit to catch the guilty parties who set off the dynamite in the tunnel."

"I'd like to hear about that, sir."

"Well, we've questioned all the independent woodworkers, but we've turned up nothing. We have no suspects."

"Oh. Well, I'm sorry to hear it. Whoever did it are murderers. They need to be punished to the fullest extent of the law."

"I agree. We won't let up on it. My plan is to question each one again and again until somebody breaks and spills the truth."

"Yes, sir."

Koblin eased back in his chair and let a broad smile brighten his beefy face. "The main reason I wanted to talk to you tonight is to tell you about the special meeting I have set up with Chur's citizens in your honor."

Erik frowned, tilted his head questioningly. "In my honor, sir?"

"Yes. As the town's burgomaster, I want to publicly honor you for the excellent and unselfish work you did in saving so many lives on the train. You're a hero for sure."

Erik's handsome features flushed. "I'm no hero, Mr. Baume."

"Oh, but you are, my boy! The meeting will take place at the spot where one day soon we are going to build the new town square. It is set for ten o'clock in the morning day after tomorrow."

"But, sir, I don't deserve—"

"None of that, now!" said Baume, raising a palm as if to hush him. "I've also alerted the burgomasters in the nearby towns of Feldis, Parpan, Arosa, and Lenzerheide. The news of the tunnel being dynamited, the wreck of the train, and the heroism of Dr. Erik Linden has reached the ears of the people in those towns, and I know once the burgomasters make the special meeting in Chur known to their citizens, many will come."

Still embarrassed, Erik said, "Mr. Baume, what I did was only what a medical doctor should have done. There was nothing heroic about it. I don't deserve any special honor."

The burgomaster laughed heartily. "Oh, but you do, indeed!" Pointing a thumb at his chest, he added, "And I am about to have the honor of becoming your father-in-law!"

Erik felt a warmth spread through his chest at those words, and was about to comment when Koblin said, "Even though I want nothing to do with your religion, Erik, I want you to know that I will be proud to have such a dedicated physician as my son-in-law. You are a real hero!"

Metryka and her mother were bringing hot coffee to the parlor, and both stood in the open door of the parlor to hear Koblin's words.

Moving into the room with Metryka carrying the tray that bore the coffeepot and cups, Kathlyn smiled at Erik and said, "And I am also proud that you are going to be my son-in-law, Erik. Very proud."

As Metryka set the tray down on the coffee table between the two men, she felt tiny needles slithering down her spine. Now that Erik had become a hero in her father's eyes, it was going to be even more difficult for her when she had to tell him that she had broken it off with Erik.

Wanting to get it over with, Metryka said, "Papa, are you about through talking to Erik? I'd like some time with him tonight."

"Not by any means, honey," said Koblin. "I have much to discuss with him."

Mother and daughter left the parlor and went to the sewing room together. Kathlyn was making herself a new dress for the wedding and wanted Metryka to see how it was coming along.

Koblin dominated Erik's time for the rest of the evening, and Erik left just before midnight without having time alone with Metryka.

That night Metryka had a battle trying to get to sleep. She tossed and turned, but slumber eluded her. The more she contemplated telling Erik it was over between them, the harder it was to ease her mind so she could fall asleep.

When dawn cast its gray light through her bedroom window,

Metryka still had not slept a wink. She rolled over, pulled the pillow over her head, and told herself she must get the task over with very soon. She dreaded facing Helmut at the office, knowing the first moment they were alone he would ask if she had told Erik.

It was almost noon when Amelia Folchert looked up from the desk in the clinic office and saw Metryka Baume come through the door. "Hello, Metryka," said Amelia. "What can I do for you?"

Metryka noted that every chair in the waiting room was occupied by patients. Looking at the nurse, she said, "Amelia, I really need to see Dr. Linden. I have to talk to him."

"Is it an emergency?" queried Amelia.

"Well, not really what you would call an emergency, but I do need to talk to him."

"I wish I could tell you it was possible, dear," said Amelia, "but he is very busy seeing patients who have been waiting for him to return home from Bern. Some of these people you see here have been waiting for over two hours, and there are more due in this afternoon. He won't have a minute to talk to you until his day is finished."

Feeling frustration, Metryka said, "All right. Thank you."

As she headed back to the factory, she felt a bit of nausea wash over her. She had already faced Helmut's irritation when she told him that morning she had not yet told Erik. Now, she had to return to the office and be questioned again.

When evening came, Metryka was held nearly half an hour past quitting time by Durbin Thorpe, who wanted to go over some financial papers in preparation for Eiger Wilhaus's upcoming visit to the factory. When she finally was able to leave, she hurried to the clinic, figuring with so many patients to see, Erik would probably still be there.

She found the clinic closed and rushed to Erik's apartment, but learned from the landlord that he had not been home since leaving for the clinic early that morning.

Her frustration increased. She headed for the Linden home. Erik was no doubt having supper with his family, as usual.

When the Linden door opened in response to Metryka's knock, Ludwig's smiling face greeted her.

"Metryka!" said Ludwig. "Come in."

Stepping into the foyer, Metryka said, "Ludwig, I need to see Erik."

"Well, that may be a while," came the bad news. "Erik was summoned to the Betcher farm about half an hour ago. Olaf Betcher's oldest son was terribly upset. He told Erik that his father had been gored by a bull. There's no telling how long he might be there."

"Oh. Well, just tell him I came by. I'll try to see him tomorrow."

"Sure will," said Ludwig. "Sorry."

"Nobody's fault," she said, covering the frustration and anxiety she was feeling.

As Metryka slowly headed for home in the gathering darkness, she was feeling discouragement on one hand but relief on the other. She wanted to get it over with, but she very much dreaded the moment she had to tell Erik the truth. She had been spared that moment once again.

Her head was throbbing. It had been a long and very trying day. All afternoon, every time she and Helmut found themselves alone, he had badgered her about telling Erik. And every effort she tried, she was thwarted one way or another.

Metryka was tired from lack of sleep. There had also been the trauma of being on the scene at the train wreck and the strain at work over the impending trouble, not to mention the constant pressure within her own mind to get alone with Erik and relieve herself of the burden she had been carrying.

With lagging steps and pounding headache, she reached her own yard and turned toward the house. Suddenly she saw a dark, shadowy form beside the large tree that stood at the corner of the front porch.

The last thing she wanted to see was Helmut waiting to meet her and question her relentlessly once more. He moved out of the shadows as she drew near, and keeping his voice low, said, "Well, is it done?"

"No, it's not," she said with a sigh, rubbing her temples.

"Why not?" His voice was rough.

"Because I have not yet been able to see him, that's why. He's out at the Betcher farm. Olaf Betcher has been gored by one of his bulls."

Anger was evident in Helmut as he snapped, "Well, just when are you going to do it? June 25? I'm getting sick and tired of—"

"Helmut, I'm doing the best I can," she said, raising a palm toward him. "Please trust me with this, all right?"

He could tell by her voice that she was about to cry.

"All right?" she said, sniffling.

Guilt took its own toll on Helmut Thorpe. "I'm sorry, sweetheart," he said and folded her into his arms.

She sniffed again, swallowing hard. "I'm doing the best I can," she said with a squeak in her voice.

"I know. I know. Honey, I'm really sorry for badgering you about it. I...I guess I'm so afraid of losing you back to him that I've become a bully. I don't mean to hurt you or put more pressure on you than you already have. Please forgive me."

"Of course," she said, sniffling again, and sliding her arms around him. "This will be over soon, my love, and then everything will be out in the open. Somehow I will get this taken care of tomorrow. No matter what. Now you must go."

Bending down, Helmut kissed her lightly and walked away, instantly being swallowed by the darkness.

She stood there for a long moment, wiping the tears from her cheeks, then took a deep breath and went into the house.

"Is that you, Metryka?" came her mother's voice from the parlor.

"Yes, Mama," she answered, moving into the parlor.

Both parents were sitting in their overstuffed chairs where they had been discussing the events of the day.

Kathlyn focused on her daughter's face. "Are you all right, dear?"

"All except for a pounding headache, Mama," she responded, touching fingertips to her temples.

"Find Erik?" asked Koblin.

"No, Papa. He's out at the Betcher farm. One of Olaf Betcher's bulls gored him."

"Oh. Sorry to hear that. Do you know how bad it is?"

"No. I guess we'll have to wait till tomorrow to find out."

"Mm-hmm."

"Well, I'm sorry you didn't get to spend some time with Erik this evening, honey," said Kathlyn.

Koblin chuckled. "She'll have plenty of evenings with him when they get married."

Metryka tried to smile. "I'm pretty weary from the strain at the factory. I'm going to bed early. I'll see you in the morning."

Metryka kissed the cheeks of both parents and climbed the stairs to her room.

Closing the door, she leaned her throbbing head against it, shut her eyes, and thought, *Oh, how glad I will be when all of this pretense is over!*

She pushed away from the door and moved toward the dresser, pulling the pins from her hair. Placing the pins on the dresser, she looked at herself in the mirror and ran her fingers through her tresses, massaging her scalp lightly, trying to ease the pain of the headache.

She went to the closet and returned a few minutes later in her nightgown. She poured water from the pitcher on the small table into the basin next to it. Dipping her hands into the water, she splashed it into her face repeatedly, then began washing her hands and arms.

Making fast work of her nighttime ablutions, she soon doused the lantern on her nightstand and climbed into bed, her eyelids drooping before her head touched the pillow.

Snuggling cozily into the covers, she whispered to herself, "Tomorrow. I will get it over with tomorrow."

This was her last thought as sleep overtook her.

Ten

At 9:45 the next morning, people were gathering in the open area where one day Chur's town square would be built. The stores and shops were closing for the special meeting. The warm spring air was fragrant with pine and spruce and the morning sun brought a cheerfulness all its own to the scene.

By ten o'clock almost every citizen of Chur was there, along with dozens of people from surrounding farms and the nearby towns of Feldis, Parpan, Arosa, and Lenzerheide.

A nervous Dr. Erik Linden was standing at the forefront of the crowd next to Burgomaster Koblin Baume, letting his eyes roam over faces familiar and unfamiliar. Baume was ready to begin but was patiently waiting for stragglers to get out of their buggies and wagons and join the crowd.

Standing beside Erik was Dr. Joseph Danzig, who was excited about the opportunity Koblin Baume was going to give him to speak to the crowd about his young partner.

Erik leaned close to Danzig. "Now, Doctor, please don't embarrass me by using a bunch of flowery words. All right?"

The old man smiled, bringing deep crinkles to the corners of his eyes. "I will only speak the truth, son. I promise."

At that moment, Erik's line of sight fell on his friend from Vaudron, Dr. Glynn Domire, who was threading his way through the crowd toward him. Domire stopped to speak to Erik's father and mother then proceeded to the front. As he drew up, he flashed a smile and said, "Good morning, Dr. Linden."

As they shook hands, Erik said, "How did you know about this meeting?"

Domire chuckled. "A little bird told me."

"And that little bird's name?"

Overhearing the conversation, the burgomaster turned toward them and said, "The little bird's name is Koblin Baume. You know—your future father-in-law."

"I didn't know you were inviting people from as far away as Vaudron, sir. I—"

"Oh, I didn't invite people from Vaudron. Just Dr. Domire. I figured since he is a friend of yours and he was there at the tunnel to help you, he should be here to tell the crowd about your heroic work. So I wired him, asking him to come."

Erik shook his head. "Heroic work. I just did what any doctor would have done."

"With his own leg banged up so he could hardly walk?" said Baume.

Again, Erik shook his head, but gave no reply. While a few more stragglers were pulling in, he let his eyes stray over the faces in the crowd and saw his close friend, Dr. Kenton Prinoth, who had a practice in Lenzerheide. At that moment, Prinoth's gaze met Erik's and he waved, smiling broadly. Erik waved back.

When the last of the stragglers had joined the crowd, Koblin Baume raised his hands to get attention. Little by little the talking subsided, and when he waved his hands and lifted his voice calling for quiet, he soon had the entire crowd ready to listen.

"Ladies and gentlemen!" he said loudly. "Welcome! The citizens of Chur and those of our farm community wish to welcome our neighbors from Feldis, Parpan, Arosa, and Lenzerheide! We are glad that you have come to help us honor the hero in our midst!"

Every eye was on Dr. Erik Linden as the crowd broke into applause, punctuating it with loud cheers.

Erik's features tinted as he looked at the crowd and gave them a sheepish smile. His gaze touched Metryka, who was standing with Justina and Dova. She was applauding vigorously, saying something to Justina.

When the applause died down and the crowd grew quiet, Baume proceeded to tell the story of the explosion in Nidwalden Tunnel, which wrecked the Chur-bound train, pointing out that Dr. Erik Linden was aboard the train because he had been the graduation speaker at the Bern University Medical School.

As he was speaking, Baume's line of sight fell on the face of Alexander Metternik, who was flanked by his group of independent woodworkers. Baume wondered if Metternik himself had anything to do with sabotaging the tunnel, though he had been perfectly calm and collected during the police interrogation. Baume told himself it just couldn't be. Metternik was known to get into fights in Chur's taverns when he was drinking, but Baume could not believe that the man would order such a thing to be done by his men. Yet somehow, neither could Baume convince himself that any of the woodworkers would have done such a horrible thing without Metternik's approval.

Koblin Baume told the crowd that in the crash caused by the explosion, Dr. Erik Linden's left leg was injured. He went on to explain how Dr. Linden labored to care for the injured passengers in spite of the severe pain he was experiencing from his own injury, and that he had saved many lives, including the life of Eiger Wilhaus. As he mentioned Wilhaus, he pointed to him sitting in the wheelchair. Baume dwelt for several minutes on the Wilhaus situation, explaining that due to a severe injury, Mr. Wilhaus had gone into heart seizure. He then lauded Dr. Linden for laboring successfully to save Mr. Wilhaus's life.

This brought ooohs and ahhhs from the crowd, and a few people near the group of woodworkers heard one man say the doctor should have let well enough alone.

Looking at Wilhaus in his wheelchair, Baume said, "Mr. Wilhaus has asked to say a few words about our hero."

Again, the use of the word *hero* brought a flush to Erik's features.

Zugg Hinwill rolled the wheelchair to the front and stood beside his boss while Wilhaus gave testimony as to the dedication to preserve human life and relieve suffering that he had seen in Dr. Erik Linden.

Hinwill then gave his own brief speech on the subject.

As Hinwill was pushing the wheelchair to its original spot, people were applauding.

Baume then introduced Dr. Glynn Domire of Vaudron—whom he had mentioned in the story—and asked Domire to tell the people what he saw when he arrived at the tunnel many hours after the explosion.

Domire had the crowd's rapt attention as he told them how amazed he was to see what Dr. Linden had accomplished...especially having very little in the way of medical supplies with him. He described surgery after surgery that Linden had performed adeptly, the latter few without anesthetic, yet each one being successful.

When Domire was finished, people were applauding and shouting out praise to Dr. Erik Linden, who stood, head slightly lowered, looking at the ground.

Baume waited for the applause and shouts to subside, then introduced Dr. Joseph Danzig. The elderly physician spent some five minutes extolling the fine character and excellent workmanship of his young clinic partner.

Koblin Baume then motioned to the owner of Chur's print shop, who stepped forward and handed him an official looking paper.

Holding the paper up for everyone to see, Baume said, "Only these who are standing up close can read the large print on this document, folks, so let me tell you first that it is a Certificate of Courage and Accomplishment that I have had made up by our local printer. The name in large print is that of Dr. Erik Linden!"

There were more cheers and applause, then Baume read the entire document to the crowd and presented it to the young doctor.

There was a rousing ovation from the crowd, then the burgomaster asked Erik to speak.

Obviously embarrassed and a bit flustered, Erik looked at

Metryka, his family, then the crowd. "Ladies and gentlemen, I am deeply honored by your attendance here, by what these gentlemen have said about me, and by this certificate. However, let me say to you what I said to Burgomaster Baume a little earlier this morning. I only did what any doctor would have done, given the same circumstances. I do not see myself as a hero."

Erik was interrupted by people shouting out that he indeed was a hero.

Erik shook his head. "Ladies and gentlemen, I have only one more thing to say. The engineer and the fireman were killed instantly on impact, as were a couple of the passengers. Other passengers died before I could get to them. But I am thankful for those whose lives I was able to save, and the injured ones that I was able to help. I want to give praise to my Lord and Saviour Jesus Christ for giving me the strength and the ability to accomplish what I did...for without Him, I could do nothing."

Erik stepped back and let Koblin Baume have the center of attention.

After much cheering and applause, Baume announced that tomorrow morning at eight o'clock, Eiger Wilhaus and Zugg Hinwill would meet with the independent woodworkers in front of the factory, and looking directly at Alexander Metternik, asked him to inform any and all woodworkers who were not in attendance at the moment about the meeting.

Metternik gave him a nod.

When Baume dismissed the crowd, the Linden family moved toward Erik, while many of the people pressed close to him to speak their personal feelings about his heroic deeds.

Metryka pushed her way toward Erik through the press, unaware of the sour look she was getting from Helmut Thorpe.

Erik smiled at Metryka when she moved up beside him. As people came by to speak to Erik, those of Chur and the surrounding farm community who knew them also congratulated Metryka on the upcoming wedding, some making comments about her being so fortunate to marry the hero.

While some people were waiting to speak to Eric, they gathered around the burgomaster and his wife, congratulating them on the upcoming marriage of their daughter to Dr. Erik Linden.

One man elbowed Baume's ribs playfully. "You're not fooling me, Koblin! You had that certificate printed up and called this meeting to make your future son-in-law look good."

There was a round of good-natured laughter.

While talking to his admirers, Erik noticed Dr. Kenton Prinoth standing to the side, apparently waiting for a chance to talk to him.

Another fifteen or twenty minutes left Erik with just his family and Metryka at his side, and one older couple who were patients at the Chur Clinic. When the couple had spoken their words of commendation for his work in the tunnel, they shuffled away.

At that moment, Dr. Kenton Prinoth, who was only a couple of years older than Erik, stepped up. Again, he spoke to Frederic and Mura, then to Justina and the boys. Having met Metryka before, he greeted her, then turned to Dova. Justina introduced him to Dova as her best friend. Prinoth greeted her warmly, then shook Erik's hand and said, "I've waited till now to speak to you because I needed a few minutes to tell you about something."

While the others at least partially listened, Prinoth said, "Erik, Martha and I are leaving Switzerland."

Erik's eyebrows arched. "Really?"

"Yes."

"You mean for good?"

"Yes. We are going to America to start a new life."

Prinoth now had everybody's total attention. "We've been reading much about life in America for the past couple of years, and what we have learned has fascinated us. Then a few months ago, I read in the Zurich newspaper that with the growth of the number of immigrants entering America through New York Harbor, the immigration authorities are in desperate need of medical doctors to examine the immigrants at Ellis Island."

Erik nodded. "Interesting."

"I made application with the immigration authorities in New York in early April and received my letter of acceptance on May 3. We will be leaving in less than two weeks. That's why Martha isn't with me. She's busy getting ready."

"Well, I'm glad for you, Kenton," said Erik. "If I ever have opportunity to visit America, I'll look for you on Ellis Island."

"You do that," said Prinoth. "I'd love to see you."

They shook hands again, then Prinoth told the others good-bye and headed for his horse and buggy on the street.

Frederic watched him climb into the buggy. "I hope it works out well for him."

"Me too," said Erik.

"Well!" said Mura, "It's time the hero's mother congratulates him!"

When Mura had kissed her oldest son's cheek and embraced him, Frederic did so, saying it was time the hero's father congratulated him, too.

Following that pattern, Justina hugged Erik, congratulating him. Next were Ludwig and Brandt. Still keeping up the facade, Metryka embraced Erik after kissing his cheek and told him how proud she was of him.

Dova stood shyly looking on.

Erik then smiled at Dova and said, "Well, I would say my sister's best friend shouldn't be left out."

Her heart pounding, Dova stepped up, kissed Erik's cheek, and received a brotherly hug. When Erik released her, she took a step back and looked at him with what Metryka and the others thought were admiring eyes.

But Dova knew they were adoring eyes.

It was just after seven o'clock the next morning when Burgomaster Koblin Baume stood in the meeting room at police headquarters and ran his eyes over the faces of the sixteen police officers who sat before him. Every man on the force was there, even those who had done the night shift and would normally be going home.

"Men," he said, "I don't have to tell you to be on guard and alert as we go to the factory. I am still convinced it was someone among the independent woodworkers who dynamited Nidwalden Tunnel, though our thorough questioning didn't surface the guilty parties. There are killers among them. Keep that in mind. And if they get out of hand, don't hesitate to get tough on them. If you have to crack a few skulls with your nightsticks, do it. Of course, you are only to use your revolvers if they really get violent."

The officers exchanged glances, nodding to each other.

"Any questions?" asked Baume.

Silence.

When no one spoke up, Baume let a grim smile curve his lips. "All right. You are called 'peace officers.' Let's see you keep things peaceful out there."

At eight o'clock, the burgomaster stood before the crowd of woodworkers with Durbin and Helmut Thorpe beside him. Eiger Wilhaus, looking peaked and thin, sat in his wheelchair with Zugg Hinwill standing at his side.

The factory employees stood behind the gates within the compound, looking on with grim faces.

Metryka Baume was watching fearfully from the office window on the second floor.

The sixteen police officers were spread out evenly on the fringe of the crowd, eyes roving continually.

Koblin Baume stepped ahead of Durbin and Helmut and looked at Alexander Metternik, who was centered in the crowd of somber looking men. "Mr. Metternik, are all of the woodworkers present?"

Taking a moment to turn and look over the half circle of men, Metternik finally faced forward again and said, "Yes, sir. All present and accounted for."

"Good," Baume said. Taking another step forward, he ran a fleeting glance over the face of Alexander Metternik, who was closely flanked by Arthur Wengen, Thomas Allman, and Croft Susack, then ran his gaze over the entire collection of woodworkers.

"I hope it was none of you who planted that dynamite in the tunnel. Whoever the guilty parties are, they will face murder charges when they are caught."

One of the woodworkers called out, "Chief, none of us would stoop that low. We're honest, hardworking men who are upset because our livelihood has been taken away from us, but we're not murderers."

Immediately, others lifted up their voices in agreement. While this was going on, Alexander Metternik and his three cohorts exchanged furtive glances.

"I cannot believe the guilty parties were just some men who decided to blow up the tunnel for the thrill of it," said Baume. "I am convinced they were men among this group before me. It was known by nearly everybody in Chur that Mr. Wilhaus and his two vice presidents were on that train. And as I see it, they were willing to kill as many people as they had to in order to take out the Wilhaus Industries men—especially the head of the company."

Men in the crowd were eyeing each other, some with suspicion in their eyes.

"Let me give you some statistics," Baume went on. "Seven people were killed. Twelve—including two children—were critically injured. Some of those will be maimed for life. There were forty-six others injured, but not as seriously. What a horrible tragedy! If any of you men know who is responsible, and you want to report it, you can come to me in private and no one outside of the police department will ever know who you are. I hope there'll soon be a knock on my door."

A quietness fell over the woodworkers.

"Mr. Wilhaus will now address you," said Baume and gestured for Zugg Hinwill to move the wheelchair to the center.

From his wheelchair, Wilhaus looked out over the woodworkers and said, "Gentlemen, violence is not the answer to this situation. I am offering all of you jobs in this factory, starting immediately. Granted, the pay scale will not come up to what you were making in your own wood shops, but think about it. Lower income is better than no income."

Angry voices began to fill the air, and a weakened Eiger Wilhaus looked up at his vice president and said, "Zugg, will you take over, please?"

Zugg Hinwill raised his hands and called out for the woodworkers to let him speak. When they only persisted in shouting at him in anger, Koblin Baume gave his men the nod, and they moved in, wielding their nightsticks, demanding that the woodworkers get quiet.

One angry man tried to grasp the nightstick from an officer, but was cracked on the head by another officer and crumpled to the ground.

The crowd suddenly got quiet.

"It is as Mr. Wilhaus just said, men!" Baume shouted. "Violence is not the answer to this situation! Horace Kefling just got his head cracked for resisting my men who are here to keep the peace. And keep it, we will—even if we have to crack some more heads! Now get quiet and stay that way!"

When there was absolute silence, Baume looked to the spot where two of his men were lifting a dazed Kefling to his feet. "Is he all right?"

"He'll have a headache, Chief," said one of the officers, "but he's not hurt."

"All right, Mr. Hinwill," said Baume. "You are speaking for Mr. Wilhaus. Proceed."

"Men, listen to me," said Hinwill. "Right now, we are paying the highest wages we can. It is expensive to set up a new factory. But if you will come to work for us, our factory manager, Durbin Thorpe, will be glad to have you. And I guarantee you, when the profits of the factory rise, wages will rise, also."

Another loud, angry voice came from the crowd: "Don't give us that business about low wages and the costs to set up a factory, Hinwill! Everybody in Switzerland knows that Eiger Wilhaus is filthy rich! He could pay us the kind of money we were making in our shops, but he won't do it because he's greedy and wants more money for himself!"

Other woodworkers shouted their agreement, their anger surfacing. Once more, the officers moved in, wielding their nightsticks, and it took only a few seconds for the noise to settle.

Stepping up beside Hinwill, Koblin Baume said, "Men, let me

remind you of how the factory has already benefited our town. I explained this before, but I emphasize that we are a community, and we should all work together to make it the best it can be. The factory will be much more of a benefit in the future as it prospers. We will all benefit from it."

"Right now we need our bank accounts benefited, Koblin!" shouted a man.

"That's right!" shouted another. "We're hurting! We need money to live on and to see that our families have what they need!"

"I understand!" blared Baume loudly. "But how much money did you take in yesterday, Rufus? And how much will you take in today?"

"Nothing!" cried Rufus. "Nothing!"

"That's my point," said Baume. "Something is better than nothing! I'm calling on all of you to seriously consider Mr. Wilhaus's job offer. Tomorrow you could be bringing in wages if you'll go to work for the factory. And like Mr. Hinwill just said, wages will rise as the factory's profits go up."

There were boos and hisses, and once more the police moved in to quell the trouble that was pending.

Standing at the office window, Metryka bit her lower lip when she saw one of the woodworkers swing a fist at one of the officers. A nightstick quickly put him down. Another man swore at the officers and clipped one on the jaw, staggering him. Two officers converged on him, and when struck on the head with both nightsticks, he went down, unconscious.

This served to quiet the crowd, who looked back toward the burgomaster.

"You men are fools if you keep this up," said Baume. "It isn't going to solve your problems to get your skulls cracked. Now use your heads for something besides targets for nightsticks. Take Mr. Wilhaus up on his offer and go to work at earning wages so you can provide for your families."

When a murmur began among the woodworkers, Baume looked straight at Metternik and said, "Alexander, talk some sense into the heads of your followers! If you will, no more heads will be cracked and this problem will be over. In time, everyone will prosper."

Another man shouted, "There wouldn't have been a problem at all, Koblin, if Wilhaus and his factory had stayed out of Chur!"

Many cheered him, waving their hands over their heads.

A big, burly man shouted, "You'd better think about it, Koblin! If they don't shut down this no-good factory, they're going to be sorry!"

Pointing a stiff finger at the man, Baume said, "No, it's you woodworkers who are going to be sorry! If you have plans to cause this factory trouble, Bartholomew, you'd best forget them! You'll find out what jail time is!"

A worker named Kenyon Hartwig moved through the crowd until he was close to the front and yelled, "I was just getting my shop started in my home when the factory came along, Koblin! I was barely making a living then, and now my family doesn't have enough food on the table not to mention other necessities we are going without! Do you expect us to just shut our mouths and go to work for Wilhaus like whipped dogs?"

Baume snapped back, "You ought to quit acting like whipped dogs and go to work for Mr. Wilhaus, Kenyon! As has already been said here—some pay is better than none! You've been told that it will get better as the factory prospers!"

Hartwig's face was purple as he retorted, "I can't do that! All of these men are my friends. I will not turn my back on them. We will all stick together."

The woodworkers lifted a rousing cheer at Hartwig's words.

Baume called for quiet but did not get it until his officers moved into the crowd, wielding their nightsticks.

When the noise settled, Baume said, "All of you should be grateful that Mr. Wilhaus is offering you employment."

From his wheelchair, Wilhaus said, "Chief, may I say something to them?"

"Of course. Go ahead."

Looking at the angry crowd, Eiger Wilhaus said, "This factory is very much understaffed. If you do not accept my offer, I will have to bring in factory workers from other Swiss towns. I would rather hire all of you."

"If you'd pay a fair wage, Mr. Moneybags," shouted another man, "we would take you up on your offer in the blink of an eye!"

There were cheers for the man, then it grew quiet again.

"Listen to me, men!" said Baume. "You'd better quit haggling and go to work for this man! You've heard his offer, now use your heads! This meeting is dismissed."

The officers began telling the crowd to break up, which they did. There was much grumbling of the woodworkers as they left the scene.

At the office window, Metryka brushed wisps of hair from her forehead and said to herself, "Well, that's over for the time being. Now, Miss Baume, before this day is over, you've got to get your task accomplished."

Eleven

Across the street from the factory, a small group of customers were gathered inside Faulk's Grocery. All of them, including Jabin Faulk, were standing at the large window, observing the scene in front of the factory.

When they heard the booming voice of Koblin Baume declare that the meeting was over and the crowd of woodworkers began to disperse, Jabin wiped a palm over his brow. "Whew! I was afraid there for a few minutes that the woodworkers were going to turn it into a riot."

"Me too," said Farina Combray. "I'm glad the police were able to keep it from happening."

Dova stood next to her mother holding two bags of groceries and watching the woodworkers scattering in different directions. There was a trembling in her voice as she said, "I'm sure it's not over. There is going to be violence before this thing is settled."

"Your right, Dova," said an older man in the group. "If Eiger Wilhaus doesn't close down the factory, the woodworkers are going to do something drastic again. Dynamiting the tunnel and killing seven people plus injuring a whole lot more was bad enough, but since that didn't work, they will turn to more extreme measures."

"That's for certain," said another silver-haired man, who was also holding a bag of groceries. "And when it happens, this town is going to see a lot of bloodshed. Dr. Danzig can't do much anymore. The whole thing will fall on Dr. Linden to care for the citizens who get injured."

The mention of Dr. Linden's name surfaced Dova's feelings toward him. She pictured his handsome face in her mind, and said in her heart, *Dear Lord, please take this love for Erik away. I can't stand it. I know I can never have him, and it's tearing me apart. Please, God. Take it away.*

At that moment, everyone in the store saw a group of the woodworkers coming across the street, talking among themselves. In the center of the group was Alexander Metternik.

As the group reached the boardwalk and passed by the store, Jabin Faulk said, "I can tell by the look on their faces; there's going to be trouble."

Metternik and the dozen men who walked with him moved on down the street. Flanking Metternik were Arthur Wengen, Thomas Allman, and Croft Suzack.

When they stopped at an intersection where some of the men would need to go different directions, big Bartholomew Sojak looked at Metternik and said, "Alexander, do you know who put the dynamite in the tunnel? You're our leader. Certainly you know who did it."

Metternik's shoulders stiffened. He frowned at the huge man and said, "I have no idea who did it. You don't think I would approve of killing innocent people, do you?"

Different reactions took place in Wengen, Allman, and Susack—all unpleasant.

"I didn't say you approved of it, Alexander," said Sojak, "but I can't imagine the woodworkers who did it not sharing the fact with you."

"Well, they didn't," Alexander said crisply. "They know I'd turn them in to Baume if I found out who they were."

Another in the group said, "Alexander, somehow we've got to find out who did it. If we don't stop them, they'll do something else, maybe even worse than blowing up a tunnel."

"Maybe that's what it's going to take," put in Kenyon Hartwig. "The way this whipped dog sees it, something drastic is going to have to be done before Wilhaus will raise the wages at the factory so we could make a living."

"So what are we going to do, Alexander?" asked Horace Kefling.

"I'm not sure, Horace," said Metternik. "I need some time to think on it. But I guarantee you, we are going to do something. What Eiger Wilhaus and his factory are doing to us independent woodworkers isn't right."

"How about burning the factory down?" said Hartwig.

Metternik shook his head. "No. That would be foolish. The fire could spread to other buildings in the business district, and even to houses close by."

Hartwig blinked. "Oh. I hadn't thought of that."

"Give me time to think on it. I'll contact all of you when I come up with a plan of action."

The group split up, with men moving away in three directions.

Metternik and his three cohorts headed toward the edge of town where their homes were situated.

"Alexander," said Croft Susack, "we failed to get Wilhaus's attention when we blew up the tunnel. He's still determined to have his way. Whatever we do, it will have to be exorbitant."

An evil grin curved Metternik's lips. "Well, I promise you, my friend, whatever we do will be exorbitant. We'll get his attention next time."

Soon the four men separated, each heading to his own home.

When Alexander Metternik neared his yard, he saw Horace Kefling, Bartholomew Sojak, and Kenyon Hartwig waiting for him under one of the huge pine trees in front of the house.

They moved toward him as he reached the edge of the yard.

"Alexander," said Kenyon Hartwig, "we'd like to talk to you."

"All right. I'm listening."

"I suggested burning the factory down," said Hartwig, "but hadn't thought that we could make innocent people suffer if the fire spread to other buildings. Well, we've been discussing another measure. How about we break into the factory at night and smash the machinery?"

Metternik touched his chin thoughtfully. "This had passed through my mind a few times, but the first man Baume will come after is me."

"We thought of that," said Kefling. "We'll break in after dark, smash up the machinery, and get out quick. You won't have to be involved."

"Wilhaus, Hinwill, and Thorpe will know it was woodworkers," said Sojak, "but they won't know which ones. But maybe he'll get the message that we mean business. We know Baume will go after you first, so we figure you have to be home when we do it and have some neighbors in, so they can testify that you were home when the break-in happened."

Metternik grinned. "I like it, boys. I like it. The factory can't operate with its machinery out of service, yet nobody will get hurt." He paused. "Just one thing."

They waited for him to declare it.

"I'd like for Croft Susack to go with you. Croft is very sharp. He'll help you to do it right."

"Fine with me," said Kefling. "That all right with you guys?"

Hartwig and Sojak both nodded.

"We'll go talk to Croft right now," said Sojak.

"You'll do it tonight?" asked Metternik.

"Yes," said Hartwig. "About eight-thirty. Be sure you have company in your house so they can tell the police you were there."

"I will. Do it fast and get out of there."

"We will," said Kefling. "All right, guys, let's go talk to Croft."

That evening at the Linden home, the family discussed the problem at hand while eating supper. As often happened, Metryka Baume had been invited for the meal.

Metryka had slept no better than she had since Erik had returned from Bern. The task before her was taking its toll on sleep and her appetite.

While the conversation went on over the meal, Erik took notice of the deep purple smudges under Metryka's eyes, evidence that she had not been sleeping well. He covertly watched her pushing the food around on her plate and not eating it. *I've got to find out what's bothering her,* Erik thought as he observed the play of emotions flitting across her face.

"I'm so glad it didn't turn into a riot," said Frederic, placing his coffee cup in its saucer. "From what I was told, it came close."

"Mm-hmm," said Ludwig. "Brandt and I talked to Mr. Faulk when we went to the store for Mama this afternoon. He said the police were using their clubs to subdue the worst troublemakers. Even knocked one woodworker completely unconscious."

Mura shook her head. "It's too bad the police have to use such measures, but it's better than letting a riot break out. But I wonder how long the police can control them." She set her soft gaze on Erik's fiancée. "Metryka, I really worry about you working there in the factory office. Who knows what the woodworkers will do? It could be very dangerous for you."

Metryka laid her fork down. "Surely they wouldn't do anything to the office staff."

"I'm afraid they might," said Erik. "I've thought about this too. If they could dynamite the tunnel, not caring who they killed or injured, they wouldn't hesitate to harm the office staff if they decided to launch an attack on the factory."

Frederic swallowed the food in his mouth. "Son, maybe the woodworkers didn't put the dynamite in the tunnel. It might have been done by someone who has something against the railroad."

Erik smiled. "That's my father: always willing to give the benefit of the doubt. I hope you're right, Papa, but I have this feeling deep inside me that it was the woodworkers. I think they were trying to kill Eiger Wilhaus, hoping that his violent death would cause the other leaders in Wilhaus Industries to close down the Chur factory. And how much better if they could take out Agno Lutrey and Zugg Hinwill, too?"

"That's the way I see it," spoke up Brandt. "And if we're right, and it was the woodworkers who did it, I'm sure it was only a handful of them. The majority of them wouldn't approve of what was done."

"I believe you're right, Brandt," said Justina, "but the way things almost got out of hand today, that handful just might incite others to do something violent at the factory. Bloodshed would speak with a loud voice to the Wilhaus people."

"Right," said Mura.

Ludwig said, "Since Alexander Metternik is the leader of the woodworkers, it was probably him and a few others who put the dynamite in the tunnel."

"I don't think so," said Metryka. "Papa told me that when Alexander Metternik was questioned by him and his officers at police headquarters the other day, he seemed very upset toward whoever did it and promised Papa and the other officers if he found out that it was woodworkers who did it, he would report it to them."

Ludwig said, "Well, it looks like whoever did it is going to get away with it. People were killed. That makes the guilty parties murderers, but they're going to get away with their awful crime."

"Not necessarily," said Erik.

Ludwig frowned. "What do you mean?"

"God knows who did it, and in His own way, He can see that the guilty parties are caught."

Looking around the table, Frederic saw that everyone was through eating. "Erik is right. God knows who dynamited the tunnel. I suggest we go to prayer right now and ask the Lord to see to it that the heartless murderers are caught."

"That's a good idea, Papa," said Erik. "Let's talk to the Lord about it."

"All right," said Frederic. "How about you leading us, son?"

Heads were bowed, and while Erik led in prayer Metryka's eyes were closed, but her mind was not on the words he was saying to God. Rather, she was once again practicing what she was going to say to him when she got him alone.

She was so engrossed in her own thoughts that she was unaware of his amen, and was startled when after a long moment Erik laid a hand on her arm. "Metryka, are you all right? We've finished praying."

When she opened her eyes and raised her head, she found herself the center of attention. Blinking nervously, she looked into Erik's troubled eyes and said, "Oh. Yes. I'm all right. I've just got so much on my mind lately. I'm sorry."

"Well, part of it has to be this woodworker problem," said Mura. "Honey, I really wish you wouldn't work there at the factory until this whole problem is settled. It's just too dangerous."

"I'll talk to my parents about it, Mrs. Linden," said Metryka, her nerves strung tight. Then she said to Erik, "As soon as I help your mother and Justina with the dishes, could we walk over and see how our new house is coming along?"

Mura reached over and patted Metryka's arm. "Honey, you don't have to help with the dishes. You and Erik need some time together alone. You should go now, before it gets dark."

"But I really should do my part, and—"

"It's all right, dear. Justina and I will be glad to do your part so you and Erik can check the house and have some time alone while you're doing it. Go on now."

When everyone stood up, Mura moved to Metryka and hugged her. "We're getting so excited. It won't be long now, till you're part of this family."

"Your wedding dress will be finished in another day or two, honey," said Justina. "Dova and I are very pleased with how it's turning out. We hope you will be, too."

Metryka felt herself crushed in a vise of panic. This facade must not go on any longer. She had to get Erik away from there and tell him the truth. Her voice came out scarcely above a whisper. "I...I'm sure I will be." She turned to the doctor. "Let's go, Erik."

Justina took a step closer, frowned, and cocked her head. "Metryka, is something bothering you, honey? You seem...well, ah...distracted."

Metryka put a hand to her forehead. "It's just all this pressure brought on by the problem with the woodworkers. If somehow they are able to make Mr. Wilhaus close down the factory, I'll be out of a job, and—"

"As of June 26 you won't need a job, sweetheart," said Erik, putting an arm around her. "Dr. Erik Linden's wife won't have to work outside of the home."

Metryka looked up at him, trying to smile, but she could barely create one. "I appreciate that," she said. "Well, we really should be going."

The sun had gone down as Erik and Metryka stepped off the porch of the Linden house and headed down the street with Erik holding her hand. The western sky was growing dim with a faint glow low on the horizon.

Dread of what she was about to do was like a wild beast inside Metryka, clawing violently at her stomach. She could feel cold sweat on the back of her neck.

They were almost at the end of the block when they saw a couple from the church coming. Both Karl and Lorna Jochim waved and called to them.

When Metryka felt Erik squeeze her hand and pull her to a stop, her heart plummeted. *More delay!*

The Jochims drew up, and Karl said, "Well, if it isn't the lovebirds!"

Lorna embraced Metryka, saying, "I can just imagine how excited you must be, dear. The biggest day of your life is coming up! Except for the day you got saved, I mean."

Metryka squeezed her, stepped back, and painted a smile on her face.

"Out for a stroll?" asked Karl.

"A little more than that," said Erik, noticing again that Metryka was not herself. "We're going to check on our new house and see what progress has been made since I left for Bern."

Karl nodded. "We've been talking to folks around town about the Nidwalden Tunnel being dynamited. Metryka, since you're in the middle if this woodworkers' controversy as an employee of the factory, what do you think? Did some of the woodworkers plant that dynamite?"

Metryka ran a dry tongue over equally dry lips. "It would seem to me that they did, Mr. Jochim. I'm sure that's my father's opinion."

"Mm-hmm. And what about you, Dr. Linden? You were on the train. Do you think the tunnel was sabotaged by the woodworkers?"

"Seems it would have to be them, sir," said Erik. "I can't think of anyone else who would want to blow up the tunnel. It was timed for the dynamite to go off just as the train arrived at the spot where it was set. If the train had been ten seconds earlier, the blast would have gone off when the three coaches were in the middle of where the dynamite was set. Probably everybody would have been killed."

"Terrible thing," said Lorna. "I hope your father catches the vile murderers, Metryka."

Metryka said, "Me too, Mrs. Jochim."

"We just prayed to that end with my family," said Erik. "Like I said at the supper table, God knows who did it, and in His own way, He can see to it that the guilty parties are caught."

"That's good thinking, Doctor," said Karl.

"Well, Erik," said an anxious Metryka, "we really should get over to the house before it gets dark."

"Right," said Erik. "Nice to talk to you, folks. We really need to keep moving."

The Jochims bid them a good evening, and Erik and Metryka were once again on their way toward the new house.

Dusk was gathering as they walked at a hurried pace.

Erik looked down at Metryka with eyes of love and took hold of her hand. Instantly, he felt it trembling. "Sweetheart, did our talking to the Jochims about the woodworkers upset you?"

Swallowing hard, Metryka stammered, "N-no, Erik. It w-wasn't that. I...I h-have something very important to t-talk to you about, and it's got my nerves stretched tight."

"Oh? Has something bad happened? I mean, something other than this woodworkers' situation and the threat of losing your job?"

"Yes."

"Well, honey, I've noticed that you haven't been yourself since you came to the tunnel. But I promise I'll do everything I can to take care of whatever is bothering you."

Metryka nodded in the gathering darkness, feeling a nausea creeping into her already jittery stomach. "We're almost to the house. We can talk in there."

As they neared the front porch, Metryka's voice quivered as she said, "Erik, I've...I've been wanting to talk to you about this for some time, but you have been too busy for me to get alone with you."

Chuckling dryly as they stepped up on the porch, Erik let go of her hand "I know the pace has been hectic lately." He placed his key in the lock, turned it, and opened the door. "Once Dr. Danzig retires and the clinic is mine, honey, I'll take in a partner who can carry a full load. Then I'll have plenty of time for my new bride."

Metryka waited silently while Erik struck a match at a small table in the foyer and lit the lantern. Adjusting the wick to give off plenty of light, he shook the flame from the match, dropped it on the table, then turned and smiled at her.

"Sweetheart, you're looking at the happiest man on the face of the earth. I, alone, am the man on this earth who is going to marry Metryka Baume. Soon you'll be my bride, and we can begin our married life together. I can hardly believe it. Erik Linden is going to marry the most beautiful and wonderful woman in all the world. No wonder I'm so happy."

Metryka's tongue seemed glued to the roof of her mouth. She was struggling to make her tongue function properly so she could get the words out, but before she could do it, Erik folded her in his arms and said, "I've been waiting all day for a kiss."

Suddenly she stiffened in his arms and blurted out, "Erik, I can't marry you!"

While he looked at her blankly in amazement, she pushed herself out of his arms. Forgetting all of her carefully rehearsed words, she said, "You heard me right. I can't marry you. The wedding is off."

Erik felt as if he had been hit in the stomach with a battering ram.

He was shaking his head, expressionless, almost paralyzed at her words.

"Wh-why?"

Metryka had not planned on speaking so sharply, but once the pent-up words and feelings started pouring out she was helpless to stop them. Her words tumbled rapidly off her tongue as she said, "To put it plainly, Erik, I am not in love with you. I thought I was, but I was wrong. I'm in love with another man. When I took the job at the factory, I—"

For one small second, the shocked, hurt look in Erik's eyes was almost her undoing, but the sentiment soon passed, and she once again let the words tumble rapidly off her tongue.

"When I took the job at the factory, I soon found myself truly falling in love with Helmut."

A glassy look formed in Erik's eyes. "Helm…Helmut?"

"Yes. He's really everything I want in a man, Erik."

"This…this has been going on for some time, I take it."

"Yes."

While Erik was looking at her as if he had found himself in a horrible nightmare and couldn't wake up, Metryka said, "I'm deeply in love with him, and he is very much in love with me. We're going to get married soon."

There was a long moment of silence as Erik stared at her with his wide, glassy eyes. "But…but Helmut doesn't even claim to be a Christian. How can you possibly marry him?"

Having lost the fear and dread that had gripped her at first, Metryka pulled her lips into a thin line, gave him a cold look, and said levelly, "Erik, none of this is meant to hurt you. I still admire you as a human being, but you might as well hear it right now. I only pretended to become a Christian for your sake because I thought at that point I was in love with you. But I've got to be honest about it: I find all of that church nonsense quite boring and very repugnant. My father is right when he says this born-again rigmarole is nothing but foolish fanaticism."

Erik frowned. "Metryka, you've heard what God says in His Word. If you die without being truly born again, you will spend eternity burning in hell. Without Jesus in your heart as your Saviour, and without your sins being washed away in His blood, you will die in your sins. You will stand before God at the white throne judgment, and the Lord will make all your sins known to the whole universe, then you will be cast into the lake of fire where you'll weep and wail and gnash your teeth in the flames forever and ever. Whatever you do, don't go on without Jesus. Don't let anything or anybody keep you from—"

"My father says there is no such thing as hell, Erik, or heaven, for that matter. He says there is no such thing as an afterlife. When we die, that is the end of us."

"But—"

"I don't want to hear any more about it, Erik," she cut in, throwing up her hands. "I'm going home now."

Feeling like his heart had been cut out with a dull knife, Erik said with strained voice, "I'll...I'll walk you home."

Twelve

Metryka Baume stepped out onto the front porch of the house ahead of Erik, a feeling of tremendous relief washing over her. Though she disliked hurting Erik, the fact that she had accomplished the dreaded task eased the strain on her nerves. Now she could face Helmut, knowing he would be pleased with her. They could show their love for each other openly and look forward to their future together.

While Erik was locking the door, Metryka ran her gaze up and down the street. Lantern light was winking in windows, and the shadowed forms of a few people could be seen on porches and in yards.

Turning from the door, a brokenhearted Erik moved up beside Metryka, took her by the arm, and guided her down the steps. He lifted his eyes overhead to see a myriad of stars twinkling in the vast infinitude of night sky and felt a broad space of deep desolation within himself.

As they headed down the street Erik said in a dull voice, "This is going to hit my sister and Dova pretty hard, Metryka, after all the work they have done on your wedding dress."

"I'm sorry about it, Erik," Metryka said evenly, "but it cannot be helped. I certainly shouldn't marry a man I don't love. You wouldn't want to marry me, knowing I'm not in love with you, would you?"

There was a moment of dead silence, then Erik said, "No."

Metryka came to a halt, which caused Erik to do so. Looking up at him in the dim light afforded by the stars, she said, "As I said earlier, Erik, I still admire you. And I want you to know that I want the best for you. I believe you are going to have great success in the clinic when you buy out Dr. Danzig. And—and I'm sure you will find the right young woman to marry. Then the two of you can enjoy the house you are having built."

A disagreeable feverish sensation formed in the center of Erik's chest and began to spread. It was like hot liquid. "The house. Well, I'm not sure what I'll do with the house." As he spoke, they were in motion once again.

They had gone almost an entire block when Erik said, "I'm really concerned about your attitude toward the Lord and the Bible, Metryka. No matter what you've done to me, I don't want you to end up in the lake of fire."

"I won't," she said stiffly. "There isn't any hell, Erik. It's just one of the Bible's many fairy tales concocted by fanatical men to frighten people."

"If there isn't any hell, why did God send His Son to die on the cross? What was His purpose?"

"Papa says Jesus Christ was just a victim of the day. He tried to start a religion and it didn't work. He got Himself crucified, and that was the end of it. There wasn't any resurrection. Just another Bible fairy tale. What they call Christianity today is just built on vague memories of a Man who tried to go against the philosophical grain of the rest of the world and failed."

They were nearing the Baume house.

"Metryka, your father is dead wrong on this. God's Word has proven true every time it has been tested by skeptics, and—"

"Erik, I don't want to discuss it any further," she said coldly. "You have your belief and I have m—"

Metryka's words were suddenly cut off by the sharp sound of

gunfire stabbing through the night, followed by loud shouts.

Both of them stopped and looked in the direction of the business district of town, where the sounds came from. Abruptly, there were more shots.

"The factory!" said Erik, taking hold of Metryka's arm and hurrying her toward the house. "I've got to get over there!"

Just as they reached the porch, the door burst open, and Koblin Baume came out, looking toward the business district as more shots were fired. His attention was then drawn to Erik and Metryka as Erik ushered her up the steps.

"I'm going over there, Chief," said Erik. "I'm sure it's at the factory."

Kathlyn appeared at the door, eyes wide as she looked at her daughter, then back at her husband. "Koblin, what is it?"

"Gunfire at the factory," replied Koblin. "I told the police officers on night duty to be on the alert in case the woodworkers tried to break into the factory. Take Metryka in the house. Erik and I are going over there."

"Oh, my!" gasped Kathlyn. "Please be careful."

Mother and daughter stood together on the porch and watched the two men as they ran in the direction of the factory and were swallowed by the night.

More gunshots punctuated the darkness.

"Come on, honey," said Kathlyn. "Let's go inside."

When they moved into the parlor, where two lanterns lit up the room, Kathlyn looked at Metryka, noting that her features were a bit drawn and colorless. "Are you not feeling well?" she asked.

"Why?" said Metryka, batting her eyelids in a show of astonishment at the question.

"You're pale, and you look like you're carrying the weight of the world. What's wrong?"

Metryka looked down at the floor, took a deep breath, and met her mother's gaze. "Mama, there...there is something I have to tell you and Papa. Later. But right now, I just want to go to my room."

"Now honey, I'm your mother, and I can tell it's something serious. This concerns me. You can tell your father whenever he returns home, or even tomorrow, if he's late getting back. But I want to know what's bothering you."

Metryka bit her lower lip, looked at the floor again for a long moment, then met her mother's gaze again. Ejecting a sigh, she said, "All right, Mama. I'll tell you. But it will be best if you sit down."

At the Metternik home, Ora Metternik was carrying a tray bearing a steaming coffeepot, along with cups and small plates with slices of spice cake on them. She smiled at Victor and Lillian Bowerbank, their neighbors from across the street, whom her husband had invited to spend the evening with them. Ora had been surprised at Alexander's sudden desire to have the Bowerbanks over, but when he reminded her the Bowerbanks had entertained them at their house last, Ora quickly gave in and hurriedly baked the cake.

"Those sure sounded like gunshots to me, Alexander," said Victor, as he watched Ora set the tray down on the coffee table. "Do you suppose there's trouble at the factory? Your fellow woodworkers making a disturbance, I mean."

"I hope not," said Metternik. "If we lived closer to the center of town, we could be sure whether those were gunshots or not."

"From what I was told by people who were near the factory this morning," said Lillian, "some of your men really showed their tempers. They just might do something daring, like set the factory on fire."

Ora poured coffee into all four cups and handed them to her guests, then to her husband. "I don't think most of them would do anything like that," she said, setting the tray down and picking up two of the plates with cake slices on them. "There are only a few who would do anything that bad."

"Probably the same few who dynamited the Nidwalden Tunnel," said Victor. "You've got some real bad apples somewhere in your barrel, Alexander."

Metternik watched his wife hand the plates to their guests. "It looks like it. I sure hope they haven't done anything else. This controversy with the Wilhaus people has got to be settled in a peaceful manner."

When Koblin Baume and Dr. Erik Linden turned onto Chur's main street, they looked toward the factory and saw a crowd gathered. Increasing their speed, they soon drew up in front of the factory. When the citizens saw who they were they made room for them to get to the center of the activity, which was inside the fence, in front of the main door.

By the light of the lanterns held by many men, they saw several policemen bending over five men who lay on the ground, bleeding. Durbin and Helmut Thorpe were standing over them, anger etched on their faces. Grocer Jabin Faulk was standing with them.

Dr. Erik Linden rushed to see about the wounded men. A quick glance told him he had some serious wounds to tend to. Having taken an oath to save lives to the greatest extent of his ability, he shoved his own recent devastation and hurt into a dark recess of his aching heart. A prayer for guidance and wisdom was on his silently moving lips as he observed the carnage before him.

Moving from man to man, Erik assessed what needed to be done, making mental priorities based on the degree of the wounds.

Upon seeing the burgomaster arrive, Officer Armant Lefler stepped up to meet him. "Chief, there were four woodworkers who broke into the factory and started smashing machinery. It just happened that Jabin Faulk was doing some work in his store and heard them smash in a door. He ran through the streets toward the police station to report it, and met up with me a couple of blocks from here. He told me what he heard, and I quickly got the attention of these other officers with my whistle.

"We ran here to the factory, and just as we arrived, the four woodworkers were coming out the main door. I shouted for them to halt, but they were armed, and started shooting. While we were exchanging shots, one of the woodworkers ran away. We hit the others, and as you can see, they're down."

"I also see Officers Anton Zrelak and Rubel Molner down," said Baume.

"Yes, sir. One of our men is on his way to Dr. Linden's apartment right now. I'm glad he was with you."

"Me too," said Baume, focusing on his two wounded men, who were being examined by a kneeling Dr. Linden at the moment. "How bad are they hurt?"

"Zrelak has a bullet wound in his side, sir," said Lefler. "Not very deep. And Molner has a bullet in his upper left arm."

Moving close to where the three woodworkers lay with Lefler at his side, Baume said, "Let's see who we have here."

Baume's eyes fell on the large form of Bartholomew Sojak, who was gritting his teeth in agony. His right pant leg was soaked with blood just above the knee. Next to him lay Horace Kefling, whose shirt was blood-soaked in the center of his chest, and beside Kefling was Croft Susack, whose shirt was soaked with blood in the midsection just above his belt.

At that instant, Dr. Erik Linden stepped up to the burgomaster. "Chief, we've got two men in critical condition. Croft Susack and Horace Kefling. Bartholomew Sojak isn't critical. He's got a slug in his leg, and the bone is broken."

"And what about my men?"

"Officer Zrelak has a flesh wound in his side. Nothing dangerous. And Officer Molner has a slug in his arm. He's not in any danger. I need you to recruit some of your men and some of the townsmen to carry all of them to the clinic so I can go to work on them. And I need somebody to go to Dr. Danzig's house and bring him to the clinic. I'm going to need his help."

Baume looked at Lefler. "Let's get the doctor the help he needs."

A quarter hour later, three of the wounded men were being laid on cots in the clinic's surgical and examining room; Susack and Kefling were being placed on surgical tables under Dr. Linden's directions.

Durbin and Helmut Thorpe had carried Officer Molner, and when Molner was on his cot, the Thorpes stepped up to Erik.

"Pardon me, Doctor," said Helmut, "but why are those two troublemakers being given preference over the two wounded officers?"

Helmut's presence brought back Erik's devastation earlier that evening. Setting cool eyes on him, he said, "I'm treating them in the order of the seriousness of their wounds. Now excuse me. I've got to get busy."

Father and son exchanged glances, shrugged their shoulders, and left.

Outside, Koblin Baume was giving two of his officers instructions to stay at the clinic in case of trouble from the wounded woodworkers as he noticed Durbin and Helmut Thorpe come out the door and hastily move down the street.

"I'll be staying for a while, myself," Baume said to the officers. "Let's go in."

When Baume and his two officers stepped into the back room, they saw Erik looking closely at the wound in Croft Susack's midsection. At the same time, the door opened and Dr. Joseph Danzig entered, with both of his nurses at his side.

Erik looked at them and said, "Am I ever glad to see three of you!"

Dr. Danzig, looking drawn and weary, said, "Where do we begin?"

Swinging his eyes toward the cots, Erik said, "Louise, Amelia, I need you to quickly bandage Officers Zrelak and Molner to stop their bleeding as much as possible, then do the same for Bartholomew. When you've done that, one of you can help Dr. Danzig, and the other one can help me. Dr. Danzig, I've examined each man here, and I find Horace in the most critical condition. Croft is next. If you will go to work on him, I'll begin immediately on Horace."

"Of course," said Danzig, moving toward the table where Susack lay.

The nurses hurried toward the men on the cots.

Erik looked at the burgomaster and his two officers and said, "You gentlemen can wait out in the office. We'll keep you advised."

Erik then moved to the table where Horace Kefling lay with a bullet in his chest. Instantly, Koblin Baume stepped up and said heatedly, "Erik, you should take care of my wounded officers completely before you even look at these troublemakers! So what if they are in worse condition? If they die while you're working on my men, too bad. They're getting what they deserve."

Erik's face settled into a grim mask. Looking the burgomaster square in the eye, he said, "Chief Baume, upon becoming a physician, I took an oath to do everything in my power to preserve all human life and so did Dr. Danzig. And we will both do just that. I have assessed the degree of each man's wounds, here, and I find the two men on these tables in the most dangerous condition. Therefore, we will work on them first."

Baume held the young doctor's steady gaze for a few seconds. "All right if I talk to Sojak?"

"Just for a few minutes. I mean very few."

Baume nodded, turned away, and moved to the cot where Bartholomew Sojak lay. The nurses were working hurriedly, bandaging the two wounded officers.

Bending over Sojak, whose eyes were closed, Baume said, "Bartholomew, I want to ask you something."

The man opened his eyes, which were dulled with pain. He made no verbal reply.

"I was told," said Baume, "that there were four of you woodworkers who broke into the factory and smashed machinery."

Sojak worked his jaw and swallowed with difficulty. Still he said nothing.

Anger blazed in Baume's eyes. "I want to know who the one was who ran away."

Sojak licked his lips. "Can't tell you."

"You mean you won't tell me."

"All right. I won't tell you. All of us are sticking together. You won't find out from me, no matter what."

Face flushed, Koblin Baume said, "I could beat it out of you!"

"In front of these women and the doctors?"

Baume wheeled, moved back to where Erik was working on his patient and said, "I'm leaving two officers here just in case any of these no-goods give you trouble. I'll be back in the morning."

"See you then," said Erik without looking up.

At the Metternik home, the Bowerbanks were about to leave when there was a loud knock at the front door.

"Excuse me," said Alexander. "I'll be right back."

Opening the door, Metternik found himself looking into the red face of Burgomaster Koblin Baume. "I want to talk to you!" gusted Baume.

Feeling suddenly shaky inside, Metternik said, "Of course, Chief. Come in."

The woodworkers' leader knew what the visit was about, and to settle quickly that he had been home all evening, he led the burgomaster into the parlor and said to his wife and guests, "Chief Baume wants to talk to me. All right if they listen, Chief?"

"Makes no difference to me," Baume said, clipping his words.

"Sit down, Chief," said Metternik, gesturing toward a chair.

"I'll stand, thank you," Baume said.

"We'd better be going," said Victor.

"No need to rush away," commented Metternik. "What was it you wanted to talk to me about, Chief?"

"I want you to tell me if you know anything about the woodworkers who broke into the factory and smashed machinery tonight."

The Bowerbanks looked at each other.

"I don't know a thing about it, Chief," Metternik said. "Please don't tell me that there was shooting. We thought we heard gunfire a while ago."

"There was shooting, all right. Four of your men broke into the factory, and when my officers got there, they were just coming out. Your men had guns, and when they were told by my officers to halt, they opened fire. Two of my men were wounded."

"I'm sorry to hear that, Chief," Metternik said, putting a sincere tone in his voice.

"Three of your men were wounded, too, Alexander. All five wounded men are at the clinic. Dr. Linden says Horace Kefling and Croft Susack are critical."

Metternik's blood seemed to chill. "Wh-who was the third?"

"Bartholomew Sojak. He'll probably live. Dr. Linden isn't too sure about the other two."

"You said there were four woodworkers."

"Yes."

"Who was the fourth one?"

"I don't know. Why don't you tell me? I couldn't get Bartholomew to tell me."

Putting on an innocent face, Metternik said, "I have no idea, Chief. Those men know I wouldn't approve of them breaking into the factory. They did it on their own."

Baume looked him in the eye. "Have you been home all evening?"

"Sure have. You can ask Victor and Lillian. They came over about seven-thirty."

"That's right, Chief," said Victor. "He's been here with us ever since we got here."

Ora spoke up. "Chief Baume, certainly you don't think my husband would take part in such a thing. Or even condone it."

"All I know is he's their leader, ma'am. I can't feature them doing what they did at the tunnel and now here at the factory without his approval."

Ora's face lost color.

Turning to Metternik, Baume said through his teeth, "If I find out you had anything to do with the break-in or the explosion in the tunnel, Alexander, you will face the full punishment of the law."

With that, the burgomaster stomped out of the house, slamming the door.

Ora rushed to her husband, flinging her arms around him. "Oh, Alex, how can he think you would be a part of any of this?"

Holding her close, Alexander looked toward his guests and said, "Sweetheart, Koblin is just desperate. Since I'm the leader of the woodworkers, he naturally assumes I either had a part in the dynamiting of the tunnel and the break-in at the factory, or I at least condoned it. My name will be cleared if he ever catches the ones who did it."

Ora sighed. "I sure hope he catches them soon."

"Me too," said Victor. "It has to be an awful thing for you, Alexander, to have Koblin think you're guilty when you're not."

"It isn't easy," said Metternik, "but he'll apologize if and when the guilty parties are caught."

"Well, he will catch them," said Victor in a comforting tone. "Koblin is good at what he does. Whoever did these things will get caught."

Alexander Metternik felt a cold ball of ice form in his stomach.

At the Baume home, Kathlyn and Metryka sat at the kitchen table, sipping hot tea, while the teapot gave off steam on the stove. Kathlyn knew her husband would want some when he came home, especially when he heard about the broken engagement.

"Well, honey," said Kathlyn, meeting her daughter's teary gaze, "you have to follow your heart. I certainly can't fault you for breaking it off with Erik. You should marry the man you love."

A smile worked its way across Metryka's careworn face. "Oh, thank you, Mama. Having you so understanding about it has helped me more than you will ever know."

"I'm glad," said the tenderhearted mother.

Metryka used a hanky to dab tears from the corners of her eyes. "But, Mama, I'm still uneasy about telling Papa. Especially after that big meeting he had for Erik, and the certificate he had printed up. Papa seemed so proud here lately that I was going to be the wife of Chur's leading physician. What if—what if—"

"What if what?"

Metryka sniffed. "What if Papa gets real angry with me for breaking off the engagement?"

"It may bother him at first, Metryka," said Kathlyn, "but once the shock wears off, he will be fine. Especially when you tell him you're going to marry Helmut. This woodworker problem has drawn your father very close to both Durbin and Helmut. Believe me, it will be all right."

"Oh, Mama, you are such an encouragement."

Both of them heard the front door open and close.

"There he is now," said Kathlyn, as the sound of Koblin's heavy footsteps echoed down the hall.

When he entered the kitchen, he ran his gaze over both faces. "I thought you two would have gone to bed by now."

"We wanted to be up when you came home," said Kathlyn. "Come sit down. I've got some tea hot for you."

"Sounds good," he said, and moved toward his chair at the head of the table.

Kathlyn began pouring tea into a cup she had ready on the cupboard.

Koblin looked at his daughter, "Honey, are you all right? You look like you've been crying."

"Well, there's something I want to share with you, Papa," said Metryka, "but first, tell us about the gunfire at the factory."

Kathlyn set his steaming teacup in front of him. Koblin took a sip, then told them about the shooting incident at the factory and the condition of the wounded officers and woodworkers.

The tea had cooled some by that time. He drank half the cup, set it down and said, "I hate to say this, Metryka, but I'm quite miffed at your future husband. I tried to get him to treat my police officers first in spite of the fact that Croft Susack and Horace Kefling are more seriously wounded, but he refused. I mean, what's wrong with him? Those woodworkers not only broke the law by breaking into the factory and smashing machinery, but they shot two police officers. I told him to let those woodworkers die if necessary and to take care of Zrelak and Molner first. If they die, they deserve it." He took another sip of tea. "But, no. Erik went to work first on Susack and Kefling."

"Dear," said Kathlyn, "you have to remember that Erik took an oath to preserve every human life possible. He—"

"He reminded me of that," said Koblin. "But when men turn themselves into criminals, they ought to be treated as such."

"How about a new subject?" asked Kathlyn.

"All right," said Koblin. "I've had enough of the woodworkers and their underhanded tactics for one day. What's the new subject?"

Kathlyn smiled, sent an assuring glance at her daughter, and said, "Metryka said she has something to share with you."

"Oh. Sure. What is it, honey?"

"Well, Papa," Metryka said, feeling the jitters in her stomach, "I made a big change in my life this evening."

"Oh, good. Did you give up that Christianity nonsense?"

"Well, as a matter of fact, I did."

Koblin's bushy eyebrows hiked up. "You did?"

"Yes. In fact, I told Erik tonight that I never believed it in the first place—that I just acted like I did so he would want me. I told him I've really never stopped believing what you have taught me all my life. The Bible is a fairy tale, and there's no afterlife. When we die, that's the end of us. No heaven...no hell."

Koblin laughed. "So how did he take it?"

"Not good. But he didn't take it good when I broke off the engagement, either."

Shock registered in the man's eyes. "You—you broke off the engagement?"

"Yes, Papa. I haven't told anybody about it because I felt Erik should hear it first. With him going to Bern, and everything that's happened since the tunnel explosion, I haven't had a minute alone with him until tonight. I told him I couldn't marry him because I'm in love with Helmut Thorpe."

"Helmut! Really?"

"Yes."

"Well, what do you know? And Helmut feels the same about you, I assume."

"Yes. We're going to get married pretty soon."

Koblin thought on it for a moment, then said, "As you know, I was quite proud that you were going to marry a doctor, but I'm so relieved to know I don't have to enter that church building to walk you down the aisle that I could shout. I like Helmut. I'll be proud to have him as my son-in-law." He paused. "You will have just a civil ceremony, won't you? Like right here at our house?"

"Yes. We've already agreed on that."

"Good! Then I'm satisfied."

Jumping off her chair, Metryka hugged her father's neck, kissed his cheek, and said, "I'm so happy! Thank you, Papa. You and

Mama have made me feel a whole lot better about this."

Koblin put an arm around his daughter, and looked up into her eyes. "Honey, you said Erik didn't take it so good when you broke off the engagement. He was probably pretty mad, huh?"

"No, Papa. He was hurt. But he didn't show any anger."

"Hah! Well, take it from me, honey. He's mad, all right. He's just holding it inside. But you watch, sooner or later, he'll try to get back at you."

It was almost two o'clock in the morning when Dr. Erik Linden sighed, looked around at Dr. Danzig and the nurses, and said, "Horace just died."

He lay aside his scalpel and drew a sheet up over Horace Kefling's face.

"This woodworker thing is going to take more lives, son," said the aging physician. "I'm wondering if Croft is going to make it."

Nurses Louise Levron and Amelia Folcher kept a close watch on Bartholomew Sojak and the two officers while both doctors worked on an unconscious Croft Susack.

When the doctors had done all they could to stop the internal bleeding in Susack's stomach, they stitched him up. It was just after three o'clock when they finished, and Dr. Danzig looked like he was about to collapse.

Erik said, "Doctor, I'm going to have one of the officers in the waiting room take you home."

"I won't argue," said Danzig. "I am very, very tired."

At 4:00 A.M., Erik told the weary nurses to go home and get some rest. They argued that he needed rest himself, but he told them someone had to stay with the patients, and since he was their boss, it would be him.

"How about if we just lie down on some spare cots right here, Doctor?" asked Louise. "Then we could spell you at times so you could get some rest, too."

"Yes, Doctor," said Amelia. "Let's do it that way."

Erik grinned. "I appreciate the offer, ladies, but like I said, since I'm boss here, you will do as I say. Don't show up back here before eight o'clock."

Louise shook her head and smiled. "All right, boss, but if we find you collapsed, what then?"

Erik chuckled. "I'll be fine. Go home."

Thirteen

Dova Combray and Dr. Erik Linden were holding hands as they walked the bank of a gurgling stream. They moved from the level land toward the steep trails that led into the high country of the Swiss Alps under a brilliant blue sky.

The day was warm and the single eye of the sun sent its bright beams down on the smiling couple as they strolled along leisurely, happy to be in each other's presence.

The trees were lushly covered with wild grapes and berry vines, and the meadows stood knee deep in grass. They made their way higher in the foothills, and as the path beside the stream grew steeper, they soon were climbing along a jagged ridge of blue granite. After a while the air cooled with the elevation, with the breeze that picked up, and with the deep shade of the pines that surrounded them.

When they reached a plateau where they could peer between the towering treetops and see the lofty, snowcapped peaks high above them, Erik squeezed Dova's hand and stopped. They were standing beside the rushing stream, its music in their ears.

From somewhere nearby, they could hear the sound of lumbermen sawing on a tree.

Erik looked lovingly into Dova's pale blue eyes. The breeze was toying with her long blond hair. Touching the soft locks and brushing them back from her face, he said, "My precious Dova, I love you with all of my heart."

Her pulse quickened pace as he kissed her tenderly.

When their lips parted, she reached up and stroked his cheek. "Erik, darling, I love you so very, very much."

They kissed again, then she laid her head on his chest.

She could feel the throb of his heart as he said, "Dova, you have always been the one I love."

With her own heart pounding, she looked up into his kind eyes, "But I thought it was Metryka you loved. Why haven't you told me this before?"

Erik started to answer, but his words were cut off when the loud voice of a nearby lumberman pierced the air: "Timber-r-r-r!"

Suddenly they were aware of a tall pine falling toward them. Looking up with the shadow of the tree spreading around them, Erik grasped Dova's arm and yanked her out of the tree's path...

Suddenly Dova sat bolt upright in her bed, gasping for breath. Cold sweat was on her brow as she blinked and looked around her bedroom. Silver moonlight flowed through the windows, illuminating the room with its soft glow.

Mopping her brow with the sheet, she said in a low whisper, "It was a dream, Dova. Only a dream. The man you love is going to marry Metryka Baume. Not Dova Combray."

Taking a deep breath, Dova lay back, put her head on the pillow, and pulled the covers up to her chin. Closing her eyes, she said, "Lord, I...I must ask you once more to forgive me for having thoughts and dreams about Erik being in love with me. I'm in love with him, but he is in love with Metryka. Please, Lord. Take this love I have for him out of my heart. Please. It just hurts so much..."

And Dova slowly drifted back to sleep.

The sun was lifting into a partly cloudy sky at 7:45 the next morning when Metryka arrived at the factory and spoke to men who were making their way into the wood shops.

When she entered the office, she found Durbin and Helmut Thorpe standing over Durbin's desk, each holding papers in their hand. They turned and looked at her, smiling.

Helmut moved toward her. "Have you heard about the shooting here last night?"

"Yes."

"Our neighbor, Walter Henske, is a woodworker, as you know. He came over to our house about an hour ago and told us about the break-in, the machinery being smashed, the three woodworkers being shot, and the two officers."

"Do you know how they are doing?"

"Not yet," said Durbin, laying the papers on his desk. "After I meet with the men and we assess the extent of the damage, I'll go to the clinic and see what I can find out. I'm certainly concerned about Officers Zrelak and Molner."

"Father," said Helmut, "do you want me to go down with you while you talk with the men?"

"No need, son," said Durbin. "As far behind as we are with the paperwork, you need to stay on it. You and Metryka, both."

Even as he was speaking, Durbin was moving toward the door. Without another word, he was gone.

Helmut looked down at the papers in his hand, shook his head, and said, "With all of these woodworker problems taking up our time, I really have gotten behind. How about you?"

"I have, too," replied Metryka, "but probably not as much as you."

She took a step closer to him, a strange light gleaming in her eyes. "Darling, even though you need to get on your paperwork, can I have a minute or two? I have something to tell you."

A smile spread over his face. "You...you told Erik?"

Smiling broadly herself, she nodded.

"Oh, wonderful!" exclaimed Helmut, folding her in his arms. "I want to hear all about it!"

As Durbin Thorpe moved among the factory workers, he found some of the men trying to repair the machines that had been damaged, while others were doing their normal jobs. He found them very angry at the four woodworkers who had smashed the machinery, and every one of them showed concern for the two wounded police officers.

The hope was also expressed among them that the fourth man who had broken into the factory and managed to escape during the shootout would be caught and severely punished.

Dr. Erik Linden was leaning over Croft Susack at eight o'clock that morning when Nurses Amelia Folchert and Louise Levron entered the clinic.

He turned his weary eyes on them and said, "Good morning, ladies. Did you get some sleep?"

"We did," said Amelia, "but you didn't."

"So how are the patients, Doctor?" asked Louise as they drew up to him.

"As you can see, Croft is unconscious again," said Erik. "He's so torn up inside, I don't think he's going to make it. He's bleeding internally again, and I can't get it stopped. Bartholomew is still critical, but a little better. Our two police officers over here are doing well. They'll be fine in a couple of weeks. The families of all four have been in. I explained the condition of each man in the office, but didn't let them come back here. I sent them home. Mrs. Susack wanted to stay, but she has two sick children Dr. Danzig has been treating, and I told her she should be home with them."

Amelia focused on Erik. "Now, how about a report on you?"

The doctor frowned. "Me?"

"Yes, you. Pardon me, but you look like death warmed over. You're worn out, Doctor."

"We want you to go home and sleep for at least a few hours," said Louise. "Dr. Danzig will probably be in a little later. We'll watch over these men till then."

Erik shook his head. "I don't think Dr. Danzig will make it in at all today. Don't you remember how weary he looked before he left here? No, I must stay."

"Till you really do collapse?" pressed Amelia.

He gave her a lopsided grin. "Tell you what. I'll take a cot in my office and lie down for a while. But I want to be near in case I'm needed."

The nurses looked at each other, then Amelia said, "All right, but you won't sleep like you would if you went home."

"Maybe not, but neither of you is a doctor. You are great nurses, but you are limited in what you can do. I'll lie down in there, but if there's the slightest need for my services on any of these men, you are to call me immediately. Understood?"

"Yes, sir," said Amelia.

"Louise?"

"Yes, sir."

Erik went to a corner in the room, picked up a canvas cot, and headed for the door.

Before he reached it, Amelia said, "Dr. Linden, you've got to put something in your stomach. You haven't eaten in a long time. I'll go over to the bakery and get you some sweet buns, and I'll make you some nice hot coffee. Louise can watch over the patients alone until I get you taken care of."

Erik shrugged. "All right."

With that, he carried the cot through the door, passed through the outer office, and entered his private office. He set the cot down and stared at it. His exhausted body was begging for rest, but suddenly he was afraid to lie down and take his mind off his patients lest the pain in his heart be given rein to take over his thoughts. Metryka's face was suddenly before him. He shook his head as if to dislodge her from his thoughts, but she was still there. He sat down on the cot and put his hands to his face.

In the clinic's kitchen, which was at the rear of the building, Amelia built a fire in the stove and prepared a large pot of strong coffee. Leaving it to brew, she hurriedly left by the back door and went two doors down the street to the bakery.

Moments later, she returned to the kitchen, carrying a sack of sweet buns. Quickly making up a tray, she carried it into the doctor's office and found him sitting on the cot, rubbing his tired eyes.

Placing the tray on his desk, she said, "Now get some of this into your stomach, Doctor, then lie down and sleep."

The aroma of the hot coffee penetrated Erik's senses. Looking up at Amelia through bleary, bloodshot eyes, he stood up, giving her a smile of gratitude. Sniffing the aroma, he said wearily, "Dear lady, that is exactly what I need."

Amelia poured him a large mug of the brew, added a heaping teaspoonful of sugar and poured a dollop of thick cream from a small pitcher. Stirring it with the spoon, she set it on his desk.

Erik sat down at the desk, took a couple of small sips, then waited for it to cool a bit.

The silver-haired nurse placed a pair of warm sweet buns in front of him.

"Thank you, Amelia," he said, "but I really shouldn't take the time to do any of this. Croft may need me."

"None of that now, young man," she said in motherly fashion. "You will perform your work much better if first you take care of yourself. Louise and I will be in there with the patients, giving them all the care possible. If we need you, we know where to find you. You get those buns and the coffee down, and then get some sleep."

She left the room, closing the door firmly behind her.

Erik drank the coffee and ate the buns while trying to force his mind to stay on the wounded men and not let any stray thoughts go to Metryka and his sorely damaged heart. Wearily, he lay down on the cot and was about to fall asleep when Louise came in and said, "Dr. Linden, I'm sorry to bother you, but Alexander Metternik is out here and insists he must talk to you."

Sitting up, Erik rubbed his eyes. "All right. Bring him in. I'll talk to him in here."

Erik had just placed the cot against the far wall when Alexander Metternik came through the door. "Dr. Linden," he said, "I'm sorry to bother you. I came to see how my men are doing, and your nurses told me that Horace died last night. They said Bartholomew is critical, and Croft is even more critical. I've got to know what you think about them."

Rubbing his eyes again, Erik said, "I'm optimistic about Bartholomew, Alexander, but I can't say that about Croft. The bullet tore his insides up pretty bad. He's bleeding internally. I was able to slow the bleeding, but I couldn't stop it completely. Only time will tell."

Alexander nodded, rubbing his unshaven chin. He had laid awake most of the night, thinking about Koblin Baume's threat if he ever found out he had anything to do with the tunnel explosion or the break-in at the factory. In the wee hours, he had decided there was no way Baume would ever know his part in either crime. The only way Baume could ever know was if one of the woodworkers told him, and they would never do that. There was a bond between all of the independent woodworkers, and they would always stick together and protect each other. They would especially protect their leader.

With this in mind, Metternik would carry on his seeming innocence and make everybody outside of his closest friends among the woodworkers think he was a peaceful and kind man.

Laying a hand on Erik's shoulder, Metternik said sincerely, "Dr. Linden, I want to thank you for the tireless effort you have put in here. Your nurses told me you were with those wounded men all night, without a wink of sleep."

"Just doing what a man of my profession ought to do, Alexander," he said humbly.

"Well, I just want to express my appreciation for what you're doing. I know Horace's death was something you couldn't prevent. And if Croft doesn't make it, it will be no fault of yours. Bartholomew, too, if he dies." He rubbed the back of his neck. "But Officers Zrelak and Molner are going to be all right, your nurses said."

"Yes."

"Well, I'm glad. And I appreciate the work you have done on them, too."

"I wish this whole thing with the factory hadn't happened," said Erik. "I understand what you and your friends are facing, but wouldn't it be better to take Mr. Wilhaus up on his offer than to have this bloodshed?"

"I'm really thinking we should," said Metternik. "Maybe I should have spoken up at the meeting. I just never thought things would get ugly like this. If I only knew who put that dynamite in the tunnel..."

"So you have no idea."

"None whatsoever. I was shocked when I learned who the woodworkers were that broke into the factory. I...I've got to somehow convince the rest of them that violence and property destruction is not the answer."

"I appreciate your concern," said Erik. "The stronger you put that to your men, the better off everybody will be."

"I'm going to do my best, Doctor," said Metternik. "Well, I'd better go. Thank you for talking to me."

Louise stuck her head in. "Dr. Linden, Durbin Thorpe is here and would like to see you when you're through with Mr. Metternik. I told him you need to get some rest. He said he wouldn't stay long."

"He can come in now, ma'am," said Metternik. "I'm about to leave."

Kenyon Hartwig was in his wood shop, cleaning up sawdust left there since his last job some two weeks previously. There was a tap on the door. When he opened it, Alexander Metternik said, "Your wife told me you were out here. We need to talk."

"Sure," said Hartwig. "Come in."

As Hartwig closed the door, Metternik turned and said, "I would assume that you know the story of what happened since you ran away from the shootout last night."

"Yes. By listening to the neighbors."

"Did you know Horace died?"

"Yes. His oldest son came to tell us. Too bad."

"Yes. I was just at the clinic. It doesn't look good for Croft, either. Bartholomew is considered critical, but not as much as Croft."

"And the officers?"

"Dr. Linden says they will be fine. I'm sure nobody got a good look at you last night before you took off. So you're in the clear. Might be good if you sort of keep a low profile for a few days."

"I was thinking the same thing. Just till things cool down."

"Right. Well, I've got to go see a couple of my men. See you later."

Alexander Metternik's next stop was at the home of Thomas Allman. While they walked together toward Arthur Wengen's house, Metternik told Allman of Horace Kefling's death and brought him up to date on the condition of Croft Susack and Bartholomew Sojak.

When they arrived at the Wengen home, Metternik took both men into Wengen's wood shop privately. Wengen was shocked with the news about Horace Kefling dying. Then Metternik explained about the other two wounded woodworkers.

With a steely look in his eyes, Metternik said, "That factory has got to be put out of business. I've been giving it a lot of thought. We've got to do something even more drastic than what we did in the tunnel."

"Like what?" asked Allman.

A wicked grin curved the leader's mouth. "If we were to take out Durbin Thorpe and his son, it would throw a real wrench in the works and cripple the factory. Our next move would be to take out Eiger Wilhaus, himself. Even Zugg Hinwill. It would be too hard to get those two right now, since they're staying at the hotel. We'll have to wait for the right opportunity. But eliminating the Thorpes will begin the crippling process quite well. What do you think?"

Thomas Allman pulled at an ear nervously. "I don't know, Alexander. We killed seven people when we dynamited the tunnel. I hate to kill anyone else. Can't we—"

"Can't we what?" snapped Metternik. "Get down on our knees

and beg them to close the factory? Come on, Thomas. Use your head. We don't have a choice in this matter. We have to put that factory out of business or try to sell our homes and go somewhere else to open up our own shops. But where? Not in Switzerland. Wilhaus would eventually put a factory somewhere near enough to us to put us out of business again. We have to act now!"

"He's right, Thomas," said Arthur Wengen. "We can't let this situation go on. I agree with Alexander. We need to take out Durbin and Helmut right away, then go to work on doing the same to Wilhaus and Hinwill."

Allman sighed. "I guess we have no choice."

"That's more like it, Thomas," said Wengen, patting him on the back. "When do you want to go after the Thorpes, Alexander?"

"Very soon," said Metternik. "We'll have to do it at night so we won't be seen. Let me think on it. I'll come up with a plan within a day or two."

That evening, Alexander and Ora Metternik were eating in one of Chur's small restaurants. Alexander's back was toward the door as they talked about Eiger Wilhaus's offer of jobs to the independent woodworkers and his stubbornness concerning the wages.

Suddenly, Ora looked past her husband and said, "Here's some of Wilhaus's people now. Durbin and Lynelle Thorpe. Hmm."

"What?"

"Helmut is with them, and he's got Metryka Baume on his arm."

Alexander's scalp pulled back from his forehead. "You mean it's like they are together? On a date?"

"Sure looks like it to me. She's snuggled up very close to him."

Alexander shook his head. "I wonder what Dr. Linden would think of this?"

"Well, since their wedding is only a couple of weeks away, I'd think he wouldn't like it at all."

"They're sitting down at the table behind you," said Ora.

"Don't look at them. Ignore them."

Soon the waitress took the orders from the Thorpe group, and while the Metterniks ate quietly, they overheard the conversation that was going on at the next table. Durbin, Helmut, and Metryka were talking about how they had gotten behind in their paperwork at the office because of the problem brought on by the independent woodworkers.

Helmut said, "Father, I'm going to go back to the office and work tonight. Maybe I can catch up a little on my paperwork."

"Excellent, son," said Durbin. "I'll take your mother home, first. Then I'll go look in on Mr. Wilhaus and Zugg at the hotel. From there, I'm going to the clinic to see how Croft and Bartholomew are doing. After that, I'll join you at the office. If we work till midnight, we should make at least a small dent in it."

"Sounds good to me, Father," said Helmut.

"All right. Let's do it. Maybe we'll have to work a few nights for a while to get caught up."

The conversation at the Thorpe table was interrupted at that moment as the waitress appeared, carrying a steaming coffeepot and a tray of cups and saucers.

Alexander couldn't reveal it to Ora, but he already had his plan formulated to take out Durbin and Helmut Thorpe. He was glad the opportunity had presented itself so quickly.

He and Ora were eating their dessert when the meals were delivered to the Thorpe table. As soon as the Metterniks were finished, Alexander said, "Well, let's go home."

As the Metterniks stood up to leave, Lynelle Thorpe caught Ora's eye and smiled at her. "Hello, Ora. Nice to see you."

"You, too," said Ora, returning the smile.

Alexander pushed his chair under the table, and as he turned to escort Ora out of the restaurant, Durbin Thorpe looked at him and said, "Hello, Alexander."

Without a smile, Metternik nodded and said, "Good evening, Durbin," and quickly ushered Ora toward the door.

Durbin watched them till they moved outside. "As hard as I try, I still can't trust that man."

"Same with me," said Helmut.

"Tell you what, Mr. Thorpe," Metryka said to Durbin, "I'll just go with Helmut to the office tonight, too. Maybe with all three of us attacking our paperwork, we can make a big dent in it."

Durbin smiled at her. "All right. I appreciate it. You're going to fit into this family in a wonderful way, Metryka."

"Thank you, sir. I'm glad you feel that way."

Lynelle took hold of Metryka's hand across the table. "We both feel that way, dear."

"All three of us do!" said Helmut. "Especially me!"

As the Metterniks entered their house, Alexander quickly lit a lantern in the parlor and said, "Honey, I forgot to tell you that I set up a meeting with a couple of the woodworkers for eight-thirty tonight. We have to work on just how to approach Eiger Wilhaus about raising the wages at the factory so we can make a decent living. Sorry. It slipped my mind until just now."

"It's all right, darling," said Ora. "I understand. Something's got to be done soon, or all of us are going to be hurting financially."

"Right. I'm glad you understand. I should be back before midnight."

When Arthur Wengen had led Alexander Metternik and Thomas Allman into his wood shop and fired up a lantern, he said, "All right, Alexander, let's hear it."

Running his gaze between his two friends, Metternik said, "The solution for taking out Durbin and Helmut was laid generously in my lap just about an hour ago."

Wengen and Allman listened intently as Metternik told them about the conversation he overheard at the restaurant between Durbin Thorpe and his son.

"All we have to do is wait till Durbin gets back and joins Helmut in the factory office," he said breathlessly. "It won't be hard to shoot them both down while they're in the office."

"Great!" said Wengen. "Tonight the crippling of the factory begins!"

At the Chur Hotel, Zugg Hinwill was helping Eiger Wilhaus into his nightshirt when they heard a knock at the door.

Easing the elderly man into a sitting position on the edge of his bed, Hinwill said, "You sit right there, sir. I'll be right back."

Hinwill opened the door. "Well, hello, Durbin. Come in. I was just putting Mr. Wilhaus to bed." Calling over his shoulder, he said, "Mr. Wilhaus, it's Durbin."

Wilhaus smiled at Durbin as he drew up beside the bed with Zugg at his side. "I appreciate your coming by, Durbin. Any more news about the wounded officers?"

"Yes, sir. I was just at the clinic. Dr. Linden was sleeping in his office, but Mrs. Levron told me they are still doing quite well."

"Good. And the two woodworkers?"

"Susack isn't doing well at all, but there seems to be a bit of improvement in Sojak."

Wilhaus rubbed his bony jaw. "Gentlemen, the woodworkers have already lost that Kefling fellow. It sounds like they may lose Susack. In their minds, this is our fault. I'm afraid there is going to be more violence."

"Me too, sir," said Durbin. "I wish they would just be reasonable and take the jobs you have offered them."

Zugg Hinwill cleared his throat nervously. "Mr. Wilhaus, I...I—"

"Yes, Zugg?"

"Well, sir, I would like to suggest that you seriously consider offering them higher wages. I really believe in the long run it would make everything better. I know you really don't want to have to bring in workers from elsewhere in the country, but the factory desperately needs more workers right now. If we hired these Chur men, the factory would be fully staffed immediately. The profits would soon make up for what it cost the factory to hire Alexander Metternik and his friends."

Wilhaus frowned. "The idea of giving them higher wages really goes against the grain, Zugg, but let me give it some serious thought. We'll talk about it some more tomorrow."

Fourteen

At the Chur Medical Clinic, Dr. Erik Linden was sitting at his desk eating hot potato soup that had just been brought to him by Amelia.

Standing over him with concern written all over her face, Amelia said, "Doctor, I hate to nag you, but you only slept for a little more than two hours this afternoon. And that was fitful sleep. You were restless the whole time. Do you realize how long it has been since you have been in your bed and had some genuine sleep? I'm really afraid you're going to collapse on us."

Swallowing a mouthful of soup, Erik picked up his coffee cup, took a sip of the steaming black liquid, and said, "Amelia, with Croft in such critical condition, I just can't go home. This soup and coffee are helping to revive me some. As soon as I'm through here, I'll go back to Croft, and I want you and Louise to go home. Both of you are worn out."

Amelia shook her head, looked at the ceiling, then down at her boss. "Dr. Erik Linden, I really do think you are the most stubborn man I have ever met. Louise isn't going to go home any more than I am. If you're staying, so are we."

"But—"

"No buts, Doctor. I know Croft is very critical. What if sometime in the night he takes a turn for the worse and you have to open him up again to try to stop the internal bleeding? You're going to need help. You won't have it if we're not here."

"I realize that, but if you're both so fatigued that you can't function to do what's needed to assist me in the surgery, Croft may die, anyway."

"I understand what you're saying, Doctor, but his chances are better if we're here to help, in spite of the fact that we're a little tired. Tell me I'm wrong."

Holding his spoon in ready position to dip it into the soup again, Erik stared at her silently.

"All right," she said. "That settles that. I'll go tell Louise we're staying as she and I had planned."

As she headed for the door, Erik said, "You mean as you had connived."

She stopped, flashed him an impish smile, and hurried out the door.

A few minutes later when Amelia returned, Erik had the soup bowl turned up, drinking what was in the bottom.

"Louise is in full agreement, Doctor. We're staying the night."

"All right. I'll bring another cot in here, and the two of you can at least get some sleep. If I need one or both of you, I know where I can find you."

"Well, our sleeping in here on cots wasn't exactly in the plan. We—"

"It is now," he said, rising to his feet. "You're a good cook, Amelia. You'll make some man a good wife someday."

"Tell my husband that, will you?"

"Sure," he said, heading for the door. "I'll get another cot, and—"

The door came open, and Louise said, "Doctor, Croft is getting worse. His midsection is beginning to bloat. It has to be the internal bleeding."

"I was afraid of this," said Erik, and hurried past her.

Both nurses followed him and drew up to the table as he pulled back the sheet over the unconscious Croft Susack and began examining his middle. After a few minutes, he said, "I'm not going to open him up again just yet. He is bloating, yes, but I want to watch him closely before I do surgery again. I'll carry another cot into my office, then while you two are getting some sleep, I'll keep a close watch here."

"Sleep?" said Louise, looking surprised.

"Yes," said Erik, heading for the corner where empty cots were stacked. He picked it up, heading for the door. "I just told your partner that you can stay on one condition: that you lie down on the cots and get some sleep. If I need either or both of you, I'll holler."

Moments later, the doctor was standing over Croft, checking his pulse. The door opened and Louise said, "Doctor, Koblin Baume is here. He wants to check on his men and the woodworkers."

Erik nodded. "Send him in. You two do what I told you."

Seconds later, Chur's burgomaster came through the door. While moving up to the table, Baume cast a glance at the two officers who lay sleeping on their cots in the dim light of a single lantern on the far side of the room. "So how are my men, Erik?"

They are doing as well as can be expected," replied Erik, still in the process of taking Croft Susack's pulse, his eyes on the pocket watch in his hand.

"And these two?"

"Just a second," said Erik, his fingers pressed to Croft's left wrist.

Baume watched silently.

"All right," said Erik, slipping the watch into his pocket. "Bartholomew is still critical, but showing improvement. Croft isn't good at all. I'm afraid he isn't going to make it."

Koblin nodded silently. "Erik, you look like you're about to collapse. Haven't you had any rest?"

Covering a yawn, the young doctor rubbed his droopy, bloodshot eyes. "I got a little this afternoon."

"And since these two troublemakers are in the worst shape, you're spending your time with them, right?"

"Right. My nurses are keeping check on Zrelak and Molner."

"Well, in my opinion, Zrelak and Molner would get well faster if the doctor would spend his time with them instead of these no-good troublemakers. They deserve to die, anyway. It's their own fault they got shot."

Erik gave him a dry look. "Need I remind you once more of my oath?"

"No. I just think it's warped."

Erik's attention was on the patient. "You're entitled to your opinion."

There was a moment of silence, then Koblin said, "Erik, before I go, I want to say something to you about my daughter."

Metryka's face flashed onto the screen of Erik's mind and intensified the pain in his heart. "Yes?"

"I hope Metryka's jilting you won't make you bitter toward Kathlyn and me."

"Of course not. It's not your fault, nor your wife's. And though Metryka has hurt me deeply, I have no bitterness toward her, either."

Koblin's eyes widened. "You don't?"

"No. And I have none toward Helmut."

The burgomaster shook his head. "I don't get it. Certainly I expected that you'd really harbor some deep bitterness toward those two."

Erik's attention was on his patient again. "When a man harbors bitterness toward someone who has hurt him, Chief Baume, it only dries him up on the inside."

"Well, I'm a bit surprised to hear this, Erik. You'd have every right to want to lash back at them. But I am glad to know your feelings about this. I'll be going. You really ought to get some rest, you know."

Erik nodded. "As soon as I can."

Koblin Baume pivoted and left the room, closing the door quietly.

At the factory office, Durbin Thorpe stepped through the door to find Helmut and Metryka in each other's arms beside her desk. They both looked at him and smiled, but made no move to pull apart.

Durbin chuckled. "You two won't get any work done this way."

"We only took a few seconds to share a kiss," Helmut said defensively. "Up until then, we've both been working hard. We heard you coming, but figured you'd understand, now that you know about us."

Durbin chuckled again, heading for the window. Drawing the curtains closed, he said, "A few seconds, huh? Well, then, I guess that's all right." He headed toward his desk. "You really should have closed those curtains."

"Why?" asked Helmut.

"Anybody who wanted to could have looked in."

"Not without us hearing their approach." Helmut frowned. "You mean the woodworkers, don't you?"

"Yes. Who knows what kind of trouble they're going to stir up next. No sense making targets of yourselves."

"I hadn't thought about it, Father. I really should have been more careful."

Before sitting down at his desk, Durbin said, "You know, I've been seeing love light in the eyes of both of you for quite some time."

"You have, Father?"

"Oh, yes. I couldn't quite put it all together with Metryka being engaged to Erik. I thought you were simply developing a close friendship, but since you broke the news to your mother and me, I understand now. I'm glad you have each other and are planning your future."

Helmut and Metryka smiled at each other.

"Well, lovebirds," said Durbin, dropping onto his chair, "let's get back to our work."

Durbin opened a drawer, took out his revolver, and laid it within close reach on the desk.

As she moved to her own desk, Metryka felt a chill slither down the center of her back. She had an aversion to guns, other than rifles used in hunting game and putting meat on family tables. Revolvers made her uneasy.

Metryka noticed Helmut do the same thing with his revolver as she was sitting down in her chair. Another chill danced down her spine.

Soon, all three were poring over their own paperwork.

Metryka tried to concentrate, but found herself glancing at the guns on the other two desks. The sight of them soured her stomach. Fear crawled into her mind, uninvited, unwanted. The woodworkers had blown up Nidwalden Tunnel in an effort to kill Eiger Wilhaus. When they broke into the factory, they were carrying guns. They wouldn't hesitate to use them again.

The fear that had seized her was like a razor, poised and ready to slice into her rapidly beating heart.

Attempting to ignore it, she put her mind on the work before her.

An hour passed.

Soon the night chill had worked its way into the office. Helmut rose from his desk, stretched his cramped limbs, and set his soft gaze on the woman he loved.

Metryka looked up and twitched her shoulders as a chill ran through her.

"Are you cold, honey?" asked Helmut, which caused Durbin to look up from his desk.

Metryka rubbed her upper arms. "Yes. Very. But most of it is coming from inside my body."

Helmut frowned. "What do you mean?"

Running her eyes to both weapons, she said, "The presence of those guns. The fact you have them on your desks tells me that something is doubtlessly going to happen. It has put a cold fear in my heart that no amount of heat can dispel."

Moving to her, Helmut bent down, kissed her cheek, and said, "Don't you worry, now. Both of us know how to use these guns, so we'll protect you if trouble comes. I'll build a fire in the stove."

As Helmut walked to the stove and began preparations to start a fire, Metryka looked at Durbin. He gave her an assuring smile. "Helmut is right, Metryka. No need to be afraid. We'll protect you."

Forcing herself to put her attention on her work, Metryka did her best to make progress on it. She was aware of Helmut as he got the fire going and went back to his desk.

A short time later, the stove was popping, and the office was becoming cozy with warmth. Metryka looked toward Helmut to find him watching her. She smiled at him.

"Better?" he asked.

She nodded. "The fire has helped to take the chill out of the room. If only something could take the chill out of my heart." A small frown of worry puckered her smooth brow.

It was exactly eleven-thirty when Metryka looked up from her work, glanced at the clock on the wall, and covered a yawn. At the same instant, father and son both raised their heads, setting their eyes on her.

"It'll be midnight soon," she said. "Do you want to keep working, or call it a day?"

"I'll need to go a half hour or so past midnight," said Durbin. "If you and Helmut want to leave, you go ahead."

"I need about that much time, too," said Helmut.

"I'm almost finished with what I expected to get done tonight," Metryka said, rising from her desk. "Since the stove is hot, it won't take but a few minutes for me to make us some nice hot tea."

The hands on the clock were at ten minutes till twelve when Metryka set a steaming cup of tea in front of Helmut, then did the same for his father.

Durbin stretched his arms, yawned, and stood up. "Think I'll take a short break and stretch these legs."

"Not a bad idea," said Helmut, shoving his chair back and standing to his feet.

While both men moved to the open area near the door and window carrying their cups, Metryka sat back down at her desk and set her own cup close at hand. "I'll go ahead and get this last report done."

Lurking in the deep shadows down on the street, Alexander Metternik, Arthur Wengen, and Thomas Allman—guns in hand—were focused on the window of the office. Durbin and Helmut Thorpe were silhouetted sharply against the curtains, sipping tea, with the lantern light behind them.

"See?" said Metternik. "Just like they said in the restaurant—there they are, just the two of them. I told you they would make it easy for us if we remained patient. Let's cripple the factory real good right now."

Up in the office, father and son were facing each other standing about three feet apart, as Helmut asked, "Did you get to talk to Mr. Wilhaus about seriously considering raising the wages so the woodworkers would come to work for us?"

"Yes. He said he would give it some thought."

"Good. I'd think he would rather put out more money than to risk any more problems with Metternik and his bunch. There have been more than enough tragedies already."

"I think he'll come to that conclusion. All the money in the world won't buy back the lives of people who have already been killed, and—"

Suddenly a gunshot pierced the night and the slug shattered the window, passed between them, and plowed into the wall. Stunned, Durbin and Helmut ducked down just as a barrage of gunfire sent bullet after bullet through the window, shattering more glass. The slugs ripped the curtains, making them fly, and chewed into the wall, striking pictures and plaques, which caused some to ricochet and rip into walls and furniture.

Both men were crawling toward their desks to get their guns. They saw a terrified Metryka out of her chair, down on her knees, face white, eyes wide.

"Get down flat, honey!" said Helmut as he grabbed his revolver and began crawling back toward the window.

There was a pause in the gunfire, as the shooters reloaded.

"We'll shoot back from both ends of the window," Durbin said in a low voice. "You take the right. I'll take the left."

Again, shots rang out from the shadows down on the street. More slugs tore through the curtains, hitting the back wall of the office and sending some ricocheting every direction.

Staying low at the window, father and son returned fire, aiming at the muzzle flashes of the blazing guns in the darkness below.

Down in the shadows, Alexander Metternik swore and hissed angrily, "I didn't expect them to have guns!" He fired another shot through the window, and instantly two more shots came from the Thorpes, plowing ground dangerously close.

Allman and Wengen each fired off another shot.

Metternik sent one more slug through the window, "Let's get out of here! The police will come any minute!"

Up in the office, Helmut cocked his ear toward the window. "They're running away!"

"Let them have it!" said Durbin, unleashing rapid shots into the darkness where he could hear pounding footsteps and vaguely make out three forms running down the street.

Helmut did the same as fast as he could cock the hammer and fire.

Suddenly one of the three fleeing shooters let out a cry and went down. The others kept running.

"We hit one!" Helmut shouted with elation. He looked back toward the spot where Metryka had flattened herself on the floor. "We got one of them, Metryka! We got—"

Helmut's words were cut off by the sight before him. Metryka was sprawled on the floor, face down. Between her shoulders, there was a crimson spot spreading on her dress.

"She's been hit!" gasped Durbin, heading toward her.

Helmut reached her first, dropping to his knees. "One of the ricocheting bullets hit her in the back!"

They both saw that Metryka was unconscious and bleeding profusely.

Helmut's face was a mask of horror. "We've got to get her to Dr. Linden!"

Even as he spoke, Helmut let his revolver slip through his fingers and carefully turned Metryka over. Sliding his hands under her body, he hoisted her into his arms and stood up.

Shouts could be heard in the street below.

Durbin rushed to the door and opened it. "Hurry, son! She's in bad shape!"

As Helmut carefully followed his father down the stairs with the limp form of Metryka in his arms, they saw a few townsmen—some with lanterns—gathered around three policemen who were kneeling around the fallen gunman.

One of the townsmen gasped as the Thorpes drew near. "Oh no! Metryka's been shot!"

"Three of them were shooting at us up in the office!" said Durbin. "They hit her! We're taking her to the clinic."

Officer Armant Lefler sprang to his feet. "You must have fired back."

"We did," said Durbin. "Who did we hit?"

"Thomas Allman."

"He dead?"

"No, but he's hit bad. We were about to take him to the clinic."

Helmut was already twenty yards ahead of his father. Durbin ran to catch up.

Lefler said to the officers, "Bring Thomas. I'm going on ahead with them."

At the clinic, Erik had opened up Croft Susack's midsection again, in an attempt to stop the internal bleeding. Amelia Folchert was at his side, sponging blood from around the incision. Louise Levron had been left on her cot in Erik's office to try to get some sleep.

"That had to have been gunfire, Doctor," said Amelia.

"Without a doubt," said Erik. "Apparently the woodworkers have done something else. There'll be someone carried in here shortly, unless whoever got shot was killed."

Shaking his head as he began stitching up the incision, Erik said, "I don't think this is going to help him much, Amelia."

"You've done all you can," replied the nurse.

Suddenly the door came open, and Louise came in, rubbing her eyes. "Did you two hear those gunshots?"

"Yes," said the doctor. "We couldn't tell just where in town they were coming from. When I heard the door open just now, I thought it might be someone bringing in a wounded person."

Looking down at the patient on the operating table, Louise asked, "Were you able to stop the bleeding?"

"Not completely. I'm afraid he's not going to make it."

Suddenly they heard rapid, heavy footsteps in the office, and before Louise could get to the door, it swung open. Officer Armant Lefler held the door open as Helmut came through, carrying the limp, bleeding form of Metryka with Durbin on his heels. Lefler said, "Doctor, some woodworkers fired on the factory office. These three were working late. Metryka was hit."

"Over here, Helmut," said Erik, pointing to an adjacent operating table. "Amelia, finish up here for me."

Amelia, nodded, took the needle and thread from the doctor's hand, and continued making stitches.

Louise moved up quickly beside Erik as he said, "Lay her face downward, Helmut."

Helping Helmut place Metryka correctly on the table, Erik ripped away enough of her dress to get a good look at the wound. He glanced at the face of the unconscious Metryka, which was turned toward him. It was devoid of color, and the deep red of the blood on her dress glared in contrast.

Erik was shocked at the myriad of emotions running through him. He knew at that moment that his love for Metryka had not dimmed at all.

Looking at Durbin and Helmut, he said, "I'll need you gentlemen to wait in the outer office."

"All right," said Durbin.

"My men are on their way with Thomas Allman, Doctor," said Armant Lefler. "There were three gunmen who fired into the factory office. Durbin and Helmut had guns and returned fire. They wounded Thomas, but the other two got away."

At that moment, heavy footsteps thumped on the office floor, and the door of the operating room came open. The two officers came in, carrying Thomas Allman.

Erik said to Louise, "Have them put him on that table over there, and check his condition for me, please."

Louise nodded, met the officers, and led them to the designated table. Erik noticed that Allman was conscious, gritting his teeth in pain.

"Let's go out to the office, men," said Lefler, "so the doctor and his nurses can do their work in here."

All but Helmut headed toward the door and quickly were out of sight.

Helmut set level eyes on the obviously weary doctor. "You must save her life."

Meeting his gaze, Erik said, "I'll do everything I can."

A frown penciled its way across Helmut's brow. "Even though she has left you to marry me?"

At Susack's table, Amelia's head came up, registering shock at Helmut's words. Louise turned around, eyes wide, showing the same kind of shock.

Still looking at Helmut levelly, Erik said, "What Metryka did will have no bearing on my effort to save her life."

Satisfied, Helmut wheeled without another word and joined the other men in the outer office.

Louise resumed cutting away Thomas Allman's shirt so she could assess the wound in his back. It was obvious to her that he had been running away from the gunshots coming from the factory office when he was hit. Over her shoulder, she said, "Doctor, I didn't know about Metryka jilting you."

"Neither did I," said Amelia, resuming her stitching work on Croft Susack.

Erik did not reply. He was too much engrossed in studying Metryka's wound. Bending low over her, he whispered to her as if she could hear him, "Metryka, I will do everything in my power with the help of almighty God to save your life."

Fifteen

While studying Thomas Allman's wound, Louise Levron spoke to Dr. Erik Linden. "Doctor, how bad is her wound?"

"Very bad," responded Erik. "You know what a ricocheted bullet always looks like."

"Fragmented, with several sharp edges."

"And you know what it does when it rips into a person's body."

"Tears it up something fierce."

"Well, that's what this one did. She's torn up bad. It chewed a large hole in her back and lodged itself dangerously close to her heart. I've got to go after it, Louise. You'll have to do what you can for Thomas." He paused, and without taking his eyes off Metryka, said, "Amelia, are you about finished there? I'm going to need your help doing this surgery."

"Just finishing, Doctor," said Amelia. "I'll be right with you."

As Erik was preparing Metryka for surgery, he heard Allman breathing hard and moaning. "Louise, what about Thomas?"

"He is in very serious condition, Doctor."

"How serious?"

Louise turned to look at Erik, noting that he was shaking his head and blinking to clear his vision as he was using antiseptic to clean around Metryka's wound. "I'm concerned for his life, Doctor. I'll do my best, but the wound is bad. The bullet struck him in the back and went almost all the way through his body. It is lodged just under the skin of his chest. He's bleeding profusely internally."

Allman grunted, moaned, and closed his eyes, still gritting his teeth.

For a moment, Louise kept her gaze on the weary physician as he rubbed his eyes again, obviously weary, and obviously deeply concerned about Metryka. A deep sigh that evolved into a low groan pushed past Erik's lips as he looked down at the woman he still loved with all of his heart.

Louise said, "This isn't right, Doctor. You should not be operating on her. You have been here at the clinic, virtually without rest for two days. You are much too tired to take on anything this serious. Your body and your mind are too exhausted to adequately perform surgery on her."

Looking at Louise through tired, bloodshot eyes filled with hurt, he said, "You're right, but I have no choice. Neither you nor Amelia are qualified to do it. You and I both know that Dr. Danzig is in no condition to attempt it. His days of performing surgery are over. If I don't do it, Metryka will surely die."

"But you are too worn out," argued Louise. "Send one of those officers out there in the office to Vaudron to bring Dr. Glynn Domire."

"She's right, Doctor," said Amelia, moving up on the opposite side of the table. "You are much too tired to attempt the surgery. Send for Dr. Domire."

Erik rubbed his eyes and shook his head. "It would take too long. She would die before Dr. Domire could get here. It's got to be done right now."

The nurses exchanged hopeless glances.

"Amelia," said Erik, "bring the scalpels from the cupboard while I have a quiet talk with the Lord."

Erik could hear Amelia's obedient footsteps as he bowed his head with a hand on Metryka's arm and said with his lips moving silently, "Lord, I need Your help. You know Louise and Amelia are right. I shouldn't attempt this surgery in my fatigued condition. But You know I have no choice. Her life is hanging by a thread."

Abruptly a verse of Scripture he had committed to memory many years previously made its way into his clouded mind. Psalm 61:2. "From the end of the earth will I cry unto thee, when my heart is overwhelmed: lead me to the rock that is higher than I."

"Thank You, Lord," he said just under a whisper.

While the nurses looked on, Erik rubbed his palms over his eyelids and the stubble of beard growing on his cheeks. When he looked at Amelia, then Louise, they glimpsed a look of sheer determination in his eyes.

Giving him a nod and a smile of assurance, Louise turned back to her own patient. Amelia reached over Metryka's form, patted Erik's arm, and said in a low tone, "Let's get it done."

Erik looked down at Metryka's ashen features and breathed out the words: "Hang in there, Metryka. With God's help, we can do this."

Taking a deep breath, Erik flicked a glance at Amelia and reached for a scalpel that lay on a tray on the cart next to the table.

A fearful Thomas Allman—lying on his stomach as Louise worked at sponging blood from the edges of his wound—looked up at her and said with trembling voice, "You said you're concerned for my life."

"Yes, Thomas. I had to tell Dr. Linden my honest opinion of your condition. I wish it could have been out of your hearing."

He licked his lips. "You're right. I am going to die."

"Please don't give up, Thomas," she said softly. "I'm doing my best to care for you till Dr. Linden is finished with Metryka and can do the necessary surgery on you."

"It won't do any good," Thomas said flatly. "I'm going to die. I know it."

"Please don't give up, Thomas," Louise said, her own voice quivering.

"I want to talk to the police officers, ma'am," he said weakly. "Now, please. I've got to clear my conscience before I die."

Alexander Metternik and Arthur Wengen huddled in the deep shadows of the woods near Wengen's house.

What little light the stars shed on them revealed fear on Wengen's strained features. "Alexander," he said in a tight voice, "we'll be caught for sure if Thomas is still alive and tells the police who was with him tonight."

"He may have been killed instantly when that bullet hit him, Arthur," said Metternik. "But if not, he won't tell the police who was with him. He has always been a true friend."

"I know, but he really wasn't with us on this idea. We shouldn't have had to work at it to convince him. He was a weak link. You saw how nervous he was. All you had to do was say what you did about crippling the factory right now and he cut loose, wanting to get it over with. If he'd hit one of the Thorpes, it wouldn't have been so bad. But missing them both messed up the whole thing."

"I can't argue with that. It also resulted in his getting shot. But I still say if he's alive, he'll never tell Baume, or any of the police officers, who was with him."

"I sure hope you're right. So what do we do now?"

"Just go home and act like nothing has happened. Our wives won't know the difference, and neither will anybody else. Nobody can prove we were with Thomas tonight."

Visibly shaken, Arthur said, "Right. Then you go home, and I'll do the same."

At the clinic, Louise Levron opened the door of the operating room and called toward the office, "I need you officers back here! Thomas wants to talk to you!"

With that, she wheeled and hurried back to her patient. "I called them, Thomas," she said. "They'll be here shortly."

"Th-thank, you, ma'am," Thomas said, his voice fragile.

Intent on what they were doing, Erik and Amelia heard two officers enter the room and move toward the table where Louise hovered over Allman.

One of the officers said, "Ma'am, Officer Lefler left here a few minutes ago. He's on his way to the Baume home to notify Metryka's parents that she's been shot. Neither Helmut nor his father want to leave."

"I understand," said Louise. "Her parents should know about it as soon as possible."

Amelia watched intently as Dr. Linden began probing through flesh and bone in search of the fragmented bullet that was buried in Metryka's back.

Erik soon found his hands shaking. He stopped probing, laid the scalpel down, and folded his hands, trying desperately to control their shaking.

Amelia's heart went out to him, but she could think of nothing to say.

I'm so very tired, Erik thought to himself. I really shouldn't be doing this. *Also, my emotions are deeply involved here. It isn't good to be doing surgery on someone I still feel so close to.*

He closed his eyes. "Lord," he said speaking just below a whisper again, "help me. I can do all things through Christ which strengtheneth me. Help me, please."

With a hand that seemed to grow more steady, he picked up the scalpel.

Cautiously he continued probing for the slug. While doing so, Erik thought of how Metryka had broken his heart and left him feeling dead inside. How could she have been so deceitful? How could she make a pretense of becoming a Christian and carry it off so convincingly? And how could she so easily destroy their promising future almost without blinking an eye?

Erik paused for a moment and used his upper arm to wipe the haze of fatigue from his eyes. He shook his head in an effort to clear it, then proceeded with his probing.

He heard Allman say, "Mrs. Levron, would you step away so I could talk to these officers, please?"

Louise nodded and moved up beside the doctor as he continued to dig in search of the slug. Amelia was keeping the blood sponged up around the wound and keeping watch on Metryka's eyes in case she started to regain consciousness.

Without taking his eyes off his work, Erik said, "Louise, would you check her pulse for me?"

"Of course, Doctor," said Louise, and took out the pocket watch that she used for that purpose.

One of the officers said, "What did you want to see us about, Thomas?"

The doctor and the nurses could hear every word as Allman said in his frail, shaky voice, "I'm not going to make it. I know I'm not. I...I can't die without clearing my conscience."

He gasped, drew a ragged breath, and gasped again.

One of the officers started to call for Louise, but refrained when Allman said clearly, "It was Alexander Metternik, Arthur Wengen, Croft Susack, and me who put the dynamite in the tunnel."

The officers exchanged glances.

Allman gasped again, swallowed hard, and went on. "Tonight... it was Metternik, Wengen, and I who opened fire on Durbin and Helmut at the factory office. I...I'm sorry Metryka was hit. We didn't know she was in the office."

The officers looked at each other, and one of them said, "Metternik was at the bottom of this all the time. Just as the chief thought."

"He put on a good act," said the other, "but I have felt all along that he was guilty. Like the chief has said several times, if he wasn't actually in on it, he was giving orders."

"Well, this testimony will fix him. Doctor, you and these ladies heard what Thomas said, didn't you?"

"We did," replied Louise.

Allman gasped, drew in a shuddering breath, and raised his head from the pillow. Letting go of Metryka's wrist, Louise moved to Allman's side. He gasped again, arching his back, then went limp, staring vacantly into space.

Louise pressed experienced fingers on the side of his neck, held them there a long moment, then pushed his eyelids shut. "He's dead,

Doctor," she said, then pulled the sheet up and covered his face.

Again the officers exchanged glances, then one of them said, "Dr. Linden, I hope you will be able to save Metryka's life. We'll excuse ourselves, now. We have a couple of arrests to make."

Farina Combray and her daughter were sitting in the parlor when Adolf came in and said, "Well, I found out what all the shooting was about. Durbin, Helmut, and Metryka were working late at the factory office. Three woodworkers opened fire on them from outside, shooting through the window. Seems Durbin and Helmut kept guns in the office, and they started shooting back. The woodworkers apparently got scared when bullets began to come their way and turned and ran. One of them got hit and went down. They've taken him to the clinic."

"Who was it, Papa?" asked Dova.

"Thomas Allman."

"Thomas?" said Farina, her jaw, dropping. "I would never have thought he would be in on something like that. Do the police know who the other two were?"

"No," said Adolf, letting his gaze swerve to Dova. "Honey, I hate to tell you this, but Metryka was hit with a ricocheting bullet. She's at the clinic, and I'm told she's in pretty bad shape."

Suddenly Dova felt a numbness clutch her chest. Her breath was tight in her lungs as she said, "Oh, Papa! That's terrible! I've got to go to her."

Farina moved to her daughter and took her in her arms as Adolf said, "I'll go see how she is, honey. You stay here with Mama."

"No, Papa!" Dova said, shaking her head as tears surfaced. "She's one of my closest friends. I must go to her. Please."

"All right," sighed Adolf. "I'll take you."

"We will take you, Dova," said Farina. "Let's go."

The Combrays moved out the door and hurried through the dark streets toward the clinic.

With the faithful nurses at his side, Erik battled his fatigue in a sincere effort to save the life of Metryka Baume.

Bending over her, he probed deeper and deeper into her back, and finally felt the scalpel touch metal. "I found it!" he said, picking up a pair of forceps. When he had a grip on the jagged-edged slug with the forceps, he laid the scalpel aside and took a deep breath. "Louise, would you mop my brow for me, please?"

The younger nurse wiped his forehead with a cloth, and gave it a final touch by mopping his cheeks.

"Thank you," he said, keeping his attention on the spot where he had a grasp on the slug.

"Anything else either of us can do, Doctor?" queried Amelia.

"Just don't bump the table in any way," he said, bending down closer. "This slug is very, very close to her heart. It's going to be tricky to get it out."

Pinching the slug tightly with the forceps, Erik took a short breath and held it. He blinked at the fatigue-induced haze on his eyes to clear them, knowing he must be extremely careful. The heart was thumping as if it was making a strong appeal for life.

Louise looked at him, wishing he was not so tired. She could see Amelia from the corner of her eye, knowing she was thinking the same thing.

Erik looked at his blood-soaked hands, and squeezed firmly on the forceps. It was a tense moment for himself and the nurses as he began to slowly extract the prickly metal from the depths of Metryka's body. As he was pulling the slug toward him, his hands began to shake, and suddenly the sharp edges of the slug punctured the heart.

The heart ruptured and blood spurted. Erik gasped. "Oh no! Oh no!"

The heart's thumping accelerated for a few seconds, gushing more blood through the punctures then it stopped.

"Oh, Doctor!" breathed Amelia, her face losing color.

Louise felt her own heart pounding as Erik dropped the forceps and began delicately massaging Metryka's heart in a gallant attempt to induce life. His hands trembled as he stopped to see if it would beat on its own.

But the heartbeat was gone.

Erik made another attempt, ejecting a nasal whine as he tried desperately to make it beat again. When he stopped, there was no change. He stared at the lifeless heart in disbelief.

Louise tenderly touched his arm. "Dr. Linden," she said softly, "there is nothing more you can do. Metryka is dead."

Moving up on his other side, Amelia laid a hand on the other arm and said, "You did all you could do, Doctor. She really didn't have a chance, even before you went after the slug."

"That's right," said Louise. "There was too much damage in there. She never could have survived."

Erik's features looked glazed and as unnaturally white as the face of an alabaster figurine. The grief he felt was carved in every hollow of his face.

Looking down at Metryka, Erik felt a wave of nausea wash over him.

She died lost, he told himself. *She died without Jesus.*

His shoulders slumped as he brushed tears from his cheeks.

Suddenly they were aware of Koblin Baume's loud voice in the outer office, and the familiar voice of Officer Armant Lefler saying, "Chief, you have to understand. Dr. Linden and his nurses must not be interrupted during the surgery."

"That's my daughter back there!" boomed Koblin.

"Chief, get a grip on yourself," said Lefler.

"Honey, listen," they heard Kathlyn saying in an attempt to reason with her husband, "if you go back there and disturb Dr. Linden, you could endanger Metryka's life."

"All right, all right!" said Koblin. "But somebody better come out here pretty soon and tell us how she is!"

Louise covered Metryka's face with the sheet. "Doctor, I'll go tell the Baumes."

"Thank you for the offer, Louise," said Erik, slowly shaking his head, "but it's my responsibility."

"Then we'll go with you," Louise said softly.

Both nurses followed him as he headed for the door, his shoulders drooping.

When the three of them stepped into the outer office, the heads of Koblin and Kathlyn whipped around. Durbin and Helmut came off their chairs, and Officer Lefler turned toward them.

The nurses moved up close to the doctor as Koblin stepped forward. "How's my daughter, Erik?"

With chalky face, Erik ran a glance at Kathlyn, who stood a couple of steps behind her husband, then looked into Koblin's eyes. "Met—Metryka just died on the operating table. I did everything I could to save her."

Helmut let out a heartrending wail and his father put an arm around him. Kathlyn broke into sobs, throwing her hands to her face. Officer Lefler looked on in mute sorrow.

At that moment, Dova Combray and her parents came in. They could tell by the atmosphere in the office and Kathlyn's sobbing that something was seriously wrong.

Koblin Baume stood glaring at the doctor, his big body shaking and his eyes round and hot. The fury in him was violent enough for everyone in the room to feel the wash of its force. "Don't give me that 'I did everything I could to save her' drivel!" he roared. "You could have saved my daughter's life, but you chose not to do it!"

Dova let out a sob, her knees going watery. Adolf put an arm around her to hold her up, and Farina took hold of her hand, giving it a tight squeeze.

Helmut could be heard weeping and sniffling as his father spoke to him in a hushed voice.

"Chief, listen to me," Erik said in a low tone. "There was nothing else I could have done for Metryka. The ricocheted slug did terrible damage inside her body and was lodged close to her heart. The heart ruptured as I was attempting to extract the slug. I—"

Eyes bulging, Koblin spat, "I still say you could have saved her if you wanted to! You—"

"Chief, listen to me!" cut in Louise. "Dr. Linden is very fatigued, and should not have had the responsibility of such serious surgery, but he was the only surgeon available to do it. Certainly Dr. Danzig could not have done it. He is not able to perform surgery anymore. Dr. Linden most certainly did everything that could possibly have been done for Metryka."

"That's right," put in Amelia.

Louise stepped to Kathlyn and put her arms around her, trying to give her some degree of comfort since it was not forthcoming from her husband. Kathlyn clung to her.

Koblin's face was beet red. "Erik!" he boomed. "If you hadn't spent yourself taking care of those low-down, dirty woodworkers, you would've been in proper condition to do the surgery on my daughter! You should've let Susack and Sojak die. The world would be better off without them."

Jaws squared, Erik said, "I took an oath when I became a physician, Koblin. I meant it when I said I would do everything in my power to save human lives—and I have done it. I did it in trying to save Metryka. When I probed into the wound, I saw immediately that there was little or no hope to save her. I can tell you now, that no matter what I did, she wouldn't have made it. I am fatigued, yes. My hands were shaky, yes. But I did everything possible to try to save her."

"That's the truth, Mr. Baume," spoke up Amelia.

"You're a lying hypocrite, Linden!" screamed Baume, ignoring Amelia's comment. "You let Metryka die on purpose!"

"I did not."

"Yes, you did! Don't tell me it didn't anger you when she told you the wedding was off!"

Dova's head bobbed at this news.

"It hurt me more than I can ever put into words," Erik said, keeping his voice level. "But I wasn't angry."

"Bah! You let my daughter die because she left you for Helmut Thorpe! It was 'get even' time, wasn't it?"

Erik felt totally defeated. His mind and body were more weary than they had ever been in his entire life. In addition to this, he carried the awful knowledge that the girl he loved died while he was performing surgery on her. He looked at the angry father with bleary, bloodshot eyes and said, "You can think what you want, Koblin, but I know in my heart I did everything I could to save your daughter's life. Her leaving me for Helmut had no effect on my effort to save her."

Koblin only gave him a cold stare.

Erik stepped around him, moved up to Metryka's mother as Louise stood with an arm around her, and made eye contact with her. "Kathlyn, I am so sorry you have lost your daughter. Please believe me. I did everything any doctor could have done to save her life."

Wiping tears, Kathlyn nodded and once more began to sob.

Erik then moved to Dova. Looking at her with misty eyes, he opened his mouth to speak, but the words caught in his throat.

She patted his arm and looked up at him in compassion as tears spilled down her cheeks.

Erik choked, cleared his throat, patted her arm in return, and managed to say, "I...know you and Metryka were good friends. I'm sorry you've lost her."

"There is no blame on you whatsoever, Erik," she said loud enough for Koblin Baume to hear. "No one who really knows you could ever accuse you of letting her die on purpose."

Now blinded by tears, Erik pressed a smile on his lips. "Thank you," he said, then slowly turned. He passed through the door of the examination and operating room, shoulders bent low, and softly closed it behind him.

Sixteen

When the door closed behind Dr. Erik Linden, Koblin Baume stared at the closed door for a long moment. "Helmut, I can't arrest him and prosecute him for letting Metryka die, because I will never be able to prove it. But I'm positive he let her die to get even with her for leaving him for you."

Kathlyn wiped tears and said, "Koblin, you're talking that way because Metryka's death has you terribly upset. You'll feel differently later."

"Never!" he said flatly.

"Well, you're wrong, Chief," said Louise Levron. "I know that wonderful man. He would never purposely let anyone die. I'm sure he was hurt by Metryka when she told him the wedding was off, but your daughter's death was not a result of Dr. Linden's revenge."

"Right," said Amelia. "Don't blame Dr. Linden for Metryka's death. Blame Thomas Allman and the other two woodworkers—whoever they are—who fired those bullets into the factory office."

"These ladies are right, Chief," said Durbin Thorpe. "The guilty parties are those three woodworkers. What they did was nothing short of murder, even if they didn't know Metryka was in the office when they opened fire. They were trying to murder Helmut and myself. You and I are on the same side in this woodworker war, and I respect you, but you are calling Dr. Linden a murderer. He is no such thing."

"My father is right, Chief Koblin," said Helmut. "Dr. Linden gave of himself completely to save every wounded man who was brought in here from the other shoot-out. He was totally fatigued by the time we brought Metryka to him. Metryka's dying was no 'get even' thing. Certainly you will not feel that way when you get over your grief."

Koblin's bushy eyebrows arched. "Get over my grief, Helmut? Never! Erik Linden let my daughter die when he could have saved her!" Turning to his wife, who was still in Louise Levron's arms, he said, "Let's go home, Kathlyn. We'll make arrangements to have the undertaker pick up Metryka's body tomorrow."

Kathlyn was sobbing again.

Louise hugged her. "My heart goes with you, dear."

Kathlyn stroked her cheek. "Thank you."

The Combrays stepped up to the Baumes.

"I'm so sorry about Metryka," said Adolf. "But Koblin, you mustn't blame Dr. Linden."

Koblin stiffened, but did not reply.

Both Farina and Dova embraced Kathlyn, speaking their condolences, then spoke them to Koblin.

Amelia hurried to Kathlyn, hugged her, told her how sorry she was for her loss, and thanked her for not accusing Dr. Linden as her husband was. Kathlyn afforded her a weak smile, but did not comment.

As Koblin ushered Kathlyn toward the outside door, Officer Armant Lefler said, "I'll go with you, Chief." He bid the others good night and followed the Baumes out into the darkness.

Dova looked toward the door where she last saw Erik. "Papa, Mama, I need to go to Erik. He needs comfort."

"It's getting late, honey," said Louise. "Your parents no doubt want to get home. Amelia and I will do what we can to comfort him."

Dova frowned, and suddenly her eyes were brimming with tears. "I appreciate your offer, Mrs. Levron," she said with a grateful smile, "but I really would like to talk to Erik myself." She looked at her parents. "Is that all right?"

"Of course," said Adolf. "We know he means a lot to you because he is your best friend's brother."

"Go on back, honey," said Louise. "If Dr. Linden needs Amelia and me, tell him to let us know. Otherwise, we'll wait here with your parents till you come back out."

"Thank you," said Dova as she beelined for the door.

Turning the knob quietly, Dova looked in and saw the doctor standing over the examining table where Croft Susack lay. She slipped in, closed the door quietly behind her, and before taking another step, she prayed in her heart, *Dear Lord, give me the wisdom I need to help him. Please put the words in my mind that I can speak to him...words that will help soften the blow he has suffered. Help me to encourage him. Not for my sake, but for his, and for Your glory.*

As Dova moved quietly toward Erik, she saw him shaking his head as he was pulling the sheet up over Susack's face. Suddenly sensing her presence, he turned and looked at her. "Dova," he said softly.

Dova's heart went out to him. She beheld a beaten man. There was such anguish in his features that he was almost unrecognizable.

Erik's features were like granite as he said in a choked voice, "Croft just died, Dova. It...it seems my surgical skills were not enough for him." He scrubbed a shaky palm over his eyes. "They weren't enough for Metryka, either."

"No, Erik," she said, moving up close to him. "Don't blame yourself. I'm sure you did everything that could have been done for Croft, and for Metryka too. I heard you tell Chief Baume when you began the surgery, you saw there was little or no hope for Metryka. You said that no matter what you did, she wouldn't have made it."

Erik's face pinched and reddened. Shaking his head, he said, "Little or no hope. But if it was even little hope, there was still hope. I...I failed, Dova. Maybe she could have been saved by a doctor with better skills."

"But Erik, both of your nurses said you did everything for Metryka that could have been done."

Tears bubbled in his eyes. "They were just being loyal, Dova. I'm not the skillful surgeon they make me out to be. I realize that, now. It was my hand that was removing the slug when its sharp edges punctured her heart. Maybe another surgeon with a more skillful hand—"

"Don't talk that way," Dova said, taking hold of his arm. "It wasn't your fault. You did everything possible to save her life. You didn't fail. As far as I'm concerned, you are the best physician and surgeon in all of Switzerland."

Brushing the tears from his eyes, Erik focused on Dova's lovely face. His heart being so heavy with grief, Dova's sweet voice and her comforting words pulled him to her like a magnet. More tears spilled down his cheeks as he folded her in his arms, held her close, and said with trembling voice, "Oh, Dova, you are such a kind and true friend."

While Erik held her, Dova's heart went out to him for the grief he was experiencing. But there was more than his grief in her mind.

In Erik's tight embrace, she found her dreams fulfilled. She was in the arms of the man she loved. She quickly told herself that his feelings toward her were only as a friend, but still…he was holding her. She would grasp any kind of attention that came from him.

After a long moment, Erik released her. As he was brushing tears from his cheeks with the back of his hand, he looked into her eyes. "Thank you for being a true friend."

"Erik, I'm so sorry about Metryka's death. I know you loved her very much. But I'm also sorry for the way she hurt you. I had no idea that she had fallen in love with Helmut. It had to have crushed you when she told you."

Erik drew a shuddering breath. "That it did. But the Lord knows I held no bitterness toward her. I certainly didn't let her die because she had jilted me. That much I can say for certain."

"Chief Baume is being totally unreasonable to accuse you of such a thing, Erik," she said. "Both your nurses told him how unjust he is in this, and so did Durbin, and even Helmut. I hope he thinks it over and realizes how wrong he is."

"So do I, but I don't know if he will ever change his mind."

She patted his arm. "Well, even if he doesn't, you must go on with your medical career in this town. Everyone else respects you and has the utmost confidence in you."

He worked a smile onto his lips. "Thank you."

"I need to go now," she said. "My parents are waiting for me. Oh, yes...Mrs. Levron told me to tell you if you need her and Amelia, to let them know. Otherwise they would stay with my parents till I came out. I...ah...should have told you that when I first came in."

"It's all right. I needed your kind words and sweet voice at the very moment you came in. The Lord sent you to me. Thank you for your concern and for your help."

Seeing the pain in his eyes, Dova said, "I'll be praying for you."

Then rising on her tiptoes, she planted a tender kiss on his cheek. As she was heading for the door, Erik said, "Thanks again."

Without breaking stride, Dova looked back over her shoulder and smiled.

When she closed the door behind her, Erik struggled to speak past the lump that had formed in his throat, and said in a whisper, "Thank You, Lord, for giving me a friend like Dova."

Wearily, he made his way to a small desk that stood next to the medicine cabinet and sat down. Dropping his head into his hands, he allowed his thoughts to go over every procedure he had done during his effort to save Metryka's life.

An anguished moan escaped his lips as he raised his head and looked toward the ceiling. "Oh, Lord, You know I wanted to save Metryka's life. You know I would never have let her die just because she threw me away. I...I wish my hands had been more steady, Lord. I wish I was a better surgeon. I wish—well, wishing won't change anything."

Slowly, Erik lowered his head into his cupped hands atop the desk, and choked on a sob. "Lord, Koblin may infect others in this town with his accusation. Help me to deal with it if he does.

And…help me to deal with the guilt I am feeling. Did I fail? Did I?"

While he wept, Dr. Erik Linden asked the Holy Spirit to comfort him and bring quietness to his soul.

As Koblin and Kathlyn Baume entered their house, Kathlyn said through her tears, "Koblin, I know you're hurting because our precious daughter is dead. Your anger toward Erik is controlling you to the point that you've forgotten that I'm hurting too. You haven't said a word to comfort me, nor even bothered to take me in your arms and hold me."

The big man shook his head. "I'm sorry, honey," he said, folding her in his arms.

Kathlyn burst into uncontrollable sobs, clinging to him with her head pressed against his chest. They held each other for several minutes.

When she gained control of her emotions, Kathlyn said, "Koblin, please don't make this accusation against Erik in front of anyone else. He is loved and respected in this town."

Moving her back so he could look into her eyes, he said, "He won't be loved and respected when I get through with him. He let Metryka die because she jilted him, Kathlyn. Can't you see that?"

"No, I can't. Erik Linden is not a murderer!"

Letting go of her, he turned his back on her. "You're blinding yourself to it! Like I said at the clinic, I can't produce proof that he let her die to get even with her, but I know it's so!" With that, he stomped through the house, entered Metryka's room, and slammed the door.

Kathlyn threw herself on a couch, and once again was sobbing uncontrollably.

Alexander Metternik was lying awake in the darkness while Ora was sleeping beside him. His mind was churning as he thought of Thomas Allman lying in the clinic with a bullet in him. He wondered if he was still alive. He thought of Croft and Bartholomew too.

Hatred boiled up in Metternik's heart as he thought of Eiger Wilhaus, who no doubt lay peacefully sleeping in his bed at the hotel.

Through clenched teeth, Metternik hissed in a low whisper, "It's all because of you, Wilhaus! If I thought I could get away with it, I'd be over there at the hotel right now and blow you into eternity! It was your rotten greed that caused you to build that despicable factory in Chur so you could add to your fortune. You didn't care what happened to the independent woodworkers and their families. All that mattered was your getting richer. If the woodworkers and their families went hungry and lost their homes, what did you care?"

Suddenly there was a loud knock at the front door of the house. Ora stirred in her sleep.

Metternik sat up and swung his feet over the side of the bed. The dim light in the room from the starry sky showed him his robe draped over the back of a chair. While he was donning the robe, the knock was repeated, only louder.

Ora rolled over in the bed, mumbling something sleepily.

"Go back to sleep, honey," he said, and hurried out of the room.

The third knock was heard as Metternik was lighting a lantern in the hallway. Rushing to the door, lantern in hand, he slid the bolt and opened it to find four police officers standing there. Two of them had lanterns.

Officer Nathan Mosford stepped up. He was in a position to block the door from shutting if necessary. "Alexander Metternik, you are under arrest for planting the dynamite in Nidwalden Tunnel and causing seven people to die. You will face seven counts of murder for that."

"What?" gasped Metternik. "I had no part in dynamiting that tunnel! Just because I'm the unofficial leader of the independent woodworkers doesn't mean I sanctioned it, and certainly doesn't mean I had a hand in it personally. You're mistaken, Nathan."

"No, I'm not mistaken," said Mosford, lips drawn into a thin line. "And neither are these other officers. We also know you were one of the three men who fired into the office at the factory tonight. Metryka Baume was in the office with Durbin and Helmut Thorpe, and one of the bullets hit her. She's in critical condition. If she dies, you will have eight counts of murder to account for in court. We are also arresting you for firing into the office with the intent to kill."

Blinking in surprise to learn about Metryka being in the office, Metternik said, "I'm telling you, I had nothing to do with either incident!"

"Oh, but you did," Mosford said stiffly.

"You can't prove it, because it isn't so!" gusted Metternik.

Officer Nathan Mosford gave him a bland look, turned, peered into the dark shadows near a huge tree, and said, "Officer Plante, bring your prisoner over here."

Metternik's eyes flicked to the spot. His heart felt like it flipped over in his chest as he saw the officer move into the light, leading a somber-faced Arthur Wengen, who was in shackles.

Seeing Metternik's widened eyes, Mosford said, "Alexander, Thomas Allman died tonight at the clinic, but before he did, he asked to talk to Officer Plante and myself. He didn't want to die without making a confession of his guilt in the crimes. While clearing his conscience, he told us that it was you, Arthur, Croft Susack, and himself who planted the dynamite in the tunnel and the three of you, minus Susack, who fired your guns into the factory office tonight."

Metternik swallowed hard. His mouth was suddenly dry. "Now look, I—"

"Don't bother to lie about it, Alexander. When we arrested Arthur, he broke down and confessed for you and himself. Like I said, you are under arrest for the tunnel incident and the incident at the factory tonight."

Metternik's face flushed and his hate-filled eyes narrowed on Wengen.

"A couple of us will come in while you put some clothes on, Alexander," said Mosford. "We've got a nice uncomfortable cell ready for you."

All the starch seemed to go out of Alexander Metternik. Nodding solemnly, he backed up so Mosford and another officer could come through the door.

Early the next morning, a weary and solemn Erik Linden entered his parents' home as Brandt met him at the door. The sweet aroma of breakfast cooking met his nostrils.

"Erik, you look like you fought a war all by yourself," said Brandt as the two of them walked down the hall toward the kitchen.

"I feel like it, little brother," said Erik.

As the two of them entered the kitchen, the family was just sitting down to the table. "I was right, Mama," said Brandt. "It was him."

"Oh, I'm so glad," said Mura. "I'll set another place."

Before her mother could get out of her chair, Justina jumped up, saying she would take care of it.

Erik slumped onto his normal chair and sighed.

"Son," said Frederic, "we know about Metryka being shot last night. How is she doing?"

The fatigued young doctor sighed again. "She died, Papa. I couldn't save her."

"Oh no!" gasped Ludwig.

The rest of the family showed their shock by their facial expressions.

"You can tell us about it while we eat, son," said Mura. "I'm so sorry about Metryka. So sorry."

Erik met her gaze silently.

Justina set plate, cup, saucer, and silverware before her oldest brother, kissed his cheek, then sat down at her own place.

Frederic led in prayer, and as the family started eating breakfast, Erik began by telling them of being jilted by Metryka, and how she said she was in love with Helmut Thorpe. The family was stunned.

He went ahead and told them that Metryka had admitted she only pretended to become a Christian to gain his favor, and that she had said she never left her father's philosophy concerning the nonexistence of a heaven or a hell.

"Oh, my," said Justina. "That means—"

"She knows better now," Frederic finished it for her in a sad tone.

When the family adjusted to this shock, Erik proceeded to tell them the whole story of what had happened at the clinic the past two days.

As he closed off, he said, "I haven't left the clinic all that time until a few minutes ago, when Dr. Danzig arrived at Louise's bidding so I could go home and get some rest."

"Son," said Frederic, "do you really feel that Koblin will spread this accusation that you let Metryka die because she jilted you?"

"He seemed quite determined to do so when he left the clinic last night, Papa."

"How could he believe such a thing?" Mura said, shaking her head. "Erik, we know you did everything you could to save Metryka's life."

"For sure," said Frederic.

"Why, that's to accuse you of murder!" said Justina. "Preposterous!"

The boys spoke their agreement.

"I know my family would never think I'd do a thing like that," said Erik, "but that doesn't mean the town will feel the same way when their burgomaster spreads the word."

"Son," said Frederic, "the people of Chur love and respect you."

"But will they when Koblin gets through with them, Papa?"

"Well, the Lord knows the truth, Erik. You must leave this whole mess in His capable hands. He knows that in spite of the fatigue you were experiencing, you did everything you could for Metryka. Let almighty God fight the battle for you. He has the power to protect you and your medical career."

"That's right, honey," said Mura. "The Lord has His perfect plan for your life, and He will see that it is fulfilled."

"And as for Metryka dumping you for Helmut, Erik," said Justina, "the Lord allowed that to happen because He has someone else for you. I know that's not the main thing on your mind, but one day it will be, and that special young lady will come marching into your life. You just wait and see."

"Sis," said Erik, managing a smile for her, "you're a pretty special young lady, yourself." His weary eyes lit up. "Oh! I didn't tell you.

Your best friend and her parents came to the clinic last night. And before they left, Dova came to me in the operating room just after Croft Susack died, and abundantly blessed my heart with the encouragement she gave. She's really a good friend."

"That she is," said Justina. "I know she thinks a lot of you."

Soon breakfast was over, and as everybody was rising from the table, Mura said, "Erik, you're undoubtedly worn out completely. Why don't you just use your old bed here in the house and get your sleep?"

"Thanks, Mama," he said, "but I can make it to my apartment. I'll get a good bath, then sleep till late this afternoon."

The sun was setting in the western sky when Erik awakened in his own bed. Rising, he thanked the Lord that he felt better, then heated water and shaved. He was combing his hair after shaving when there was a knock at the door.

"Why, Pastor Helms!" said Erik at opening the door. "Come in."

As Pastor Trevor Helms stepped into the apartment, Bible in hand, and Erik closed the door, he said, "Your father came to my office and told me the whole story, Erik. He told me you'd be sleeping till sometime this afternoon. I'm glad to see that I didn't awaken you."

"Would have been all right if you had, Pastor," said Erik. "Come. Sit down."

As they sat down on overstuffed chairs facing each other, the pastor told Erik how sorry he was that Metryka had jilted him, that she was shot, and that she had died without the Lord. They discussed the weight they felt in their hearts because Metryka had gone into eternity lost.

Helms then told Erik that Koblin Baume indeed was spreading his accusation all over town.

Erik said, "Pastor, my greatest fear now is that I could lose my practice. Dr. Danzig and I are close to closing the sale of the clinic between us. Koblin's vicious attack on me could ruin it all."

"God might have something to say about that, Erik," said the preacher, opening his Bible. "Let me show you something."

Erik picked his own Bible up off the small table next to his chair.

"Psalm 91:1 and 2," said Helms. "You follow while I read it aloud.

> He that dwelleth in the secret place of the most High shall abide under the shadow of the Almighty. I will say of the LORD, he is my refuge and my fortress: my God; in him will I trust."

Erik nodded. "Yes."

"Erik," said the pastor, "I'm sure you have read this passage many times before, but I want to point out something very special here."

"Yes, sir?"

"First, note the word 'secret.' The secret place of the most High. Psalm 25:14 says, 'The secret of the LORD is with them that fear him.' And, of course, this is speaking of those who know the Lord Jesus Christ as personal Saviour, who have been truly born again and washed in His precious blood."

"Amen."

"So only God's born-again children can know the secret of the Lord, right?"

"Right."

"I mean, you might as well undertake to describe a sunset to a person who has never had their sight, or beautiful music to a person who has never had their hearing, as to talk of God's secret place to someone who is a stranger to His grace and His salvation. The secret place spoken of here is that place of intimate communion and fellowship with our heavenly Father, which puts us under His protective shadow. Even carnal Christians do not inhabit that secret place, because they allow sin in their lives to keep them from it. It takes a close, loving walk with the Lord to dwell there."

"I agree, Pastor," Erik said with conviction.

"Erik, as your pastor, I know you walk close to Jesus. The secret place is a place of nearness to Him. And this puts you under the protection of His shadow. A child walking with you abides under your shadow. You are never far from him. You keep him in sight, within reach. He is ever in your protection. Understand?"

"Yes, sir. It's beautiful."

"Now, here you are with false accusations being leveled against you by Metryka's father. But the Lord knows they are not true. You need not fret yourself about what will happen to your medical career. When a Christian finds God's secret place, he finds the place of eternal calm. You are dwelling in the secret place and abiding under the shadow of the Almighty. There is no other place as safe as this. Just dwell there, and let your Saviour work out His will in your life. In spite of Koblin Baume's untrue accusations, the Lord can and will protect you."

Misty-eyed, Erik set his gaze on the man of God. "Thank you for pointing these things out, Pastor. You have strengthened and encouraged me more than I could ever tell you."

"That's what pastors are for, Erik. You physicians minister to the physical body. We pastors minister to the soul."

"Well, I wish I did as good a job with the physical body as you do the soul."

Helms smiled. "You're an excellent physician, Erik. And don't let anybody tell you any different. Let's pray together."

Seventeen

Dr. Erik Linden stood at the front window of his apartment and watched Pastor Trevor Helms as he climbed into his buggy and drove away. "Bless him, Lord. Thank You for giving me such a wise and tenderhearted pastor."

Turning from the window, he went back to the overstuffed chair where he had sat while talking to the pastor. Picking up his Bible, he turned again to Psalm 91. He dwelt on the first two verses for several minutes, then read the entire Psalm.

Tears filled his eyes when he read in verses 14 and 15 what God said concerning the person who dwells in the secret place:

> Because he hath set his love upon me, therefore will I deliver him: I will set him on high, because he hath known my name. He shall call upon me, and I will answer him: I will be with him in trouble; I will deliver him, and honour him.

"Lord," he said, thumbing the tears from his eyes, "You are so good to Your children. You know this child of Yours is in trouble. Koblin Baume seems set on destroying me. I am also battling doubts about my own surgical skills. You say right here in Your Word that when I call upon You, You will answer me. You say that You will be with me in my trouble and deliver me. I am looking to You for that deliverance. I know from Scripture that You do not always deliver Your children from their troubles immediately, but in Your own perfect timing, You do deliver them. Help me, Lord, to grow closer to You in these trials, and help me to learn from them that I might serve You better. I always want to—"

Erik's prayer was interrupted by a knock on the door. Closing the Bible, he wiped away the tears, rose from the chair, and hurried to the door.

Two lovely faces were smiling at him as he opened the door.

"Justina! Dova! Come in."

As his sister and her best friend entered the apartment, Justina said, "We came to see if you were all right."

Closing the door, Erik said, "I'm much better. The long sleep refreshed me marvelously, and Pastor Helms's visit refreshed me even more."

"Justina thought he had probably already been here," said Dova. "I'm sure he was a blessing to you. He's such a wonderful pastor."

"A blessing he was, and a wonderful pastor he is," agreed Erik.

As the three of them sat down in the apartment's small parlor, Erik said, "Let me show you what Pastor pointed out to me in Psalm 91."

Erik read them Psalm 91:1 and 2, and repeated the pastor's words of comment on the verses.

Both young women were acquainted with the verses, but were very much touched by the emphasis on the secret place where every born-again child of God can dwell safely.

Dova said, "Erik, I have spent time in this passage on many occasions over the years, and I love what Pastor Helms showed you about the secret place. I recall one time that I was meditating on these two verses, and it struck me that not only is the secret place a place of safety, but it is the secret place of God's love. We know God loves lost people and desires to save them, and we know He loves His wayward children who will not dwell as close to Him as they should, but only those children of God who dwell in the secret place can really experience His love to the fullest. It is the secret place of God's love."

"That is so true, Dova," said Erik, noticing for the first time just how beautiful she was.

"We rob ourselves of so much if we don't walk very, very close to Him," said Justina.

"Yes," agreed Dova. "And something else I love in this passage. The word 'shadow.' What a fascinating word! Just think about it. There cannot be a shadow without light. So the secret place is a place of brightness. Scripture says if we walk in the light as He is in the light, we have fellowship with Him."

"That's good," said Justina. "So by dwelling in the secret place, we walk in His light, and at the same time we abide in the shadow of Him who is our refuge and our fortress."

"What a place to be!" Dova said jubilantly. "When I am in my Lord's shadow I can reach forth my hand and touch Him, and I can lift up my eyes and see His wonderful face!"

Erik smiled, shaking his head in wonderment. "Thank God for His marvelous blessings!"

"Yes!" said Dova. "We have such a wonderful Lord!"

"That we do," said Justina, "and He will take care of you, Erik."

Erik smiled.

"Well, Dova," Justina said, rising from her chair, "we need to be going."

Erik walked them to the door, saying how much he appreciated them coming by to check on him.

Justina hugged him tightly. "I love you, Erik, and I am praying for you."

"I love you too, sis," he said. "And thank you for praying."

Justina stepped back and smiled at Dova. "I'll give you permission to hug him too."

The lovely blonde giggled. "I was going to hug him even without your permission!"

Justina laughed, and watched as Dova and Erik embraced.

"I love you too, Erik," she said, as the handsome doctor held her in his arms. "And I'm praying for you."

"I love you, Dova," Erik said softly. "Thank you again for being such a special friend."

While the embrace lasted, Dova desperately wanted to tell Erik she was in love with him but refrained.

As the two young women moved out the door, Dova noticed a look in Justina's eyes which told her that maybe she wasn't fooling her best friend at all. Nothing was said on the subject however as they walked down the street to the corner, then went their separate ways.

The next day, at the graveside service in the Chur cemetery, a minister from a neighboring town was presiding as a large crowd huddled close, making small circles around nearby grave markers. He read two brief passages of Scripture, then commented on them.

The Linden family stayed on the fringe of the crowd, accompanied by the Combrays. From time to time, Dova glanced at Erik, who was standing between his parents. The grief etched on his face touched her heart, and she silently prayed for God's comforting hand on him.

It was a cloudy day, but the clouds in the sky were not as heavy as the clouds in Erik's heart. Metryka had died while he was performing surgery on her. She had taken her last breath and her heart had beat for the final time while he was extracting the deadly bullet from her body.

The minister drew his brief message to a close, and while Kathlyn Baume could be heard sobbing, he prayed over the sealed coffin. He then made his way to the place where the Baumes were seated, spoke some soft personal words of comfort, and stepped aside.

The mourners stood in a long line and passed by slowly, speaking their own words of condolence to the heartbroken parents. The Lindens and the Combrays remained slightly aloof until the last people in line were speaking to the Baumes.

Most of the mourners had left the cemetery, but a few people were huddled in small groups near the coffin, talking in low tones as the Combrays spoke to Koblin and Kathlyn. Some were saying how glad they were that one of the three woodworkers who fired into the factory office had paid with his own life, and that the other two were in custody to face justice for their deed.

When Adolf, Farina, and Dova had spoken their condolences, they moved a few steps ahead and waited as the Lindens spoke to the Baumes.

Kathlyn was dabbing at her tear-filled eyes as Mura took hold of her hand, saying in a low voice how sorry she was about Metryka's death.

Frederic laid a hand on Koblin's shoulder and said, "Chief, my heart goes out to you. I'm sorry about your loss."

Koblin had been staring emptily at the ground and was unaware that it was the Lindens who were bringing up the end of the line. He looked up at Frederic, surprised, then ran his hot glare to Justina, who was next. He focused on Ludwig and Brandt, who stood behind Justina, then set his angry gaze on Erik.

Looking back at Frederic, Koblin spat hatefully, "You're sorry, are you? Well, it was your lying hypocrite son who killed her! You ought to be sorry!"

Heads turned in the groups that stood close to the coffin.

Kathlyn, who was saying something to Mura, stopped and turned to look at her husband.

Koblin rose to his feet, a wrenching combination of emotions on his flushed face. He pointed at Erik. "You filthy murderer! We ought to hang you. My daughter's dead because you let her die! She got wise and dumped you for Helmut Thorpe. You had your revenge, didn't you, Doctor? You could have saved her, but you just stood there in that clinic and let her die"

Erik was aware of the remaining mourners staring at the scene. His heart sank.

"Now hold on, Burgomaster Baume!" countered Frederic Linden. "My son is not a murderer. He did everything to save Metryka's life in spite of the fact that she jilted him. He is a Christian, and an excellent physician. I resent your—"

"Aw, shut your mouth, Frederic!" roared Baume. "I don't care what you resent. It's my daughter lying dead in that coffin, not yours!"

"You shut your mouth, Baume!" came a feminine voice, surprising everybody.

Baume's head whipped around at the outburst with a shocked intake of breath.

Every eye went to petite Dova Combray, who was stomping stiffly toward the burgomaster. Color ran high on her ivory cheeks as she drew up, threading her way between Mura and Frederic Linden and stopping less than a yard from the stunned burgomaster, who looked as if he couldn't believe what he was seeing.

Breath sawing in and out of her throat as her blue eyes flashed fire, Dova looked up at the big man towering over her. "Where do you get the unmitigated gall to accuse Dr. Linden of murdering your daughter? That is the most absurd thing I have ever heard!"

Arching his back, Baume said, "Now, see here, girl, your insolence will not be tolerated! Do you realize who you are talking to?"

"I'm not blind nor deaf! Of course I do. You're this town's burgomaster, and you're Metryka's father. I was Metryka's friend, sir, as you well know. And I'm very sorry that her life had to end so prematurely, but you are as wrong as wrong can be to accuse Dr. Linden of letting her die because she jilted him. Metryka died at the hands of Alexander Metternik, Arthur Wengen, and Thomas Allman! Not at the hands of Dr. Linden. Put the blame where it belongs!"

The small remnant of mourners were looking on wide-eyed, especially Dova's parents and the Linden family. No one had ever seen this side of her before. Erik's heart was banging his rib cage.

"He could have saved her, but he didn't!" boomed the burgomaster. "He let her die on purpose!"

"Nonsense!" blurted Dova. "He's a life saver, not a life taker. Dr. Linden is the epitome of everything a doctor should be. If this is not true, why was he so honored by the University of Bern Medical College? Tell me that. And why did you, Chief Baume, give Dr. Linden the Certificate of Courage and Accomplishment for his outstanding work in Nidwalden Tunnel, where he saved so many lives in spite of severe pain he was suffering from?"

There was a dead silence in the cemetery as Koblin Baume stared down at the small young woman for a long moment, the crowd looking on.

Turning to a stunned Kathlyn, he lifted her by the arm and said, "Let's go."

As Baume led his wife among the grave markers toward the road that ran by the cemetery, Kathlyn looked back at Dova and silently mouthed, *I'm sorry.*

Dova felt a hand touch her arm, and turned to see Erik looking down at her. Suddenly a look of total shock registered on her face.

"Er—Erik," she stammered, "I...I don't know what came over me. I'm sorry. I...I know I've embarrassed you." She bit her lower lip. "I'm normally a shy person. I don't know where I found the words, let alone the nerve to speak them."

Dova's hands went to her temples as she dipped her head. "Oh, Erik, please forgive me for causing a scene. I shouldn't have. Especially at a funeral."

Everyone looked on as Erik took both of her hands in his. "Dova, look at me."

She raised her head and met his gaze with tears in her eyes.

Deeply touched by her bold defense of him, Erik said, "What you did took a lot of courage. I cannot tell you how much I appreciate your loyalty. You really are a true friend."

A shy smile tugged at the corners of Dova's mouth.

Erik folded her in his arms and said, "Thank you for being my ally in this battle."

As Dova silently enjoyed being in Erik's arms, Justina regarded her best friend with a new appreciation. She noted the look of satisfaction on Dova's face and smiled to herself as a knowing light danced in her eyes.

In the days that followed, Erik tried to draw strength from Psalm 91:1 and 2, but was still having an inward conflict. Many times a day, while he was working on patients at the clinic, he found himself thinking about the night he performed surgery on Metryka in the attempt to remove the jagged bullet from her body. He knew he was fatigued to the point that ordinarily he would not have tried to do the surgery, but reminded himself that he had no choice.

But doubts continued to assail him. Did he really do everything that any qualified surgeon would have done for Metryka? Or could he have done more, and saved her life?

With his patients depending on him and needing his undivided attention and loving care, he tried to shake the doubts from his mind. He must concentrate on the work at hand.

Exactly one week from the night Metryka had died on the operating table, Erik lay in his bed with a new moon shedding its silver light through the windows. Try as he might, he could not keep the entire scene from going through his mind.

When the moment of Metryka's death came in his memory, Erik sat up in the bed and said, "Oh, Metryka, how I loved you! No one but God knows the pain and anguish that went through my entire being when you told me you had never really been in love with me. My heart seemed to rip loose from its roots, Metryka. Oh, how cheated I felt, never to have actually been loved by you. And then…then to learn that you had only pretended to become a Christian. And to have you make a mockery of the Saviour's death on the cross for you by faking a profession of faith. It's almost more than I can bear, to think about you dying lost."

Lying down again, Erik buried his face in the pillow. "And dear Metryka, it grieves me deeply that your father really believes that I let you die to get back at you for what you did to me. Never, Metryka. You know me better than that. If somehow we could talk, I know you would tell me you don't believe it."

Once again, Erik could hear the voice of Koblin Baume's accusing words echoing through his head. He put the heels of his hands to his ears as if that would stop Koblin's booming voice from getting through to his mind. But the words kept coming: fierce, cutting, accusing him of something he could never do.

For quite some time, he lay there and did battle with the memories of that awful night in the clinic when Metryka took her last breath, and her heart beat the final time. This kept alive the unpleasant parade of thoughts of the events that followed, which persisted in marching through his brain.

Somewhere in the deep of the night, Erik finally lay still and quiet, and soon began to feel drowsy. An owl hooted in a tree somewhere nearby, and he fell asleep.

It seemed he had been asleep only minutes when Erik's eyes popped open. He was lying on his side. There was someone in the room. He could feel it. Rolling onto his back, he saw her standing at the foot of the bed.

The sight of her tightened his chest with bands of cold iron, flexed the muscles of his arms, and brought ridges to the sides of his neck. Heart thundering, he sat bolt upright. "Metryka!"

Moonlight streamed through the windows, and the shadows in the room seemed frozen. The curtains hung like sheets of lead. His mouth tasted metallic.

The moonlight fell with horrible clarity on the swollen features of Metryka Baume. She was clad in the blood-spattered dress in which she had died. Her lips were black and pulled back over her teeth in a hateful grimace. Every feature was fixed and livid as she set her haunting eyes on him, with nothing but the whites showing. Her whole face wore a ghastly expression of abhorrence as she hissed, "You let me die, Erik! You let me die! Oh, you're right. I know it wasn't revenge for my jilting you that caused it. It was your bungling hands! If you were the surgeon everybody thinks you are, you would have extracted that bullet without puncturing my heart."

Erik's mouth was dry as a sandpit. The white, blank eyes seemed to burn into his brain.

"Who's next, Erik?" Metryka said in ridicule. "Who will have to die next because of your bungling hands?"

Erik suddenly sat straight up in the bed, gasping for breath, a sheen of sweat on his face. "No! No, Metryka! I didn't bungle. I—"

His pounding heart felt like it would rip through his chest as he blinked and rolled his eyes around the room, searching for the accusing specter.

Wiping his face with the sheet, he lay back down. He thought the horrible dream through, hearing again Metryka's accusing words in the chambers of his imagery. Then he thought of his own words to Koblin Baume on the night of Metryka's death: "Metryka just died on the operating table. I did everything I could to save her."

But now, in his bedroom with the haunting nightmare fresh in his mind, he said aloud, "Did I? Did I really do everything possible to save her? Or am I a bungler? Was it my own incompetence that cost Metryka her life?"

Throwing his hands to his face, he wept, and said, "Dear God in heaven, did Metryka have to die because I failed her?"

Rolling his head back and forth on the pillow, Erik heard Koblin Baume's harsh words echo through his mind: "Don't give me that 'I did everything I could to save her' drivel! You could have saved my daughter's life, but you chose not to do it! You're a lying hypocrite, Linden. You let Metryka die on purpose! You let my daughter die because she left you for Helmut Thorpe. It was 'get even' time, wasn't it?"

His reply to Koblin's accusations jumped into his mind: "You can think what you want, Koblin, but I know in my heart I did everything I could to save your daughter's life. Her leaving me for Helmut had no effect on my effort to save her."

But with the cold sweat beading on his brow, the young doctor suddenly found himself plagued with doubt. Did I really do all I could, or was there a subconscious bitterness deep inside me that I allowed to take control? Did I really let her die because she jilted me?

Erik shook his head. "No!" he wailed. "I couldn't have done that! I just couldn't! I took an oath..."

Then his words to Dova after Croft Susack died came to mind: "Croft just died, Dova. It...it seems my surgical skills were not enough for him. They weren't enough for Metryka, either."

Rising from the bed, Erik began pacing the room by the pale moonlight that was coming through the windows. "Lord Jesus," he said, wiping the perspiration from his face, "I just can't believe I held a subconscious bitterness toward Metryka and let her die when I could have saved her. I know I didn't. I know it. The oath I took when I became a physician wasn't just on my lips. It was in my heart. It was in my bones. It was in my very being. Yes, in my subconscious too. I know I couldn't have let her die on purpose."

He stopped pacing, rubbed his temples, and said, "Then, it has to be—"

He swung his gaze to the mirror above the dresser and squinted questioningly at his dim reflection. Moving up to the mirror, he looked himself in the eye. "Then it has to be my lack of skill. That's why Croft died. I was right. My surgical skills weren't enough for him. And...how about Metryka? When I was removing the bullet from her body, was it my fumbling hand that caused her heart to rupture? If...if it was my lack of skill that caused her to die, I should never do surgery on anyone else. I don't deserve to ever hold a scalpel in my hand again."

His body went rigid as he stared at his image in the mirror. Squaring his jaw, he picked up a wooden match that lay at the base of the lantern, struck it, and lifting the glass chimney, lit the wick. Raising the wick so the flame was high, he carried the lantern to the bed stand and picked up his Bible.

Turning to Psalm 91, he read verses 1 and 2 aloud. Tears misted his eyes as he looked heavenward and said with quivering lips, "Dear Lord, as I dwell in Your secret place, I need You as a refuge and a fortress from myself. It's my fault. I should have been able to save Metryka, but I failed. I...I can't give up my medical career, but I must never wield a scalpel again. I must never subject anyone to my surgical bungling again. Oh, help me. Help me."

As the next morning passed while Dr. Erik Linden cared for one patient after another in the clinic, he was taunted with his failure to save Metryka Baume and Croft Susack. Though he quoted Psalm 91:1 and 2 to himself over and over many times while doing his work, he could not shake the conviction that his days as a surgeon were over.

At one point, when he had just given medicine to an elderly man and watched him shuffle out the door of the examination room, he carried the man's file folder to the office and laid it on a small stack of folders on Amelia Folchert's desk.

Running his gaze over the faces of those who sat in the waiting area, he said, "All right, Amelia, who's next?"

"Mrs. Wyant, Doctor," said Amelia. "She's scheduled to have an examination on her hand. You remember—the one she burned with boiling water?"

Smiling at the woman as she rose from her chair, Erik said, "Oh. Yes. Of course. Is it still giving you some pain, Mrs. Wyant?"

"Yes, Doctor," replied the middle-aged woman as she drew up to him. "I think maybe it has picked up some infection since you dressed and bandaged it for me."

At that moment, Dr. Joseph Danzig came in the front door, having just made a house call on an expectant mother. He greeted the patients in the waiting area, then smiled at Mrs. Wyant and greeted her.

As Erik started to escort Mrs. Wyant into the examining room, he paused and said, "Dr. Danzig, I need to talk to you sometime today, if you can spare a few minutes."

"Of course," said Danzig. "We'll find time."

About an hour later, both doctors were working on patients on adjacent examining tables when Louise Levron came in from the office and rushed up to Erik. "Dr. Linden, a farmer just brought in his seven-year-old boy. He needs emergency surgery. The boy fell off the barn roof, and a broken rib has punctured his lung. Amelia looked at him outside in the wagon, and his father is carrying him in now."

Sudden cramps hit Erik's stomach, and he broke into a cold sweat. Turning to Dr. Danzig, he said, "Doctor, I'm not up to doing surgery right now. Do you think you can handle a punctured lung?"

Danzig gave him a puzzled look. "Why, ah…I'm sure I can."

Moments later, with the patient prepared for surgery by both nurses, Dr. Danzig went to work on the boy in spite of the fact that his hands were a bit shaky. When the surgery was done, and Danzig told the nurses all would be well, Erik left the patient he had on the table for a moment, and said, "I'm glad to hear the boy is going to be all right."

"It would have been better if you had performed the surgery, Doctor," said Danzig. "My hands were shaking pretty badly. But, thank God, I was able to get it done."

"Yes," said Erik. "Thank the Lord. Ah…Doctor, you remember I need to talk to you."

"Well, since we have a waiting room full of people, it will have to be after we close the clinic."

"That's fine."

"All right. In fact, son, I've been wanting to have a talk with you, too. We'll take care of both subjects after we close up."

"Yes, sir," said Erik. "That will be fine."

Eighteen

Late that afternoon when the last patients had been seen, the clinic was closed, and the nurses had gone home, the two physicians sat down in Dr. Danzig's office to talk.

Danzig eased into his chair behind the desk, and his partner sat down on a wooden chair in front of the desk.

Looking very tired, the silver-haired physician said, "Well, my boy, what is it you wanted to see me about?"

Erik smiled. "You said you have been wanting to talk to me, so I'll let you go first."

Danzig leaned back in the comfortable chair, nodding. "All right. You and I have talked for better than a year now about the inevitable day arriving when I would step down and sell you my half of the partnership. Well, Erik, that time has arrived. I've come to the place where I know I must retire from practicing medicine. Age has caught up with me, and I simply cannot do it any longer. It is time to enact our plan. You can find yourself a new partner and go on with the clinic's great work. Chur is growing, and your practice will grow with it."

As Erik listened politely to the doctor's words, he was chewing on the inside of his mouth. His nerves tightened and knots were forming in his stomach.

Danzig looked at him expectantly. "Well?"

Rising from the chair, Erik drew a deep breath and let it out through his nostrils. "Dr. Danzig, this brings us to what I wanted to discuss with you."

Danzig raised bushy eyebrows. "Oh?"

Erik began pacing nervously. "Sir," he said, moving his hands in and out of his pockets, "I must explain something to you."

"I'm listening."

"Well, sir, this isn't easy for me, but I have to be honest with my longtime friend and mentor."

"All you've ever been is honest with me, Erik."

"Y-yes, sir," stammered the youthful physician, still pacing. "Today, when I declined to perform the surgery on that little boy, I know it befuddled you."

"To say the least."

"Well, sir, I'm having doubts about myself as a surgeon."

Danzig frowned. "You mean you're letting those accusations Koblin Baume is spreading all over town get to you. Don't let it bother you, son. God knows, I know, and you know that you didn't let Metryka die in order to get even with her for jilting you."

Erik stopped, looked him in the eye, and said, "I had to make sure I didn't have some subconscious bitterness toward her that caused me to just allow her to die when I could have saved her. I've got that settled, Doctor, but my doubts have to do with my own surgical skills, that I don't have what it takes to do surgery. I can't get it out of my mind that I failed in my work and let both Metryka and Croft Susack die by sheer incompetence. And I'm afraid that's exactly what I did."

"Nonsense," Danzig said flatly. "You're an excellent surgeon. You've taken marvelous strides in your surgical work for such a young man."

Erik began pacing once more. "Dr. Danzig, I appreciate your confidence in me, but I can't get over the fact that two people are dead who might have lived if a competent surgeon had operated on them. I failed them. I can never put a scalpel in my hand again. I can do all other things required of a physician, but surgery is out for me. I can never perform surgery again."

Dr. Joseph Danzig rubbed his chin, his eyes following Erik as he moved back and forth like a caged animal. Erik was like a son to him, and his heart was deeply touched as he watched the doctor pace nervously in the room, the look of anguish deepening with each step. "Erik," he said softly, "you are not the first surgeon to have a patient die under the knife and blame himself. I've known of several to have this happen. You have a promising career ahead of you as a physician and a surgeon. Don't let this situation defeat you."

"I can agree with the 'physician' part, sir," said Erik, "but two people dying the same night with me wielding the scalpel is too much. I understand your need to retire, though I wish it never had to happen."

Stopping, he stepped to the desk and looked down at Danzig. "I need to ask a favor of you, sir."

"And that is?"

"Will you stay on here and do whatever surgeries are necessary until I can find a new partner? Then I'll have the new partner do all the surgeries. I simply don't trust myself to hold a scalpel. Therefore, I shouldn't endanger patients by attempting to do surgery on them. Will you grant me the favor?"

Danzig looked at him for a long, silent moment while thoughts were filtering through his mind. He knew the best thing for this young man to do was to get back up on the horse, so to speak. But as he observed the look of fear and determination in Erik's eyes, he knew it was of no use to try to argue him into it.

I'm so tired and ready to retire, he thought, *but with God's help I can go on a little longer.*

Sighing deeply, Danzig rose to his feet and walked around the desk. Giving the hurting young doctor a comforting pat on the back, he looked him square in the eye and said, "Son, I'll grant your request. I'll stay on until you've found a new partner."

A smile of relief spread over Erik's handsome face. "Oh, thank you, sir! I appreciate it more than I could ever tell you."

"I know that," said the aging physician. "But I want you to listen to me."

"Yes, sir?"

"You are an exceptionally talented man, Erik. In time you will overcome your self-doubts, and once again you will be the great surgeon that you have been."

Erik met his tired gaze, but did not comment. In his heart, he was sure it could never happen. He would go on with his medical practice, but a partner would have to perform all of the surgeries.

"Do you have a man in mind for your new partner, Erik?" asked Danzig.

"Yes. I've been thinking about Dr. Glynn Domire."

Danzig's brow furrowed. "But he already has his own practice."

"I think Glynn might be interested though, because Vaudron is such a small town and hasn't grown in size for the last forty years. Chur, on the other hand, is growing. It offers a much better opportunity. I think he'd rather be a partner here with me than to have his own practice in Vaudron."

Danzig rubbed his chin thoughtfully. "You're probably right. So when are you going to talk to him?"

"Tomorrow, if you will handle the clinic by yourself so I can go."

"Of course."

"All right. I'll rent a horse at the stables and ride for Vaudron early in the morning."

As Erik was nearing his parents' house for supper, he saw his father coming up the street from the opposite direction. They met at the front yard at the same time.

"Working a little late, Papa?" said Erik.

"Yes. So did you hear how the trial turned out?"

A blank look etched itself on Erik's face. "Oh! It was today, wasn't it? I've had my mind on so many things, I forgot it was today. So how did it go?"

"Let's go on in. I can tell everybody at once."

The aroma of supper cooking met their nostrils as father and son stepped into the house. Ludwig and Brandt were just coming out of the parlor. Both smiled at them, and Ludwig said, "Just in time, Papa, Erik. Mama just called from the kitchen that supper is ready."

"Oh, there you are!" came Mura's voice from the kitchen door at the end of the hall. "We were about to start eating without you two."

As they moved that direction, Frederic said, "I had to finish up a small job before I could leave."

Mura moved up, kissed her husband, then looked at her oldest son. "And your excuse, Dr. Linden?"

Erik kissed his mother's cheek. "No excuse, Mama. A reason."

"Oh. All right. What's your reason for being late?"

"I had to have a talk with Dr. Danzig, and we just couldn't get to it till after we closed the clinic. It was an important matter and couldn't wait till later."

They moved into the kitchen as Erik was making his explanation.

Justina was setting steaming bowls on the table. Smiling at her father and oldest brother, she said, "Papa, Erik, I'm glad you made it before we started eating. Get your hands washed. Supper's ready."

Moments later, the family was seated around the table. Frederic called on Brandt to offer thanks for the food.

As the steaming bowls were being passed around and plates were being filled, Mura looked at her husband and said, "Honey, did you happen to hear how the trial turned out?"

"Oh. Yes. When Erik and I met up outside, I asked him if he had heard about it. He hadn't, so I said I'd tell everybody at the same time. Metternik and Wengen were convicted on eight counts of murder and sentenced to hang."

"How soon will they hang, Papa?" asked Brandt.

"They will be executed publicly at sunrise tomorrow," said Frederic. "The gallows is already set up on the spot where the new town square will be built."

"I know there has to be progress," said Erik, "but it saddens me that any of the violence sparked by the opening of the furniture factory ever happened. My heart goes out to the woodworkers, but killing people is not the answer."

Everyone spoke their agreement.

"I hope this conviction will send a message to the woodworkers," said Ludwig. "This town doesn't need any more violence."

"For sure," said Justina. "I just wish Mr. Wilhaus would be willing to pay higher wages at the factory so the woodworkers would have jobs and things could settle down."

"I look for the union to come in," said Erik. "That could change things."

"Yes," said Frederic. "For the better, I hope. We all know there has been violence in other parts of Switzerland because of the union, and in many European countries too. I sure hope that won't happen when they come in here."

"Maybe the execution of Alexander Metternik and Arthur Wengen will work as a safeguard against any more violence in Chur," said Mura. She looked at Erik. "This important matter you had to discuss with Dr. Danzig—anything we should know about, son?"

Erik's face lost color. "Well...yes."

"What?" asked Frederic.

Erik laid his fork down. "Actually, Dr. Danzig wanted to talk to me, too. He said he wanted to put our plan for me to buy his half of the partnership into motion. He is ready to retire."

"Bless his heart," said Justina. "He has worked hard all these years. He deserves some rest."

"He does," agreed Erik. "All I did was ask him to stay on with me and do any surgeries that come along until I can get a new partner. I'm going to Vaudron tomorrow and talk to Dr. Glynn Domire about becoming my new partner. I think he will. As soon as he's here, Dr. Danzig can go into retirement. I'll have Glynn do the surgeries, then."

Frederic showed his puzzlement. "I don't understand, Erik. Are you saying you aren't going to perform surgery anymore?"

"Exactly. I can't do it, Papa. Not since I let Metryka die on that operating table. Croft Susack, too."

Everyone at the table looked stunned.

"Son," said Mura, "you did the best you could for both of them."

"I did, Mama. But my best wasn't good enough. I believe a competent surgeon could have saved both lives."

"Erik, you are a competent surgeon!" said Frederic. "You mustn't let these two deaths keep you from saving lives."

Erik shook his head. "No, Papa. I can never perform surgery again. I failed Metryka, and I failed Croft. I can go on as a physician, but not as a surgeon."

Frederic set tender eyes on his oldest son. "Erik, you will get over your self-doubts in time. Don't give up on yourself as a surgeon."

Erik sighed. "I wish I could believe that, Papa, but I don't. I can never use a scalpel again."

"Well, honey," said Mura with a thin smile, "you can't keep your Papa and me and your siblings from praying that the Lord will change that."

Erik managed a lopsided grin. "Guess I can't."

"Well, I'm glad you're going to offer the partnership to Dr. Domire," said Frederic. "I really like him."

The rest of the family agreed.

There was a silent moment while they ate, then Ludwig said, "Erik, I sure hope all this talk that Koblin Baume is spreading won't hurt your practice as time goes on."

"Me too," said Erik. "My practice is in the Lord's hands. I'll just have to trust Him to protect me from Koblin's onslaught."

At sunrise the next morning, Erik swung into the saddle at the stables and trotted the bay gelding toward the west end of town. As he crossed the main thoroughfare, his attention was drawn to a large crowd that was gathered at the open area where the town square would one day be laid out.

Pulling rein, Erik focused on the scene.

A half dozen policemen surrounded the gallows where two ropes dangled from a heavy beam, each with a hangman's noose swaying in the morning breeze. Burgomaster Koblin Baume stood at the trip lever at one end of the platform as two policemen were guiding Alexander Metternik and Thomas Allman up the gallows steps, their hands bound behind their backs. The wives of the condemned men could be heard wailing loudly.

Erik goaded the gelding into a gallop and headed out of town.

By the time Chur was out of sight, the morning sun had risen above the eastern elevations behind the lone rider, sending bright golden shafts to tip the pine trees that surrounded him.

Running his gaze in a panorama, Erik decided it was a beautiful day for a ride. The clear, cobalt sky overhead was dotted with puffy white clouds lazily riding the breeze. The wildflowers were in early bloom, and covered the ground as a colorful carpet. Only a few weeks ago, snow blanketed it all in whiteness.

Birds of various plumage were busy building nests in the trees to shelter their offspring. Their ardent chirping as they called to one another filled the air with a sweet sound of music. Spring green leaves in the birch and aspens made their own statement as they fluttered in the breeze.

After a while, Erik let his mind go to his problems as he kept the horse at a brisk walk. Once again, the horrid moment when Metryka died on the operating table came before him. With it came the guilt that he had failed to save her life, when another surgeon might have done it. While reliving the horror he had felt that night, Erik was oblivious to the beautiful surroundings of the Swiss countryside and failed to appreciate the glorious day that God had created for him.

Erik's mind was dark and heavy with his guilt when the horse stumbled slightly, but it was enough to rouse him from his dark thoughts. Straightening in the saddle, he shook his head as if to clear his mind, patted the horse's neck, and prodded him into a trot.

Looking around him, he was once again struck with the uplifting brilliance of the sunshine, the music of the birds in the trees, the beauty of the day, and the bright colors of the wildflowers that God had given him to enjoy.

"Hey, Erik," he said to himself aloud, "this is the day the Lord has made. Rejoice and be glad in it."

The snowcapped peaks of the Alps came into view in the distance.

"Please forgive me, Lord," he said, looking skyward. "I shouldn't let my troubles get to me so that I fail to see the wonders of Your handiwork all around me. And I mustn't ignore Your great shadow while I dwell in the secret place."

A smile crept over his mouth, and a peace descended on him as he rode on, giving God glory for His goodness.

It was midafternoon when Erik rode into Vaudron and soon drew rein in front of Dr. Glynn Domire's office. Dismounting, he stepped inside and found Domire's nurse smiling at him from behind the desk. There was no one in the waiting area.

"Hello, Dr. Linden," said the nurse warmly.

"And hello to you, Mary," said Erik. "It's nice to see you again."

"How's the leg?" she asked.

"It's healing quite well," he replied.

"I'm glad. And how are things at the clinic?"

"Quite busy. Dr. Danzig and I have little time to get into trouble."

Mary laughed.

"I'm here because I need to talk to your boss. Would there be a time today I could see him?"

"Oh yes. He's in his office right now with a young couple who learned only last week that they are going to have a baby. Dr. Domire is giving them some instructions about prenatal care, and should be finished in a few minutes. His next appointment is in an hour, so there will be time for you to see him."

"Great! I'll just sit down over here and stop bothering you."

"Dr. Linden," said Mary, chuckling, "you are not bothering me."

"You're so kind," he said, heading for the waiting area. "If I fall asleep, wake me when he's ready to see me, all right?"

"All right," she said, shaking her head and smiling to herself.

Erik was reading a Zurich newspaper some ten minutes later when the young couple emerged from Dr. Glynn Domire's private office, thanking him for his help. The excitement of the coming baby showed on their faces.

Mary was about to call Domire's attention to the fact that Dr.

Linden was there to see him when Domire spotted him sitting in the waiting area. "Well, look who's here! The hero of Nidwalden Tunnel."

As Erik was heading toward him, Mary said, "Dr. Domire, Dr. Linden rode here from Chur this morning. He wants to talk to you."

Smiling broadly, Domire said, "Well, come on into my office. It's always a pleasure to be in the presence of such a hero."

Erik looked at Mary, rolled his eyes as he passed her desk, and entered the office ahead of Domire.

Mary giggled to herself as the door went shut.

It was early afternoon the next day when Erik Linden entered the office at the clinic to find Joseph Danzig standing by the desk in conversation with both nurses.

Greeting Amelia and Louise with a warm smile, Erik looked at his elderly friend and mentor and said, "Got time to talk?"

"We can talk right here," said Danzig. "I have filled Louise and Amelia in on what's happening."

"Oh. All right, then. I am happy to announce that the Chur Medical Clinic will soon have a new partner!"

"Wonderful!" exclaimed Amelia. "Louise and I wish our beloved Dr. Danzig would never have to retire, but since it has to happen, we are very happy to know Dr. Domire will be coming."

"Yes," said Louise. "He is a fine man. We will be glad to work with him."

"I'm glad he felt his opportunity was greater here than in Vaudron," said Danzig.

"Me too," said Erik. "He will be coming as soon as he can sell his practice to another doctor. He already has one in mind, and he feels the man will want to do business with him."

"The sooner the better," said Danzig. "This old man is ready to retire."

"Sir," said Erik, "did you explain to these ladies about my not wanting to do surgery anymore?"

"He did, Doctor," said Louise, "and Amelia feels just like I do.

Such talent and skill should not be wasted. We believe that in time, you will be back to the operating table again."

Erik forced a thin smile. "Dr. Domire said the same thing. I don't think so. But I'll be here to handle all other parts of the practice."

Three weeks passed, with Danzig performing what surgeries were necessary at the clinic. Dr. Glynn Domire arrived, and Danzig officially retired. The new partnership was formed with the help of one of Chur's attorneys, and immediately the people of the town made Dr. Domire feel quite welcome.

On the morning of the second day Domire was in the clinic, Dova came into the office with a white cloth wrapped around her left hand. Both doctors were at the desk, talking to Amelia and Louise, and saw her come in.

Moving toward her swiftly, Erik said, "Dova, what happened?"

"I burned my hand cooking breakfast. Hot grease."

"Well, let's go back to the examining room so I can take a look at it," said Erik.

Dova nodded, spoke to the nurses, then said, "Hello, Dr. Domire. Nice to see you again. And welcome. I'm very happy you're here."

"Me too, Dova," said Domire. "These are such nice people to work with."

"All three of them are special," said Dova, as Erik guided her toward the door of the examining and operating room.

Erik sat Dova down on the edge of an examining table, and carefully removed the cloth so he could assess the burn on her hand. After examining it, he said, "This isn't too bad. Are you in a lot of pain?"

"Some."

"Let me give you some salicylic acid mix before I work on the burn."

When Erik had treated the burn with salve and wrapped it loosely with gauze, Dova said, "You're such a good doctor. I hardly felt any pain at all while you were working on my hand."

"I'm sure the salicylic acid helped," he said.

"Some, of course, but it was the tender, capable hands of the physician that really made it feel so good. The same hands that one day soon will be doing surgery again."

"I appreciate your kindness, Dova," Erik said softly. "But I won't ever be able to do surgery again."

"Well, your sister and I don't believe that. Justina and I have spent time in prayer together lately about it."

Erik grinned. "Oh, is that so?"

"Yes, Doctor, that is so. You will do surgery again."

Looking deeply into Dova's blue eyes, he said, "Thank you, Dova, for being such a true and caring friend."

Meeting his gaze, Dova wished she could tell him that what she felt for him was more than friendship, but kept it to herself. *Maybe someday,* she thought.

Nineteen

At the same time Erik was treating the burn on Dova Combray's hand, Durbin Thorpe and his son were at their desks in the factory office looking over applications that had been made by several women who were interested in filling the vacancy left by Metryka Baume.

Holding up one application, Durbin waved it at Helmut and said, "So far, I like this one best. Rachelle Monniak."

"I'm sure she would make a good bookkeeper," said Helmut. "I think I lean more toward her than any of the others we've discussed. Rachelle is—"

Helmut's words were cut off by the sound of heavy footsteps on the stairs outside. When they were on the walkway, Helmut left his desk and headed for the door. Before the knock came, he opened the door. Two well-dressed men came in. One looked to be in his mid-forties. The other, Helmut thought, would be close to sixty.

"Good morning, sir," said the older of the two. "My name is Edgar Folsheim, and this gentleman is Malo Licktin. We are officials of the Grutliverein Labor Union. And you are…"

Regarding them with unmistakable scorn, he said, "I'm Helmut Thorpe, assistant manager."

"We need to see Mr. Durbin Thorpe," said Licktin.

"Bring them in, Helmut," came Durbin's voice, edged with irritation.

Helmut made a silent gesture for them to enter. They quickly made their way to Durbin, offering their hands. Durbin shook them both lackadaisically, and waited for the men to speak.

The labor union officials were used to cold receptions by management, but they would not be denied.

"Mr. Thorpe," said Folsheim, "may I remind you that Swiss government law says we are allowed to make contact with your employees and talk to them about joining the union on factory property."

Durbin said coolly, "You don't need to remind me. It is fresh in my mind daily."

Reluctantly, Durbin and Helmut took the union officials into the workplace of the factory and called a meeting of the employees. Durbin made a brief speech to the employees, advising them that by law he must allow the union officials to speak to them, but added emphatically that they also had a choice whether they joined the union or not. The only stickler was that all the employees had to go one way or the other. If the majority voted to go with the union, all employees would have to do so.

Folsheim and Licktin offered membership in the Grutliverein Labor Union to the factory employees. They explained that if the employees joined the union, it would give the union the power to force the factory to raise wages and improve working conditions.

The union officials answered questions from the floor, and worked hard to convince the employees to unite and join up. They explained that they would return in three weeks. They wanted the men to think it over and come together in unity so their wages and working conditions would be vastly improved.

Durbin Thorpe stepped forward as Folsheim and Licktin were about to leave and told his workers to stay put. He wanted to talk to them before they went back to work.

When the union officials were gone, Durbin told his employees that when Eiger Wilhaus returned to Bern a week ago, he predicted that the union would show up soon, and left instructions for him and Helmut to counter them by telling the factory employees they would be better off in the long run if they refused to join the union. The factory's profits were showing improvement already, and soon their wages would be raised.

Helmut warned the workers of the union dues they would have to pay, whereas if they refused to join the union, one day they would be much better off financially and have no dues to pay. He encouraged them to unite, even as Folsheim and Licktin had said, but they should unite against the union and stick with Mr. Wilhaus in total unity.

There was an uproar of voices, and the Thorpes saw immediately that the factory workers were divided on the issue. Durbin quieted them and said they needed to get back to work.

When the men had gone back to their work, Durbin and Helmut discussed the situation. They knew if the men did not unify, there was going to be real trouble.

The next day, word of what happened at the factory had spread to the independent woodworkers, and Ashton Cray, the man who had replaced Alexander Metternik as leader, called for a meeting in his barn.

Every woodworker was in attendance as Cray stood before them and said, "Men, I learned about Folsheim and Licktin being at the factory yesterday just after noon, so I've had some time to think about it. Here's what I would like to suggest to you. Let's take Eiger Wilhaus up on his job offer, then when we've been hired and the vote comes whether or not to join the union, we'll lend weight to the present employees who want to unionize, and it will be done."

"I agree, Ashton," spoke up Kenyon Hartwig. "Then when the union moves in, everybody will be making decent wages, and we can go on with life as usual."

"Right," said Cray. "So let me hear it, men. Is this what you want to do?"

To a man, they all agreed.

"Good!" said Cray, who was a tall, thin man of fifty. "We'll present ourselves at the factory first thing tomorrow morning, and tell Durbin Thorpe we're taking Wilhaus up on his job offer."

The next morning, when Durbin and Helmut arrived at the factory, they found Ashton Cray and all the other independent woodworkers collected near the gate. Some of the factory employees were talking to them.

Helmut said, "I wonder what this means."

"I have a feeling we're about to find out," Durbin said with an edge to his voice.

As father and son drew up to the small crowd, Ashton Cray stepped up to them and said to Durbin, "I think you know I've taken Alexander Metternik's place."

"I heard that," said Durbin. "What can I do for you?"

"We've all come to take Mr. Wilhaus up on his job offer."

Durbin and Helmut exchanged frowning glances, then Durbin said, "I don't know that the offer still stands, Ashton. I'll have to send him a wire and ask him. I'll do it right away, but it will probably take a day or two to get a reply back. Why don't you come to the office and check with me day after tomorrow."

"Will do," said Cray. "Thanks."

Having heard the conversation, the woodworkers walked away with their leader. The employees who had been in conversation with them hurried into the building.

When the two entered the office, Helmut said, "I don't like the smell of this sudden change of heart, Father. They no doubt know about Folsheim and Licktin showing up here yesterday, and that there'll be a vote when they return in three weeks. Seems to me that Cray and his bunch want to get hired as soon as possible so when it's time for the vote, they will cast their votes to join the union. With their number added to the men who already are for joining the union, they would have a good chance of swinging it."

Durbin nodded solemnly. "I'm sure you're right. I think Mr. Wilhaus will see through it, too."

Two days later, a smiling Ashton Cray entered the factory office and said, "Good morning, Durbin, Helmut. Have you heard back from Mr. Wilhaus?"

"We have," said Durbin, not bothering to smile. "Mr. Wilhaus said he knows why you and your friends suddenly decided to take him up on his offer."

Cray frowned. "What do you mean?"

"Mr. Wilhaus said you're doing this so you can help swing the vote to unionize the factory. Therefore, he has withdrawn his offer."

Cray's face grew mottled. "He's got it all wrong." His tone was short and abrupt. "My men and I are hurting financially and need jobs. That's why we came to accept his offer."

"Well, like I said, the offer has been withdrawn. However, Mr. Wilhaus said to tell you that after the factory employees have voted on the union question, he will consider making the offer again—if unionization is voted down."

Cray stared at him blankly for a few seconds. "Well, thanks for sending the wire." He left the office, dreading what he had to tell his woodworkers.

When the Linden family sat down for supper that evening—with Dova as Justina's guest—everyone saw the glum look on Erik's face.

After Frederic had led in prayer and the food was being passed around the table, Mura fixed her gaze on her oldest son. "Erik, you seem troubled, honey; is something wrong?"

Erik painted a thin smile on his lips. "I don't want to bother you with it, Mama. It's nothing new."

"You talking about Koblin Baume's attack on you, son?" asked Frederic.

Erik nodded. "He's continuing to use his powerful position as burgomaster to talk me down to the citizens of Chur. It's getting worse. Some of my longtime patients are asking for Dr. Domire when they come into the clinic, no matter what illnesses or injuries they have. When Amelia or Louise have questioned them about why they are particularly asking for Dr. Domire instead of me, they make flimsy excuses, but it is quite evident that it stems back to what Koblin is saying."

Dova set compassionate eyes on the man she secretly loved. "Erik, I'm so sorry. It just isn't right that he should be allowed to do this."

Erik shrugged. "He's the top law officer in this town. Who's to stop him?"

"God can," Dova said quickly. "We need to pray hard about it."

"We've prayed a lot," said Mura, "but we need to get more earnest about it."

Dova was directly across the table from Erik. Reaching toward him, she patted his hand and said, "I promise. I'm going to pray earnestly about it. You shouldn't have to suffer for something you didn't do. The Lord will answer in His own way."

"That's right," said Frederic. "If we pray hard enough, the Lord will definitely take care of the matter."

"How do you think the Lord will take care of it, Papa?" asked Justina.

"I don't know, but like Dova said, He will do it in His own way. And that will be the right way."

That night as Erik lay in his bed in the apartment, his heart was heavy over the devastating effect Koblin Baume's vicious attack was having on his medical practice.

"Lord," he said in a choked voice, "what should I do? It bothers me because Glynn is feeling guilty for taking my patients. But it's no fault of his, as I've told him. And You know that it hurts me deeply because these patients are willing to believe what Koblin is saying. My life is miserable, Lord. It's difficult enough to have lost confidence in myself as a surgeon but when even my longtime patients snub me, it's almost more than I can bear."

At this point, a hot lump filled his throat and tears welled up in his eyes. "Lord, it's been going over and over in my mind what Dova said at supper tonight: I shouldn't have to suffer for something I didn't do. And then we prayed You would answer in Your own way. And when Papa commented on it, he said Your way would be the right way. If...if there's something I should do, Lord, please show me. Bring it into my mind. I want to do Your will."

Suddenly a face flashed onto the screen of Erik's mind. His friend, Dr. Kenton Prinoth...

Edgar Folsheim and Malo Licktin returned to Chur as promised, and entered the office at the factory. They were ready for the vote to be taken. Still treated coolly by Durbin and Helmut Thorpe, they were led to the workplace where the employees were called together.

Once more, Durbin addressed the men, telling them things would go better for them in the long run if they voted against joining the union.

The union officials tried not to show their irritation at his words.

Malo Licktin then addressed the workers, saying exactly the opposite of what Durbin had said.

It was Durbin's turn to cover his irritation.

When the vote was taken, the employees were split right down the middle.

Edgar Folsheim turned to Durbin with a grim countenance and said, "We've got a stalemate here, Mr. Thorpe. I'm sure you know the law requires a majority vote one way or the other for the issue to be settled."

"Yes," said Durbin, nodding slowly.

"I would like to address the men."

"The law says I have to let you," said Durbin.

Edgar Folsheim spoke to the factory workers, waxing eloquently, doing everything he could to give them sound reasons why they should vote to unionize.

When he had finished, he ran his gaze over their faces and said, "I want you men to have time to seriously consider what I have just told you. Mr. Licktin and I will come back in another three weeks, and the vote will be taken again."

Dova Combray stepped into the foyer of the apartment building where Erik Linden lived, carrying a shallow pan. In the pan was a chocolate cake, still warm from the oven.

Knowing that the man she loved was suffering at the hands of Koblin Baume, and believing that he was still in love with Metryka's memory, she wanted to comfort him. She climbed the stairs to the second floor and knocked hesitantly on his door. When she heard his footsteps approaching, she put on a happy, smiling countenance, not wanting him to see the heaviness in her heart reflected in her eyes.

When Erik opened his door in response to the knock, a wide smile spread over his face. "Well, hello, Dova! What have we here?"

"I saw Mrs. Levron on the street this morning, Erik. She told me you're still being mistreated by your patients because of what Koblin Baume is doing. I...I thought maybe a chocolate cake would help cheer you up."

"Well, bless your heart," Erik said, his face brightening. "I really appreciate your caring so much about my feelings. Please come in."

A bit off balance at the invitation, Dova said, "Th-thank you, but it...it wouldn't be proper for me to come into your apartment."

A crooked grin captured his mouth. "It is quite proper, young lady, since my sister and brothers are here."

"Oh! Well, of course," she said, stepping in.

Justina, Ludwig, and Brandt were coming toward them as Erik closed the door.

Brandt held out his hands. "I'll take the cake, Dova! It was so nice of you to bake it for me!"

Everybody laughed as Dova placed it in Brandt's hands.

Justina hugged her best friend. "We heard every word that was said, honey, and we really appreciate your doing this for our big brother."

"We really do," said Ludwig. "Especially if we get to eat some of it!"

Dova smiled.

Justina took the pan from Brandt, then turned to Dova and said, "Come with me to the kitchen. We'll make some coffee to go with this treat. You gentlemen sit down here in the parlor. We'll be back shortly."

Not wanting to miss one moment in Erik's presence, Dova looked at him hesitantly, then smiled at him, sighed quietly, and followed her friend. Having seen Dova's expression, Justina grinned to herself.

Twenty minutes later, Erik and his brothers looked up to see the two young women enter the small parlor. Dova was carrying a tray that bore a steaming coffeepot and five cups. The tray Justina carried had five plates piled high with large slices of chocolate cake.

When Brandt dug into his piece of cake, he flashed a smile at Dova. "I'm sure glad you wanted to cheer Erik up!"

Ludwig laughed. "Me too! Anytime you want to cheer our big brother up again, Dova, let us know!"

While the small group ate cake, drank coffee, and talked about various things, Justina managed to watch Dova surreptitiously for signs of her true feelings toward Erik.

When Dova thought no one was paying particular attention to her, she gazed at Erik and allowed a look of pure love to hover in her eyes.

Aha! Justina thought to herself. *I saw it, Dova! Sweet lovesick girl, I think it's time you and I had a little talk. As soon as I can arrange some private time with you, we'll have ourselves a chat.*

A secret smile tugged at the corners of Justina's mouth as she contemplated what magic might be in the air.

The next evening, after a day of being snubbed by more of his patients due to the continual crusade against him by Koblin Baume, Erik arrived at his parents' home for supper. Upon entering the kitchen, he was pleased to find that Dova was once again a guest for the evening meal.

Justina noted the look in Dova's eyes when Erik spoke to her. She would have her private conversation with Dova soon.

While Mura was stirring a steaming pot, she smiled at her oldest son. "Guess what, honey! It's your favorite tonight—chicken and dumplings."

"Well, bless you, Mama," he said, moving up and kissing her on the cheek.

While they were eating, the subject of Koblin Baume's vengeful deeds and their effect on Erik came up.

Frederic said, "Son, I don't know how you can stand it. It has to hurt you deeply when the patients you have taken care of ever since you went to work with Dr. Danzig won't let you take care of them anymore."

"That it does, Papa," Erik said, meeting his father's gaze. "The pain goes pretty deep."

Dova wanted to jump up, wrap her arms around Erik, and tell him she would love his pain away if he would let her. But this desire had to stay in her own heart.

As the meal progressed, Mura noticed that even though she had prepared Erik's favorite meal, he was absently picking at his food and had eaten very little. "Erik," she said, deep lines forming in her brow, "is something wrong with the chicken and dumplings?"

This question captured everyone's attention.

"No, Mama," Erik replied, shaking his head slowly. "I...I just don't have much appetite."

"Honey, I know this Baume thing is bothering you, but you've been eating better than this, even when it wasn't your favorite meal."

Erik sighed, pushed his plate aside, and clasped his hands on top of the table. "I have something to tell all of you," he said in an unsteady voice, "and it isn't going to be easy. I guess now is as good a time as any."

While silent apprehension held the small group in its grip, Erik let his gaze take in each dear face as if he were trying to commit it to memory. When his eyes fell on Dova, they lingered a bit longer, for he saw something in her gaze that mystified him, something he had never noticed before.

Blinking to break the spell that held him, he looked around at the group and said, "All of you know that my life has been quite grievous ever since Metryka died on the operating table and her father started his campaign against me."

Heads nodded.

Erik cleared his throat nervously. "I know you've all been praying that the Lord would stop Koblin from doing this. And you know it hasn't happened. Dova, you said the other night that the Lord would answer our prayers in His own way."

"Yes," said Dova, nodding.

"And Papa, you said whatever way the Lord answered, it would be the right way."

"Of course," said Frederic.

"Well, He has answered in a way I had not even imagined, but in my heart I know it is the right way. I...ah...I'm going to leave Switzerland and go to America."

A shock wave washed over the group.

A small moan of dismay escaped Dova's lips. She quickly covered her mouth with a palm, looking around the table to see if anyone had heard it, but they were so stunned at Erik's announcement they obviously had not.

Finally, Frederic was able to find his voice and say, "Son, how did this come about? Why are you leaving us?"

"Papa," said Erik, "one night when I was praying for God to stop this Koblin Baume thing, He brought someone to my mind, sharp, clear, and in a positive manner." He paused slightly. "My friend, Dr. Kenton Prinoth."

"Yes?" said Frederic, still in shock.

"Dr. Prinoth is now in New York City, working at Ellis Island in New York Harbor."

"This is where they check the immigrants through into the country, isn't it?" said Mura in a weak voice.

"Right, Mama. Dr. Prinoth is one of the physicians who does the medical examinations to see if the immigrants can be allowed into the country. You may recall that he was here for the special—" Erik choked, coughed. "For the special meeting when Koblin gave me the...the certificate."

"Yes," said Frederic.

"Well, at that time, Dr. Prinoth told me he was going to America to become one of the Ellis Island doctors. When the Lord brought him to my mind, I wrote him a letter that night and mailed it the next day. He wrote me right back and told me there is a shortage of doctors at Ellis Island. He gave me the name of the Ellis Island authority to contact if I wanted to come. I did, stating my education and experience, and I was offered a job by wire. I sought counsel from Pastor Helms on this, and after much prayer, I am sure it is God's will for me to leave here and go to work for the United States Immigration Department. This will keep me in the medical work that I love, but it will also remove me from private practice so I will no longer have to face doing surgery."

While the family and Dova Combray were looking at each other, still stunned by the news, Erik said, "I have already sold my half of the clinic to Dr. Domire, and I'm booked on a French ship to America, which will leave La Rochelle, France on August 9. I will depart from Chur for La Rochelle on August 2."

Mura gasped. "Erik, August 2 is only five days from now!"

"Yes, Mama."

"Why...why haven't you told us this before now?"

"Yes, Erik," said Justina. "Why?"

"I felt it was better to get everything settled, then tell all of you just a few days before my departure time. I thought it would be easier on everybody."

Dova's heart was pounding, but she did not let on.

Ludwig and Brandt seemed still in shock.

Wiping tears, Mura said, "Son, I know what the present circumstances are doing to you. I can't blame you for leaving Chur. But I just wish you weren't going so far away."

"Me too," said Frederic. "It will be hard to see you go all the way across the Atlantic Ocean to America, Erik, but I understand that this is probably the only place you can go and still do your medical work without being in a position where you would be expected to perform surgery. But I say again, son, I believe in time that you will be able to wield a scalpel once more."

Justina's voice quivered as she said, "I believe that day will come too, but even then, Erik couldn't practice medicine in Chur anymore because of what Koblin Baume has done."

Erik smiled at her, left his chair, bent down and put his arms around her. "I'm glad you understand, sis."

"We all understand," said Mura, "but it's still going to be awfully hard to have you so far away."

Erik stepped to his mother, leaned over, and hugged her. Kissing her cheek, he said, "My new job gives me a month off annually after I've been there a year, Mama. I'll be home next August to get some more good chicken and dumplings!"

Twenty

In spite of the sadness they felt upon hearing Erik's plans to leave his homeland and go to America, everyone at the table laughed at his comment about returning home for chicken and dumplings.

When the laughter settled, Dova said, "Erik, are you aware that Franz and Elizabeth Vagner live on Manhattan Island?"

The familiar names sparked Erik's interest. The middle-aged couple had been patients at the clinic. They were Adolf and Farina Combray's best friends and faithful members of the church. They had gone to America to live some two years ago.

"I knew they lived somewhere within the five boroughs that make up New York City," said Erik, "but I didn't know any more than that. So they are in Manhattan. And I understand they have a shoe store, just like they did in Chur."

"Yes. My parents keep in touch with them by mail. Their store is doing quite well. They found a good Bible-believing church within a couple of blocks from where they live and are very happy with it."

"Well, I'm glad for them," said Erik. "I'll sure have to look them up when I get settled on Ellis Island."

"That's why I brought them up," said Dova. "At least you'll have friends close by."

"That'll help," said Erik.

"The Vagners' latest letter came just a few days ago. Mama let me read it. In the letter, they told of a recent visit they made to the Statue of Liberty and how much they enjoyed it."

Erik nodded. "I'm looking forward to seeing that statue myself. I'm told it is a sight to see."

"Must be," spoke up Ludwig. "I read that it's three hundred and two feet high, from its pedestal to the tip of the torch."

Brandt's mouth dropped open and his eyes widened. "Three hundred and two feet! Really?"

"Yes."

"Wow! You could see all the way to Europe from that high."

"Well, almost," chuckled Erik.

"Was there anything else of interest in this latest letter from the Vagners, Dova?" asked Mura.

"Yes. They told us if we ever came to New York for a visit, we could stay in their home. Then they jokingly said if I wanted to come and live in America, I could live with them."

"I'm sure they would take you in if you really did move there, though," said Mura. "They are such sweet people. I'm glad you will have them close to you, Erik."

"Yes," said Erik. "And thank you for bringing me up to date on the Vagners, Dova. I'll look them up for sure."

Later that evening, Justina and Dova walked into Justina's room and sat down on the edge of the bed.

Justina sighed and said, "What a jolt! I wouldn't have been shocked at all to hear Erik say he was going to some other city in Switzerland to practice medicine. But America! It's so far away."

Suddenly Dova threw her hands to her face and burst into tears.

Justina's brow furrowed. She put an arm around Dova's shoulders. "Honey, what is it?"

Drawing a shuddering breath, Dova looked at Justina through her tears and said shakily, "Justina, I...I can't stand to see Erik go!"

"Well, sweetie, we'll all miss him, but—"

"May I bare my heart to you?" said Dova, stifling a sob.

"Why, of course. I'm your best friend."

"I'm in love with Erik, Justina! So very much in love with him!"

Justina left the bed, picked up a handkerchief from the dresser, handed it to her friend, and sat down beside her again. When Dova had wiped away the tears from her cheeks, Justina took both of Dova's hands in hers and with a twinkle in her eye, said, "I knew it! I just knew it. You are a pretty good actress, sweetie, but you revealed that love several times when you thought no one was looking. I've suspected it for quite a while. In fact, I was planning on getting you alone and talking to you about it."

Dova sniffed, blinked at fresh tears. "You were?"

"Yes. Of course, this was before I knew my brother was going to America." Justina took a deep breath. "How long have you felt this way toward Erik?"

"I've loved him since I was about twelve years old. Of course, always from a distance. He used to tease me a lot and pull on my pigtails. I loved every minute of it. As the years passed, I fell deeper and deeper in love with him."

Justina squeezed Dova's hands. "Oh, honey..."

"All these years I've carried a torch for him, Justina. Being in your home a lot, I got to know him better, and seeing him at church helped too. And I'll never forget how crushed I was when he started dating Metryka. Then when they announced their engagement, I thought I was going to die. In fact, I almost wanted to die."

"Bless your heart."

"Justina, before he fell in love with Metryka, I used to imagine what it would be like if he fell in love with me and asked me to marry him. I told myself I would be such a good wife to him. And even after Erik and Metryka were engaged, I had the same thoughts, and over and over I had to ask the Lord to forgive me. Erik was going to marry Metryka, and I knew I shouldn't be thinking like that."

"Well, Metryka's gone, honey. I just wish it had been you he fell in love with. He wouldn't have gotten his heart torn out."

"That's for sure. I would never tear his heart out. I love him too much to ever hurt him." Dova paused, then went on. "But to Erik, I'm just that little girl who is his sister's best friend. He doesn't notice me as a woman. Oh, I love him so much! I tried to stop loving him when he became engaged to Metryka. I begged the Lord to take the love I felt for him out of my heart. But He never did, Justina. It's still there right now, and stronger than ever."

Justina let go of Dova's hands and tenderly stroked her cheek. "Honey, with Metryka out of Erik's life, I think it is quite possible for him to see you as a woman. A very beautiful woman, I might add."

"But how, Justina? I can never make him notice me as someone other than that little girl who is his sister's best friend with the Atlantic Ocean separating us."

"Well, honey, I'll tell you this much. Erik thinks an awful lot of you. He brings your name up quite often. Especially since all of this Koblin Baume thing has happened, and you have stood by him in it. What you did that day at the cemetery to defend him really put you high on his list as a true and loyal friend."

"I'm glad for that, but I'm afraid that's all he'll ever see in me—a friend. Especially with him going thousands of miles across the ocean."

"Maybe the Lord has left the love for Erik in your heart, in spite of your prayers for its removal, because He has plans to bring the two of you together."

Dova dabbed at her tears with a handkerchief. "How? He'll be in America. I'll be here in Switzerland."

"Don't ever put a limit on God, Dova," said Justina. "If He wants you and Erik to marry, He can work it out. Just trust Him, and wait on Him."

"Oh, I wish I could tell Erik that I am in love with him," said Dova. "But it's not proper for a young lady to do so."

"You're right. But I could tell him for you."

Shaking her head, Dova said, "No, no. Don't do that. If Erik felt anything romantic toward me, he would show it. He would feel undue pressure if you told him I was in love with him."

Justina nodded. "I understand. I won't tell him. But I wish he could know. Maybe there are feelings in his heart toward you that he just hasn't revealed."

"I'd love to believe that, but if those feelings were there, he would reveal them." Tears were flowing again from Dova's eyes.

Embracing her, Justina said, "Don't give up, honey. Like I said, if God wants you and Erik together, He will work it out. Just trust Him and wait on Him."

"All right," Dova said through her tears. "I'll leave it in God's hands and wait."

"That's my girl," said Justina, easing back and looking into her tear-filled eyes. "I love you, sweetie."

Dova gave her a watery smile. "I love you too."

On Tuesday, August 2, 1892 the Linden family, along with many friends from church—including Pastor and Mrs. Trevor Helms—gathered at the railroad station to see Erik off.

Dova stood beside Justina, and when it was time for Erik to board the train, Dova waited while everyone else embraced Erik and told him good-bye. When it was finally Dova's turn, she moved up to him, feeling like her heart was breaking in two.

Erik smiled at her, and gave her a brotherly hug. Then releasing her, he took hold of her hands and peered into her eyes. "Thank you one more time, Dova, for being such a true and loyal friend. You will be in my thoughts."

Dova unwittingly let the love she felt for Erik surface in her eyes.

He saw it immediately, and thought, *There's that mysterious look again. I'm not imagining it, but I'm not sure what it means.*

Her heart was beating so hard she wondered if Erik could hear it. Squeezing his hands, she managed to say, "I'll miss you, Erik."

Squeezing back, he said, "I'll miss you too."

For the final time, the conductor was calling for all passengers to board.

As Erik let go of her hands and picked up his hand luggage, he saw tears gush into Dova's eyes. She quickly turned away to hide her face.

He started to say something, but decided against it. Saying one last good-bye to his family and the group, he quickly boarded the train.

Justina moved up and put an arm around the weeping Dova.

Having entered the nearest coach, Erik took a seat by a window and waved at the group as the train chugged out of the station. His eyes settled on Dova, who waved with tears coming down her cheeks.

On the night of August 9, Erik came out of a small bookstore at the wharf in La Rochelle, France, and placed the book he had purchased in his valise. The book, entitled, *The Settling of America* was printed in both French and English. He bought the English version, planning to read it on the voyage across the Atlantic Ocean. He knew it would help him to understand much about the country he would soon call home.

He took a few steps from the bookstore and let his gaze run up and down the docks. Gas lamps positioned every thirty feet or so along the way cast erratic ribbons of light across the harbor, dancing among the four ships at anchor. He took in the ship's massive size. It was well lighted, and excited passengers were already moving about on all three decks, looking it over. Two huge smokestacks were belching smoke as the engines in the ship's bowels prepared for departure.

Joining the line of passengers who were in the process of boarding, Erik let his eyes stray to the majestic bow of the ship, and the bold red lettering high up on its side: *F.R.S. VERSAILLES.*

The brochure placed in his hand at the ticket office informed Erik that "F.R.S." stood for Francaise Republique Ship, and that it was named Versailles after the French city where King Louis XIV had his opulent palace in the seventeenth century.

Soon Erik was moving up the gangplank amid chattering passengers, and upon showing his ticket to one of the ship's stewards, was given instructions on how to best reach the third deck where he would find his first-class cabin.

As he was making his way across the main deck toward the stairs that led to the upper decks, Erik saw the greater part of the passengers being directed to the lower part of the ship into steerage, where the poor people would make the journey. He saw fear on many of their faces, and noted that the majority of them were dressed in worn and tattered clothing. Some of the children were frightened and were crying. "Bless their hearts," he said. "They're going to America to find a better life. I hope all their dreams are fulfilled."

Soon Erik was on the third level and made his way to cabin number four on the port side. While he was taking items from his luggage and placing them in dresser drawers, he heard the ship's bell resound across the dark harbor. Even as echoes of the bell were being carried by the breeze into the night, the ship pulled away from the dock and began moving due westward out to sea.

An hour later, passenger traffic on the decks and catwalks dwindled to nothing, and like the rest of the passengers aboard, Erik Linden was bedded down and fell asleep.

When Erik stepped out of his cabin the next morning, the sun was just lifting off the ocean's eastern horizon into a clear blue sky. The only blemish overhead was the coal smoke that rose from the huge smokestacks, roiled into the air over the stern, and lifted skyward. Behind the *Versailles,* the underwater propellers churned the water white, leaving spreading trails. The sea was clear and sapphire blue, and the ocean surface pleasingly smooth.

By the time Erik came out of the dining room after enjoying a delicious breakfast, passengers young, old, and in between littered the decks. Some sat on wooden benches bordering all three decks, some leaned over the rails, and others sat in deck chairs.

Greeting passengers he encountered on his way back to the third deck, Erik was soon at his cabin door. Noting a deck chair close by, he decided he would sit there while getting started on the book he had bought at La Rochelle. Stepping inside while leaving the door open, he picked the book up off the dresser, where it lay next to his Bible. Just as he turned back toward the door, he found a small, wiry man in a white uniform looking at him. Gold epaulets hung from his narrow shoulders. A silver beard ran the fringe of his jaw from temple to temple, and a mustache to match rode his upper lip. Though he was small, there was a definite ruggedness about him and a dogged look in his sea-blue eyes. Erik estimated him to be somewhere between sixty and sixty-five.

Speaking in French the wiry man said, "Good morning, sir. I am the ship's captain, Harve Rochforte." Glancing at the paper on the clipboard he held, he added, "I believe you are Dr. Erik Linden."

Shaking his hand, Erik replied in French, "I am glad to meet you, Captain Rochforte." *This is a crusty old sea-dog ship captain if I ever saw one.*

Looking again at the paper on the clipboard, Rochforte said, "You are from Chur, Switzerland."

"Yes, sir."

"Are you a medical doctor?"

"Yes, sir. I'm going to America to serve as an examining physician for immigrants at Ellis Island in New York Harbor."

"May I ask, Doctor, if you know English?"

"I sure do," Erik answered in English.

"Good!" said the captain in English. "I'm trying to improve my English, so we will use it, all right?"

"Excellent!"

"Fine. Our ship's doctor is an American, Dr. Linden. He was hired by our shipping company about a year ago. He is the one who got me started learning English."

"Where in America is the doctor from?" asked Erik.

"Chicago, Illinois. Like me, he is a widower. His name is Dr. Stanley Miller. I know he will be eager to meet you. Did you have your own practice in Chur?"

"A partnership with one other doctor."

"I see. I want to say that I'm happy to have you aboard."

"Thank you."

"I haven't seen Dr. Miller yet today, but when I do, I'll tell him about you. Like I said, he will want to meet you. Well, I have to meet the rest of my first-class passengers, so I will be on my w—"

The captain's eyes had fallen on Erik's Bible, which lay on the dresser. "I see you are a Bible reader."

"I sure am."

"It looks very much like the Bible my wife used to have."

"You mentioned, Captain, that you are a widower. I gather your wife was a Bible reader too."

Rochforte's throat clogged a little as he said, "My wife and four-year-old son died of a rare fever forty-one years ago, while I was at sea, Doctor."

"I'm so sorry, sir," said Erik. "But I'm glad to know that your dear wife loved God's Book."

"She sure did," said Rochforte, rubbing the back of his neck. "She was a sweet and devoted Christian lady."

"I'm glad to hear it," said Erik. "And what about Captain Harve Rochforte? Is he a Christian?"

The captain's wrinkled features tinted. "Ah...no, sir. My wife became a Christian just before she gave birth to our son. She talked to me about it every time I came home, you know, about being born again and that kind of thing. But, well, I had no interest in it."

"Captain, I'd be happy to show you what the Bible says about it," Erik said.

"Oh. Well, right now, I have to see my other first-class passengers. Nice to have met you, Doctor. You'll no doubt be getting a visit from Dr. Miller."

With that, Rochforte hurried away.

Standing at the door of his cabin, Erik watched the bowlegged captain move along the catwalk and stop at another cabin. "Lord," he said softly, "please let me talk to him some more. I would love to see him come to know You."

That evening as Erik was sitting alone at a table in the spacious dining room, he looked up to see a man in a white uniform approaching.

Erik smiled as the man said, "Dr. Erik Linden?"

"Yes," said Erik, rising to his feet and extending his hand.

Clasping Erik's hand, the man said, "I'm Dr. Stanley Miller. Captain Rochforte told you about me."

"Yes. Glad to meet you," said Erik, estimating Miller to be in his early fifties.

"Same here," said Miller. "I'd like to have some time with you, Doctor, so I can get to know you. Right now, I'm on my way to look at an expectant mother who is having some problems."

"I understand," said Erik. "I'm from Switzerland on my way to live in America. Maybe you can teach me some things about your country."

"Of course. It's a long way to New York Harbor yet. We'll get together. Well, I must go. Glad to have you aboard."

As the days passed at sea, Erik spent a great deal of time sitting on the upper deck in various places, reading his new book. At times he closed the book and his eyes, put his head back, and let the soft breeze and the warm sun melt the cold chunk of ice he had been carrying in his heart since Metryka's betrayal.

He missed his family dreadfully and thought of them often. He missed Dova Combray too, and found her repeatedly on his mind. He kept thinking of the mysterious look in her eyes and the way she squeezed his hand at the railroad station and of the tears she was shedding as the train pulled away.

Once when Dova's lovely face was focused sharply in his mind, he moved his lips silently, saying, "Dova, you are a wonderful girl. You're going to make some man a marvelous wife."

Suddenly, it struck him. As lovely and sweet as Dova was, he couldn't remember ever seeing her with a young man. He wondered why, thinking she should have many prospective beaux.

As he read the book, and the ship carried him closer to American soil, the more excited he became. He was ready for his new job and the new life that lay before him.

One day, he let himself imagine what America was really like. "Lord," he said, "I know You have a plan for my life because I'm

Your child. Help me to be pliable to Your perfect will. Lead me to the church You want me to join, and bless me with Your sweet presence. Use me for Your glory, Lord."

As the sea breeze caressed his face, a gentle quietness filled his heart and mind.

A week after the ship had embarked from La Rochelle, the two doctors finally were able to get together. They struck up a friendship, and talked medicine to their hearts' content. Erik did not share with Miller his aversion to ever using a scalpel again.

The *Versailles* was almost halfway across the Atlantic Ocean when heavy clouds began to build up and the wind was gaining force, producing white caps on the surface of the deep waters.

Erik was walking along the rail on the main deck and studying the coming storm when he came upon an elderly woman who was gripping the rail, trembling, and looking at the approaching clouds with terror in her eyes.

Laying a gentle hand on her arm, Erik said, "Ma'am, I'm a medical doctor. Is there something I can do to help you?"

Glancing at him just enough to get a glimpse of his face, she looked back at the storm, and spoke in a tremulous whisper that Erik could barely hear. "I…I was in a storm at sea a few years ago, Doctor. And…and the ship almost went down. I…I've never gotten over it. I didn't want to make this voyage, but there was no choice. My husband died, and I'm going to America to live with my only son and his family."

"You're alone on the ship?"

"Y-yes, sir."

Erik could tell the woman was on the verge of hysteria. "Come," he said. "Let me take you to the ship doctor's quarters. We'll get you some medicine that will help you."

In Dr. Miller's quarters, the frightened woman was given a strong sedative, and Miller had a woman take her to her cabin. He expressed his appreciation to Dr. Linden for helping the woman.

On the way back from the doctor's quarters, Erik heard a male voice call his name. Looking around, he saw Captain Harve Rochforte standing on the bridge, motioning for him to come up.

The wind was plucking at their clothing and the ship was beginning to roll and sway with the tossing waves as Erik came to Rochforte. "Dr. Linden," said the captain, "I saw you talking to that elderly woman and then take her to Dr. Miller's office. Is she all right?"

"Just frightened of the storm, Captain," said Erik. "She told me she was in a bad storm at sea some years ago, and the ship almost went down. Dr. Miller gave her a sedative and had a lady take her to her cabin. She's all right for the time being."

Rochforte nodded. "Well, it's going to get worse, I'm sorry to say. I've been in many a storm in my years at sea, and this one looks as threatening as any I've ever seen."

"Well, sir, I've already been praying that the Lord will protect the ship when the storm hits and not let it be damaged."

Rochforte scrubbed a gnarled hand over his eyes and said, "I have to admit something, Doctor. Even though I've been a seaman nearly all my life, I still get scared when I see a storm coming on the ocean. More than anything, I fear drowning."

"Well, sir," said Erik, "you would not need to be afraid of dying, no matter how it would come, if you knew the Lord Jesus Christ as your own personal Saviour."

The captain's eyes misted. "My wife used to say the same thing, Doctor."

"She was right. Captain Rochforte, you need to be born again, just like your wife told you. This comes by repenting of your sin and receiving the Lord Jesus as your Saviour. No one knows when they are going into eternity. You need to settle this matter without delay."

The ship suddenly rocked from a huge wave that slammed it on the starboard side. Both men had to grab the railing to keep from falling.

While salty spray struck them in the face, Erik said above the roar of the ocean, "Captain, I'd be glad to sit down with you and talk about it."

Shaking his head, Rochforte said, "No time now, Doctor. Right now the storm is about to hit us in all its fury. I need to be back at the controls. Better get to your cabin."

As Erik made his way down the metal stairs from the bridge, clinging to the railing, he said, "Lord, please let me lead that man to You."

Twenty-one

Within three hours after the heavy clouds were first sighted, the ship was in the midst of a fierce storm. Powerful winds drove the falling rain savagely against the ship. As the ship pitched and bobbed, high seas broke over the bow, sprayed across the decks, and splashed against staterooms, bridge, and wheelhouse.

Captain Harve Rochforte sent out his deckhands and pursers to make sure the passengers stayed off the decks. The first- and second-class passengers were confined to their cabins on the upper decks, and those in steerage were jammed together in the bottom of the vessel.

In the cabin on the main deck, which was both his quarters and his office, Dr. Stanley Miller looked up to see Dr. Erik Linden come through the door, drenched.

"I was just about to send for you, Doctor," said Miller, handing him a towel. "There are already reports of seasick people in steerage, and it won't be long till those on the upper decks will be getting sick, too."

Dabbing at his wet face and hair, Erik said, "I figured you could use some help. Where can I best serve?"

"Steerage," said Miller. "I'll have some of the deckhands make sure you have plenty of water to give the sick ones. You know what vomiting does to dehydrate a person."

"Yes, sir."

"As you probably already know, the ship's sick bay is down on the level of the engine rooms and steerage in the stern."

"Yes," said Erik. "The captain mentioned that when we were talking one day. And as I understand it, only first- and second-class passengers can be treated in sick bay at a time like this."

"Right. The sick passengers in steerage have to stay where they are. I have deckhands down there already as a cleanup crew."

Handing the towel back, Erik said, "I'll get on down there."

"Be plenty careful on the way," said Miller. "It's quite dangerous out there on deck right now."

"Will do," said Erik, and moved out into the storm. He almost ran into two deckhands who were carrying a woman to Dr. Miller's quarters.

When he reached steerage, Erik found that many children and adults were already very sick.

Erik had been working in steerage for some two hours when he was kneeling over a cot, trying to get water down a nine-year-old boy who had been vomiting repeatedly since the storm broke. The boy's parents stood over them, bracing themselves against a steel pillar to keep from falling.

From one end of steerage to the other, infants and small children were wailing, and older children and adults were moaning in agony, wishing the storm would subside so the dizziness in their heads and the nausea in their stomachs would go away.

The moans and wails rose above all the sounds that came from outside of the ship: the constant dashing and splashing of giant waves against the sides of the vessel, and the howling of the storm as the wind surged through the doors.

While putting water down the sick boy's throat, Erik heard the young mother begin to weep and cry out that the ship was going to sink. He looked up to see her husband with his arms around her, and heard him tell her the ship would not sink. But she continued to weep, saying no ship could stand this kind of pounding by a storm.

Looking up at her, Erik said, "Ma'am, your husband is right. The ship isn't going to sink. I was talking to a seasoned deckhand on my way down here to steerage, and he told me there is nothing to worry about. Shipbuilders know the seas often have powerful storms, and they build the ships accordingly. Literally thousands of ships have weathered storms like this for centuries. Please don't be afraid."

At that moment, Erik saw a deckhand coming toward him, doing his best to keep his balance as the ship rolled and pitched.

Bending over him, the deckhand said, "Dr. Linden, my name is Chad Delozier. We need you at Dr. Miller's quarters right now. It is an emergency."

"Someone hurt?"

"Yes, sir. Dr. Miller."

Erik looked at him, eyebrows raised. "Dr. Miller is hurt?"

"Yes, sir. He was on his way from the sick bay in the stern to a stateroom on the second level, carrying his medical bag. I happened to be on the main deck, and saw him as he was climbing the stairs. Just as he reached the second level, the ship pitched severely. The wet deck caused him to lose his footing, and a gust of wind hit him at the same time. Its force drove him into the railing and over it. He fell to the main deck."

"Oh no. Is he hurt bad?"

"He thinks his left shoulder is dislocated, and the arm is definitely broken. One of the pursers and I carried him to his quarters. We laid him on the examining table. Dr. Miller sent me to come and tell you he needs you as soon as possible."

Erik nodded, looked up at the boy's parents, and said, "One of you will need to get more water down him. He will dehydrate if he doesn't get another full cup. It will take time, but keep working at it."

"I will do that, Doctor," said the mother. "And thank you for the encouraging words about the stability of the ship."

Dr. Miller was in absolute agony when Erik Linden and Chad Delozier entered the oversized cabin. Purser Randel LeTreve was standing over Miller. Chad introduced him to Erik, who then quickly moved up beside the table and said, "Chad says your left arm is broken, and you think your shoulder is dislocated.

Through clenched teeth, Miller said, "Yes."

"Well, let's just have a look. I'll do my best not to cause any more pain than is necessary."

Teeth still clenched, Miller said, "How many times have I heard that come out of my own mouth?"

Chad said, "Dr. Miller, I'll look in on you later. If it's all right, I'll go back down to steerage and help the other deckhands with the sick ones."

Miller nodded.

As he opened the door, Chad said, "Take good care of him, Dr. Linden. We need him."

"I'll do my best," responded Erik.

It took only a few minutes for Erik to determine that the shoulder was indeed dislocated, and where the arm was broken. Confirming this to Miller, he told him he would put him under with chloroform and go to work on him immediately.

With the table rocking while the ship rolled and pitched, Dr. Stanley Miller nodded grimly.

While Randel LeTreve looked on, Dr. Linden took a bottle of chloroform from the medical supply cabinet and picked up a folded cloth.

Returning to the table, he set his eyes on the purser and said, "Randel, even though Dr. Miller is going to be under the chloroform, I'll need you to hold him steady for me while I set the arm and the shoulder. Can you handle that for me?"

Randel's eyes widened and his jaw slacked. He swallowed hard. "Y-yes, sir. I'll do my best."

Erik soaked the cloth with chloroform and placed it gently over Dr. Miller's mouth and nose. While he waited for the anesthetic to take effect, his mind flashed back to Metryka and the horror he felt when she died under his hand on the operating table. Again he silently told himself he would never be able to do surgery.

Even as he did, the voice of Dova Combray echoed through his mind, saying she knew he would perform surgery again one day.

Erik shook his head. Several people had told him the same thing. Why was it Dova's voice he heard?

When his patient was under, Erik removed the cloth. "All right, Randel. It's time. I want you to brace one of your thighs against the table to help hold it against the wall, and grip Dr. Miller on his chest, with both hands. Put your weight behind it and hold him as still as you possibly can."

Nervously, Randel took the position described, his hands trembling.

"You all right?" asked Erik.

Randel nodded, licked his lips and said, "Yes, sir. I…I've just never done anything like this before. But I'll do my best."

Placing his hands on the dislocated shoulder, Erik looked at the purser. "Ready?"

"Yes," said a determined Randel LeTreve. "Go ahead."

Erik went to work on the shoulder, and with hands that had put dislocated shoulders back into place before, he soon had it done. In the process, the anesthetized patient jerked and twisted, but the purser held him fast.

"Now the arm," said Erik, releasing a pent-up breath.

Randel watched as Dr. Linden ran his fingers over the swollen forearm, feeling the exact lines of the broken bone beneath the skin, then aligned it with a quick snap.

At the sound of the bone, Randel's knees turned to mush, and his eyes rolled back in their sockets. The anesthetized patient arched his back and let out a moan.

Erik looked up just in time to see Randel collapse on the floor in a dead faint.

Erik shook his head, telling himself he would have to fit Dr. Miller with a sling for his arm and shoulder before he could see to Randel.

When a quarter hour had passed, the sling was in place, and Randel was still out cold. With Miller still under the influence of the anesthetic, Erik covered him with a light blanket, did what he could to stabilize the table against the pitching wall, and knelt beside his other patient.

Gently slapping one cheek and then the other, Erik called Randel's name repeatedly. There was no response. Erik quickly jumped to his feet and went to the medical supply cabinet. In one of the drawers, he found what he was looking for. Moving back to Randel, he knelt down and passed the vial of smelling salts under his nose.

Randel's head rolled back and forth, then in a few seconds he was coughing and sputtering. His eyes came open and took on a wild look as he tried to sit up. Gripping his shoulders, Erik helped him to a sitting position.

Randel blinked his eyes, trying to focus on the doctor's face. "Wha' happen, Dr. Linden?" he asked in a shaky voice.

"You fainted," said Erik. "I guess it was when I snapped the broken bone in the arm back in place."

A sheepish look claimed the young steward's face. "Oh, Doctor, please don't tell anyone I fainted. I would never live it down."

Patting his shoulder, then helping him to his feet, Erik said, "I assure you, Randel, your secret is safe with me."

Randel sat down in a chair, and Erik went back to his other patient. While he was checking the sling to make sure it was right, the door came open, and Captain Harve Rochforte came in, closing the door behind him.

The bowlegged man glanced at a white-faced Randel LeTreve, then hurried up to the table where Dr. Miller lay. "Dr. Linden, Chad Delozier told me what happened. How is he?"

Erik explained what he had to do to Dr. Miller, assuring him that Miller would be all right after his arm and shoulder had healed. It should take about eight to ten weeks.

Rubbing his bearded chin, Rochforte said, "I'm sure glad you were aboard to take care of him, Dr. Linden. Since he will be incapacitated for the rest of this voyage I need to ask if you will do the medical work till we get to New York."

"Be glad to," replied Erik.

"Thank you, Doctor," the captain said with a sigh. "That relieves my mind." He then set eyes on the purser. "What's wrong with Randel? He looks a little peaked."

"I had him holding Dr. Miller down while I put the shoulder and broken arm in place," said Erik. "I think it wore him out."

"Oh," said Rochforte. "Well, thanks for helping him, Randel."

"Glad to do it, sir," said Randel.

Turning back to Erik, Rochforte said, "Dr. Linden, I think the storm is letting up. The wind is dying down, and there's some light showing behind the clouds."

A smile tugged at the corners of the doctor's mouth. "Good. None of us will complain about that."

"Well, I must get back to the bridge," said the captain. "Ah…Dr. Linden, could I get you to come to my cabin for a little while tonight? I need to talk to you. Say…about eight o'clock?"

"Certainly, sir. I'll be there. How long will it take the ocean to settle down once the storm is over?"

"Oh…three or four days."

"Really?"

"Yes. It's a big ocean, Doctor."

Erik grinned. "I know that, but I didn't think it would take that long."

Rochforte chuckled. "I guess we all learn something every day, don't we?"

"I guess we do. See you tonight."

"See you tonight," echoed the captain, and hurried out the door.

At precisely eight o'clock, Erik knocked on the door of the captain's cabin.

Opening the door, Harve Rochforte smiled, and said, "Come in, Doctor."

Erik smelled coffee brewing as he stepped in. Rochforte closed the door and said, "Have a seat there at the table, and I'll pour you a cup of coffee."

When the captain had poured a cup for the doctor and one for himself—placing them in holders that were fastened to the tabletop—he said, "Doctor, ever since our conversation about dying, I haven't had a good night's sleep. I...I want to be ready for death, whenever it might come. I want to know I'm going to heaven."

A wide smile spread across Erik's face. "I've been praying that this would happen, Captain. I'll run to my cabin and get my Bible."

"No need," said the man. "I have my wife's Bible in my dresser drawer. Be right back."

While Harve Rochforte was going after the Bible, Erik said in a low whisper, "Thank You, Lord. You've been working in his heart, and he's ready."

Harve sat down and said, "I've carried this Bible with me all these years, but I've only read in it a few times." He then handed it to Erik.

Accepting it with a smile, Erik quickly opened it to the first chapter of Mark and laid it before him, saying, "Read these verses aloud, Captain. Verse 14 and 15."

Reaching into his shirt pocket, Harve pulled out a pair of wire-rimmed spectacles. "Now after that John was put in prison, Jesus came into Galilee, preaching the gospel of the kingdom of God, And saying, The time is fulfilled, and the kingdom of God is at hand: repent ye, and believe the gospel."

"All right, Captain," said Erik, "there are two commands given by Jesus Christ in verse 15. What are they?"

"Well, the first is to repent, and the second is to believe the gospel."

"Right. Do you know what it means to repent?"

"Yes. Mattie—that's my wife—explained it to me. Repentance is a change of mind that results in a change of direction. Mattie said when a sinner repents before God, he is showing sorrow for the sins he has committed against God and is turning from his unbelief to put his faith in Jesus Christ to save his hell-bound soul. It also includes asking forgiveness for your sin."

Erik grinned. "Sounds like she taught you well."

"Yes, but this stubborn old fool wouldn't do what she told me."

"So I don't have to convince you that Harve Rochforte is a guilty sinner before a holy God."

"No, sir. I know there's a verse in there somewhere that says all men have sinned and come short of the glory of God. Harve Rochforte is a hell-deserving sinner."

"Just like Erik Linden," said the doctor. "If I got what I deserved, I'd be in hell already."

The captain nodded.

"Captain," said Erik, "in Acts chapter 17, we're told that God has commanded all men everywhere to repent. Peter wrote in his second epistle that God is not willing that any should perish, but that all should come to repentance. That's simple enough. According to Scripture, to perish is to spend eternity in a burning hell. No repentance of sin results in eternal hell."

Harve nodded and nervously adjusted his position on the chair.

"Now, what was the second commandment there in Mark 1:15?"

"Believe the gospel."

"That's it," said Erik. "Paul wrote in Romans 1:16 that the gospel of Christ is the power of God unto salvation to everyone that believes. If they don't believe on the Christ of the gospel, they certainly don't believe the gospel."

Flipping a few pages, Erik stopped at John chapter 3, handed the Bible to Harve, and said, "Read verses 17 and 18."

Harve focused on the passage. "For God sent not his Son into the world to condemn the world; but that the world through him might be saved. He that believeth on him is not condemned: but he that believeth not is condemned already, because he hath not believed in the name of the only begotten Son of God."

"Is that plain enough, Captain?" asked Erik.

"Yes, sir. It's the unbelief that condemns a person to hell."

"Right. It's refusing to believe the gospel and to put your faith in the Christ of the gospel that lands you in hell when you die. Now, let's look at God's definition of the gospel, so we know what we must believe to be saved."

Erik went to 1 Corinthians chapter 15 and handed the Bible to Harve again. "Please note that Paul says in verse 1 he is declaring the gospel unto the readers of the epistle. See that?"

"Yes."

"All right. Read verses 3 and 4, Captain. Here's the gospel."

Harve nodded and adjusted his spectacles. "For I delivered unto you first of all that which I also received, how that Christ died for our sins according to the scriptures; And that he was buried, and that he rose again the third day according to the scriptures."

"All right," said Erik. "Paul goes on to declare the good number of Christians who had seen Jesus alive after His resurrection but the gospel we are to believe if we are to be saved is found in verses 3 and 4. Paul also wrote in the epistle to the Galatian churches that there are those who pervert the gospel. He warned that anyone who perverts it will be accursed. That's to be condemned to hell. A gospel perverter is condemned already because he has not believed, remember?"

"Yes."

"Now, Captain, gospel perverters add to it things that are not here, saying it takes other things to bring salvation. Tell me, are your good works in the gospel?"

"No, sir."

"Then living a good life won't save you, will it?"

"No."

"Is baptism in the gospel?"

"No."

"How about religious rites and deeds?"

"No."

"Is there a church in the gospel?"

"No."

"Is there anyone in the gospel other than Jesus Christ?"

"No."

"Then to add anything or anyone to the gospel is to pervert it, right?"

"Yes."

"And what happens to people who teach or believe a perverted gospel?"

"They're accursed."

"Right. So according to the true gospel it was Christ's blood-shedding death on the cross, burial, and resurrection that provides salvation for sinners if they will repent of their sin and believe it. Do you see that?"

"Clearly, Doctor."

"All right. You said your dear wife talked to you about being born again."

"Yes."

"Jesus said we have to be born again to go to heaven. John 1:12 says this happens when we receive God's Son. Ephesians 3:17 makes it clear that we receive Jesus into our hearts. Now let me show you how all of this takes place."

Erik turned in the Bible to Romans chapter 10 and handed it to Harve. "Now read verse 13, Captain."

Again, Harve adjusted his spectacles. "For whosoever shall call upon the name of the Lord shall be saved."

"All right. In order to be saved, Captain Harve Rochforte must repent of his sin, believe that Jesus died on the cross for him, was buried for him, and came out of the grave for him, adding nothing to this. Do you believe that, Captain?"

Tears were welling up in the captain's eyes. "Yes."

"Then what do you have to do to be saved?"

"Turn to Jesus in repentance, acknowledging that I am a lost, hell-bound sinner, ask Him to come into my heart and save me."

Looking him square in the eye, Erik said, "When do you want to do that?"

"Right now!" came the answer.

Then and there, while the *Versailles* bobbed up and down on the restless sea, Dr. Erik Linden had the joy of leading the captain to Jesus Christ. While Harve Rochforte called on the Lord to save him, Erik was praising God in his heart for answered prayer.

Four days after Captain Harve Rochforte became a Christian, the Atlantic Ocean had settled down. Everyone on board was happy that the water was calm.

On the fifth day, Dr. Erik Linden was in the private portion of Dr. Stanley Miller's quarters, checking the sling he had made for the arm and shoulder. They heard the outer door open, and the voice of the captain called, "Dr. Linden, are you in there?"

Excusing himself to Miller, Erik stepped into the clinic area and said, "Yes, sir. What can I do for you?"

"We have a boy in steerage, Doctor, who is having severe abdominal pain. Can you come?"

"Certainly," said Erik. Moving to the inner door, he told Miller he had a boy in steerage to look at and would see him later.

Arriving in steerage with the captain at his side, Erik found a seven-year-old boy in a great deal of pain. When he had examined him with his parents and the captain looking on, he felt a coldness wash over him like an icy ocean wave.

"What is it, Doctor?" asked the boy's father.

"Appendicitis, sir," replied Erik.

"You can operate, can't you?" asked the mother.

Now it was cold chills dancing down the doctor's backbone. Swallowing hard, he said, "Y-yes, ma'am. The surgery must be done immediately. If not—"

"The appendix could rupture and kill him," said the father, finishing it for him.

Erik nodded. He had his medical bag with him, but upon leaving Chur, he had purposely avoided putting scalpels in. To the captain, he said, "I need to get him up to Dr. Miller's office quickly."

Fifteen minutes later, with the boy's parents sitting in the office part of the ship doctor's oversized quarters, Dr. Erik Linden administered ether to the boy in the examining room while Captain Harve Rochforte was washing his hands thoroughly in hot, soapy water in order to comply with the doctor's request for help while performing the surgery.

Soon the boy's eyes closed, his tense body began to relax, and his rapid breathing became slow and regular.

Erik's heart was banging his ribs so hard he could feel it throb through his whole body. A mental picture of Metryka lying on the operating table at the Chur clinic tried to force its way into his mind, but he prayed in his heart, *Lord, please take it away! I must have no distraction. This boy will die if I don't open him up right now. Help me. Help me.*

Suddenly, another picture took its place. It was Dova Combray smiling at him. He beheld the confident look in her eyes, as she said, "You can do it, Erik. I believe in you."

Erik took a deep breath, looked at Rochforte, and said, "Captain, I explained how you are to sponge up the blood around the incision."

"Yes." Harve nodded. "I'll do my best."

Erik managed to form a smile, nodded, then began feeling the boy's rigid abdomen for the appropriate place to make the incision. Picking up a scalpel, he said in his heart, *I can do all things through Christ which strengtheneth me. Help me, Lord. Take these hands. Please guide them to perform correctly. Calm my pounding heart. Help me to save this boy's life.*

A calmness descended over Dr. Erik Linden's entire being, and he quickly made the incision with a steady hand.

An hour had passed when the anxious parents looked up to see the doctor and the captain emerge from the examination room.

A relaxed smile graced Dr. Erik Linden's face as he said, "Your son will be fine. The surgery went well. He'll be up and moving around in a few days."

That night as Erik lay in his bed, he said, "Lord, I want to thank You once again for helping me as I did the appendectomy. You know the vow I had taken with myself that I would never attempt to perform surgery again. Praise Your precious, wonderful name! I really can do all things through You."

His mind went to Dova. He could almost hear her saying, "See? I told you!"

Smiling to himself in the darkness, he said, "Dova, I really miss you. You are the sweetest—" Erik clamped a hand over his mouth. *What was I about to say?*

His mind was spinning. He had always thought of Dova as just a good friend, but at that moment, he pictured her in a totally different light.

Two days later, Erik was in the captain's quarters, giving him Scriptures to help him grow in his newfound life, when a knock came at the door.

Opening the door, the captain found Chad Delozier looking at him with worried eyes. "Yes, Chad?"

"Captain," said Chad, "I was told Dr. Linden is here."

"I am," said Erik, moving up beside the captain. "What can I do for you?"

"We need you at cabin number 127 right now," said the deckhand. "Mrs. Storel has been having some problems with her pregnancy. Dr. Miller was keeping check on her before he fell. I think she is about to have her baby."

When Erik and the captain arrived at cabin 127 on the second level, they found Paula Storel's husband in a terrible state.

While Paula lay on the cabin bed, moaning in pain, Jacque Storel wrung his hands nervously and explained to Dr. Linden that their doctor in France told them Paula would have to have her baby by cesarean section because of the unusual bone structure of her hips. He approved of the ocean voyage though, thinking she would go full term, which was some six weeks away. They had planned to be in Philadelphia, Pennsylvania, with Paula under the care of a new doctor long before the baby was born.

Erik quickly examined Paula while Jacque and the captain waited on the catwalk outside, then went to them and said, "Mr. Storel, this early labor was probably caused by the storm we had a few days ago. She was no doubt jostled quite a bit when the ship was pitching and bobbing on the rough sea."

"It was a little more than that, Doctor," said Jacque. "Paula actually stumbled and fell here in the cabin during the storm, but she seemed all right afterward."

Erik turned and looked at Paula writhing in pain on the bed. "I must do the surgery immediately, Mr. Storel. Captain Rochforte helped me do surgery on a boy a couple of days ago. Is it all right if I have him help me on your wife?"

"Of course, Doctor," said Jacque, wringing his hands.

"All right. We need to get her to Dr. Miller's quarters right now."

Moments later, as Dr. Erik Linden was preparing to do the cesarean section on Paula in the clinic area of the ship doctor's quarters, he realized he was once again in a position he could not avoid. He must do the surgery immediately, or mother and child would both die.

With a prayer in his heart, he began the operation with the sweet voice of Dova Combray at the back of his mind, telling him he would soon be over the fear.

When the surgery was done, Erik thanked God in his heart. The cesarean section was flawless, and he had delivered a small but healthy baby girl. Both mother and father were pleased with the doctor's work and were thrilled to hold their first child in their arms.

Some three hours after the baby's birth, Dr. Linden returned to the examination room to find Paula holding the tiny baby close to her heart and the proud father standing beside the table.

As Erik stood next to Jacque, Paula with tears in her eyes lifted a hand to clasp the doctor's. "Thank you, Dr. Linden," she said. "You did a wonderful job."

"With God's help, Mrs. Storel," Erik said humbly. "I'm thankful He could use me to do what had to be done."

When Paula released his hand, Erik bent over and ran the back of his hand along the sleeping baby girl's soft, silky cheek. As he did so, he spoke to the Lord in his heart. *Dear Jesus, thank You for guiding my hands again, and for getting me beyond my fear of ever performing surgery again.*

After spending a few more moments with the Storels, Erik told them he would be back in a little while to check on mother and baby again, and stepped out onto the deck.

The lowering sun was turning the western part of the ocean a bright golden hue.

Drinking in its indescribable beauty, Erik stood there and quickly found himself reliving the moment that Metryka had died on the operating table. "Thank You, Lord," he said quietly. "Now I know I did everything I could to save Metryka's life."

A huge sigh of relief escaped his lips as he headed for the stairs that led up to the third level. "Dova, I wish you could know about the two operations I did today. If you knew, I can just hear what you would say: 'I told you so!'"

Climbing the stairs, Erik decided he could do surgery on a regular basis again, and told himself he would go on and take the job at Ellis Island, but that one day, he would open his private practice somewhere in America.

Twenty-two

At the Grutliverein Union headquarters in Zurich, first vice president Henry Wimms looked up from the papers he was studying at his desk as his secretary came in from the outer office. She was carrying a yellow envelope, which was still sealed.

"Yes, Helna?"

Drawing up to the desk, she said, "Since Mr. Safford is not here, sir, I thought you should see this telegram that just came from Chur."

Smiling, Wimms said, "I'm sure our esteemed president would want me to handle anything to do with the Chur factory situation in his absence, Helna."

Taking the envelope from her hand, he thanked her. Helna left the office as Wimms was slitting the envelope with a letter opener. When he took out the sheet of paper and began reading it, a frowned clouded his brow. By the time he finished reading it, his face was red. Dropping the telegram on top of the desk, he stood up, took a deep breath, let it out through his nostrils, and headed for the door.

Stepping into the outer office, Wimms said, "Helna, I need you to get Edgar Folsheim and Malo Licktin in my office immediately."

"Yes, sir," said the secretary, rising from her desk. "I know they are both in their offices. I'll have them here shortly."

Less than ten minutes later, Folsheim and Licktin were sitting down in front of the first vice president's desk.

"What is it, sir?" asked Folsheim. "Helna said it was urgent."

"Most urgent," said Wimms, picking up the yellow sheet of paper. "I have a telegram, from an anonymous source in Chur. It was addressed to Mr. Safford, but I'm glad he's out of the country right now. He wouldn't approve of what I'm about to do, but you men know I don't mind doing something that might be considered underhanded if it is of benefit to the union."

Both men smiled thinly and nodded.

"The message," said Wimms, "is that Durbin Thorpe has been meeting every day with his factory employees, doing everything possible to convince them to vote against going union. From what I'm told, Thorpe has been quite nasty in his comments about us."

"Who do you think sent the telegram, sir?" asked Licktin.

"Has to be a factory employee who wants to go union."

"That's what I was thinking."

"Me too," said Folsheim.

"You two are little more than a week away from returning to the Chur factory for the vote," said Wimms. "It seems to me something has to be done about Durbin Thorpe. He's in our way."

"I agree," said Folsheim. "From what we were able to learn when we were there, this man has a strong personality and a persuasive way about him. It is my opinion that he will keep the union from getting in there."

"How about you, Malo?" asked Wimms. "You of the same opinion?"

"I am," said Licktin. "Especially with him talking down the union as your anonymous friend has reported. He is definitely in our way. "

"That's all I needed to hear from the two of you," said Wimms, rising to his feet. "I figured this was what you would tell me. But I wanted to be sure before I put the wheels in motion."

As Folsheim and Licktin stood up, Wimms tilted his head down, looked at them from the tops of his eyes, and said, "Gentlemen, this conversation never happened. Understand?"

"Yes, sir," said Folsheim.

"Yes, sir," echoed Licktin.

Wimms followed them into the outer office, watched them enter the hall, then said, "Helna, I need Albert Conreid and Hans Nikolta in my office immediately."

"I'll get right on it, Mr. Wimms," said Helna.

Some twenty minutes had passed when Henry Wimms looked up from the telegram he was rereading and saw his two favorite henchmen enter his office.

A sneer was on both faces as they drew up to the desk.

"You got a job for us, Henry?" asked Albert Conreid.

"Mm-hmm. Sit down while I tell you about it."

After filling the two men in on the situation and letting them read the telegram, Wimms said, "I want you to go to Chur and make Durbin Thorpe disappear. Understood?"

"Understood," said Hans Nikolta, grinning wickedly. "Mr. Durbin Thorpe is about to do a vanishing act."

Matching the wicked grin, Wimms said, "Talk to Edgar and Malo before you go. They can give you Thorpe's description and tell you anything else you need to know."

"Will do," said Conreid.

Two days later, it was midmorning in Chur as Albert Conreid and Hans Nikolta sat in a buggy across the street from the Wilhaus Furniture Factory.

"That's got to be the office up there," said Nikolta, looking up toward the large window on the second level.

"From what Edgar and Malo said, only Thorpe and his son work up there, even though there was a third desk."

"Well, we'll just have to decide exactly how to do it when we get up there."

"Fine, Albert," said Nikolta. "As usual, you do the talking, and I'll follow along."

They were about to step out of the buggy when Conreid touched his partner's arm. "Someone's coming out of the office."

As the young man emerged through the door and headed toward the stairs, Nikolta said, "That has to be the younger Thorpe. He fits the description Edgar and Malo gave us."

"Good. Maybe we'll be fortunate enough to catch Durbin up there alone."

They watched Helmut Thorpe walk briskly down the street. When he was out of view, Henry Wimms's henchmen hurried across the street and up the stairs.

"Good morning, sir," said Albert Conreid when Durbin Thorpe responded to his knock. "Are you Mr. Durbin Thorpe, the manager here?"

"Yes," said Durbin.

"Well, sir, my name is Emery Dyck, and my partner here is Gregory Bruman. We understand that you are having serious trouble with the Grutliverein Union."

"You could call it that," said Durbin. "As usual, they are trying to muscle their way into the factory, and I'm doing all I can to stop them."

"Well, sir," said Conreid, "Mr. Bruman and I are bitter enemies of the Grutliverein Union, and we are opposed to what they do to good legitimate businesses just to fill their own pockets. We both had companies of our own but were finally forced out of business because of the union. We are here to help you if you would like."

A smile worked its way over Durbin's face. "Come in."

As the two impostors stepped into the office, they were glad to see that no one else was there.

"I'm between bookkeepers, gentlemen," said Durbin, closing the door. "Usually there would be a young lady here to make coffee for us. I have a new one hired, but she won't start until next week. I could try, but I'm not very good at it."

"Coffee isn't necessary, Mr. Thorpe," said Nikolta.

Looking relieved, Durbin bid them sit down in the two chairs that stood before his desk. "Tell me more."

"We know about Edgar Folsheim and Malo Licktin having been here a couple of weeks ago," said Conreid, "and we know how the vote went the first time. We know they're coming back in another week to oversee another vote."

Looking puzzled, Durbin asked, "How do you know all of this?"

Hans Nikolta chuckled. "We have a man on the inside at the union office in Zurich. He keeps us informed."

"We have a plan that will help you convince all, or at least the majority of your employees to vote against unionizing the factory, Mr. Thorpe," said Conreid. "It has worked in many places all over Switzerland, and it will work here."

"Sounds good," said Durbin. "And what do you charge for implementing your plan?"

Conreid gave a figure which sounded reasonable to Durbin, and followed by saying, "Of course, Mr. Thorpe, the factory is only obligated to pay us if our plan results in the employees voting against going union."

"Well, I'm ready to listen," said Durbin.

Even as he was speaking, footsteps were heard on the stairs outside.

Rising from his chair, Durbin said, "Sit tight. I'll take care of whoever it is."

Opening the door, Durbin found factory foreman George Capen smiling at him. "Good morning, boss," said Capen. "Do you have time to go over those wood orders with me?"

"Ah…not right now, George. How about this afternoon? Say about three o'clock?"

"Sure. See you then."

Durbin closed the door, sat down at his desk again, and said, "Now, let's hear about your plan."

Conreid looked toward the door. "Tell you what, Mr. Thorpe, it would be best if we do this where no one can disturb us. We have a horse and buggy outside. How about we take a little ride into the country while we talk?"

Durbin grinned. "Sounds good to me. I could use a little fresh air."

While Durbin was leaving a note for Helmut, simply telling him that he had to leave but would be back soon, Wimms's henchmen exchanged furtive smiles.

Laying the note on Helmut's desk, Durbin said, "I'll run down and tell my foreman that I'll be gone for a little while. Then we can go."

"We'll meet you at the buggy," said Nikolta. "It's directly across the street."

Two miles outside of Chur to the west, Dova Combray had just delivered a dress she had made for Martha Dolberg, one of her regular customers.

Leaving the small cottage, Dova walked along the narrow, shaded lane to the road, and headed back toward town. The sun was shining out of a clear sky and a soft summer breeze was blowing.

Soon Dova's attention was drawn to a buggy that was coming toward her with three men in the single seat. As the buggy drew near, she studied the three faces and recognized the man in the middle.

Smiling, she waved and called out, "Mr. Thorpe! Hello."

Durbin smiled and tipped his hat. "Hello, Dova."

Dova ran her gaze to the faces of the other two men and wondered who they might be.

Conreid and Nikolta noticed the girl focusing on them and both got a good look at her.

As the buggy rolled on down the road, Hans Nikolta said, "Who's the pretty girl?"

"Her name is Dova Combray. Her father is Adolf Combray. He owns the Chur Hardware Store in town."

Looking back down the road, Nikolta could barely see Dova through the dust raised by the buggy's wheels. She was walking briskly toward Chur. "Really a pretty girl," he commented.

"Well, gentlemen," said Durbin, "let's hear your plan."

The sun was lowering in the western sky when Helmut Thorpe stood on the walkway in front of the office and called down to the foreman, who was leaving for home. "George!"

Capen stopped, smiled up at Helmut. "Yes?"

"Are you sure my father didn't say anything about where he was going?"

"He didn't volunteer that information," said George. "He said he left a note for you."

"He did, but there isn't a word in it that says where he was going."

"As I told you, he was supposed to meet with me about those wood orders at three o'clock. So I assume that wherever he went, something came up to delay his return."

"All right," said Helmut, worry evident on his face. "See you tomorrow."

Helmut locked the office and hurried home.

When he entered the house, his mother was dusting the parlor. Giving him a smile, she said, "Is your father with you?"

"No. I was hoping he would be here."

"Here? He always walks home with you."

Helmut explained to his mother about the note, and that his father had spoken to George Capen that morning, saying he was leaving for a little while.

"But he never came back to the office, Mother," Helmut said.

Lynelle Thorpe's brow furrowed. "This is strange, son. If he isn't home pretty soon, we'd better go tell Koblin about it."

Twilight was on the land when Koblin Baume responded to the knock on his door and found Lynelle and Helmut on his front porch. He could tell by their faces that they were upset.

"May we come in, Koblin?" asked Lynelle. "We need to talk to you."

"Of course," said the burgomaster, the door opening wider.

As they stepped in, Kathlyn appeared, picked up immediately that something was awry, and said, "What's wrong?"

"Durbin's missing," said Lynelle, tears welling up in her eyes.

"Missing?" said Koblin.

"Yes," sniffed Lynelle. "I'll let Helmut explain."

When Helmut had told the story, Koblin Baume shook his head and said, "I hate to say this, but because of what's been going on with the independent woodworkers, I fear they have done something to Durbin."

Lynelle gasped, and Helmut put an arm around her shoulders.

"I'll take a couple of my officers right now," said Koblin. "We'll go to every woodworker's home and question them. It'll take quite a while, so you go on home. I'll come there and let you know what I find out."

It was an hour past midnight when the burgomaster and two of his officers appeared at the Thorpe door. Helmut invited them in, and when they were led into the parlor where Lynelle sat, handkerchief in hand, Koblin said, "Lynelle, Helmut, we have questioned every woodworker and come up with nothing. They all say they know nothing about any of their own wanting to harm Durbin. Usually, this kind of questioning will surface something solid if there is anything underhanded going on. I really believe they're telling us the truth."

"So what now, Chief?" asked Helmut.

"I'll form a search team at sunrise, and lead it myself," said Koblin. "We'll search the entire town and surrounding area. I'll let you know one way or the other as soon as I can."

A few miles west of Chur, farmer Wald Malford finished breakfast, told his wife he was going to do some fence repair along the irrigation ditch, and left the house carrying shovel, hammer, and nails.

While making his way along the bank of the ditch toward the spot where the fence had been damaged by one of his bulls, something caught his eye. The lifeless body of a man was lying face down on the bank with the head and shoulders submerged in the water.

Eyes wide, Malford dropped his tools, and ran to the body. Bending over, he grasped the man's ankles and pulled him out of the ditch. Then taking hold of the shoulders, he turned him over. A gasp escaped his lips. "Durbin Thorpe!"

Not wanting to disturb any clues that might have been left behind by whoever had murdered Durbin, Malford dashed to the house. Panting for breath, he told his wife of his discovery, and that he was going to ride to town and report it to the police.

Within minutes, Wald Malford was in the saddle, riding the lane that led to the road. When he turned onto the road, he put the horse to a brisk trot.

Seconds later, Wald saw two policemen on horseback coming toward him. Snapping the reins, he put the horse to a full gallop.

At ten o'clock that morning in Zurich, Helna entered Henry Wimms's office with a yellow envelope. "Another telegram, Mr. Wimms," she said, handing it to him. "It's from the telegraph office in Feldis."

"Thank you," said Wimms, picking up his letter opener as Helna returned to the outer office. He knew Feldis was some thirteen miles from Chur. The telegram would be from Conreid and Nikolta. He slit the envelope open and unfolded the yellow paper.

The wire was coded so as not to alert the telegraph operator in Feldis of any covert dealings. Decoding it, Wimms learned from his two henchmen that the job they were sent to do had been accomplished. They added, however, that because of an unforeseen circumstance, there was some unfinished business to be taken care of before they returned to Zurich.

As the buggy moved slowly down the street past the Adolf Combray home at midmorning, Albert Conreid said in a low voice, "That's the place, Hans. Her father being well-known in town made it easy for us to find out where she lives without raising any suspicion."

"It's a shame to have to kill such a pretty girl," Nikolta said almost sadly.

"Yes, but if we don't, she could identify us," Conreid said. "She has to die."

"I know."

"We'll get her tonight, if we have to kill the whole family to do it."

By noon, word had spread over most of Chur about Durbin Thorpe's body being found on the Malford farm.

When Adolf Combray arrived home for lunch, he found his wife and daughter in the kitchen. Kissing one, then the other on the cheek, he said, "I suppose you've heard about Durbin Thorpe."

Both women looked at him in puzzlement.

"No, we haven't," said Farina. "We haven't been out the door all morning. What about Durbin?"

Dova's widened eyes were fixed on her father as he said, "Wald Malford found Durbin's body half submerged in the irrigation ditch on his farm this morning. Turns out Lynelle and Helmut reported him missing last night to Koblin."

Farina's mouth sagged.

Dova's face went a pasty color.

"Koblin has already stated officially that it was murder," said Adolf. "He doesn't think it was the independent woodworkers who did it, but hasn't completely ruled them out because of what some of them did before."

Dova stood immobile. Her hand went to her mouth as her eyes became twin pools of alarm. Waves, cold and black, were lashing at the edges of her consciousness.

Noting the effect of the news on her, Adolf laid a hand on his daughter's shoulder and said, "Honey, are you all right?"

Farina stepped closer. "Dova, this is horrible news, but is there something else that has you upset?"

Dova's lips quivered a few seconds before she could speak. The words came out shakily. "Papa, Mama, yesterday morning when I was on my way back from Martha Dolberg's house, I...I saw Durbin in a buggy with two men. They were coming from town. I spoke to him, and he spoke back, calling me by name. The men looked at me, too. Do...do you suppose those were the men who murdered him?"

Folding his daughter into his arms, Adolf said, "They probably are the ones, all right. If you saw them coming from town on that road, they would have been going in the direction of the Malford farm."

"You say Durbin called your name, and the men looked at you, honey?" said Farina.

"Yes."

"Oh, Adolf," said Farina, her features turning gray, "those men might decide to come after Dova, since she could identify them."

"That's highly possible, honey," said Adolf. "We're taking her to Koblin right now."

When Dova told her story to Koblin Baume and two of his officers at the police station, she gave them the best description she could of the two men she had seen with Durbin Thorpe.

Baume and the officers told the Combrays that Dova must be careful. It would be best that she not be out on the streets for a while. Baume commented that since the killers were not woodworkers that Dova would have recognized, they were probably long gone, but it would be best if Dova stay in the house till further notice from him.

That night at the Combray home, the window shades were drawn throughout the house.

Hiding in the shadows close by, Albert Conreid and Hans Nikolta were keeping a close watch. Though they could not see inside the one-story house, they were able to make out the three family members moving about by the shadows they cast on the window shades. They agreed on which female shadow was Dova. She was a little shorter and somewhat slimmer than her mother.

Skulking about in the dark as the night grew older, the two killers were finally able to see Dova's silhouette as she entered her room about ten o'clock.

"Looks like she's retiring for the night," whispered Nikolta.

"Uh-huh," said Conreid. "And we'll see that she goes to sleep forever."

Inside the house, Dova slipped into bed while her parents stood just outside her door in the hall.

"Good night, honey," said Farina. "I know your nerves are on edge, but try to get some sleep."

"I will, Mama," she said, reaching up to douse the flame in the lantern on the table beside her bed.

"Good night, sweetheart," said Adolf. "I love you."

"Me too," said Farina.

"I love you both," Dova said tenderly.

Adolf and Farina moved down the hall by the dim light that flowed from the door of their bedroom.

Lying in total darkness, Dova felt uneasy. She tried to relax, but her nerves were tense and her body rigid. Throwing back the covers in the total darkness, she fumbled for her robe that was draped on the back of a chair and stepped out into the pitch-black hallway. When she reached her parents' bedroom, there was no light beneath the door. Tapping lightly, she said in a low voice, "Mama, Papa, can I come in?"

"Sure, honey," came Adolf's voice.

Pushing the door open into solid darkness, Dova said, "I...was wondering if we could pray together one more time for God's protection on me."

"Of course, honey," said Farina. "Come over here and get between us like you used to do when you were little."

Suddenly a series of gunshots were heard from just outside the house, along with the sound of shattering glass.

Dova took a breath to scream, but her mother was out of bed

and covered her mouth while Adolf was padding down the hall in the dark toward Dova's room.

As he reached the open door, he heard rapid footsteps outside, fading into the night. By the clear sound, he knew the glass was gone from the window. The shooters had fled.

Voices were heard outside, which Adolf recognized as belonging to the neighbors. They were carrying lanterns.

Adolf returned hurriedly to the other bedroom, put on trousers, shirt, and shoes while telling his wife and daughter that the shooters had run away.

When Adolf stepped out onto the front porch there were several people in the yard, holding lanterns. One man called out, "Adolf, was anybody hit?"

"No, praise the Lord!" replied Adolf. "But if it weren't for God's protection on Dova, she would have been hit."

When the neighbors went into the Combray house with Adolf, and lanterns were taken into Dova's room, Farina and Dova joined them.

Window glass was splattered all over the floor, along with the glass from the chimney of Dova's lantern. The pillows and bedding had been ripped to shreds by the bullets, and there were holes in the wall, and the bed's headboard was splintered.

Trembling as her mother kept an arm around her, Dova said shakily, "Papa, it had to be the men who saw me speak to Durbin. They were taking him into the country to kill him...and now they want to kill me."

Shortly thereafter, Koblin Baume and three police officers sat in the Combray parlor while Dova sat between her parents on the couch.

Baume and his officers agreed that the same men who killed Durbin Thorpe had just tried to kill Dova because they feared she could identify them.

"I've ruled out the woodworkers completely," Baume said to the Combrays. "I can't imagine the woodworkers hiring professional killers. They wouldn't have the money, anyhow. I think the killers are connected to the union."

"Really?" said Adolf.

"Yes. It took me a while to come to this conclusion, but I think Durbin's stiff resistance to the union had them afraid he would keep them from getting into the factory. Though most of the union leaders are good men who are trying to do right for labor in Switzerland, there often is a faction within a union who are ruthless and dissident.

"I feel confident this is what we are facing. Dova innocently got herself involved by being on the road at the time the killers were taking Durbin out in the country to kill him. And I fear that when they learn that they didn't kill her tonight, they'll try again. For their own safety, they must silence her."

Dova looked at her parents fearfully.

"Adolf, Farina," said the burgomaster, "you've got to get Dova clear out of the country, and I mean in a hurry. These men no doubt are hired killers, and they won't give up till they kill her."

Both parents were holding Dova tightly.

"I would have given her some protection," said Koblin, "if it had entered my head yet that it could be killers hired by the union. I'll leave several officers around the house for the rest of the night, and I'll keep some of them posted as guards around the clock till Dova is out of the country. But do it quickly."

The next morning, Adolf went to Pastor Trevor Helms's house and told him what happened, saying he needed him to come and talk to Dova.

While they were walking toward the Combray house, Adolf told the pastor what Chief Baume had said about getting Dova out of the country. Helms agreed, saying it was the only sensible thing to do.

When they got to the house, the pastor sat down with the family and opened his Bible. Looking tenderly at Dova, he said, "I want to encourage you. Let me read something to you from Psalm 91."

While Helms was reading the entire Psalm, Dova recalled that it was the same passage the pastor had used to encourage Erik.

When he had finished reading Psalm 91, Helms took Dova back

to verses 1 and 2. After spending several minutes on verse 2, pointing out that God was Dova's refuge and fortress, he took her to verse 1 and showed her that as God's faithful child, she was dwelling in the secret place of the most High, and therefore, she was abiding under the protective shadow of the Almighty.

"So you see, Dova," the pastor said in conclusion, "the secret place is your place of safety."

Commenting that Dr. Erik Linden had shared with her what the pastor had shown him in the midst of his great trial, Dova said finally, "Thank you for sharing it with me too, Pastor. It really is a comfort to my heart."

Helms smiled at her, then running his gaze to both parents, he asked where they were planning to send their daughter.

"You remember that Franz and Elizabeth Vagner are living in New York City, Pastor."

"Yes."

"Well, in letters they have jokingly said that if Dova ever wanted to come to America to live, she could live with them. Farina and I have discussed it. We are sure they would take her in if we sent her to New York. This is what we are going to do until the danger is past."

"We also discussed it with Dova," said Farina.

"And how do you feel about it, Dova?" asked Helms.

Dova took a shallow breath, cleared her throat and said, "Pastor, I don't like the thought of leaving Mama and Papa and my friends, as well as leaving my country in order to be safe, but since this is what my parents feel is best, I will do as they say. I have no doubt that the Vagners will welcome me with open arms."

"Well, it won't be forever, honey," said Adolf. "As soon as we are sure that these men who killed Durbin and tried to kill you have been caught and punished, you can come home."

"That's the way to look at it," said the pastor. "The main thing is to keep you safe as far as is humanly possible. The Lord expects you to do that. And behind it all, Dova, you dwell in His secret place."

"Yes," said Dova. "I'm so thankful for that."

"Since there isn't time to correspond with the Vagners before putting Dova on a ship, Pastor," said Adolf, "I'm going to write a letter to them and send it with her. I'll explain the whole situation and ask them to keep her until she can return home and be safe."

"I know it will all work out," said the pastor. "Let's have a time of prayer, and ask the Lord to keep His mighty hand on this precious girl all the way to the Vagners' front door."

Twenty-three

Dr. Erik Linden was standing at the railing on the port side of the main deck as the *F.R.S. Versailles* pulled into New York Harbor under a crystal blue sky on Monday afternoon, September 12. The rest of the passengers lined the railing with him, eager to get a glimpse of the Statue of Liberty.

Erik gazed toward the city and its maze of tall buildings, then let his eyes run back toward the Atlantic. The sun-kissed water was an enchanting blue with shining waves and white foam alongside the hull of the ship.

Suddenly a teenage boy shouted in French, "There she is!" He was pointing at the magnificent statue ahead on the left.

All eyes were immediately fastened on Lady Liberty, who stood on her pedestal, holding a torch in her raised right hand and a tablet in her left. Some already knew that inscribed on the tablet was the date: July 4, 1776.

Erik's eyes misted, and a lump rose in his throat. To him, the lady with the torch held high represented the liberty he would have in America from the gossiping tongues of the Chur citizens who blamed him for letting Metryka Baume die.

"Thank You, Lord," he breathed, "for the peace You have given me in that matter. In Your perfect timing, You designed it so I would have to perform those two surgeries aboard ship. Now I can live free of the guilt I was carrying, thinking I had failed Metryka, and I can look forward to one day having my own practice wherever You lead me. And I can perform all the surgical operations that come my way. I'm excited about my new life in America, Lord. Thank You for the secret place, and thank You for Your protective shadow."

Soon the ship slowed to a halt some two hundred yards from Ellis Island, and Captain Harve Rochforte gave command to the deckhands to drop anchor.

Erik let his gaze rove over the island, which was actually divided into three sections. All three of its buildings shared the same bit of earth and were joined together by a long windowed walkway. In the complex was the main administration building, the hospital, and the large apartment building that housed most of the island's employees. The island was resplendent with beautiful trees, bushes, and green lawns. Abundant in supply were a myriad of seagulls that fluttered about the island.

Soon Erik was in line with the rest of the passengers as they were crossing gangplanks from the lower level of the ship to board the ferryboats that were pulling up beside the *Versailles.*

While watching the gangplanks being dropped into place, Erik felt a tap on his shoulder. He turned to see Captain Harve Rochforte smiling at him. Rochforte shook Erik's hand, thanked him sincerely for leading him to the Lord, and wished him a happy life in America.

Soon Erik was on a ferryboat with some one hundred other passengers bobbing along the harbor waters, heading for Ellis Island. He studied the island once more, then ran his gaze to the Statue of Liberty a few hundred yards away. His heart skipped a beat at the sight of her.

Moments later, Erik found himself standing in line in the huge room at the administration building that served as the medical facility. While waiting for his own medical examination, he looked both directions, searching the booths for a glimpse of Dr. Kenton Prinoth.

After about twenty minutes in line, he spotted Prinoth moving along the back side of the booths, then saw him enter a booth some fifty or sixty feet away. Leaving the line he was in, he hurried to the line in front of the booth where his friend had gone, and joined it at the rear. He would be longer now getting his examination, but it would be worth it to see his friend and have him do the examination.

Within an hour, Erik found himself with just an elderly man in front of him. His eyes were fixed on Dr. Kenton Prinoth as the doctor motioned to the elderly man, telling him he was ready for him.

Suddenly Prinoth's line of sight fell on Erik. His eyes widened and a smile broke across his face. Telling the old man to sit down, Prinoth rushed up to Erik and said, "Well, look who's here! I've been waiting for you to show up! How was the voyage?"

"Quite pleasant," said Erik. "We had one storm that was pretty rough, but other than that, it was good."

As the two men shook hands, Prinoth said, "After I examine you, I'll get one of the other doctors to take my place here, and I'll take you to one of the immigrant interrogators. There won't be very many questions for him to ask you, since you've been hired as one of our doctors. Then I'll take you to the administration office and we'll get you signed up on the medical staff."

"I'm ready," said Erik.

When Erik was all signed up and ready to start work the next morning, Kenton took him to the Ellis Island employees' apartment building. As they entered the three-story building, Kenton said, "You're in apartment 212 on the second floor. As you will see, we doctors get special treatment by the administration because we are the island physicians. Our apartments are larger and fancier than the others."

"I wouldn't ask for that," said Erik, "but since it's laid in my lap, I'll take it."

When they reached the door of apartment 212, they found Erik's trunk and one large suitcase sitting there, which had been delivered by the ferryboat people. Kenton helped him carry them inside, then said he needed to get back to his booth. They would have supper together that evening in the dining hall.

Placing his overnight bag on the couch, Erik looked around the apartment. He was pleasantly surprised at how spacious and charming it was. A large, dark walnut four-poster bed dominated the single bedroom with a dresser and chiffonier. The bed looked soft and comfortable, with a dark blue quilted spread and pillow cases to match. Two hunting scenes hung in gold frames on the walls, and a painted stand held a large pitcher and bowl with a mirror above it. The large windows were draped in the same shade of blue as the bedspread, with a wide white stripe around the edges.

In the parlor area, there were two overstuffed chairs that matched the couch, which had a dark oak coffee table in front of it. The chairs sat at an angle near one of the windows, and a small rolltop desk and chair had been placed against one wall. The walls were decorated with still-life paintings, along with a portrait of Abraham Lincoln.

The white brick fireplace caught Erik's eye, and even on the warm summer day, he could picture a fire burning there brightly in the winter.

Slowly turning in a circle, he smiled and said, "This will do nicely. Yes, indeed. Very nicely."

Wanting to get settled in at once, Erik unpacked his bags and trunk. He then left the building to take a leisurely walk around the island and get his bearings in his new home.

Two days later Erik pulled his rented buggy up in front of the Vagner home in Manhattan. He was warmly welcomed by the Vagners, who invited him to stay for dinner.

Upon hearing the story, the Vagners told Erik they were happy he was there, but sorry for the reason he had to leave Chur. They were also happy to hear news from home. They invited Erik to their church, and he was pleased to tell them he had next Sunday off and would be there.

~~~

As time passed, and Erik worked happily in the medical facility on Ellis Island, he found his thoughts often going to Dova Combray.

One night as he lay on his side in his bed with the sound of the waves slapping the shore of the island in his ears, he was about to drop off to sleep when suddenly Dova's beautiful face appeared on the screen of his mind.

Rolling onto his back, he looked through the windows at the starlit sky and said in a whisper, "Erik, old boy, you're really missing that sweet girl, aren't you? Have your feelings changed toward her? Is…is it no longer just friendship?"

He took a deep breath and sat up, leaning his back against the headboard. "It is *more* than friendship. Could it be love?"

His mind went once again—as it had countless times since boarding the ship in La Rochelle—to the last time he saw Dova. He could almost feel her squeeze his hand like she did then. And he could see her again, standing on the depot platform as the train took him away, tears streaming down her cheeks.

"That squeeze, Dova," he said in a low voice, "and those rivers of tears on your face…do you feel something more than friendship for me too?"

Five days after the gunmen had tried to kill Dova Combray, she had a tearful good-bye with her mother, the Lindens, and the Helmses at the house, and under cover of darkness, was taken by her father and two police officers to the Chur railroad station. The train that would take her all the way to La Rochelle, France, was to leave at midnight.

One of the officers stepped into the chosen coach first, and after looking the passengers over, waved for the others to follow. Adolf Combray kept an arm around his daughter as they entered the coach with the other officer on their heels.

Allowing Dova to choose the seat she wanted, Adolf placed her overnight bag in the rack above, then folded her into his arms as the
~~~

officers moved away, one to stand at the front of the coach, and the other at the rear. Every passenger who entered the coach would be carefully scrutinized.

Others were boarding hurriedly as the conductor stood on the platform outside, calling for all passengers to get on the train.

The officer at the rear of the coach noted a tall, slender man in a cream-colored summer suit with hat to match come through the door, carrying an elegant cane. The man, who appeared to be in his late thirties, wore a thin mustache and carried a valise. He watched the man choose a seat a couple of rows and across the aisle from where Dova would sit. He took up a friendly conversation immediately with a well-dressed woman about his age who was sitting next to the window. The officer decided the man was all right.

Looking up at her father, Dova said, "Papa, it's so hard to go off and leave you and Mama. Are you sure there isn't some way for me to stay home and still be safe?"

Looking into his daughter's eyes that were misty with tears, Adolf said, "No, little one. This is the only way to make sure you don't become a target for the hired killers. Your mother and I couldn't live with ourselves if we didn't do everything we could to assure your absolute safety."

As the conductor's voice was heard making the final call for boarding, Adolf cupped Dova's face in his hands, thumbed away the tears that stained her face, and kissed one damp cheek and then the other. "Go with God, my precious little one. I'll see you again soon. I love you."

"I love you, too Papa," she said, raising up on her tiptoes to plant a kiss on his cheek.

Dova sat down on the seat, which she would occupy by herself, and slid next to the window. Leaning close, Adolf said, "Be sure to find Erik as soon as you get to Ellis Island. Since he will be at the very place where you will be examined, it shouldn't be hard. Just tell someone in authority you are a friend of Erik's and need to see him. Like I said earlier, tell Erik what has happened in your life, and ask him to help you get to Manhattan and the Vagner home. You have the letter, don't you?"

"Yes, Papa. It's right here in my purse."

The train's bell was clanging and the whistle blew. Adolf kissed the top of Dova's head, told her once more that he loved her, and hurried off the train.

As the train pulled away, Dova waved to her father, who was standing on the platform with the officers. Fresh tears welled up in her eyes as her father disappeared from view.

When the train was out of the depot, moving westward across the dark landscape, Dova dried her tears, laid her head back, and thought about her future.

Her mind ran to Erik, and her heart quickened pace as she thought about seeing him again. She knew Erik would understand the fear she had of the men who had tried to kill her and would be a comfort to her.

A warmth flooded her heart as she pictured the handsome face of the man she loved. *Maybe,* she thought, *just maybe this is the Lord's way of giving Erik and me a chance. At any rate, it's nice to know that he will be there, and if God is in it, Erik will learn to love me as I do him.*

Turning her face to the window, all she could see at first was darkness, but as she looked upward, she saw countless stars twinkling brightly and the moon hovering over a faraway hill. Dova sighed, and in a low voice, said, "And we know that all things work together for good to them that love God, to them who are the called according to his purpose." A slight smile curved her lips. "*All* things, Lord. Even professional killers trying to kill me."

When the rising sun kissed the windows sending its golden light into the coach, Dova awakened and rubbed her eyes. The steady rhythm of the clicking wheels beneath her and the sway of the coach had lulled her to sleep, and she had slept well all night.

Stretching her arms, she covered a yawn, and let her gaze drift through the car. She noticed a man across the aisle looking at her. He quickly averted his eyes, eased down on the seat, and tipped his cream-colored hat down over his brow.

A bit fearful, Dova glanced at the man periodically for quite a while, but he seemed to be sleeping. She took her Bible from her purse, and by the sunlight that filled the coach read Psalm 91. She concentrated on verse 1, drawing strength and courage from it. She reminded herself that the secret place was her haven of safety.

Upon arriving in La Rochelle, Dova hired a buggy to take her from the railroad station to the harbor. During the ride through the city, Dova thought of the man in the cream-colored suit. She had caught him looking at her on several occasions during the trip from Chur. Each time, he had looked away quickly, but had never ventured to speak to her.

She sighed, telling herself she was rid of him now. He wouldn't be around, walking with his fancy cane and looking at her furtively. She would be on the ship, and he would be wherever he was headed in La Rochelle.

Soon the buggy pulled up to the docks, and Dova eyed the ship that waited to take her to America, to safety, and to Erik. As the driver helped her out of the buggy and a porter took her large suitcase to put it on the ship for her, Dova was about to turn and head for the ticket office when she saw a buggy pull up behind her. The tall, slender man in the cream-colored suit was in the buggy, along with two men and the woman he had sat by on the train. Dova's heart thumped in her chest.

She hurried toward the ticket office, venturing a look over her shoulder. The strange man was helping the woman out of the buggy.

Just before she entered the ticket office, Dova looked back again. The woman was walking with the other two men, and the man in the cream-colored suit was ahead of them, moving briskly toward the ticket office.

There were three lines inside the ticket office. Dova watched the strange man from the corner of her eye as he stepped in the line next to hers. She was out of the office and heading across the dock toward the gangplank while the man was purchasing his ticket at the counter inside.

When she reached the gangplank, she hurried onto the ship quickly. Pausing on the deck as a steward looked at her ticket and told her how to find her cabin, Dova looked down to see the man moving toward the gangplank. He was not looking at her. This gave her some relief.

Maybe he meant nothing at all by looking at her. Maybe it was just her imagination. She had thought that possibly the union people who were after her had somehow found out she was going to America, and had sent a man to see that she didn't get there alive.

The next day, as the ship was on its voyage across the Atlantic, Dova was coming out of her cabin on the second-class deck when she saw the man in the cream-colored suit emerge from the cabin next to hers.

Cold chills were born at the center of her spine and spread quickly through her entire body.

Two male passengers were coming along the walkway together. The man noticed them, and as he turned the key in the lock of his door, he nodded at Dova, touched the brim of his hat, and hurried away.

Later that day, Dova was sitting on a deck chair near the starboard rail on the second level. Her head was laid back, and her eyes were closed. Suddenly she heard children laughing as they ran past her in their play. She opened her eyes to look at them, and as they passed from view, her peripheral vision alerted her of someone standing at the rail nearby. When she turned to see who it was, her blood turned to ice.

The strange man was looking at her.

He averted his eyes again and stared out to sea.

Frightened, Dova told herself it was not just her imagination. There was no question about it. The man was after her. Was it just happenstance that he was in the cabin next to hers? Absolutely not. He had learned her cabin number from one of the ticket agents and purposely took the one next to hers.

He definitely was not one of the men she had seen with Durbin

Thorpe in the buggy the day he was murdered, but she was sure he was part of the union's deadly faction. Dova told herself she must make sure to stay where there were other people at all times.

With her stomach soured, she left the deck chair and headed for her cabin. Without looking back, she felt the eyes of the man boring into the back of her head like twin beams of awful light.

Entering her cabin, she locked the door, picked up her Bible, and sat down at the small desk. Hands trembling, she read Psalm 91:1 and repeated it over several times. "Lord, I'm asking You to keep me in Your secret place...my only place of safety."

Dova Combray had her bags packed and ready early on the morning of the day the ship was to drop anchor near Ellis Island in New York Harbor.

Too excited to sleep, she was up while it was still dark and the moon was being swallowed by the ocean on its western rim. Once her packing was done, she waited till sunrise, and kept watch through the window of the cabin until passengers were milling about on deck in good numbers.

Stepping out of the cabin, Dova looked eastward to admire the sunrise. A brilliant gold-filled sky presented itself for her view, augmented by a bright orange-red sun peeking over the horizon, shooting fiery darts out across the water.

The New York coastline soon came into view, and the decks were filled with people pushing toward the rails to get a look at the new land that many of them would soon call home.

Dova thought of Erik, who had no idea she was coming back into his life. And then there were the Vagners, who had no idea she would soon invade their lives and be a guest in their home. She was almost overwhelmed at the enormity of her situation, but the one in whose shadow she abode spoke peace to her racing heart at that moment.

As the ship swung into New York Harbor and steamed inland, Dova stood amid the crowd of passengers on the port side of the main deck, taking in the marvelous sights. In the corner of her eye, she kept the strange man in the cream-colored suit in view.

Soon they were passing the awesome Statue of Liberty with the torch of freedom held high in her upthrust hand. Dova longed for freedom from the man who had been her unwanted traveling companion since she left Chur.

When the ship dropped anchor amid other ships and Dova boarded a ferryboat for Ellis Island, she noticed the man shove his way past a line of people in order to get on the same boat. Again, fear struck her heart. She told herself if he wasn't after her, he wouldn't have done that.

As Dova arrived at Ellis Island and entered the large cavernous building, she was astounded at the crowds of people and the raucous babel of languages being spoken, few which were familiar to her.

However, knowing English, she was able to read the signs and follow the directions to the place where she would have her medical examination. As she moved that way, she noted that armed guards were positioned about the place, observing the crowds.

When she took her place in line before one of the many booths, Dova surveyed the hundreds of people in the building, jostling their way from place to place, looking frightened and lost. Babies were fussing, and small children were crying. Dova knew most of them were tired and hungry and feeling the same fear their parents were experiencing. The mothers especially looked worn and weary.

At that moment, Dova saw a matronly looking woman clad in a black bombazine dress and white apron moving about the crowd, talking to the immigrants and helping them join the lines in front of the proper booths. Then Dova noticed other women dressed in the same manner, doing the same thing from one end of the building to the other.

"Amazing," Dova murmured to herself as her own line moved slowly toward the booth ahead.

A few minutes later, Dova spotted the man in the cream-colored suit, nonchalantly leaning against a nearby wall, but positioned so he could see her.

When she was finally met by the doctor assigned to the booth, she gave him the information he requested, including what country she was from. After he had checked her eyes, ears, and throat, and said she was free to pass to the part of the building where she would be questioned by the immigration authorities, she said, "Doctor, are you acquainted with Dr. Erik Linden?"

"I sure am," he replied with a smile. He snapped his fingers. "Come to think of it, Dr. Linden is from Switzerland. You know him from there, I presume."

Before Dova could answer, she heard her name called above the din of the place, and looked up to see a surprised Erik Linden hurrying toward her. He was smiling from ear to ear.

Erik took Dova completely by surprise as he folded her in his arms, saying, "Dova! I can't believe this! It's so wonderful to see you!"

Easing back in his grasp, Dova smiled and said, "It's wonderful to see you too, Erik."

"What are you doing in America?" he asked, light dancing in his eyes.

"If we can have some time together, I'll tell you. I was just asking the doctor if he knew you. I would have found you if you hadn't found me first." She glanced toward the strange man to see if he was still there.

He was.

"Did you pass the examination?" asked Erik.

"She did," the doctor answered for her, and handed Dova her papers.

Taking her by the arm and guiding her a few steps away, Erik asked, "Can you remain on the island after you're questioned by the immigration authorities, Dova?"

She smiled and nodded. "As you will see, I can't go anywhere without your help."

Looking puzzled, he told her where to wait for him in the next building.

"I'll be there," she said, flicking a glance toward the man in the cream-colored suit again.

Erik frowned. "You seem ill at ease, Dova. I know this is often the case with immigrants on Ellis Island, but, well, I have to ask if you're all right."

Meeting his gaze, Dova said, "Can we step aside a little farther and talk? Or are you busy at the moment?"

"Not too busy to talk to you."

When they had moved to a spot of relative privacy, Dova said, "Over there against the wall to your left. Do you see the man in the cream-colored suit with the fancy cane?"

"Yes."

Noting that the man was looking another direction at the moment, Dova explained that he was on the train with her, and on the ship, and without question, was following her.

"Are you sure?" he asked, giving the man a hard look.

"Absolutely," said Dova, then gave him a brief but detailed version of why she had come to America.

Erik's features crimsoned. "So he's following you to do what his cohorts in Switzerland failed to do. Well, he's in trouble now! You wait right here. I'll get some of the armed guards. We'll take care of him!"

While Dova watched, Erik collected four guards and approached the man.

At the scene—out of Dova's hearing—the strange man found himself quickly surrounded by the guards. Face flushed with anger, Erik moved up close as the man stiffened at the sight of the guards, and said, "Who are you, mister? You understand English?"

"I understand English," came the level reply. "My name is William Anson."

"And you're from Switzerland?"

"Yes."

"I want a straight answer from you, mister!" said Erik. "Why have you followed Miss Dova Combray all the way from Chur?"

Expecting Anson to deny it, Erik waited, eyes aflame.

The guards laid their hands on their holstered revolvers as Anson reached inside his coat. One of them grabbed his wrist and said, "Hold it!"

The guns came out of their holsters quickly and were trained on the stranger. The guard who had hold of Anson's wrist, reached inside his coat, and pulled a revolver from his shoulder holster.

"Just as I thought!" said Erik. "You were going to kill her the first chance you got!"

Shaking his head, Anson said, "I wasn't reaching for the gun, sir. I was wanting to show you my identification. I am a private investigator from Zurich. May I produce the identification, now?"

"Go ahead," said one of the guards.

Anson took a slender wallet from the inside pocket of his coat and handed it to Erik.

Erik opened it and read the papers. Handing it to a guard, he said, "Looks like he's who he says he is."

The guard read the papers, nodded, and handed the wallet back to Anson.

"In my other pocket is a letter, sir," said the private investigator. "It is from Mr. Adolf Combray, in his handwriting. I'm sure the girl will recognize it. Mr. Combray told me all about the professional killers who are after his daughter, and why. He hired me to stay close to her all the way, and see that she arrived safely in America."

Erik's flushed face began to resume its natural color. "Well, this puts a new light on things."

"May I show you the letter? I was supposed to introduce myself to Miss Combray when she was safe at the Franz Vagner home in Manhattan and give it to her."

"Of course."

Anson produced a sealed envelope.

Opening it and taking out the letter, Erik read it and smiled. "Tell you what, Mr. Anson, I'll take over for you at this point. You can go on back to Switzerland. I'm a very close friend of Dova and her family. I'll see that she gets safely to the Vagners. If you would like to talk to her and verify what I'm telling you, feel free."

Anson grinned. "I'm convinced that you are her friend, sir. These guards seem to know you."

"We do," said one of the guards. "He is Dr. Erik Linden from Chur, Switzerland, and is on our medical staff."

"I do need to have Miss Combray sign a paper I have in my wallet," said Anson. "It's for her father, so he will pay me."

"Of course," said Erik. Turning to look at Dova, he found her watching the scene intently. Smiling, he motioned for her to come to him.

There was still apprehension in Dova's eyes as she drew up.

"Dova," said Erik, "this man is William Anson, from Zurich. He is a private investigator. Your father hired him to see to it that you arrived safely in America."

Dova's head bobbed. "I...I had no idea."

Handing her the letter, Erik said, "Your father gave him this. He was to put it in your hands when you were safely at the Vagner home in Manhattan."

Her eyes fluttered as she unfolded the sheet of paper and read the letter. "It's Papa's handwriting, all right." Embarrassment showed on her face as she said, "I'm sorry, Mr. Anson. I know my father loves me very much, but I had no idea he would do something like this to protect me. Thank you for watching over me so well."

"It was my pleasure, miss," said Anson.

"He has a paper you need to sign, Dova," said Erik. "So he can prove to your father that he saw you safely this far. I'm taking over for him at this point. I'll see that you get to the Vagner home safely."

Anson produced the paper and a pencil. When Dova had signed it and William Anson had gone, Erik thanked the guards for their help. Taking Dova by the arm, he said, "Come on. I'll take you to the place where you can be questioned by the immigration authorities."

As they were making their way through the crowd of immigrants that milled about the building, Dova said, "I was so frightened of that man, Erik. And all the time, he was there to protect me. Remember when you told me about Pastor Helms using Psalm 91 to encourage you?"

"Yes."

"Well, he did the same for me. I had no idea how emphatically the Lord would prove that first verse to be true."

Erik looked heavenward and said, "Thank You, Lord, for the safety of the secret place of the most High!"

Twenty-four

When Dova met Erik at his booth after finishing her question-and-answer examination, he took her to an area where there were chairs and couches and made her comfortable in a big chair.

She explained that her parents wanted her to go to the Vagners and tell them her story, knowing they would take her into their home until she could safely return to Switzerland. She showed Erik the letter her father had written to the Vagners, explaining the attempt on her life, and asking them to keep her until further notice.

Standing over her, Erik said, "I'll put you in a room tonight in the dormitory where the part-time employees stay. I'll take tomorrow off, and we'll go to the Vagner home together. You rest now."

"I will, thank you," she said, smiling up at him.

"I get off at five-thirty. I'll come and get you, and we'll eat supper together at the employees' dining hall."

At six o'clock that evening, Dova sat across the table from Erik in the dining hall, still weary, but very hungry.

Having never seen some of the concoctions that she found before her, she bravely sampled each one.

Noting Dova's careful approach to the food, Erik chuckled. "I know it's foreign to you, Dova, but you'll get used to it. I did. And I've come to like the food that seemed so strange to me at first."

"I hope it will be the same for me," she said, managing a smile. "I like this coffee all right, but I probably should have tried the tea."

Rising from the table, Erik said, "I'll get it for you. Do you like cream and sugar in your tea?"

"Yes."

Minutes later, Erik returned to the table carrying a tray with a cup of tea, as well as cream and sugar.

Dova smiled warmly. "Erik, you're a lifesaver!"

He laughed. "That's what doctors are supposed to be, aren't they?"

When Dova and Erik arrived at the Vagner home on Fifth Avenue late the next morning, she was happy to see that Manhattan's Central Park was directly across the street. Dova commented on the beauty of the park as Erik helped her out of the buggy.

When Elizabeth Vagner responded to the knock on her door, she was shocked to see Dova with her former family physician on American soil. Quickly inviting them in, she explained that Franz was at the shoe store, but would be home for lunch.

Over European-type tea, Elizabeth listened as Dova and Erik told her the whole story. Immediately, Elizabeth assured Dova she had a home with them as long as she needed it. She also gave praise to the Lord for Dova's safe journey, and both Erik and Dova told her how precious Psalm 91:1 had become to both of them.

At Elizabeth's bidding, Erik carried Dova's luggage into the guest bedroom on the second floor, and Dova complimented Elizabeth on the beauty and charm of the room. She then hugged her and thanked her for taking her in.

At noon, Franz came home for lunch, and was every bit as stunned as his wife had been to see Dova and Erik. When he was told the story over lunch, he also welcomed Dova to their home, giving praise to the Lord for His mighty hand on both young people.

As the days came and went, Erik went to Manhattan as often as he could, although he did not have a wealth of spare time. There was always a welcome at the Vagner home, and the four of them spent many hours together talking over special times in their homeland.

On the second Sunday Dova had been with the Vagners, Erik arrived as planned to walk with them to church. Before they left the house, Erik showed Dova a letter that had just come from his parents.

Believing that Dova no doubt was in New York by then, Frederic and Mura wanted both of them to know that the men who had tried to kill Dova had attempted a union-related killing in Geneva, and had been gunned down by police. They were professional killers, Albert Conreid and Hans Nikolta. An investigation by the Swiss government revealed that they had been hired by the Grutliverein Labor Union's first vice president, Henry Wimms, to kill a shoe factory owner in Geneva who was adamantly resisting unionization. Wimms had been arrested and would go on trial shortly.

The letter went on to say that the union had decided to stay away from the factory in Chur. Eiger Wilhaus had returned to the factory, made Helmut Thorpe manager, and raised the wages generously. All the independent woodworkers were now happily employed at the factory.

Feeling much relief, Dova and Erik seemed to be walking on air as the foursome headed for church.

That afternoon after Sunday dinner at the Vagner home, Erik and Dova took a walk in Central Park. The heat of the summer had faded, and the glorious colors of autumn painted the leaves on the trees vividly. Many leaves had already fallen, and as they walked—each lost in their thoughts—they playfully kicked at the colorful leaves with each step.

In his private thoughts, Erik wanted desperately to tell lovely Dova that he had fallen in love with her, but refrained because he wasn't sure how she felt toward him. That mysterious look appeared in her eyes quite frequently, but he didn't know how to find out if it meant what he hoped it meant.

In Dova's private thoughts, she knew she was more in love with Erik than ever, and wanted to tell him. But it was improper for a young lady to do so.

That evening when Erik entered his apartment, he went directly to the small rolltop desk, sat down, and penned a letter to Justina. He told her how he felt about Dova, saying he needed her sisterly help. He asked if Dova had ever said anything about having special feelings toward him.

The next morning, he posted the letter in the outgoing mailbox in the main building on Ellis Island.

Erik continued his trips into Manhattan, wanting to spend as much time with the woman he loved as possible. They went to church together, sometimes went shopping together on Fifth Avenue, and took more walks in Central Park. Each wanted to tell the other how they felt, but because of past circumstances, were not able to find a way.

On Friday, October 21, Erik received the reply from Justina. When he opened the letter, it said in large letters:

> You loveable dope! I know for a fact that Dova has been in love with you from afar since she was twelve years old! Haven't you ever noticed that as beautiful and charming as she is, she has never had a beau? It's because she felt she could never love anyone but you. Go tell her you are in love with her! Your declaration will be received with open arms!
> With love and anticipation,
> Justina

Tears were in Erik's eyes as he said to himself, "I have to work tomorrow, but on Sunday afternoon, I'm taking Dova for a buggy ride to the beach in Manhattan. We're going to have a little talk!"

It was a spectacular fall day as Erik pulled the buggy to a halt in the parking lot on the beach at midafternoon on Sunday. They were on the southernmost tip of Manhattan Island, looking out across the Upper Bay.

Erik helped Dova out of the buggy, and kept a hand on her elbow as they walked slowly along the beach. A soft breeze was blowing, and the bay was pale blue with white crests swimming lazily toward shore and washing up on the sunlit beach.

Farther out on the bay where it spread into the Atlantic Ocean, the water gradually became a darker blue, and Eric and Dova spotted a trio of ships coming in toward the harbor.

They drew up at a rocky point and stood quietly, taking in the breathtaking sight. Off to the right was Bedloe's Island where Miss Liberty stood, waiting to welcome the incoming ships.

Erik's mind was busy. He was trying to think of the best way to approach Dova with his declaration.

Dova looked up at him and said, "I was thinking about the letter from your parents. With those men dead who tried to kill me, and that vice president who evidently ordered it behind bars, I'll probably be getting a letter from Papa quite soon saying I can come home."

Erik was still searching for words as he looked into her eyes.

"I'll miss you," she said softly.

A stray breeze blew a tuft of Dova's hair across her face. Without even thinking about what he was doing, Erik let his finger brush the curl away from her eyes. His hand tarried there, then he lovingly caressed her cheek. She looked up at him, and as if her hand had a mind of its own, it came up and her fingers closed on his hand.

"Dova," Erik said with a quiver in his voice, "I am very, very much in love with you. I started falling in love with you before I ever left Switzerland, but I didn't realize it till I was on the ship. I...don't know how you feel about me."

Her eyes were locked on his as she found her voice and said, "Oh, my darling Erik. I have been in love with you since I was twelve years old. When you used to tease me and pull my pigtails, every time you pulled one, I fell deeper in love with you."

"I had no idea. To me, you were just my sister's best friend and a close friend of mine."

"About the time I was going to try to find a way to let you know how I felt, you started dating Metryka. Then you became engaged. I just backed off, thinking all hope was gone."

"But the Lord had His plan for us," Erik said, looking deeper into her soft blue pools.

Dova blinked at the excess moisture that welled up in those eyes.

In that golden moment of time, the love that God had given Erik and Dova for each other shone brightly between them.

"Dova," he said breathlessly, "I...I—"

"What, darling?"

"Will you marry me?"

It was like heaven had opened up to shower its blessings.

Dova's voice was a melodic alto. "Yes! Oh, yes! I will marry you!"

The words they had both spoken were an enchanting musical accompaniment, an audible means to bring their faces closer together, to touch temples, and then to turn their heads ever so slowly until their lips came together.

Holding her close as both their hearts throbbed, Erik said, "I told you shortly after you arrived here about my performing the surgeries aboard ship and getting past the mental block I had about ever doing surgery again."

"Yes," she said, clinging to him.

"And I told you that within a year or so, I want to go wherever the Lord leads here in America, and get back into private practice."

"Yes, and I think it's wonderful."

"Well, I can do it with the woman I love at my side. And that makes it even more wonderful."

"Oh, darling," she breathed, and they shared another sweet, tender kiss.

The sun was lowering in the west.

With arms about each other, the happy couple turned and set their eyes on the Statue of Liberty as her long shadow was cast over the rippling waters.

Dova looked at it for a long moment, then said, "Darling, as husband and wife, we will dwell together in the secret place of the most High and abide under the shadow of the Almighty."

Mail Order Bride Series

Desperate gold hunters of the West resorted to unconventional measures in their quest for companionship, advertising for and marrying women they'd never even met! Read about a unique and adventurous period in the history of romance.

#1	Secrets of the Heart	ISBN 1-57673-278-9
#2	A Time to Love	ISBN 1-57673-284-3
#3	The Tender Flame	ISBN 1-57673-399-8
#4	Blessed are the Merciful	ISBN 1-57673-417-X
#5	Ransom of Love	ISBN 1-57673-609-1
#6	Until the Daybreak	ISBN 1-57673-624-5
#7	Sincerely Yours	ISBN 1-57673-572-9
#8	A Measure of Grace	ISBN 1-57673-808-6

Angel of Mercy Series

Post-Civil War nurse Breanna Baylor uses her professional skill to bring healing to the body, and her faith in the Redeemer to bring comfort to thirsty souls, valiantly serving God on the dangerous frontier.

#1	A Promise for Breanna	ISBN 0-88070-797-6
#2	Faithful Heart	ISBN 0-88070-835-2
#3	Captive Set Free	ISBN 0-88070-872-7
#4	A Dream Fulfilled	ISBN 0-88070-940-5
#5	Suffer the Little Children	ISBN 1-57673-039-5
#6	Whither Thou Goest	ISBN 1-57673-078-6
#7	Final Justice	ISBN 1-57673-260-6
#8	Not By Might	ISBN 1-57673-242-8
#9	Things Not Seen	ISBN 1-57673-413-7
#10	Far Above Rubies	ISBN 1-57673-499-4

Hannah of Fort Bridger Series

Hannah Cooper's husband dies on the dusty Oregon Trail, leaving her in charge of five children and a general store in Fort Bridger. Dependence on God fortifies her against grueling challenges and bitter tragedies.

#1	Under the Distant Sky	ISBN 1-57673-033-6
#2	Consider the Lilies	ISBN 1-57673-049-2
#3	No Place for Fear	ISBN 1-57673-083-2
#4	Pillow of Stone	ISBN 1-57673-234-7
#5	The Perfect Gift	ISBN 1-57673-407-2
#6	Touch of Compassion	ISBN 1-57673-422-6
#7	Beyond the Valley	ISBN 1-57673-618-0
#8	Damascus Journey	ISBN 1-57673-630-X